I don't want you to be afraid of me," he murmured, his voice thick with need. "Tell me you don't fear me now, Ariana."

"I don't," she whispered, her parted lips glistening in the firelight. "I trust you, Braedon . . ."

Her words were lost in that next moment. Damning the conscience that urged him to keep his distance, he slipped his hand around her warm nape and pulled her into his arms. Their lips met, tentatively at first, only the merest brush of mouth on mouth, a hesitant, testing kiss that ached all the more for its sweetness.

"Ah, God," he moaned against her, trying to hold himself in check. "This will go too far, angel. Much too far . . ."

She stared up at him and smiled a virginal smile. He had never seen anything so innocent. She was so tender and yielding. So damned soft in his arms.

"Touch me," she told him, a breathless demand. "Kiss me, Braedon. Please . . ."

Other Books by Tina St. John:

**LORD OF VENGEANCE
LADY OF VALOR
WHITE LION'S LADY
BLACK LION'S BRIDE**

Books published by The Random House Publishing Group
are available at quantity discounts on bulk purchases for
premium, educational, fund-raising, and special sales use.
For details, please call 1-800-733-3000.

HEART
OF THE
HUNTER

TINA
ST. JOHN

BALLANTINE BOOKS • NEW YORK

Sale of this book without a front cover may be unauthorized. If this book is coverless, it may have been reported to the publisher as "unsold or destroyed" and neither the author nor the publisher may have received payment for it.

This book is a work of fiction. Names, places, and incidents either are products of the author's imagination or are used fictitiously.

This book contains an excerpt from the forthcoming paperback edition of *Heart of the Flame* by Tina St. John. This excerpt has been set for this edition only and may not reflect the final content of the forthcoming edition.

An Ivy Book
Published by The Random House Publishing Group
Copyright © 2004 by Tina Haack
Excerpt from *Heart of the Flame* © 2004 by Tina Haack.

All rights reserved under International and Pan-American Copyright Conventions. Published in the United States by The Random House Publishing Group, a division of Random House, Inc., New York, and simultaneously in Canada by Random House of Canada Limited, Toronto.

Ivy Books and colophon are trademarks of Random House, Inc.

www.ballantinebooks.com

ISBN 0-345-45994-6

Manufactured in the United States of America

First Edition: June 2004

OPM   10   9   8   7   6   5   4   3   2   1

For Christy C.,
and the enchantment she found with her own beloved
Hunter. May every heart be as blessed
as the both of yours were.

In a time long ago, before man knew what it was to keep time, there existed a place where light, faith, peace, and prosperity reigned. That place was called Anavrin, a kingdom of mist and magic. A secret world that thrived for untold centuries, it remained hidden from the mortal plane that surrounded it like so much shifting sand. Anavrin's people knew nothing of what lay on the other side of the veil that separated their secret kingdom from the world Outside. They lived in perpetual summer, knowing no pain or fear or vice. They knew nothing of human frailty or wickedness . . . that is, until an Anavrin princess made the tragic mistake of falling in love with a mortal man.

Her brother was king, and his queen and lady wife had just given birth to their first child, beginning a strong new branch of Anavrin royalty. As was tradition, the babe's arrival would be sanctified with a drink from the sacred cup of Anavrin: the Dragon Chalice, wrought of gold and bejeweled with four enchanted stones. The princess was honored to be the maiden chosen to fill the cup from the virgin well, a holy pool that flowed from a woodland waterfall that marked the space between Anavrin and the Outside like a curtain of dark glass.

Alone at the well, the princess heard a strange sound carrying over the rush of the falls. It was the sound of a man—a mortal man, wounded and moaning on the

*other side of the water. The princess knew no fright or
anguish, but she knew compassion, and she wanted to
ease this man's suffering. She called to him and was surprised to find that he heard her. Indeed, he could hear
her, but the sheltering wall of the waterfall concealed her
from his sight, as it had concealed all of Anavrin through
the ages. He beseeched her to come out of hiding and
help him, assuring her that he meant her no harm. The
princess knew it was forbidden to interact with folk
from the Outside; it was unthinkable to pass the barrier
of the falls. But the man's pain caused a peculiar ache in
her breast that was too great to ignore.*

*Setting the sacred Chalice beside the well, she ap-
proached the rushing waterfall and stepped to the Outside. To her dismay, the man's injury was worse than she
could have imagined. He was dying; she could see it in
his fierce but dulling blue gaze. She wiped a shock of
sweat-soaked golden hair from his brow, unveiling a
face of breathtaking appeal. He was beautiful, and she
fell in love with him at once. She had to help him, but she
knew not what to do. He begged her for water, but the
scant handfuls she drew from the pool beneath the falls
did little to quench his thirst.*

*The princess recalled the Dragon Chalice, filled with
water from the sacred well and now sitting some half-
dozen paces past Anavrin's threshold. There was power
in that jewel-encrusted cup, power enough, perhaps, to
help the man who lay bleeding in her arms. She could not
bring the Chalice to him, for well was it known that a
terrible ill would befall Anavrin if ever the cup was lost.
It was said that a great and dangerous dragon would be
unleashed upon the kingdom should its people ever lose
the cup and its protective powers. In order to save the
man as she so desperately wanted to do, the princess*

would have to bring him to the Chalice. She would have to bring him into Anavrin itself.

Certain it was the right thing to do—the only thing to do—the princess urged the man to his feet and helped him toward the falls. He was too weak to question her purpose, too weak to understand the extraordinary gift she meant to give him. The princess fed him from the Chalice and the man drank as if he had gone a lifetime without water. He drank until the color returned to his face, until the wound that tore him open ceased to bleed, then, at last, began to heal. His strength returning, the man started to draw himself to his feet. It was then that the king and half of Anavrin came thundering into the glade.

They saw the Outsider standing there, embracing the princess in his tattered, bloodstained clothes, and knew at once what she had done. The man was brought back to the royal castle and made to feel a guest in the lavish royal chambers, but behind closed doors, the king searched for a means to be rid of him. Anavrin's wise old mage brought an answer. The Outsider would be given a second drink from the Chalice, this time containing a potion that would erase all memory of the day's events. He would recall nothing of Anavrin, nothing of the princess or how she had spared his life. While the man dozed, he could be returned to the Outside none the wiser.

Upon hearing of the king's intention, the princess pleaded with him to allow the man to stay at Anavrin. She begged him as her brother to bind the man to her, pleading that he allow her to wed the Outsider. But the king would not hear of it. He warned her that she knew nothing of this man, that to permit him to stay was to put all of Anavrin in jeopardy. As planned, the king arranged to have the Dragon Chalice waiting for the man that evening at table.

What he did not expect was that his obedient sister would defy him.

Unable to bear the thought that she would lose her beloved, the princess had warned the man not to drink from the Chalice that night. She told him that she would wait for him in secret, and together they would flee Anavrin to be together on the Outside. Her beloved did not keep her waiting for long. With a mad ruckus of shouts and bootfalls following on his heels, the man burst from the castle's great hall and swept her along as they ran out to the yard and on, into the darkening woods. The princess knew the way to the well, and, within a few breathless moments, they stood hand in hand in the mist of the falls. With scarcely a backward glance, the princess leapt with the man through the waterfall, leaving behind all that she knew of Anavrin.

Nay, not all, she realized but a heartbeat later.

For bundled neatly under the man's arm was the sacred Dragon Chalice. The bejeweled vessel that had been forged for the first King of Anavrin an eon before, its four vibrant stones said to ensure the very life of Anavrin itself. Now those stones glowed with unholy fire beneath the rag that concealed the cup. The princess knew a jolt of unfamiliar alarm as she watched the Outsider unwrap the Chalice. For the first time in all of her immortal existence, she knew fear. She tasted regret, but alas, too late.

The cup seemed to hum with a peculiar pulsing power, causing the man's hand to tremble as he fought to keep hold of his stolen prize. The cup shook violently and tumbled out of his grasp to hang suspended before him. The four stones glowed more fiercely. A shot of light seemed to grow out of the center of the Chalice, so strong it fractured the treasure apart at its core. No longer a single cup, but four—each bearing one of the glowing stones—now twined together in a halo of blinding light, twisting and climbing high above the heads of the princess and the Outsider. The man tried to grab them back, but their light was too pure, too fiery. In a sudden flash, the treasure burst into vapor and simply vanished.

For the rest of his days, the Outsider lamented the loss of the Chalice. He blamed the princess for the trick that stole it away from him, but she knew nothing of the magic that had occurred. A brigand and a scoundrel, the Outsider did not believe her. Nor did he wed her, but he bred his mortal whelps on her and drove himself to madness with tales told over too much wine of a kingdom spun of gold and a jeweled cup that gave him life renewed when he was as good as dead.

Over time, his drunken ramblings grew legs of their own, feeding rumors that the Dragon Chalice and its four mystical stones did, in fact, exist—even if scattered to opposite corners of the realm. It was suggested that the man who reunited the Chalice, bringing the four parts to the whole, would be granted immortality. Indeed, legend stated that he would have wealth and happiness beyond imagining, for to claim the Dragon Chalice was to win the key to Anavrin itself.

For some, the legend was nothing more than a fairy story, the fantastic delusion of a penniless sot who was not worth his own spittle. Others believed the Chalice to be the possible salvation of mankind, a gift to be recovered and cherished as the holiest of relics. For still others, the Dragon Chalice and its secrets were very real . . . and there were those among that number who would stop at nothing to have it for their own.

❧ 1 ❧

February 1275

WINTER BORE DOWN on London like a great winged beast. Howling and angry, it darkened the midday sky as it swooped in off the sea, clawing at the town with ice-sharp talons of frigid cold and spitting a heavy, wet rain. Lady Ariana of Clairmont clutched the edge of her hooded fur mantle and drew it close to her face as she and her riding companion urged their mounts toward one of several snow-drifted dockside taverns. Clouds of gray woodsmoke belched out of a stone chimney that braced the side of the squat establishment, indicating the warmth to be had inside, but there was little else to recommend the place from what Ariana could see.

The tavern's sole window had been shuttered and nailed tight in an effort to combat the cold; the wet, weather-beaten boards rattled in weak protest as another blustery gale blew down to assail them. The winter storm had driven everyone of sense to seek shelter until the worst of it passed. Now the street and its surrounding shops and buildings seemed all but deserted, save for a few ragged souls who appeared to have nowhere else to go. Ariana wished to be out of the cold, too, but her appointment here was of the utmost importance, and she

could not let a little wind and sleet keep her from her
meeting.

Her brother's life depended on it.

She pivoted in her saddle to address the knight who
rode beside her, speaking at nearly a shout to be heard
over the swirling winds and stinging rain. "Are you certain this is the place, James?"

"Aye, my lady. The Cock and Cup, above Queenhithe,
just like he said." The Clairmont guard lifted his leather-
gauntleted hand and pointed to a snow-spattered, icicle-
fringed sign that banged and creaked over the tavern
door. "Our Monsieur Ferrand seemed a merchant of
some means. Would that he'd chosen a more suitable location for this final meeting. This place looks more a
stew than a public house."

"Never mind what it looks like," Ariana replied, despite that she shared James's misgiving. "We won't be
long delayed here, after all. Just time enough to deliver
our passage fee and accompany the monsieur to his ship
at the docks below."

James grunted, then led her toward a small stable adjacent to the tavern. They would leave their horses there
while they met with the Parisian merchantman, who had
agreed, for a not insignificant price, to transport them
across the Channel to France on the morrow. As they left
the covered shelter and dashed for the tavern, James issued a fatherly warning. "Stay well near me once we're
inside, my lady. I don't know what that beady-eyed
Frenchman is scheming, but methinks 'tis beginning to
smack of treachery."

Her gloved hands under her cloak for warmth, Ariana
felt for the small purse affixed to her girdle. Their passage fee to France—indeed, all of the coin she could
scrape together for this sudden, clandestine trip—jingled

in the bottom of that modest pouch as she followed close behind James, her booted feet sloshing through the snow and mud. Slung over her shoulder on a thick leather strap and knocking against her hip as she ran was a different purse, this one larger, heavier, the contents far more valuable. For this second satchel contained the sole purpose for her risky, unseasonable travel. The reason she left Clairmont to brave the arduous ride to London and now found herself willing to put her fate in the hands of a man like Monsieur Ferrand de Paris.

Simply put, she had no choice.

Her brother, Kenrick, had not returned from an autumn trip to the Continent, but it was not until a ransom demand arrived at Clairmont just a sennight ago that Ariana had understood the reason for his delay. He was being held captive by enemies she knew nothing about, powerful enemies who had taken an interest in something Kenrick had been studying. Ariana had but a mere month's time to assemble and deliver his ransom in secret, or her beloved brother would be killed. Meeting these considerable demands would be a difficult enough task in fair weather, next to impossible when winter was full upon the realm.

But she would not fail him. Kenrick had always been there for her, from the time she was a child—her best ally, dearest friend. She would not fail him now. God help her, she could not.

Ariana silently intoned the vow as James paused at the tavern door. "Stay close," he repeated, then clutched the iron latch in his gloved fist and pushed the thick panel open with his shoulder to let her past.

A gust of wind all but blew Ariana into the lamplit gloom of the tavern. The whistling gale seized the hem of her mantle as she crossed the threshold, whipping it about like an unlashed sail. Slick, wet snow swirled in at her feet, adding to a muddy puddle of water that had collected on the tread-worn dip in the floor just beyond the door—a puddle she did not see until she stood in it, her sodden boots taking on even more water in the long moment it took for her toes to feel the added cold. She dared not cry out as she stepped to the side of the chilly puddle, perhaps because she was too tired. Or perhaps because she was loath to call more attention to her arrival in the smoky, surprisingly crowded tavern.

As it was, a good number of heads were already raised from their cups, too many pairs of eyes rooting on the young noblewoman in the fox-lined cloak who no doubt looked as though she ought to know better than to wander this far down into the docklands of the city. Ariana removed her hood and swallowed her sudden trepidation. She squared her shoulders in a pose she hoped conveyed confidence, but she was very grateful for James's solid bulk at her back as he pulled the door closed behind him, then came to stand protectively beside her. From the corner of her eye, she saw him hook his mantle around the hilt of his sheathed sword, a clear statement that anyone with designs on her would have to first get through him.

James nodded a curt greeting to the tavern keeper. "Ferrand de Paris?"

"Aye. Over there, sir," came the reply, accompanied by a jerk of the old man's grizzled chin.

Ariana followed the gesture with her gaze, toward a table in the corner of the room. The rotund, greasy-faced French merchant was engaged in conversation with another man who was seated on a bench across from him, a broad-shouldered giant with wind-tousled, overlong hair that gleamed as dark and glossy as the richest sable against the pale gray wool of his tunic.

His back was to her, but even without seeing his face, Ariana could plainly tell that his proud carriage and demeanor marked him as a man of some consequence. He was no mere knight, for there were no spurs riding at the heels of his tall leather boots, and although he wore a sword at his hip, the center of the pommel glowed with the milky iridescence of mother-of-pearl. A nobleman, she guessed, perhaps bargaining over one of the merchant's fine treasures from abroad—or rather arguing, she amended, as she and James drew near enough to hear the stranger's deep growling voice.

"Don't insult me, Ferrand. This is a simple matter. You hired me to deliver the silks and I did it. Over a month ago. Now I want what you owe me, or I'll take it out of your vermin hide."

The man spoke the Norman French of England's noble classes, his cultured accent as smooth as a polished stone even if his threat bore the harsh and naked edge of a jagged blade. Monsieur Ferrand evidently understood the danger he provoked, for his nose twitched, and the cup he raised to his lips wobbled in his shaky hand. He set it down without drinking.

"Come now, let us settle this like gentlemen," he said, a suggestion that earned a snorted oath from across the table. "Meet me at the dock on the morrow and I will gladly pay you your fair share of the trade."

The man in the gray tunic shoved himself up off the bench, his large hands braced on the table's edge. He gave a forcible push as he rose, pinioning the merchant into the corner with the weight of the table across his torso. "You'll pay me tonight, Ferrand. I'm through with your stalling."

Ariana had supposed the man was tall when she first spied him from across the room, but she had not been prepared for the sheer enormity of his person until she found herself a scant two paces from him at the table. He grabbed his mantle from the bench and whirled away from Monsieur Ferrand with a snarl, a move that brought him face-to-face with Ariana and James, who stood at her side, now pointedly clearing his throat as if to prompt an apology from the man. No such courtesy was offered.

The dark-haired rogue drew up just short of trampling them and paused there, towering over Ariana in rude silence, a menacing expanse of muscle and scarcely contained fury. But if his considerable size and surly mood unsettled her, it was nothing compared to the jolt of horror she felt when she tipped her head back and looked up at his face. Too harsh to be handsome, he radiated an unforgiving, ruthless power that was made all the more chilling by the presence of a terrible scar that ran the diagonal length of his left cheek. The long silvery welt of skin marked an old wound that must have sliced him open from temple to jaw. It had been a savage cut, perhaps meant to kill him had the blade continued its downward path to his throat.

Ariana was vaguely aware of her hand, which had risen to hover protectively at her neck as she stared up at the stranger's angry scowl. She must have gasped upon seeing him, understandably so, but the man seemed unfazed by her reaction. Indeed, the wry twist of his lips, the narrowing of his smoke gray eyes beneath the heavy slash of his dark brows, suggested he took a measure of amusement at her fright. He stared back a moment longer than a gentleman should, taking her in, from the top of her smart little traveling hat and crispinette to the fashionably pointed tips of her sodden calf-leather boots. She distinctly heard him chortle under his breath before he tilted his head slightly, a subtle move that made a hank of his shaggy black hair fall forward to cover part of the scar, although nothing could obliterate the savagery of his face completely.

With a lingering glance at Ariana, then a belated acknowledgment of James, the man stepped around them without a word to stalk out of the tavern and into the wintry bluster outside.

"Monsieur Ferrand, are you all right?" Ariana asked, once the stranger was gone. "Who was that awful man?"

"Oh, him?" The Frenchman had extricated himself from his trapped position in the corner and now rose to greet them. "Pay him no mind, he is no one. Just one of my business associates." He wagged his hand in casual dismissal. "Sit, sit, please. Let us get on with our own business, eh?"

When Ariana moved to accept his invitation to join him at the small table, James's firm grasp on her elbow held her back. "Do all of your business associates have to threaten you before you make good on your bargains, Ferrand?"

"That man is a thief and a scoundrel, *monsieur le chevalier*. Now he seeks to add extortion to his bag of tricks. You saw him, after all, the insolent beast. Did he look like a man you would trust at his word?"

"Not especially." The Clairmont guard grunted. "But then I'm not sure you do, either."

"James," Ariana sharply interjected, shooting an apologetic smile at their host. "We don't want to insult Monsieur Ferrand, now do we? Certainly not when he has so kindly agreed to provide us transport to France. Do you forget how many inquiries we made upon our arrival in London? There was scarcely anyone willing to make the crossing as quickly as we needed. Monsieur Ferrand's assistance is greatly appreciated, and I'm sure he is a man of his word."

She could tell James remained skeptical despite her attempt to persuade him, but he said nothing more to indicate his mistrust. He knew what was at stake here. He understood the urgency—the near desperation—of Ariana's desire to get to France. James had served her family nearly all his life; he would not jeopardize Kenrick's safety any more than she would.

"Yes, well, then," said the Frenchman in the moment of silence that followed. "Shall we firm up the terms of our arrangement, my lady, or does your husband speak for you?"

"I am not married," Ariana replied, seating herself on the bench opposite Ferrand. "Sir James comes with me from Clairmont as my escort."

"The lady's bodyguard," added James, "should things take a misfortunate turn."

Monsieur Ferrand bared his teeth in a rather poorly affected smile. "A task you undertake with admirable zeal, I see. Who wouldn't, when the body one is guarding is as lovely as hers?"

Ariana did not like the implication in that statement, nor did she miss the tension creeping into James's features as he stared down at Monsieur Ferrand. "Your terms, merchant. Let's get to them without further delay and have done with this meeting."

"I believe we agreed upon seven sous sterling, did we not, Monsieur?"

Ferrand turned away from James to deal instead with Ariana. "Yes, my lady. That was the sum."

"Very well." Ariana reached for the coin pouch on her girdle and proceeded to count out the somewhat steep price of passage. "There you are," she said, sliding the small pile of coins toward the merchant seaman. "Payment in full, up-front, as you required."

The Frenchman's stubby fingers curled around the silver, which disappeared neatly into his waiting purse of fine brocade. "A pleasure doing business with you, *demoiselle*." He grinned, then signaled to a serving wench to bring him another cup of ale. "Join me in refreshment, won't you? Then I will show you to my ship. I would advise you stay the evening below deck, so we might set sail for France with the next tide."

Ariana declined when the serving woman came to the table and offered her a cup of ale. "If 'tis all the same to you, *monsieur,* would you take us to your ship now? The past couple days have been rather long and taxing. I would very much like to rest awhile in preparation of our crossing."

Ferrand grunted into his full mug of ale. "As you wish," he said, setting the drink down with a shrug. Standing up, he donned a dark blue cloak that hung on a peg of a nearby beam. "I am docked just below Thames Street at Queenhithe. This way, *s'il vous plaît.*"

They followed the merchant toward the door. A rough-looking huddle of seamen slouched at a table at the center of the room—some of Ferrand's acquaintances, evidently, for he hailed them in French and cuffed one on the shoulder as he walked by. Five hairy faces looked up at the merchant's greeting, some of them openly leering at Ariana.

"Something is wrong. I don't like the looks of this, my lady," James whispered as they stepped out into the street with Ferrand. She could feel the knight tense beside her, knew his battle instincts were on alert even before she saw his hand come to rest on the pommel of his sword in anticipation of trouble.

It did not take long to arrive.

Ferrand pulled on a pair of leather gloves as he stood beneath the sheltering eaves of the tavern roof. It was still cold and spitting drizzle, still dark as dusk though it was not long past noontide. The merchant seemed not to mind the weather overmuch. He stood there, grinning expectantly.

"Which way to your vessel?" James asked. "We don't want to stand around in this freezing muck all day."

"I told you, *serjant*," Ferrand drawled, using the derogative term for a soldier of the lower class. "I am docked at the quay below. But you'll be staying here, I think."

Ariana's gasp underscored James's vivid oath. "What is the meaning of this, Monsieur Ferrand? We paid you for passage—"

"You paid me for your passage, *demoiselle*. Not his. He stays."

James took a step forward, ready to lunge for the little merchantman. "Why, you cheating bastard. I knew you carried the stench of a thief on you."

Before he could get near enough to grab him, the group of seamen from the tavern poured out into the street behind them. Two of the big men seized James's arms and wrenched them back until his face contorted in pain. As he struggled futilely, another man stole his weapon and brandished it before him, chuckling maliciously.

"Wait, please!" Ariana cried, terrified for James and seeing her chances of reaching Kenrick in time begin to slip away. With shaking hands, she widened the drawstring of her coin purse and fumbled around for another seven sous. She thrust the handful of silver at Monsieur Ferrand. "Here. Take it. Now, please, let him go. We don't want any more trouble. You agreed to take us to France and we have paid you to do so. What more do you want?"

"This is not about the money," James said through gritted teeth as the Frenchman took Ariana's coin.

Although Ferrand did not deny it, he reached out and yanked Ariana's coin purse from her hands. There was not much left in the little pouch, but it was all she had and the loss of it sent her into a fit of rage. With a cry, she flew at Ferrand, scratching at him, kicking him, beating him with her fists.

"Pull this hissing cat off me!" he shouted to his men while he tried to fend off her assault.

She felt one final, satisfying rent of his skin where her fingernails raked his face, but then she was caught in a vise of sweat-soured wool and beefy resistance. The last two seamen each had ahold of her: one locked her arms at her sides, hoisting her off the ground, while the other grabbed her flailing legs and clamped her feet tight in his fists. She pitched and roiled, but there was no escaping their grip on her. Even her screams proved of little use, all but devoured by the howling of the winter wind.

"Take her down to the ship and lock her in the hold," Ferrand ordered. "And mind you don't bruise her too badly. Skin that fair will fetch me a handsome price on the slave market, even after I take my use of her."

"Damn you, Ferrand!" James roared. "I'll send you straight to hell if you so much as breathe on her!"

Ariana struggled anew against her bonds, fighting her captors for all she was worth as they began to haul her away from the tavern and toward an alley leading to the docks. She caught one last glimpse of James, still held by Ferrand's men and bucking like a man gone mad. The third seaman drove his fist into James's stomach, doubling him over before slamming his knee into the knight's face.

Ariana called out for her old protector, the knight who had come so willingly into this misfortune, who had warned her of the risks in trusting a man like Ferrand yet stayed at her side despite his personal doubts. She cried for him to forgive her, but she doubted he would hear. She was halfway down the alley now, icy rain stinging her face, the smell of fish and brine assailing her nostrils as she was carried nearer to the docks.

She prayed Ferrand's men would not hurt James too badly, that he would somehow overpower them and get away. He was a strong man, after all, and quite skilled as a fighter. If there was a way, he would free himself. Dear Lord, he had to.

Just as she must find a way to escape her own bonds now.

She continued to scream and thrash, determined that she would not go easily into whatever fate awaited her on Ferrand's ship. At last, her struggles were given a modest reward. She jerked and kicked, and finally got one leg free. Her booted foot thumped onto the wooden plank of the dock and within a heartbeat the other followed. The relentless sleet had slackened the knave's grasp on her enough that with a renewed bout of twisting and bucking, she was standing up on her own, still held by the arms but halfway to freedom.

Freedom, however, was a relative term, for all around her churned the foamy darkness of the Thames. In order to escape Ferrand and his men, she would either have to break past them and run back up the docks or take a frigid leap into the river and hope she would be strong enough to swim to safety somewhere along the quays.

Neither option seemed promising, but she kept fighting, kept working toward escape.

"Hold her still, will you!" barked the man who was frantically trying to recapture her legs. "The bitch is going to break my fingers with her thrashing!"

The ironlike vise around her arms and breasts tightened to the point of pain, and the man holding her chuckled now, breathing hotly against her ear. "She's a fighter, this one. Full of fire, jes the way I like 'em."

"Animals!" she cried. "Let me go! Someone help me, please!"

Her plea went wholly ignored, as she knew it would, her near hysterical screaming drowned out by the men's amused laughter and the continuing storm. Ariana heard thunder rolling somewhere behind her, a rhythmic rumble that shook the wooden planks beneath her, reverberating in the soles of her sodden boots. She was dripping wet in the cold and tiring fast, her breath rasping out of her aching lungs in thin puffs of steam. She pulled against the bonds that held her, but in truth she did not know how much longer she could fight.

"What say you give us a little taste 'fore the captain comes down, eh, *ma petite*?"

Revulsion coiled in Ariana's belly at the ale-soured suggestion that fanned her neck like a hot, groping hand. With all the strength she had left, she bent her head forward then snapped it back, hard. With a brutal-sounding smack, the back of her skull connected with the cartilage and bone of her captor's face. He howled and lost his grasp on her to clutch at his nose. Ariana lunged forward to make her escape but only managed two steps, caught at once by the second brute.

"You shouldn't have done that," he snarled. "My friend René, he is very vain about his looks."

But a broken nose was the least of the other man's present worries. From out of the gloom behind him came a dark figure, large and imposing. Ariana strained to see a face within the hooded cowl of the man's mantle, but the sleet and snow were driving down at a blinding slant now, concealing all but the massive bulk of his body and the huge broadsword that was a slash of silver in the charcoal gray of the wintry afternoon.

James! Ariana thought in a flood of panic and sudden, profound relief. It had been his approaching bootfalls she heard, not thunder. By God's grace, he had found her after all. But how had he managed to get away from Ferrand's men?

The old knight had never looked so formidable or so capable of doing harm as he did when he stalked toward René. One moment the miscreant was coughing and wheezing bloody curses at Ariana; the next, he was dead at the end of her rescuer's unforgiving blade, his slack body tumbling off the edge of the dock and splashing into the icy river below.

"What the devil—"

René's friend swore an oath and scrambled to draw his own weapon, thrusting Ariana aside with force enough to send her skidding to her knees on the dock. She crashed into a bunch of barrels that were lashed to one side the gangway, the rough oak containers and a surrounding web of cargo nets being all that spared her from a plunge into the frigid black water of the Thames.

Ahead of her some dozen paces, the two men were engaged in deadly battle. Their swords rang out above the lolling creak of the docks and the steady pelting of the storm. Ariana watched in terrified fascination as James expertly dodged each blow that came from Ferrand's man, only to deliver a barrage of punishing thrusts and swipes that left his opponent huffing and scraping onto one knee.

The seaman was well beaten. He dropped his weapon and clutched at the edge of James's cloak, begging quarter. Ariana relaxed somewhat, glad it was over. She let out a small sigh of relief, waiting for James to accept the surrender as honor would compel him to do. For a long moment, he did not move, merely stood there, his breath rolling between his lips in a frothy plume of pale steam while Ferrand's man continued to beg for his life.

Ariana brought herself to her feet as though in a daze, curious and not a little shaken. She took a hesitant step forward, in time to see that Ferrand's man would receive no mercy whatsoever. In time to see that the face concealed from her until now—the face that pivoted toward her in fury as she approached—did not belong to James at all.

It was him.

The rude stranger from the tavern—the roguish man with the hideous scar.

He hardly seemed to notice her astonishment. Indeed, he hardly seemed to have a care for her at all. His piercing gaze flicked back to the blubbering huddle at his feet. His massive sword arm came up from under his cloak, then with an ease that said he had done it a thousand times before, he flipped his weapon in a downward arc and embedded the length of steel in the other man's chest, killing him with swift efficiency and an utter lack of remorse. He retrieved his blade, wiped it clean on the dead man's bulk, and sheathed it before kicking the lifeless body over the edge of the dock. Then he turned once more to Ariana.

"Come with me," he instructed her, his large gloved hand outstretched.

"N-no." Ariana took a step backward, half stumbling over the cargo net at her heels. She shook her head, numbed by what she had just witnessed, terrified that this man was her unlikely rescuer—perhaps her only hope. "Stay away from me. I have to find James—"

"Your man is dead. They killed him, left his body in the alley up there. I saw it."

"No," Ariana whispered, her heart breaking at the thought. "No, it can't be."

"Give me your hand, *demoiselle*." He scowled at her, impatience tight around his mouth and in his tone of voice. "Your hand, lady. I mean you no harm."

Ariana stared at that extended offer of help, at the strong, steady arm reaching out to her through the misting rain and snow. Her options were few and fleeting the longer she remained on the docks. She had lost all of her coin and her means of transport to France. Heaven help her, but she had even lost James, a thought that nearly sapped what little strength remained in her shaking legs.

She stared at this scarred and deadly stranger, sensing it could be dangerous to trust him, yet knowing he was likely her only hope of surviving the night. And she had to survive. She had to figure out another way to get to France before her brother's captors acted on their threat.

He moved toward her, his boot heels thudding hollowly on the planks of the dock. His black hair was dripping and spiked where it lay against his sharp cheekbones and brow; the sinister scar on the left side of his face gleamed silver-white as he spoke. "Now, my lady.

Unless you'd rather take your chances with that whore-monger, Ferrand."

Tamping down the fear that rose to choke the very breath from her lungs, Ariana held out her hand to her unlikely savior, and went to him.

•

❧ 2 ❧

BRAEDON LE CHASSEUR was not the sort of man inclined to come to the aid of damsels in distress. That he did so now, and for a highborn girl who had regarded him with nothing short of fear and revulsion when he first laid eyes on her, should have told him this was a bad idea. One look at the haughty young woman, richly garbed and poorly guarded, indicated just how far out of her element she was. As out of place in the dockland tavern as a lamb in the midst of a seething wolf pack, she was likely to be killed or debauched before the night was through. Not that it should be any of his concern.

He should not have lingered at the Thames Street stable, where he had been waiting, sensing trouble soon to come after quitting his meeting with Ferrand. He should have walked away when he heard the scuffle and the feminine scream coming from the alley leading to the docks. He should have kept to his own affairs, turned the other way and headed for his cog, which was moored farther down the quays, near the old city bridge.

He did not need the trouble he was stirring up now, not when he had spent most of the last year and a half moving within the cover of London's deep shadowlands, a ghost of who he once had been, all but anonymous now, deliberately avoiding his old notoriety.

As it stood at present, he was but a moment from leaving the young woman there at Queenhithe when she finally blinked away her state of rattled shock and took his hand. He ran with her, off the dock and up onto the wide expanse of the wharf. Knowing that Ferrand and his remaining henchmen could not be far behind, Braedon had planned to skirt the street and follow the back of the buildings toward his boat downriver. But the girl's hesitation had delayed them a fraction too long.

Ferrand came around the corner of a building on Thames Street, his three shipmates close behind him like hulking wolfhounds, loping along at their master's heels. From the head of the alley, Ferrand paused suddenly, spotting Braedon and the girl.

"Get them!"

The men set off at a run on Ferrand's command, charging down the walkway and fanning out to head off either route of escape. One man drew a large sailor's knife from beneath his mantle. The others had swords, and so did Ferrand, who hustled down the wharf at nearly the same pace as his snarling companions, enraged and screaming like a madman.

"Ah, hell," Braedon cursed, winded from having played rescuer with the first two men and not at all looking forward to facing off against these next comers.

He was too old for this at thirty years of age. His bones ached with the relentless winter drizzle, and his head pounded with the knowledge that he could have been sleeping in his cabin right now, or better yet, warm in his bed with some pleasing female company. Instead, he stood a good chance of getting his innards spilled all over the docks in the short time to come.

"What are we going to do?" shrieked his unwanted companion in this mess, the very reason for his present predicament.

"We?" he drawled, then chuckled at the irony as his hand went to his sheathed sword. "It looks like *we* have a bit more trouble to deal with tonight, *demoiselle*."

Braedon swiveled his head, quickly scanning their surroundings, looking for someplace to send the woman where she could make a clean escape or at least be out of his way while he dealt with Ferrand and his mates. But there was nowhere for her to go and Ferrand's men were closing in. "Get back," he ordered, shoving her behind him with a sweep of his arm. "Just stay out of the way, back near the dock."

"Wait!" When he started to walk away from her, she grabbed his sleeve, her grasp surprisingly strong for such a mere slip of a thing. "Are you mad? We must try to outrun them."

"No time." Pulling his arm away from her, he drew his sword.

"But you cannot mean to fight all of them at once— they're going to kill you!"

"Perhaps." He shrugged and threw her a look that was probably more reckless than he felt. "If they kill me, *then* I advise you to run."

Stalking forward, sword at the ready, he met the first man to reach him, the one with the ugly-looking knife. Braedon dodged the first vicious strike, finding it tricky to maneuver in the slick, icy glaze that was beginning to settle on the wide planks of the wharf. He recovered his footing and lunged to deliver a counterattack, but the man saw him coming. He twisted out of the path of the blade and sliced at Braedon's sword arm, gashing him across the top of his wrist.

Braedon roared at the growing burn of the cut, but not out of pain. Feeling his flesh tear under the punishing edge of steel, seeing his blood darken the light gray of his tunic sleeve, the metallic smell of it filling his nostrils with the scent of combat and rage, wakened Braedon like a man coming out of a long, dead sleep.

He pivoted, raising his sword on a guttural oath. The blade came down, hard and heavy and fast. The man with the knife moved his arm to swing again. Not fast enough. Braedon's weapon bit into flesh and bone with a jarring thud, hacking off the man's hand in one clean strike and sending it catapulting into the darkness of the river. Seizing on the moment of horror as the man gaped at his arm, mouth open, mind too shocked to scream, Braedon swung with his blade and knocked the dying man off the pier.

"You're next, Ferrand," he taunted in lethal calm as the Frenchman closed in on him with his man. "I wager your death is long overdue."

"I'm sure we can work this out, you and I," Ferrand replied, lifting his shoulders in a casual shrug. "I have no wish for violence. If you want the wench, take her."

Ferrand grinned, but even in the hazy gray mist of the day Braedon could see the glint of fear in the Frenchman's eyes. He caught the subtle direction that was passed to Ferrand's shipmate, a flick of a glance that commanded the man to move in on Braedon from the other side. *Let him come,* he thought, pretending not to notice the trap and inching backward to lead the two men farther out onto the wharf.

The girl saw the trouble coming, too. From behind him he heard her whispered warning. "Be careful," she said, her light footsteps retreating to the back of the pier, toward safety if he survived or an isolated dead end if he did not.

Ferrand's man made his move suddenly, with a roar of bloodthirsty malice. He charged from the right and bore down on Braedon, forcing him backward on the dock while Ferrand brought up the rear. Braedon's sword crashed against the other man's, the grate of metal on metal—once, twice, and then again—swelling in the air around them. Braedon pushed against the force of his opponent's weapon, driving him back, but the man was an ox. He kept coming at him, kept artlessly swiping his blade like a cleaver.

"Kill him, you idiot!" shouted Ferrand. The merchant had since backed off from his attack. Braedon saw him slowly retreating from the fight, evidently deciding he might rather flee while he had the chance.

Braedon was not about to let him get away. He felt his boot heel snag in something on the ground at his back— a cargo net, heaped in a careless pile on the dock. Near it stood a group of large oak barrels. He grabbed the rim of one with his left hand and hauled it down in front of him, throwing the obstacle at the big man's feet. It knocked the brute off balance and lost him his weapon, which Braedon kicked away. With a bellowed oath, Ferrand's man teetered at the edge of the dock, then fell in with a splash. Braedon meant to leap in after and finish him off, but his attention was drawn over his shoulder, toward the sound of fast-retreating footsteps.

Ferrand was already halfway up the wharf and heading for his own ship.

Braedon took off at a dead run, his boots pounding the wet planks of the docks as he pursued the portly merchant coward. Bloodlust thrummed in his veins with each step that drew him closer. He reached for him and missed, a failure that only compelled him on more fiercely. With a savage cry, Braedon leaped on Ferrand and threw him to the ground. He tried to scramble away, clawing at the planks of the wharf, thrashing beneath Braedon's weight.

Latching onto his shoulder, Braedon flipped him onto his back and threw a punch into the Frenchman's face. He backed off and flung his arm out to reach for his sword, which he had lost in capturing Ferrand.

"Stand up," he ordered the merchant. The blow had dazed Ferrand. At his waist, one of his coin purses had come untied and spilled some of its boon. Braedon reached down and yanked the pouch from his belt, affixing it to his own baldric with a nimble slipknot. "On your feet, and take up your weapon, unless you prefer I skewer you where you lie."

Ferrand shook off his disorientation with a curse, coming up on one knee as he glared at Braedon. "You think I don't know you? Oh, yes," he said around a wheezing chuckle. "I know who you are, *monsieur*. I know all about you."

A queer prickle of expectation crept along the back of Braedon's neck. He stared hard at the fat little man, despising the glint of amusement that lit the merchant's gaze. He felt his hand tighten on his sword, his blood thrumming heavily in his temples. He grabbed the merchant by the shoulder of his cloak and hauled him up, his sword arm prepared to strike. "You had your chance, Ferrand. Now you die."

Braedon raised his weapon—and heard a feminine scream of terror ring out in the distance behind him at the docks. He threw a glance over his shoulder. Through the sleeting rain, he saw the young woman struggling with the man he should have taken the time to kill before setting off after Ferrand. The cur was still half-submerged in the river but coming up on the dock to get her.

"Damn it!"

Braedon had a split second to decide: finish Ferrand, or go to the girl. His every battle instinct commanded him to cut the oily little merchant down, but it would cost him precious time. Ferrand calculated the problem at the same time. He twisted slightly in Braedon's grasp, his chuckle small, but full of amusement. "Another time, *monsieur*."

Braedon felt a queer tingle start in his fingertips, a tingle that quickly spread into his hand and up the length of his arm, raising the hairs on his skin. He swung his head back toward Ferrand . . . and found he held nothing but empty air.

"Jesu," he gasped, astonished and not at all sure his eyes registered the truth.

The merchant was gone. In his hand one moment, the next simply vanished into the sleeting rain. On the wharf a few paces away from him, scrambling low to the ground, was a large brown rat. It paused—God's wounds, did it stop to look at him?—before fleeing into the shadows of the docks.

Nay.

Impossible.

The heavy sleet, the dark misting fog—all of it conspired to confuse him. His grasp on Ferrand must have slackened enough for him to slip away. The storm was pounding hard enough that it might have disguised his retreating footsteps. The sleet itself could have masked the merchant as he fled to a hiding place somewhere on the wharf.

People did not just disappear into thin air. Flesh and bone did not slip away like so much vapor.

And yet . . .

The girl screamed again, drawing Braedon's attention

away from the unsettling feeling that was prickling in his belly. He slicked the rain from his eyes and put Ferrand from his mind to focus wholly on the girl. He saw her bend down and grab something—the net, he realized when she struggled with the sodden weight of it and tossed it onto her attacker. It slowed him down, but he still managed to reach out and seize her by the ankle.

Braedon was on the dock and running toward her before her rump hit the planks.

She clung to one of the heavy barrels, shrieking as the bulk of her attacker's form lurched up out of the water. He still had her ankle, but she was fighting furiously, kicking him with her free leg and stubbornly hanging on to the barrel to keep from being dragged into the river. Ferrand's man made a grab for his sword, which lay just an arm's length from him on the docks. His fingers never gained purchase.

Braedon thundered down the dock and drove his blade into the man's spine, killing him instantly.

The girl kicked away the slack grip on her ankle and scrambled back near the barrels, her breath quavering and shallow. Braedon sheathed his weapon then reached out his hand to her.

"Are you all right?"

She nodded, but he could see that she was shaking violently, her face ashen. Beneath the skewed tilt of her ridiculous little hat, her blue eyes were wide with terror, her gaze glassy with shock. The webbed crispinette that held her thickly coiled blond hair neatly behind her head had been ruined in her struggle. Torn and drooping, the slender threads of damp silk hung limply at her neck, trembling as she did. She was a wreck, and judging from her stricken pallor, he doubted very much that she would have the wherewithal to walk away without his support.

"Come on," he growled, pulling her hood up over her head to shield her from the drizzle. "It's over now. Let's get out of here."

She took his hand, turning her face into his arm as he led her away from the carnage on the wharfs. He brought her up onto the street, then hurried around a corner that opened at the front of an old church dedicated to St. Magnus the Martyr.

"Where are we going? Please—where are you taking me?"

"To the bridge," he said, deciding just then and gesturing to a stone archway ahead of them. Sturdy chains hung between two wooden poles, marking the line where London's rule ended and the jurisdiction of London Bridge's powerful merchant class began. "You're best to wait the next few hours outside of the city in case any more of Ferrand's men come sniffing around."

Beyond the tall gray tollgate was an elevated street suspended over the Thames by no less than two dozen arches of varying sizes, which spanned the width of the churning brown river. Crowded with shops, residences, and chapels, the London Bridge was a living stretch of stone and timber and humanity that linked London town with Southwark, its seedier neighbor on the other side. Normally the bridge would be overrun with carts and people and wandering animals, but with today's inclement weather, the twelve-foot-wide street beyond the tollhouse looked all but deserted.

A guard on watch called for them to halt and pay the toll. Braedon loosened the coin pouch on his baldric and felt the girl's eyes light on him in accusation.

"That's my purse," she said. " 'Tis my money in that pouch—Ferrand stole it from me."

Braedon grunted, but he was not about to let go of the purse. The way he saw it, Ferrand owed him at least this much for his recent cheating. To say nothing of the gratitude this highborn lady rightly owed him for rescuing her from the vile French whoremonger and his henchmen. Ignoring the sullen glare he received from the girl at his side, Braedon dug into the pilfered coin purse and withdrew the two farthings it would cost them to cross. They walked briskly beneath the steep stone archway of the tollgate, sheltered momentarily from the sleet outside.

"Do you have a name, *demoiselle*?" Braedon asked her as they traversed the dark hollow of the corridor. For a long moment, the only reply was the wet sound of their boots slapping on the cobbles and echoing over the steady rush of the water some thirty feet below.

"Ariana," she answered finally, as if reluctant to divulge any information to him. "Ariana of Clairmont."

He had not heard of the place, but it was clear from the cultured timbre of her voice that she was a young lady from a good house of high degree. And he was certain, even without asking, that she did not hail from London or its nearby towns, for he would have seen her before now, and he would not have forgotten a lovely face like hers.

No, after all he had been through, ironically, he had not lost his appreciation for beauty. He remembered fine things and pretty faces, and he sometimes lost himself in pleasant memories of a life abundant with both. He did not miss the pretension of those days or the arrogance of the stupid young man he had been. So careless, so caught up in his own indulgences and blinded by his own glory. All it took now was an accidental glimpse of his reflection—in a pool of water, or in the frightened, wary gaze of a gently bred maiden like the one hurrying along beside him on the bridge—to remind him of what that life had cost him.

Braedon jerked his thoughts away from memories of the past, before more troubling reminders could surface. He and the girl came out from under the covered portion of the bridge gate and stepped back into the elements. The icy rain stung his face but he made no move to draw his hood farther over his head, well aware that his scar was in plain sight. He didn't care.

Let her look at it, he thought grimly, willing himself to ignore the furtive glances coming from over her right shoulder as they walked in silence. Let her stare like everyone else and shrink away.

He had lived long enough with the travesty of his face that he could almost count the time it would take for someone to have their fill of it and avert their eyes. Gasps and stares no longer affected him, but to his utter irritation, he found he could not bear this woman's quiet scrutiny after all. He sensed a hidden trace of pity there, and it angered him more than any open display of fear or disgust ever could. He stopped walking and abruptly turned to face her straight on.

"W-what are you doing?" she asked, frowning up at him. "Shouldn't we keep going?"

"I thought it might be easier for you to stare if I held still a while."

"Oh." Her wind-nipped cheeks reddened deeper as she quickly averted her gaze. "I'm sorry."

"For the condition of my face, or your rude perusal of it?"

She glanced up sharply. "Both."

He raised a brow.

"Neither," she corrected, huffing a little sigh of discomfiture. Her gaze flew down once more, shuttered by golden brown lashes several shades darker than her hair. A lock of that honey-colored silk peeked out from under the hood of her mantle, glossy and golden yellow against the russet red of her fox-lined cloak. She worried her lip, frowning in consternation and clearly unsure what to do with her gaze now. "Forgive me for staring. I meant no offense. I am sorry."

Braedon grunted. He wasn't looking for an apology, merely meant to make a point. But now that he had, he wondered what he had gained. He wondered at her age suddenly, which had to be less than twenty by his guess. At least a decade his junior. Too young by far, and exceedingly too pretty to be traipsing around London without a full retinue of armed bodyguards.

"This way," he said, and started walking once more. She followed along beside him, carefully avoiding looking at him at all.

Although he intended to be rid of her within a few hours and to put her out of his mind entirely not long after that, he could not curb his curiosity about the woman. And since he was cut and bleeding on account of her besides, he reckoned he had a right to know just what sort of pretty little fool he had risked his life to save.

"I hardly think whatever bauble or silk you meant to purchase from Ferrand was worth the price, *demoiselle*."

"I didn't come here to buy anything from him."

"No?"

"No. I came to London on a matter of business. Urgent business." She eyed her coin purse, which bobbed at his hip, neatly secured to his sword belt. "That money was to pay for my passage to France."

"France?" he scoffed. "What could possibly be there that you would want to brave the Channel in the dead of winter?"

"Nothing of your concern, I assure you."

She made a hasty grab for the purse, but Braedon was faster. He jerked it from his baldric and caught it in his other hand. "Your disagreement with Ferrand down there was none of my concern, either, but you didn't seem to mind me stepping in to save your silly neck." He met her haughty glare and held it. "What's in France?"

She scowled, her fine brow pinching, lovely mouth pursed. "If you must know," she said, relenting after a moment, "my brother is there. I was going to Rouen to . . . to visit him."

That was likely a lie, or at the very least, a partial truth. "Urgent business, this visit, was it?"

"That's right. He . . . he needs me, and I have to get there as soon as possible. I will get there."

Braedon snorted at her senseless determination. "Any brother who would expect his sister to brave ice squalls and rough seas for the mere pleasure of his company is either an idiot or a madman. Maybe both."

That pricked her dander. His stride was purposefully long, but Lady Ariana kept up despite their difference in size. Her boot heels clipped smartly on the planks of the street. "My brother is the most honorable man I know. He would never willingly put my life in jeopardy."

"I am glad to hear it, *demoiselle*. Then he will no doubt consider it a favor if I keep your purse and prevent you from further endangering yourself."

"A fine excuse, coming from a common thief and scoundrel," she grumbled, not quite under her breath. "I could have you arrested for stealing, you know. No doubt a man like you is wanted for any number of misdeeds."

"Your gratitude overwhelms me, my lady. Perhaps you would rather I had left you at the wharf to deal with true thieves and scoundrels? I warrant you would have lost far more than just your coin."

She grew very quiet as she absorbed the weight of his comment. Her steps slowed a bit, and the flashing impertinence he had been enjoying in spite of himself was fading quickly from her eyes. Braedon frowned, irritated that he should feel even a twinge of guilt for his goading of the girl. He stamped it out as quickly as it had come, refusing to feel anything for a foolhardy girl who would walk headlong into a den of cutthroats and criminals on a whim to see her kin on the Continent.

"Is Clairmont so far from London that no one advised you of its dangers? The docklands are no place for a lady of gentle breeding, particularly one wandering about practically without escort."

He half expected an argument, or at least a hot retort, so he was surprised when she was silent, her gaze directed out over the river as they walked an open section of the bridge. "James tried to warn me," she replied quietly. She made a regretful sound in the back of her throat. "He told me he didn't trust Ferrand, but I . . . I didn't listen. Oh, poor James! I can't believe he's . . ."

She bit her lip, evidently unable to speak the word. Turning away from him to head toward the wall of the bridge, she walked to the edge and looked out over the river. Her dainty gloved hands were braced on the waist-high wall, gripping it tightly as her shoulders quaked beneath her cloak. Despite her tenacity, she was obviously a sheltered young girl, and she had been through quite an ordeal; the weight of it bore down on her now. She turned her face against her shoulder, away from him, and softly wept.

Braedon paused, uncomfortable with this female state of distress. Perhaps he had seen too much death in his lifetime to recall what it was like to grieve. Nor did he have the patience to console Lady Ariana when he could still sense Ferrand and his mates sniffing around the docks.

"Come," he said, resisting the urge to touch her. "We should not tarry here. The sleet is getting worse again and night comes faster in a storm. We haven't far to go now."

With a shaky nod, she collected herself and turned to walk with him once more.

Braedon guided her farther down the bridge, toward the rows of countless merchant shops that clung to each side of the street, some of them built out and over the edge of the bridge, their timber overhangs supported by thick oak-hewn struts. The street was dark, cast in shadow by the looming buildings flanking it and by the *hautpas* that stretched over the narrow walkway to afford more living space to the residents while strengthening the structures on either side.

Shopkeepers' shingles hung some nine feet above the ground, high enough to permit horse and rider to pass beneath them. Colorfully painted pictures advertised the tradesmen's skills or the goods to be had within their shops. This near the City side of the bridge, the merchants catered to a higher class of customer, offering luxurious items ranging from gloves and hats and bolts of rich fabrics to maps and books and musical instruments.

Braedon passed all these shops with nary a glance, taking his unwanted charge closer to the midsection of the bridge, where the street odors mingled with the spicy tang of incense, which drifted out like ghostly ribbons of perfume from the stone walls of the famed Chapel of St. Thomas à Becket. He felt Ariana pause and knew she could not help but gaze with wonder at the beautiful place of worship. The London Bridge was renowned in places farther than the Continent, and the chapel, named for the tragic bishop killed on order of the second King Henry, was its crowning jewel.

"My lady," he said, prompting her past the towering chapel with its pointed towers and on toward another tight cluster of merchant shops.

They picked up their pace and darted beneath the sheltering canopy of another *hautpas*. "I had heard this bridge is like a city unto itself, but I had no idea it was so vast. Is this where you live?" she asked.

"Nay, but I know someone who does."

"A friend of yours?"

"Once. A long time ago." He considered her innocent question with a measure of irritation. "I don't make it a habit to keep friends."

"Why not?"

He kept walking, answering without looking at her. "It's proved too dangerous."

"Oh." He felt her gaze on him, wary with understanding. "To dangerous for them, you mean?"

"Nay, *demoiselle*. For me."

They stopped in front of a half-timbered shop at the end of the row. Braedon blew out his breath and approached the door, glancing up at the shoe-and-hammer sign that swayed from its hinge above their heads. The shingle proclaimed the resident a cobbler, but he had been a knight when Braedon knew him best. One of the greatest, most valiant men ever to wield a sword. They had fought many battles together, shared many adventures, celebrated untold victories.

But that was before. . . .

"Step out of the rain," he instructed the girl, an impatient edge to his voice.

He brought her before him under the eaves, then reached out and rapped on the old oak door. It opened a short moment later, creaking inward. From within the wedge of warmth and light, a woman about Braedon's age peered out into the drizzling rain. Her gaze flicked over the two sodden visitors standing beneath the eaves, her questioning brown eyes darting from the tall man standing back in the shadows to the girl huddled in front of him, shaking and wet.

"Good morrow, Peg."

The woman's gaze narrowed as she stared up at Braedon, now peering in scrutiny at his eyes, at the scar that jagged down the entire left side of his face. She frowned, no doubt trying to reconcile the vaguely familiar voice with the savage, wrecked face of a stranger. It took but a heartbeat for her confused disbelief to burn away into recognition.

Once it did, her round face took on a harder mien.

"Braedon," she said, her voice soft but not welcoming.

"It has been a long time, Peg. You look well."

Her mouth went tight at his pleasant greeting after more than a year of absence. A welcome absence, if the fractional closing of her door were any indication. She looked to his scar again, damage not present when last she saw him. If it raised any emotion in her to see it now, she seemed intent to swallow past it. "What do you want, Braedon? How did you find us?"

"I need to talk to your husband," he said, understanding that her wariness of him—her distrust, even after all this time—was not entirely misplaced. Braedon felt another suspicious female gaze fix on him, this one coming from Ariana of Clairmont. She likely wondered at this cool reception at the house of a so-called friend. Perhaps she felt a certain satisfaction to see it, although it hardly mattered to him what she thought. In a few hours, she would no longer be his concern at all. "Is he here, Peg?"

"Nay. Not for you." She moved forward so she blocked the entrance. Her voice was tight and low, as if to speak without being heard from within the shop. "Haven't you cost him enough? We have a new life now, as you can see."

"I won't stay long, I promise you." He gestured to Ariana with a slight jerk of his chin. "This girl is in trouble. I wouldn't have come, but I had hoped you might help—"

Peg's answering scoff was brittle. "Trouble has a way of following you, doesn't it, Braedon? Perhaps I should call for the sheriff instead."

There was a sudden shuffle of movement somewhere at Peg's back: the scrape of a chair on the wide planked floor, the irregular *clop-scuff-clop* of a heavy gait drawing near.

"Who is it, my love?" called a booming voice from out of the gloom. The dragging footsteps and dull thud of a walking cane continued to advance. "Who the devil would be out in this weather?"

Peg threw a frantic look over her shoulder, then glared back at Braedon. " 'Tis no one, husband. Just a couple of lost pilgrims seeking the nearest tavern."

Her husband's chuckle was rich and good-natured, just as Braedon remembered it. "Well, they will find not a one on the bridge. No cellars to store the ale, you see."

"Yes," Peg replied. "As I told them, they will have to look elsewhere for what they want."

She started to close the door on Braedon and the girl, but a thick forearm and a large, callused hand reached over her shoulder and pushed the panel wide. "The Bear at Bridgefoot is your closest bet, friends, but I wager you'll find a better ale at the Three Neats' Tongues on the City side . . ."

The big man's voice trailed off when his merry eyes settled on Braedon. Robert the cobbler, once known across England as Robert the Bold, stood and stared in dumbstruck silence. Though bearded now and balding, lame from the injury that had ended his years as a knight and relegated him to accept a cobbler's apprenticeship with Peg's sire, Braedon was glad to see there was still a glint of humor in his dark eyes, still a light of conspiracy in his slow-spreading smile. "Christ on the Cross. As I live and breathe . . . Braedon. Is it really you, after all this time?"

"Rob," he replied, smiling back despite himself as he reached around Ariana to clasp his old friend's hand in firm greeting.

"I've long thought you dead, my friend. You should be, after what happened that day."

Braedon shrugged off the note of concern in his friend's comment. If he had been presumed dead, it was because he had wanted it that way. He still preferred to maintain his distance from reminders of his past. It was one of the reasons he had stayed away from Rob, despite having known for some time that he was living here on the bridge, just a few hundred feet from where Braedon docked when he was in London.

"Jesu, Braedon." The graying, plump ex-knight looked him up and down, then met his gaze and grinned. "You look like hell." He shook his head and let out a deep, rolling chuckle. "You look like bloody hell, but by my vow I've never seen a more welcome sight in all my years! Come in, come in."

Peg had since drawn up beside her husband, a miserable look of regret tugging at the corners of her mouth. She loved Rob fiercely, and she would not deny him a happy reunion with an old friend, no matter how personally opposed to it she was. Braedon respected that about her, and he had no wish to add to her worries.

He would not have burdened them with his presence at all, if it had not been for the unexpected—and wholly unwanted—problem of Ariana of Clairmont. He shouldn't have gotten involved in the first place, but now that he had, he was loath to leave her adrift in the city by herself. Rob would make certain she got back home without trouble. As for himself, he planned to leave port and sail for warmer climes at the next tide.

And in a private, weary corner of his heart, he knew the trip would likely be his last.

"I'll come in, but I cannot stay. An hour at most, and then I must go."

This he said to his friend, but his pledge was directed in deference at Peg. She met his meaningful gaze before stepping aside to admit Ariana and him into her home. "We've just finished supper, but there is still some porridge left in the pot, if you'd like me to warm it along with some wine for the both of you."

She looked at Ariana, who had grown quite still and quiet in the time she had spent with Braedon on the bridge. She could see the girl was exhausted. She removed her hood and her ruined head covering, which had not done much to keep her dry amid the deluge. Thick tendrils of her long hair had come loose of their braids and now drooped over her brow, soaked like the rest of her.

She was trembling and wrung out, standing there in weary silence. She flinched when Peg came over to help her out of her soggy mantle.

"I'll just put it by the fire, where it can dry. Here, let me have that heavy bag, child."

Ariana's hands slammed down on top of the large leather satchel at her hip, as though in reflex. "Nay. Not this. This stays with me."

"As you wish." Peg gave the girl a reassuring smile that dimmed somewhat when turned on Braedon. "Your mantle, too," she said, thrusting out her hand to take his cloak.

As he shrugged out of the wet garment and surrendered it, he saw Peg's questioning gaze fix on his injured arm. "I had a small disagreement with a couple of men down on the docks. 'Tis nothing."

Peg glared up at him and clucked her tongue. "Nothing, he says, while he bleeds all over my floor. Stay put," she ordered him, some of her sternness lost in the huff of resigned exasperation she blew out. "I'll fetch some cloths to clean and bind your arm. Your lady can help you undress."

❧ 3 ❧

TIRED AND COLD, Ariana felt as though she had somehow breached a barrier to a strange new land, a land very different from her home at Clairmont. London was indeed a dangerous place, and she was alone here, save for the dubious companionship of the man who had delivered her out of harm's way and promised shelter with these good people on the bridge.

The selfsame man who had stolen her purse from Monsieur Ferrand and claimed it for his own, she hastened to remind herself when the warmth of the cobbler's shop began to thaw some of her good sense.

That the cobbler's wife could assume she and this man—Braedon, had they called him?—shared some sort of personal connection snapped Ariana out of her torpor like a hammer dropped on glass. Help him undress, indeed! She ignored the steady gaze that pierced her from where he stood and hurried after the woman, who disappeared into an adjacent room of the shop.

"You should know that man is not my . . . that is to say, we are not—"

"Is it a knife wound, or something other?"

Ariana gave an uncertain shrug. "Knife, I believe."

With a disapproving grunt, Peg opened a cabinet and took out a folded swatch of old white linen, which she proceeded to tear into several long strips. She turned and handed them to Ariana, then retrieved a small corked pot of ointment from a shelf containing an array of like-shaped containers. "Are you injured as well?"

Ariana shook her head. "I have a few bruises, but I am fine. Some bad men attacked me near the docks. They killed my friend and stole my money, but he . . . Braedon," she said, reluctantly testing the name on her tongue, "he saved my life."

Peg eyed her skeptically as she handed her the pot of salve. "Well, then. I'd say you were most fortunate. The Braedon I know would sooner walk away from people when they need him most."

She stepped past Ariana without another word, leaving her to stand there and wonder what he had done to make this woman so distrustful of him. The harsh words she greeted him with echoed back to Ariana in a cool rush of memory: *Haven't you cost him enough? Trouble has a way of following you, doesn't it, Braedon?*

Standing beside him under the eaves of the shop's front door, Ariana had looked up at him as he absorbed those words. She had not missed his slight flinch or the muscle in his jaw that went tight in reflex at his unwelcome reception. But he had not said anything to counter Peg's vague accusations.

Nor had he seemed surprised to hear his friend, Rob, say that he had thought him dead.

We all did, after what happened that day.

Ariana felt a tug of curiosity pull at her. That he had been away for some time was clear enough, but why? Who was this scarred, unreadable man who had spared her from death—or worse—at Monsieur Ferrand's hand? Who was he, and what was it that haunted him? For it was clear that he was a man haunted by something that went deeper than any flesh wound . . .

"Oh, what does it matter, anyway?" she chided herself in a stern whisper.

Shaking away thoughts of her broody rescuer, she reminded herself that she had bigger problems of her own to consider. Kenrick's ransom weighed like a heavy stone in the large leather satchel slung over her shoulder. At least Ferrand had not discovered that particular treasure. Nor Braedon, she thought with a prickle of sharp resentment. He had refused to return her coin purse, but she would fight him unto death before she surrendered the key to Kenrick's freedom.

She would wait here until she could be sure Ferrand had lost her trail, as Braedon had suggested, and then she would search out another means of getting to France. Perhaps she would sell James's fine gelding, which she prayed was still stabled with her mare back near the tavern at Queenhithe. Surely if the boon was high enough, she could find an honest ship captain willing to take her to the Continent. Perhaps she would inquire after such a captain at one of the chapels on the bridge.

Kenrick's ransom would be delivered to his captors, as planned. She would not abandon her mission to save him. She would not fail him, no matter what it might cost her.

The renewed sense of resolve bolstered her as she carried the bandages and ointment out to the other room.

Braedon was seated on a bench at a small table near the fire. He had already removed his tunic, thankfully without her assistance, and he now sat there bare-chested and wholly immodest, a cup of steaming wine caught in his hand. Peg straddled the bench beside him, cleansing the wound on his right forearm while he drank and conversed with her husband in low tones across the table. Ariana thought she heard Clairmont mentioned as she approached with Peg's supplies, but she could not be sure as the discussion ceased altogether by the time she reached the table.

"Set them there, if you will," Peg said, gesturing to the empty space of table near her.

Ariana did as instructed, her gaze locking for an instant with the unsettling intensity of Braedon's piercing gray eyes. She glanced away, feigning disinterest while Peg swabbed up the last few streaks of blood from his arm and reached for the pot of ointment. Before she could remove the cork, something began to bubble over and hiss in the fireplace.

"Ach! My porridge," Peg exclaimed, leaping to her feet. She plopped the jar of ointment down in Ariana's palm. "Dress his wound while I see about your supper."

"But I—"

"Let me help you, wife." Rob swung his legs over the bench he occupied and hobbled away from the table to follow Peg to the hearth. He lightly swatted her behind when he reached her side, then retrieved two wooden bowls from a shelf on the wall. Something he whispered in his wife's ear made her laugh softly.

Against her will, Ariana turned her gaze on Braedon. Though he said not a word, he was watching her expectantly as he took a drink from his cup of wine. The firelight danced on his skin as he moved, illuminating a fascinating expanse of sculpted sinew and hard, lean lines. A dusting of crisp dark hair spread across the planes of his strong chest. His muscled belly looked as firm as granite beneath the loose waistband of his winter hose.

Ariana felt her face flame as she considered his unclothed form, although she did not know why he should affect her so. She had seen men without their tunics on before. Indeed, very often in the summer months the knights at Clairmont would practice thus at their weapons in the yard. Kenrick had possessed no large measure of modesty around her, either, but there was something very different between her golden-haired brother's athletic physique and this man's swarthy and immense warrior's body.

If Kenrick was beautifully formed, as her friends frequently assured her he was, then this man was profane in his masculinity. Everything about him was hard and imposing, from his savaged face with its strong dark brow, blade-sharp cheeks, and stern jaw, to the iron-hewn brutality of his massive shoulders and body, which exuded an air of pure power even at rest. Heaven help her, but Ariana found it difficult to tear her gaze away from him.

"Here," he drawled from his seat on the bench, startling her gaze back to his with the deep sound of his voice. A smirk teased the edge of his mouth as he slid his cup of wine toward her on the table. "You look as though you could use this more than me. You're not going to swoon at the sight of a little blood, are you?"

"Of course not. I am no stranger to dressing wounds," she told him, meeting the slight mockery in his tone with a haughty look of offense.

She had dressed wounds, that was true enough, although she was not at all certain the sundry scrapes she had assisted with at Clairmont could compare to a knife wound like the one presented to her now. She stared at the small crock in her hand, then down at the ugly gash that had torn open Braedon's arm. It was bleeding again, less than before, but it looked painful and nasty, and she wondered how he could sit there and endure it as if it were nothing at all. As it was, she could hardly stand to look at the damage. But she refused to show her squeamishness, or to betray the peculiar tremor of awareness that coursed through her at the thought of putting herself in such close proximity to him and touching his bare skin.

Sitting beside him, her back to the table—for she was not so bold as Peg that she would lift her skirts and straddle the bench as she had done—Ariana retrieved the damp cloth and blotted away the fresh blood from Braedon's arm. Her hands were slightly unsteady as she removed the cork from the pot of ointment and set it aside. The tincture was brown and sticky, and it smelled of tree sap and spices and moist loamy earth. She dipped her finger in the pungent muck and carefully applied it to Braedon's wound.

"This cut is deep. It really should be stitched or it will leave a terrible-looking . . . scar."

She realized her slip an instant too late. She had done it again, calling attention to the scar he already bore, the knife-edge line of white that gave his face such a rough, brutal appearance. Wincing inwardly, she lifted her gaze from Braedon's arm. He was watching her with mild interest, his eyes hooded, revealing nothing of his mood.

"I'm sorry," she whispered, feeling ten times a fool and an insensitive clod. "I didn't mean . . ."

He said nothing to excuse her or put her at ease, merely looked at her as he reached out to hand her a strip of linen bandage. Ariana worked quickly. She wrapped his arm securely to seal the wound, all the while feeling his gaze on her like a physical thing, warm and weighty, menacing and yet compelling. She bent over his arm to fasten off the ends of the bindings and felt his breath stir her hair. This close, her senses filled with him—the intriguing definition and form of his muscular torso, the rain-washed, spicy scent of his skin, so warm beneath her fingertips. . . .

Nay, this was nothing like the ministrations she had provided at Clairmont. This was something vastly different. He was different from anyone she knew, and she did not know why he should affect her so. Heaven help her, but she did not want to know. She could hardly wait to get the last knot tied and put a respectable space between them.

All the better that she would soon put the English Channel itself between them.

At last Peg and Rob returned to the table. Peg carried a tray containing two bowls of steaming, yeasty-sweet porridge; Rob hobbled along beside her, one hand on his cane, the other wrapped around the neck of a decanter filled with more hot mulled wine.

"Here you are. 'Tis not much, but it should warm you some."

Peg placed the bowls on the table while Rob poured the wine. Ariana's stomach growled at the sight of the warm meal and she ate as if she had just come off a long Lenten fast. She was hungry and cold, but the wine and porridge filled her, and the heat of the fireplace enveloped her like a blanket of thick downy wool.

Though she fought it, sleep beckoned now that she was sated and warm. The lure of slumber peeled away the trauma of the day and a contented drowsiness began to descend, dimming Ariana's problems, muting the sounds in the room, dousing the light from the glowing hearth. Her eyelids grew heavy, her head a taxing weight on her shoulders. She sighed and felt herself succumbing to the quiet, needing the rest as badly as she had needed the sustenance of her meal.

She stretched her arm out on the table and slowly nestled her head in the crook of her elbow. She needed rest, but she could not afford to sleep for long. The satchel containing Kenrick's ransom hung reassuringly at her hip, a constant reminder of her task, her vow. She drew the pouch onto her lap, clutching it in her free arm, and let herself relax a bit.

She would close her eyes for just a few moments, and then she would extricate herself from this place and these people, and be on her way once more. . . .

"God's bones, Braedon. I see you here at my table and I wonder if I am sitting with a ghost."

With Peg gone to the other room and Ariana asleep like the dead on the bench beside him, Braedon glanced up and met the gaze of his old brother-in-arms. Rob's jovial mood sobered now that it was just the two of them. They shared a dark bond, having survived a hellish night that had ended in a storm of blood and flames. Like an old wound that refused to mend, being in Rob's presence dredged up vivid images of things Braedon wished he could forget.

"At least a year and a half it's been since that night, but I vow it could have happened only yesterday." Rob blew out a curse. "What kept you away all this time? How could you let me think you had perished out there on that tideswept crag like the others?"

Braedon shrugged, then took a drink of his wine, considering the day he had led five loyal men to their graves. It was supposed to have been a victory celebration, a very lucrative one, funded by a wealthy man who'd imposed upon Braedon's vaunted reputation with an irresistible offer. Retrieve a certain trinket, and he would be paid a sizable reward. Double the boon, should he also bring in the thief who stole it.

Braedon had come through—the relentless le Chasseur never failed—and he was eager to collect his promised due. Too eager, it turned out. For on the night of the exchange, what awaited him and the small band of men he trusted like brothers was betrayal by one of their own and an ensuing horrific bloodbath. Braedon should have seen it coming, but he'd been blinded by his own arrogance. Invincible, so he'd come to think. Until that night proved him worse than a fool.

That he had lived when other more worthy men had not provided little comfort, then or now. In truth, he had been trying to escape that night ever since, but it seemed no amount of running carried him far enough away from the horror of what he had witnessed.

Rob expelled a heavy breath. "Jesu, Braedon. I can still see that blade flashing down across your face. The bastard meant to lay you open. 'Tis a miracle you survived. A miracle we both did, truth to tell. The devil himself was on that cliff that day."

"Not the devil," Braedon replied. "Just a man."

Rob leaned in, lowering his voice to a near whisper. "A man whom steel can't fell?"

Braedon stared at him, then lowered his gaze to his cup, refusing to acknowledge his friend's statement. But Rob, despite being so many months away from the matter, seemed unwilling to give it up.

"It was the devil, my friend. How do you explain the evil we saw?"

Braedon shrugged. "My strike was off. I missed my mark, that's all."

"You never missed your mark—not in all the years I've

known you. Your blade struck true as ever. I saw it, and you did, too."

"I don't know what I saw."

"And what of the girl we delivered there?" Rob asked. "Don't tell me your eyes failed to see what haunts me to this day, Braedon. How do you explain the way she died?"

Braedon's jaw clamped tight at the mention of the thief he'd been sent to locate and return. A fey thing, with silver-blond hair and a timidity that seemed wholly at odds with the boldness it had taken for her to steal a priceless artifact from a man as powerful as the one who'd hired Braedon. An artifact she refused to touch with her bare hands for fear that it would destroy her. How mad she'd sounded to him. How mad it still seemed to him to think on it now.

"We intruded on some black brand of magic, Braedon. She tried to warn us. We should have let her go—her and that accursed cup she'd stolen. We should have listened to her. By the Rood, but how could we have known she spoke the truth?"

"I didn't come here to talk about her, Rob. Or anything else that happened then." His voice was clipped, an angry growl that rang in his ears. His hand was gripped tight around his tankard, but somehow he managed to effect a calmer timbre as he looked up and met his friend's uncertain gaze. "It's over, what happened that day, Rob. It is done. Let us speak no more on it."

Rob nodded. "As you wish, my friend. I did not mean to dredge up memories best left buried."

But the memories had been unearthed, and a pall of thoughtful silence descended on the small shop room. Braedon took a long drink of wine that did nothing to assuage the rise of bitter bile in his throat. With little effort, he could still see the incredible explosion of fire that had erupted atop the cliff. He could still feel his confusion—his rage—as the blood of his men began to spill all around him, chaos loosed by his own failing. He could still feel his blade cleaving the air, could hear it sing as it descended, could see it hit the flesh and bone shoulder of his enemy . . . and pass clean through without leaving so much as a scrape.

And now he could not help thinking about what had happened on the docks a short while before, when Ferrand de Paris all but evaporated from his grasp.

He shook his head, thrusting aside the illogical track his mind was wont to take, and focused on issues rooted in the here and now, namely Lady Ariana of Clairmont and his desire to relieve himself of her welfare as soon as possible. He explained the situation to Rob, who readily agreed to see her home within the week.

"Anything you need, Braedon. You know you have but to ask and I will be there for you."

He rose and took Rob's hand in a firm grasp of friendship. He did not waste words on excuses or farewells. Fetching his tunic, which had since dried before the fire, he shrugged into it and fixed his baldric around his hips. There were less than four hours until the tide came in, and he meant to set sail as soon as the river swelled enough to permit safe travel out of London.

"You won't be coming back." Rob did not pose it as a question. As always, even after all this time, he knew him well. "Where will you go?"

Braedon shook his head. "Wherever fate sees fit to carry me, I suppose."

Rob nodded, understanding. "Might you see fit to help

me carry this child to a proper bed before you go?" he asked, hooking his thumb at Ariana, who had begun to stir where she slept draped over the table.

Braedon carefully lifted her slack weight into his arms. She opened her eyes as her head came to rest against his shoulder and murmured something about taking care of her satchel. A moment later she was dozing again, as delicate as a sparrow, her arms wrapped around his neck, her breath fanning warm and light against his chest. He brought her into an adjacent room and set Ariana down on a small pallet within.

Rob was waiting outside the door when Braedon came out a few moments later to retrieve his mantle. He turned and reached for the latch on the shop door.

"Stay, Braedon. Let's talk some more. You can leave on the morrow's tide."

He paused for the slightest moment at Rob's entreaty, then without a word, he opened the door and walked into the gathering darkness outside.

Ariana was lost in a blissful dream. In the haziness of her sleep-drenched mind, she felt the inexplicable sensation of weightlessness, of being protected and sheltered, carried in strong arms away from a roiling sea of danger and placed with gentle care into a nest of soft wool. The dream stretched out, washing over her in languorous waves. Timeless, seductive.

A comforting brush of hard, warm fingers traced her cheek, then tenderly smoothed her hair. Ariana snuggled deeper into the phantom caress, deeper into the dream, relishing the feeling of safety, of quiet calm.

Through the muted veil of slumber that cocooned her, a low, soothing whisper caressed her temple, so near she could feel the words form against her brow. "Sleep, little sparrow, and godspeed. . . ."

The voice was deep and cultured, yet laced with an edge of danger. It was a warrior's voice, as rough as the calluses on his sword-worn fingertips, yet speaking words as soft as the finest velvet. There was a sadness in that voice as well. A loneliness. A solitude that touched something deep in Ariana's soul.

It beckoned to her, like a wary, wounded animal, and against everything she knew to be prudent, Ariana found herself reaching for it.

Reaching for him.

"Braedon . . ."

"He's not here, child."

Peg's voice jolted Ariana awake. She pushed herself up on the pallet that had been her bed and blinked away the cobwebs of sleep. Her hair was loose from its plaits, disheveled and hanging in her eyes. She raked it from her face and met the taxed gaze of the cobbler's wife.

"I must have been dreaming," Ariana offered, somewhat embarrassed to have called out Braedon's name in her sleep, and thankful that he had not been the one standing there to witness it himself. "What hour is it?"

Peg stood in the doorway of the small antechamber, her arms crossed over her chest. "The chapel bell will soon toll Lauds."

"Nearly daybreak?" Ariana drew aside the thin wool coverlet and pivoted to place her feet on the floor. "I have slept far longer than I intended."

"You looked as though you needed the rest," Peg said. She shoved off the doorjamb and crossed to open a shuttered window on the adjacent wall. The storm had cleared overnight. Now the bare light of the coming dawn spilled into the dark chamber and cast Peg's face in a pale pinkish glow as she looked out over the river below. "You should attend your toilette now. My husband has gone to fetch a cart and horse. He'll be back anon, and I trust you'll be ready when he returns."

Ariana adjusted her heavy leather satchel, which had twisted around to her back in her sleep. "Ready for what?"

"Why, Rob is taking you home, of course."

"Home?" she echoed, shaking her head in denial when Peg turned away from the window to meet her confused gaze. "I don't understand."

"The weather has cleared enough for safe travel, and so there is no reason to delay. 'Twas Braedon's request that Rob transport you to your home—Clairmont, is it?"

"Yes, but—" Ariana stood up, fully alert now. She knew Braedon considered her a fool to risk passage to the Continent, but who was he to interfere in her affairs? "I appreciate your willingness to assist me, but I have no wish to return home. In truth, I cannot. You see, I am on my way to France. That's why I'm here in London—to secure passage across the Channel."

Peg gave her a skeptical look. "According to Braedon, you are stranded here without escort. He told Rob that you have no means and no money—"

"Aye," Ariana retorted archly, "because he stole it from me. Well, stole it more or less. It doesn't matter. I will find a way to get where I am going. I appreciate your generosity, but I assure you it is unnecessary." She bent to retrieve her boots from the floor near the pallet, then yanked them on in a huff. "Despite what Braedon might think is best for me, I don't need to be escorted home. Nor do I need any of his charity. Indeed, I've half a mind to tell him so right this moment."

"You cannot," Peg said when Ariana straightened her skirts and made to march out of the room. "He has already left."

"Where?"

Peg gave a noncommittal shrug. "To the docks, I imagine. He's been gone a few hours. Rob said he planned to set sail on the incoming tide."

"Set sail?" Ariana asked, stunned into stillness by this information. "Whose ship does he sail?"

"His own, I expect. Braedon is not the type to serve another man."

No, she did not imagine he was. Ariana whispered a quiet oath. "When is the tide due in?"

Peg did not answer. Ariana's face must have reflected the urgent track of her thinking, for Peg suddenly reached out and placed a firm but gentle hand on her arm. "Let him go. For your own good, I tell you this now—woman to woman. There is a darkness in his heart, and if you get too close, it will consume you. Let him go, and if your paths should ever cross again, grant him a wide berth. He will only hurt you in the end, I promise you."

Ariana swallowed hard as she acknowledged Peg's warning. She saw the sincerity in the woman's dim brown eyes, heard the same in her ominous advice to keep her distance from Braedon. But more than wary of the warning, she was desperate, and she knew every hour that slid by while she remained in London took her one step closer to Kenrick's demise.

With a wordless cry, Ariana wrenched her arm from

Peg's grasp and bolted from the shop, dashing out into the waking throng that was starting to fill the street of London Bridge.

Braedon had a boat, and when he left port she meant to be on it—no matter what it might cost her.

❧ 4 ❧

"Yᴏᴜ ᴅɪᴅɴ'ᴛ ᴛᴇʟʟ me you owned a boat."

Braedon unlashed one of the lines on his cog and turned to find Ariana of Clairmont standing behind him on the wharf, regarding him in stormy accusation. He was not surprised to see her there; he had heard the terse clip of boots on the dock as she approached, and his instincts had told him it was her even before her light gait and the angry swish of her skirts and long cloak gave her away.

"Why didn't you tell me?"

He threw her a brief, dark scowl. "You didn't ask."

His curt tone should have been enough to dismiss her, but to her credit and his dismay, she remained firmly planted where she stood, hands fisted on her hips, brow pinched in haughty offense. Her departure from Rob and Peg's house must have been hasty. Her unbound, sleep-rumpled blond hair tumbled around her shoulders, devoid of hat and crispinette. The pale, delicate strands lifted in the morning breeze that blew in off the river. Her cheeks were flushed pink, but Braedon suspected their color had more to do with her ire than the chill mist of the dawning morn. She had the look of a woman who would stand firm through the most brutal tempest, and for a moment—just a moment—Braedon found himself admiring her tenacity.

"Go back to Rob and Peg's, if you have any sense. The docks will be alive with men soon, and you don't belong down here."

"I'm not leaving until you hear me out."

"Why does that not surprise me?" he groused, not quite under his breath. "Move on, *demoiselle,* before you invite more trouble for yourself."

She moved, but only to take a step toward him. "I want you to take me to France."

He laughed aloud and gave her his back while he continued to work on readying the cog to depart. "Out of the question."

"Why?"

"Because you will no doubt be more bother than you are worth. This isn't a royal pleasure barge, my lady; it's a working vessel. And even if I were inclined to take on a passenger, the last place I would take one is to France."

"Oh? Why? Have you left a string of brokenhearted women there?"

He chuckled wryly and tied off the cog's single sail with a harsh tug. "I gather you've been talking to Peg."

"She told me I should keep my distance from you. She said you can't be counted on, that you leave people just when they need you most."

Braedon rounded on her, ready to challenge that charge. He thought better of it, however, and caught himself before he was pricked into defending his old, tattered honor. He came around the thick wooden mast and leveled a hard stare on the girl. "If she said all of that, and you believe her, then why are you here?"

"I told you. I need your help."

"I have helped you," he replied. "If you didn't want what I offered, that's not my concern. My obligation to you—such as it was—is done."

She let out an affronted little gasp, her footfalls clipping behind him on the planks of the dock as he stalked away from her to check one of his cargo nets. "You stole my passage money and left me at the mercy of strangers whom I know nothing about, and now here you are, preparing to sail off without a care in the world for stranding me with no options whatsoever. You are despicable."

Her barb stung him more than he wanted to give credit, but he cast off the insult with a shake of his head and an exhaled curse. "You were safe enough with Rob. He is an honorable man. He would have made sure you got back to Clairmont in one piece." He felt the corner of his lip curl as he glanced up and met her indignant glare. "And I didn't steal your money, either."

"You most certainly did, no matter what you choose to call it. That purse belonged to me, not Monsieur Ferrand. And not you, sirrah."

He threw the web of rope netting down at his feet. "You are quite quick to judge me, *demoiselle*."

"If I am," she replied with a lofty toss of her head, "'tis only because you betrayed yourself immediately and continue to prove yourself a scoundrel the longer I see you. You, sir, are as wicked as you look."

Provoked beyond toleration, he stalked toward her, advancing to where she stood on the wharf with her chin held high, fists clenched at her sides. "You judge only what you plainly see. Is that so, Ariana of Clairmont?"

That stubborn chin climbed up a notch. "Yes."

"Then why don't you have a look in that satchel of yours and tell me what you see."

Braedon found a perverse measure of amusement in her sudden look of confusion, in the wary frown that put a crease of apprehension in her smooth white forehead. "What do you know about this?" she demanded, protectively clutching at the large, fat leather pouch and holding it to her as if she feared he might steal that, too. She unhooked the thong and toggle that held it closed, her fingers trembling in her haste to check the contents. "If you took anything from within here, I swear I will . . . *oh*."

She reached in and withdrew the small coin purse from where Braedon had placed it in the moments before he left Rob and Peg's a short few hours ago. A flush of color filled her cheeks.

"Satisfied?" He arched a brow to make his point. "Now, if you'll excuse me. As you can see, I have work to do here."

He pivoted to dismiss her bodily and heard the jingle of coins behind him. "I can pay you."

"I know how much you have in that bag, Ariana. You can't afford me." He threw a knowingly arrogant glance over his shoulder. "Besides, if I needed your money, I'd have kept your purse."

"Fine," she replied. "If that is how you feel."

"It is." He stared, unblinking, waiting for her to absorb his refusal. "Now run along, *demoiselle*. The tide is in, and I'd like not to be delayed any longer with pointless conversation."

Turning his back on her for what he hoped was a final time, he continued with the last checks of his vessel. He listened for a muttered curse or a huff of frustration. For the angry, staccato clip of boots retreating up the dock in defeat. He heard no such thing. Only the lengthy pause of contemplation—the persistent, almost audible turning of a stubborn female mind—assailing him from behind. Her gaze needled the back of his head like tiny daggers.

God's blood. He would not turn around and invite further argument. He owed the chit nothing. He would not give her the slightest concession in this—

"Very well," she said. "If my coin is of no value to you, and honor does not compel you to help me, then let us make a different bargain. There must be something else you might accept in exchange for my passage. . . ."

Try as he may to remain unaffected by the woman, her suggestion halted him where he stood. Cocking his head, he slowly swung back around to face her. She was nervous now, her slender fingers fidgeting with the furred edge of her mantle. A flush of pink filled her cheeks and she quickly glanced down.

"What do you propose?"

She seemed reluctant to meet his gaze in that moment—she was an innocent, there could be no doubting that fact, despite the sensual implication in her blurted offer. Without looking at him, she said, "Name your price . . . and I will pay it."

Tossing down the end of the rope he had been coiling, Braedon crossed the deck of the cog and leaped down onto the wharf. He strode up to Ariana, leaving not half a pace between them, and grabbed her chin between his thumb and forefinger. He tilted her face up, forcing her to meet his eyes. "What exactly is it that you suggest bargaining with, *demoiselle*?"

Wide blue eyes flicked up uncertainly, then down again, shuttered by a sweep of her long lashes. She squirmed, turning her head away from him. Her voice stammered when she finally found it, wobbling just above a whisper. "I . . . I think you take my meaning. Do not make me say it."

Braedon grunted low in his throat, a predatory sound of pure male interest that should have scared her off like a frightened hare. "If you cannot say it, Lady Ariana, then how do you intend to *do* it?"

She swallowed hard but lifted that guileless gaze once

more and met his steady stare. "I told you. Name your price. Just . . . say you'll do this for me. Take me to France. Please."

As he contemplated the sensual allure of her mouth, those lush pink lips that seemed so ripe for kissing, he wondered if he ought to test her, right then and there. Her scent—a mix of trepidation and stubborn resolve—drew him closer, heightening his body's awareness of her. All that was male in him, all that was untamed and animal, went taut with anticipation.

"You are that intent on reaching the Continent?" he challenged, his voice a soft growl, his breath steaming in the scant space between them. "Are you that determined to see your brother?"

She stared up at him in mute silence, her foolish tongue no doubt paralyzed by the weight of the bargain she was on the verge of striking. But there was no need for her to answer his question. Braedon could see the truth of it in her eyes. The determination, the desperation.

The stark, quivering fear.

Testing her, he reached up and touched her cheek, letting his fingers sift through the silky tendrils of her hair. She scarcely flinched at the contact. Only the slightest tremor of her indrawn breath and the sudden skitter of her pulse beneath his fingertips as they curled around her nape betrayed her anxiety at his touch. She held herself very still, her eyes on his as he gradually pulled her to him.

His desire thrummed as their bodies came together. At the feel of her pressed so deliciously against his thighs and abdomen, his sex stirred, his arousal swift and complete. She had to feel his interest. No doubt she saw it in his hungry gaze, in the flaring of his nostrils as he greedily breathed her in. Innocent or nay, she was old enough to know what he was about in that moment. She was far too clever not to understand what she encouraged with her rash offer. Yet she did not shriek in virginal terror or make the slightest effort to pull away.

He didn't know whether to be elated or dismayed.

Irritated, he decided, realizing just now that she truly was desperate to reach France. Desperate enough to consider giving herself to a virtual stranger—a ruthless, dangerous man, Braedon acknowledged wryly, who would be all too willing to collect on the debt when the time came.

He might have been tempted to sample some of his boon right there on the dock, if not for the rise of voices coming from farther down the wharf. Lifting his head, he turned his gaze over his shoulder and peered through a swirl of thin morning mist to where a group of sailors had gathered. The knot of rough-looking men were watching him and the girl.

Ferrand's men.

One of them pointed and gave a shout. The group started running on the man's command, heading straight for Braedon's dock.

"Damn," he cursed, shoving aside his enticing thoughts of a delectable tangle with the lady to thwart this current mayhem. "We have to go, my lady. Now."

He grabbed her by the wrist and turned to haul her onto his boat. To his surprise, she dug her heels in and resisted. "Wait! My horses," she said, shaking her head. "James's mount and mine are stabled back there, near the tavern. I can't leave them. I will need a mount once I reach France."

"Too late for that, *demoiselle*."

The sailors' shouts grew louder. Footsteps thundered on the wharf. Something whizzed over their heads and lodged in the cog's mast with a dull *thwunk!*

A crossbow bolt. One of Ferrand's men paused to load another missile, then raised the weapon and let the second bolt fly. Another took up a similar position, leaning against a barrel to prepare a further attack.

"Down!" Braedon shouted to Ariana, bringing her under his arm. Hunched over with her, he ran a couple paces on the dock, pulling them out of the arrow's deadly path. It missed its mark by a hairbreadth and splashed into the icy river. He crouched low and ran to untie the last line, releasing the cog from its slip. "If you're coming with me, *demoiselle,* come now."

With a shriek, she ran the handful of steps and gave him her hand to help her up onto the deck. Braedon shoved off from the pier and shifted the cog's wide sail to catch a gust of chilly morning air.

"Stay down," he instructed her, directing her to the forecastle at the head of the cog's deck. The elevated square structure rose up on squat, sturdy beams, one of two small watchtowers at either end of the vessel, which also served as the sole means of protection from the elements. "Stay beneath here," he ordered her. "Don't move until I tell you."

She scrambled into place with a quick nod while Braedon ran for the rudder at the stern. Ferrand's men launched a few more bolts, but the cog caught wind and was already gliding out of range, sailing off into the wide swell of the Thames.

Braedon steered the ship upriver as efficiently as he could, wondering whose head Ferrand wanted more: his, or Lady Mayhem's. He glanced to where she huddled on the foredeck, her knees drawn up to her chest, her arms wrapped tightly around them. Her eyes were wild, fixed on him as if waiting for reassurance. Her lush lower lip trembled, caught between the neat white line of her teeth.

She was shivering and scared beneath the forecastle, but she was safe.

God help her if she trusted *him* to keep her that way.

Braedon swore under his breath as he left London in his wake and headed for the estuary that would set him on a course toward the Channel.

Toward France, the place of his birth . . . very nearly the scene of his demise.

Jesu. What had he gotten himself into?

For a long while, Ariana dared not move a muscle. She remained where he ordered her, curled up beneath the forecastle and wary, listening as the sounds of London's waking quays and streets grew distant. Creaking cart wheels and the cacophony of fishermen on the docks was replaced by the brisk rustle of the cog's sail and the wet lapping of the Atlantic tide as it carried them farther out to sea. Ferrand's men must have given up their chase, or perhaps she and Braedon had simply managed to outrun them. Either way, Ariana was relieved for their growing distance, and grateful to Braedon for assisting her to safety once again—no matter how reluctant he was to provide that assistance.

She tried not to think about the bargain she had nearly made with him before Monsieur Ferrand's men drove them onto the cog. The rashness of what she had suggested—the plain foolishness of it—shamed her to the core. Thank heaven he had no time to accept the ill-conceived offer.

She watched him from across the length of the deck, where he stood atop the crenellated wooden structure opposite the one that sheltered her. His hand on the vessel's rudder, legs braced apart to absorb some of the roll of the waves, he loomed tall and impassive, like a legendary warrior of old. She saw his keen eyes scan their surroundings for further threats from all sides, his sharp mind calculating their course as he managed the cog's direction with an easy command that Ariana could not help but admire.

She found herself admiring the strength of his hands and arms as well, visually measuring the wide line of his shoulders beneath the thick gray fall of his mantle. A gusting winter breeze rolled in off the water and over the prow of the cog to riffle his sleek sable hair, tossing the dark waves about his face and shoulders.

Perhaps he sensed her eyes on him, for he glanced at her then. Considered her in steady silence.

Despite his air of cool command, the gaze he leveled on her was hot, intensely focused. He looked strangely wild in that moment, and infinitely more dangerous than Ferrand and his henchmen put together. Ariana had seen that unsettling look before. He'd worn the same a short while ago on the dock, when she made the very hasty mistake of bargaining herself in exchange for his escort to France. When every instinct in her body had warned her that he was going to kiss her—and that he might well do far more, given half a chance.

Even now the thought chased a shiver of wariness over her limbs and to places scandalously more private. She rubbed off the odd quickening of her senses and pulled her cloak tighter around her shoulders.

"There are blankets in the bulkhead below, if you're cold."

Ariana followed his gesture to a planked upright partition beneath the platform where he stood. She was cold, even within the shelter of the forecastle. The winds were growing ever more blustery the farther they headed toward open sea, and she was glad for the thought of some extra warmth. Slowly, she crawled out onto the open deck. Pushing herself up, Ariana unfolded her legs and attempted to stand.

She was not prepared for the sudden swaying of her limbs or the pitch and rock of the vessel beneath her feet. She lurched a couple of steps to the side and found herself leaning precariously close to the deck rail. Some terrifying distance below, the sea churned so dark as to be black, icy-looking waves cleaving against the sturdy hull of the cog and rolling away again in foamy white tails. Ariana let out a gasp as she gripped the rail and watched the tumble of the cold, dark ocean below.

"Steady," Braedon warned. He had leaped from his post and was at her side in a trice, catching her before she could take her next breath. He brought her away from the edge, his strong, muscled arm snaked firmly around her waist. "Have you never been on a ship before?"

"N-No."

He grunted as if he might have guessed as much. "Well, have a care. It may take you a while to get your sea legs."

Ariana nodded. He had released his hold on her, but she realized she was still clinging to him, to the comfort of his solid mass, while she struggled to regain her balance in a world gone infirm and off kilter. With some effort, she uncurled the fingers that had been clutching his mantle like a lifeline. Now that she was standing, her stomach did not feel so steady, either.

"How . . . long?" she asked, finding it difficult even to summon her voice.

"Some people never adjust." He shrugged, eyeing her with a dubious arch of his brow. "If you're lucky, 'twill pass in a few hours."

Nausea assailed her, but she would willingly suffer out this and more if it meant saving Kenrick's life. She shook her head—gently, for the added motion made her vision swim. "How long before we reach France?"

"Calais is the closest port, not quite a day's distance in fair seas. Easily more than twice that if we run into foul winter weather."

"And Rouen?"

"By sea, we would needs head for Honfleur. That could take a week."

Ariana could scarcely stifle her miserable-sounding groan at that woeful bit of news. They faced a possible sennight at sea? Her pitiful stomach lurched at the notion, but she reckoned as long as she was at the rendezvous point—alone, as her ransom instructions stated—by the next full moon, little else mattered.

Certainly not a little bout of seasickness.

When she dragged her gaze up from the rough-hewn planks of the deck, she found Braedon watching her, a knowing look on his face. "Are you all right? You look a bit green, my lady."

"Nay, I'm fine," she all but sputtered. "I am . . . just . . . fine."

She did not bother to wonder if he believed her, or even if he cared. With one hand at her mouth and the other clutching her roiling belly, Ariana dashed for the side of the cog. And not a moment too soon.

❧ 5 ❧

A COOL, DEEP darkness blanketed the world when Ariana next opened her eyes. She had been sleeping beneath the forecastle, as it was all she could do to combat the nausea that had been her constant companion for most of the voyage. Thankfully, she had not been sick since the first time, and she prayed she would last the rest of the trip without further humiliation.

Not that Braedon had contributed to her discomfiture. In his gruff way, he had been quite understanding. He had helped her back from the ship's rail, given her the supply of coverlets from the bulkhead and a flask of fresh water and some dried mint leaves, which he instructed her to take in small doses until her stomach steadied. Coming fully awake now, Ariana uncorked the decanter and swished a bit of the cool water around in her mouth. She spat it over the side of the cog as discreetly as she could, then took another drink to refresh her parched throat.

"How are you feeling?"

Sounding more annoyed than concerned, Braedon's low voice rumbled in the quiet night that surrounded them. She could tell from the direction it drifted that he was yet at the helm, vigilantly guiding them toward France regardless of the certain late hour. And it was cold, bitter cold. The February evening had grown frosty without the scant warmth of the sun, but Ariana found the bracing chill somehow inviting. She was cramped from sitting in her rumpled nest beneath the forecastle and welcomed the thought of stretching her limbs. Her lungs were starved for some fresh sea air.

"I'm better now, I think," she answered. Gathering one of the woolen blankets around her shoulders, she crawled out onto the open deck. "Have we much longer to go before we reach France?"

"We should spot Calais's shore a couple of hours before dawn."

Braedon was beyond her line of vision, standing at the rudder on the stern and all but hidden by the wide, ghostly swell of the sail. Gingerly, anticipating a sudden swoon of her stomach, Ariana cleared the structure of the forecastle and got to her feet. She put her hand out, splaying it against the smooth weather-beaten planks for added support as her legs adjusted to the movement of the boat. She was unsteady at first, but her head did not swim as it had before. Her stomach, blessedly, did not revolt.

"Better?" he asked again, giving her a moment, as if to ascertain that she was standing fully upright and not immediately clutching her belly and running for the side of the cog.

Ariana nodded, a moot effort, for if the sail did not entirely conceal her, she doubted very much that he would see the brief bob of her head amid the inky blackness of the night. Only the slimmest remnant of a last quarter moon hung above them, the sky's vast spangle of stars crowded by thin shreds of clouds so dark a gray as to be near to black themselves.

Night was deep and endless this far away from shore,

so different from the evenings she'd known back home. So tranquil, naught but the rhythmic lap of the sea, the soft jangle of the ship's lines, the ripple and sough of the large white sail. The canvas glowed against the night-black sky, billowed full above her head as if God's own breath blew down from the heavens to propel them forth.

She closed her eyes and whispered a prayer for easy passage, and for Kenrick's continued safety. She had little time to reach him, less than three weeks before the next full moon, when his captors would be waiting to receive his ransom in Rouen.

His ransom, Ariana thought with a frown. For what was not the first time, she wondered at the satchel she carried and its mysterious bulk. What did Kenrick's captors want with a pack full of scribblings and cryptic diagrams? She knew they had meant something powerful to her scholarly brother, but he had never shared any part of it with her.

Nor with anyone, so far as she knew.

Whatever secrets the satchel contained, it had been an obsession for Kenrick—one he had apparently developed while serving as a Knight of the Temple of Solomon. His duties for the brotherhood had kept him away from Clairmont for years. Finally, the summer past, he'd returned home unexpectedly, announcing that he had left the Templars. Ariana had been thrilled to see him, but her excitement dimmed upon his arrival. He had changed in the time he'd been away. He took no visitors, keeping long hours in his chamber, alone, the great oak door locked from within while he worked. On what, precisely, he would not say.

Once she and Kenrick had been dear friends, but the serious knight who came home in his place was a haunted man, aloof and distant, exceedingly private. He trusted no one.

Not even her, a fact that broke her heart.

When she had woken one morn last fall to learn that he had left for France on undisclosed business and without a word of good-bye, she did what any concerned younger sister would do. She sneaked into his private quarters to find whatever had stolen her brother away from her. It took her several days to find the satchel, and when she did, its contents provided little illumination.

Scribed in parts with an odd, undecipherable brand of Latin, interspersed with crudely rendered pictures and sprawling calculations, Kenrick's notes made little sense. What small amount she could puzzle out seemed to speak of miracles and strange occurrences, queer happenings in various places in England and France. He had chronicled pages and pages of such events, with complicated formulations linking some and crossing out others. It was nonsense from what she could see. Indeed, for a long while, days longer than the endless time she spent poring over the satchel's contents in frustrated wonder, Ariana considered the possibility that her beloved brother might well be out of his mind.

That is, until the day an anonymous missive arrived at Clairmont announcing his capture and demanding his findings as ransom. Whatever he had been working on was evidently of great interest to the villains who held him hostage. But who . . . and why?

"Now that you're awake, *demoiselle,* perhaps we should talk."

Braedon's deep voice jolted her from her thoughts. "Talk, my lord?"

"Yes. Come around where I can see you."

The thought of moving any distance on the swaying bulk of the cog chased a shiver of dread up her spine. But she took a few steps forward, inching toward the sound of Braedon's voice. She dared not look around, fearful that she would lose her footing, precarious as it was. She took another gingerly step, watching her feet move carefully on the moonlit planks of the deck. Once she had cleared the sail, she thrust her hand out to grab one of the lines that held the mast, wrapping her fingers around the taut rope to keep her balance. She was shaky, still uneasy and hesitant to move about, testing every step like a fawn on new legs.

When she finally mustered the courage to look up, she found Braedon idly regarding her from his post on the sterncastle. A bench had been built into the wooden structure, presumably to provide the helmsman a place to rest as he manned the rudder. Braedon lounged on the seat with arrogant command, his long legs stretched out before him, black boots crossed at the ankle and gleaming in the thin starlight. His left arm was flung over the back of the crenellated platform, his right hand rested on the handle that controlled the thick vertical paddle of the cog's rudder.

Although the night was dark, the large outline of Braedon's cloaked body was darker still. He was shadow on shadow, the severe angles of his face cast in harsh relief by the pale wash of moonglow that filtered down through the scuttle of drifting clouds overhead. Ariana could feel his assessing gaze focus on her across the distance of the deck.

She forced a casual brightness to her voice, but from her position center deck, her left hand curled a little tighter around the mast line. "What is it you wish to talk about?"

"Oh, many things, I assure you." The smile he offered her—that brief baring of his teeth—hardly set her at ease. "Foremost, *demoiselle,* I am wondering why it is that Ferrand de Paris might wish to see you dead."

"Me?" Ariana choked, astonished to think she might be the target of such unwarranted violence as murder. "I saw no evidence of fellowship between you and Monsieur Ferrand. How can you be certain his men weren't shooting at you?"

He released her from the heat of his gaze and tipped his head back, as though casually surveying the night sky. "Ferrand and I share a mutual mistrust, that's true. However, if he had cause to want me dead, I warrant he would have tried to do something about it long before now. Which leaves you, Ariana of Clairmont. What would a flesh peddler like Ferrand de Paris want with you?" He adjusted the rudder slightly as he spoke, and then those keen eyes leveled on her once more. "Aside from the obvious, that is."

Ariana opened her mouth to protest, but stopped herself just short of blurting out proof of her naïveté. She grasped his meaning at once and felt her ears heat like an iron cast into a roaring brazier. He would steer her into treacherous waters, if she was not careful. "I don't know what Monsieur Ferrand could have against me, save that he failed in his attempt to extort my coin."

"Ferrand is not above cutting purses, but he usually prefers bigger game. There's got to be something else he wants from you."

"Something . . . else?" With her free hand, Ariana felt beneath her cloak for the satchel containing Kenrick's ransom. "I don't know what it could be."

A prickle of suspicion wormed its way up her spine before the words were out of her mouth. Could Ferrand possibly have something to do with her brother's capture? Perhaps he knew who held him. Did he want the satchel as well—enough to murder James? Enough to want her dead, too?

Heaven help her, perhaps Kenrick's papers were of more value—and greater danger—than she realized.

"Tell me again about your business in Rouen," he said, studying her as if he scented her apprehension and meant to divine its source. "I want to know more about this urgent visit of yours with your kin, Ariana. Is your brother in some brand of trouble?" His gray eyes narrowed on her. "Or mayhap the trouble is yours."

For an instant, one fleeting, worrisome instant, Ariana considered telling Braedon her true purpose in going to Rouen. With James dead, she had no allies in this quest, no one to share her worry or assure her that everything would be all right in the end. For the first time since leaving Clairmont, she felt truly afraid.

Truly alone.

But she couldn't tell Braedon what she was involved in, not even if she believed she might be able to trust him. Kenrick's captors had demanded that she bring no one with her—even James had understood that Ariana would have to attend the rendezvous alone or risk jeopardizing Kenrick's life by not adhering to the ransom demands. She was alone in this, and she had no choice but to keep it that way.

" 'Tis as I told you," she said at last, squirming under his scrutiny. To mask the nervous tremor of her hands, she clutched at the blanket around her shoulders and worked to hold it closed. "My brother is in Rouen. He's been there for several months. Recently he sent word that he wanted to see me, and so I am going—"

"Do you think me a lackwit, *demoiselle?*"

Ariana swallowed past a knot of dismay. "N-no. Not at all."

"Good. Because I am no fool, nor do I expect you are. So let us dispense with this game of verbal cat-and-mouse. What are you carrying in that satchel of yours, and what might Ferrand de Paris want with it?"

She drew back, mouth agape, unable to utter a word for the shock and dread that lanced through her in that moment.

"Oh, come now, *demoiselle.* Did you think I haven't noticed how you guard that bag like one of your own appendages?"

Ariana's heart sank. How could she have been so careless? "It—it just contains some personal belongings from Clairmont. My private things, nothing of interest to anyone but me."

"Truly," he drawled, more challenge than question.

"Truly," she lied. Then, worse and worse: "I swear it on my life."

He was silent for a long moment, considering her through the chill gloom of the night. His eyes narrowed, his moonlit expression dubious and dangerously schooled. "You'd stand here now and wager your life on a bag that contains nothing of worth?" He mocked her with a low, rumbling chuckle. "Mayhap you are a fool, Ariana of Clairmont."

Although his sarcasm stung her pride, she breathed a mental sigh of relief. Better he think her the veriest idiot than let him wonder any longer about the satchel's contents or her clandestine purpose in going to Rouen.

"Are you hungry, *demoiselle?*"

Her nerves still jangling, Ariana merely blinked at him,

no doubt confirming his assessment that she was, indeed, lacking sense. "What?"

"Your stomach is empty and you haven't eaten all day," he remarked as though he spoke to a dull child. "Are you hungry?"

"N-no." Ariana shook her head. She could not possibly think of eating when her mind, and her stomach, were churning like mill wheels.

"Suit yourself," Braedon replied. He dug into a pack on the floor beneath the sterncastle bench and pulled out a couple of items of food. "If you mean to stand there, you may as well make yourself useful. Fetch the water flask and bring it over here. I reckon it's time you start earning your keep."

Mother Mary.

Her relief in escaping his suspicious questioning was blotted out by the dread of this new request. Not only did she have to make her way back to the forecastle shelter to get the water, but then he would have her travel the entire length of the boat and join him at the stern . . . to start earning her keep. Heaven only knew what he meant by that. Ariana was quite sure she didn't want to know.

She considered throwing herself on his mercy then and there, but she was not at all sure he would afford her any. Perhaps the precarious walk across the deck and back would bring on her nausea again. If only she could be so fortunate.

Or perhaps she would lose her footing and wash overboard, a clean end to the woeful mess she was in with this unsettling man.

Ariana refused to allow that last possibility, for her death now would be the ultimate failure. She carefully made her way back to the forecastle and retrieved the flask, then crossed the full length of the deck—some threescore paces in all, and not a trace of wooziness to show for it. Braedon was waiting for her when she reached the sterncastle. He stood at the top of the wooden ladder that led up to the elevated platform, his hands fisted on his hips as he looked down at her, a vague smile teasing his lips.

"You might make a decent shipmate, after all."

"Not that you would actually know," she said, telling herself it was silly to warm to his idle praise. "From what I have seen of you thus far, I should think you prefer to do everything for yourself. No friends to speak of, no crew . . . Do you do everything alone?"

He chuckled as if she'd just made a jest. "Not everything."

She reached up to offer him the hard leather flask. He crouched down and put out his hand to take it, but instead of grabbing hold of the decanter, his large fingers wrapped around her wrist. "W-what are you doing?"

"Helping you up."

Too late to so much as consider refusing him. Braedon's grasp was firm, his arm incredibly strong as he lifted her off the deck. Ariana scrambled to put her feet on the ladder and make the short climb, assisted against her will to the top of the sterncastle platform. The view from topside fair stole her breath.

Water glistened as far as the eye could see, the rippling black waves dappled silver by the slender moon and glittering stars. There was no horizon hemming them in, no boundaries to this fathomless world. But there was a loneliness here as well. She felt it in the chill wind that buffeted her from all sides, howling in the mast lines and shuddering in the sail. She felt it in the vastness of a world without light, without solid form.

And, inexplicably, she felt that loneliness in Braedon, too.

"It must get terribly quiet out here for days by yourself. And dangerous, I would think, to sail a vessel like this on your own."

He was seated on the bench behind her, his right hand on the rudder while the other held a joint of smoked mutton. He took a bite without answering her, turning his gaze out over the water as he chewed, his eye on a bright star overhead. "I like the quiet."

"And the danger?"

"The only danger here is dying, and it isn't much at that, if you don't live in fear of it." The water flask rolled beside him on the bench. He picked it up, pulled the cork, then tipped it to his mouth and drank. "Sit, if you like," he said, indicating the vacant spot on the other side of the rudder. "I'm not going to bite, now that I've got something else to chew on."

While she did not think it wise to put herself so close to him, Ariana was glad not to be standing any longer. The cold breeze in her face was nice, if blustery, but being so high off the deck was making her feel a bit light-headed. She plopped down beside him gracelessly, aided by the sudden rock of the boat as it sliced through a dark wave. He let go of the rudder and reached out to catch her arm, steadying her.

His touch lingered for a moment, firm and warm. Ariana squirmed beneath the intensity of his gaze and the awareness of his body's warmth so close to hers. She parted her lips to murmur that he could let her go, but he must have read as much in her eyes, for he released her arm and leaned back against the crenellated wall of the stern-castle.

"What is it about France you don't like?"

He gave a mild shrug. "I have nothing against France. Indeed, I was born there."

"But you never want to return?" To his questioning scowl, she said, "On the docks this morning, you said it was the last place you would go."

"Actually, I said it was the last place I would take a passenger."

"Is there a difference?"

He grunted, clearly becoming annoyed with this line of conversation. Evidently he preferred to be the one asking the questions, not answering them. "Yes," he said. "There's a difference."

"Does it have something to do with what happened to your friend Rob?" she pressed, aware that she was prying, but finding herself too curious about him to be completely polite. "Or mayhap it has something to do with what happened to you . . . your scar?"

He glared at her and exhaled sharply through his teeth. "You ask a lot of questions, Ariana of Clairmont. I'm beginning to think I preferred your company earlier today."

"I'm sorry. I was just . . . talking."

"I've had enough talking, *demoiselle*."

He tilted his head skyward and gently pulled the rudder a fraction to the left. He ignored her for a while, leaving her unsure what to do in the ensuing uncomfortable silence. Finally, she stood up. "I would be happy to return below now," she said helpfully. "I'm sure you need to concentrate on whatever it is you're doing." She followed the direction of his gaze up toward the stars and frowned. "What are you doing?"

"*Nachtsprung.*"

"Knockt—"

"Night-leaping," he interjected when she made a muddled attempt to say the strange word. "The Norsemen called it *nachtsprung* when they sailed their ships through the night, using the stars to guide them. They could leap the night and make up time on their voyages."

She couldn't help but be intrigued. "And that's what we're doing now, night-leaping?"

He nodded, still watching the sky. "Do you see that star there—" He pointed for her, directing her gaze. "—the bright one, just beyond the tip of the mast?"

Ariana moved in front of him so she could align her gaze with the place he indicated. "Yes! I see it."

She was so fascinated with this new knowledge that she scarcely noticed how close she stood to Braedon now, less than a hand's width between them, so close she could feel the warmth of his body permeate the woolen layers of blanket and mantle that encased her. So intrigued was she with the stars and the magic he had just shown her, she all but forgot to be afraid of him.

Her awareness of him settled in slowly. Almost pleasingly.

"Using the mast and the North Star's position near it, we can sail all night on a due course for France," he told her, his voice low and oddly soothing behind her. Still, she startled when he stood up and took her hand in his.

"What are you—"

"Here," he said, placing her fingers around the rudder's handle. "You man the helm for a while. Just watch that star and hold it steady."

"Oh. No—I couldn't possibly!"

But he had already let go and she was guiding the vessel over the water, feeling the power of the sea tug at the rudder in her hand as the cog carved through the waves. It was exhilarating, the headiest feeling she had ever known. Ariana could not stifle her thrilled little laugh, wondering if this was how the birds felt, soaring above the ground with the wind in their face.

She wanted to close her eyes and savor the feeling of freedom and power, but she didn't dare look away from the guiding star for a moment. She also realized she hadn't nearly the strength that Braedon possessed, and where he made the task look easy with one hand, Ariana was soon grasping the rudder in both of hers and putting every ounce of concentration on the task.

Behind her, Braedon shifted, coming closer to her. She felt the weight of the rudder's pull lessen, and realized his hand had come to rest next to hers on the beam. For the longest while, he said nothing. Neither did she, struck mute by the glory of the night as it sped by, and by the strange charge that seemed to enliven every particle of her being at the awareness of him standing so near her in the dark.

A strong wave rocked the cog, and suddenly the distance between them was nil. Ariana stumbled back on her heels and the length of her spine collided with the solid mass of Braedon's chest and thighs. Her face heated in spite of the crisp, chill breeze that nipped her cheeks and brow. She gasped and hastily tried to move away, but managed not even a pace before he caught her around the waist.

He held her there for a long moment in a silence that seemed to scream a desperate warning through Ariana's mind. But heaven help her, she didn't move. Could scarcely command her thoughts, much less her limbs. Her hair was winging loose in the breeze of the boat's swift pace, blowing about her head in a tangle, baring her neck to his touch. And touch he did. His fingers sifted through the mass of her hair, so gently, so intimately. He grazed the skin beneath her ear with his knuckles, then down, to the sensitive curve at her shoulder.

Although it was wrong, dangerous to allow him such liberties, Ariana could only stand there in a dazed brand of wonder. She had never been so close to a man before. Nor should she be now, a prudent voice warned in her head. Certainly not this man, this benighted, solitary soul with the haunted gaze and lethal, warrior's hands. Large, strong hands that were caressing her with incredible tenderness.

Slowly he turned her around to face him. He leaned into her, his nostrils flaring as he drew in a deep breath, scenting her as an animal might size up a mate, ravishing her senses with the mere idea of what he might intend for her—there in the middle of the ocean, with no one around to hear her even if she could find her voice to scream. But screaming seemed the last thing she was capable of doing. She had no breath in her lungs. No strength to shove him away and flee his arms, as she ought to do.

She parted her lips, though on a feeble protest or gasp of confusion, she wasn't at all sure. Nor did he give her a chance to decide. Threading his warm fingers along her jaw and cheek, he let his hand wander farther, to the nape of her neck and down along the arch of her spine. His gaze stark, glittering in the scant starlight, he pulled her to him and slanted his mouth over hers.

The first brushing of his lips against hers sent a shock of sensation through her every limb and fiber. Warm, firm, so expertly sensual, his kiss awakened a sudden burning in her very core. It alarmed her, this new experience. How heated and compelling his mouth was on hers.

How immensely dangerous to allow it to continue, even for a moment. She felt herself melting into him as his other hand came around to press against the small of her back, drawing her nearer to the flame. At the urging of his tongue, teasing the seam of her lips, she opened to him.

Heaven help her, but where her thoughts were uncertain, her body seemed to welcome him with an instinctual understanding. She brought her hands up between them, pressing her palms to the solid mass of his chest. Her intention was to push him away, but it was a feeble attempt when her fingers seemed to have a will of their own, clinging to the thick wool of his mantle where she meant to deny him and save some shred of her honor. She heard herself moan, but a roll of distant thunder swallowed it up. A flash of lightning ripped across the sky an instant later, followed by another crash in the heavens above.

It was all that saved her from a path toward certain ruin.

With a growl low in his throat, Braedon released her at last. She brought her fingers to her wet, burning mouth, a hundred oaths of outrage swimming in her head, although regretfully, none made it to her dumbstruck tongue. Instead, mute and in shock for what she'd just done, she backed away.

She didn't get far. Braedon caught her by the wrist, steadying her as the sea rocked beneath them. "The water's getting rough—too dangerous by far for you to remain up here, *demoiselle*." He was breathing hard, his keen gaze steady and potent as he stared at her. The wind tossed his sable-dark hair around his head like a tempest, as wild as the man himself. His scarred, angular face was cast in sharp relief as another jag of lightning streaked overhead, illuminating his eyes and the stark, tortured line of his mouth. "Go below, Ariana. Now."

He need not tell her twice. As soon as his grip on her arm loosened, Ariana turned on her heel and fled down the ladder to the relative safety of the deck below.

❧ 6 ❧

BRAEDON WAS UNCERTAIN what bothered him more, having to fight the coming squall—which would be fierce, by the looks of it—or the swell of lust he weathered for some time after Ariana's narrow escape from the sterncastle. He wanted the girl, and that surprised him. It angered him, for any fool could see that she was a maiden, pure and untouched, a fact that alone should have quashed her appeal in his eyes.

Should have, but did not. God's bones, but he had been closer to taking her in that moment than he cared to admit. A stolen kiss, a licentious touch . . . a brazen embrace that could have easily led to a complete and total seduction.

She had promised him that much, after all. Herself, in exchange for her passage to Rouen. That bargain had been close to his thoughts all day, even though he knew he could not hold her to it. His soul was dark, but he was reluctant to think he had sunk so low that he would look to sate his hunger on an innocent. She had suggested her bargain in haste, and despite the predatory way he once made his living, he'd never had an inclination toward rape.

He did not flatter himself that he was the sort of man who inspired breathless swoons among the fair sex—not anymore, not in a very long time—but he had yet to meet a woman who would deny his powers of persuasion once he'd set his mind to pursue her into his bed. And to Braedon's chagrin, he found he was fast becoming intent on pursuing Ariana of Clairmont.

Saved by the storm, he thought with a rueful chuckle as he gazed up at the sooty, roiling clouds.

Smoke gray and shot with lightning, the clouds that had been threatening earlier now moved in quickly, bunching together to blot out the quarter moon and snuff the stars. A roll of thunder cracked overhead, and the waves began to heave beneath the hull of the cog. Wet snow spattered his face, stinging and icy-sharp. A gust of wet wind gnashed at the sail, sucking the air from it, then filling it like a sheep's-bladder balloon.

Braedon swore a curse for the lunatic's mission that might yet spell his doom. And for what? he wondered, considering the young woman who huddled below on the deck, trusting him to see her to safety. He didn't believe for a moment that she was telling him the truth—about anything thus far.

Visit her brother, his arse. He hadn't missed the fear in her eyes, even through the distance that separated them on the deck. Nor had he missed her vehement denial that she carried anything but worthless personal effects in the satchel she so vigilantly guarded. She was lying to him, and Braedon didn't appreciate it. Particularly not when his livelihood was suddenly tangled up with hers.

Ariana of Clairmont was harboring a secret. A dangerous secret, and one he had every intention of rooting out as soon as they embarked in France.

But he doubted they would be getting there anytime soon.

The bitter wind was fast becoming a gale. It whipped his mantle around his legs and flung his damp hair into his face. Braedon leaped down from the sterncastle and ran to lower the sail. It was flapping violently; a rip had started near the top of the wide square of canvas. The winds were growing too fierce to risk leaving it up where the storm could destroy the sail, or worse, seize it in a deadly fist and capsize them. There was nothing to do but ride out the worst of the squall and pray it didn't blow them too far off course.

Ariana thought the raging seas would never calm. The storm had been swiftly brutal and bitter cold, tossing them around like a twig in a tempest. It was still blowing at dawn, though less intense, the sleet having changed to a dizzying flurry of snowfall. She was astonished they came out of it in one piece and could not have been more relieved when Braedon shouted that he spied land. She came out of hiding, blankets wrapped around her, and looked to where he stood at the rudder.

"France, *demoiselle*, off the starboard bow."

Looming in the distance over the right side of the boat were the rugged outlines of land. Shadowy dark, save for a few snow-dusted plateaus, the shore jutted out into the sea like a massive fortress wall, guarding the land. *France,* Ariana thought with an inward sigh as she hurried to the deck railing.

By God, she had done it.

She was nearly there now. *Pray, let Kenrick be safe until I find him,* she intoned silently, clasping her hands together in a solemn plea.

"Please, dear Lord," she whispered, "let him be alive."

"Let who be alive?"

She snapped her head to the side, only to find Braedon standing beside her. Amid the low howl of the wind and the concentration of her thoughts, she hadn't even heard him approach. He watched her now, a look of expectation—nay, a look of doubt—on his face. She blinked up at him, caught off guard by his nearness and a sudden humiliating recollection of the kiss he'd forced on her the night before. He stared through her, as though he had laid her bare, and the weight of his wicked gaze left her incapable of even so much as a stammered retort.

"You and I are going to have a talk, *demoiselle*. Just as soon as we dock and find shelter in Calais."

"Calais?" She was jolted out of her discomfiture, alarmed by the news that they were cutting short their journey. "I thought we were to sail for Honfleur. Is that not a closer port to Rouen?"

"It is, but we won't be sailing anywhere in this weather. We'll dock in Calais to wait out the storm. That will give you ample time to tell me precisely what it is you're involved in—"

"But I have told you—"

"—and then," he added, interrupting her, "*if* your answers satisfy me, I will consider taking you on to Honfleur and Rouen."

"You have no right to order me—"

A dark brow winged up in challenge. "Aye, *demoiselle*. I have every right, until I am compensated for my services. That is, unless you wish to pay me what you duly owe." He gave her a meaningful look that made her cheeks flame. "In which case, we can settle up now and go our separate ways as soon as we reach port."

Ariana swallowed back the knot of dread that rose to lodge itself in her throat, nearly choking on it. He could not be serious.

"Nay?" he asked, a wickedly amused smile tugging at the corner of his mouth as he watched her squirm. "Alas, more's the pity. I have been very much looking forward to collecting on that debt since last night."

She could not help but gape at him in mute appall. "How dare you suggest . . ."

"I would hasten to remind you that it was not my suggestion, *demoiselle,* but yours. 'Name your price and I will pay it.' Was that not what you said—what we agreed upon before we left London?"

"Agreed?" she gasped. "Nay, sir. We never settled on anything! You can't possibly think—surely, you are not knave enough to expect that I would . . ."

Oh, but he likely was enough of a knave to expect it, she thought grimly, hearing her voice trail off on the snowy breeze.

"Prepare yourself, my lady. We dock within the hour. Meanwhile I will consider a fitting price for your passage here."

Like the veriest scoundrel, he left her standing at the deck rail without another word. She watched in a state of torturous anxiety as he went about preparing the cog to dock. As though he had not a care in the world, he tested lines and then began to unfurl the cog's sail. The wet canvas caught the brisk winter wind as soon as it was hoisted, and a short while later they were maneuvering their way along the marsh-lined tidal inlet that led to Calais's walled citadel.

Ariana kept herself out of Braedon's path as he readied the cog to dock. The top of the sail had suffered a long tear during the storm and would have to be repaired, she heard him tell one of the fishermen on the quay. The bearded Frenchman pointed toward a squat little stone house just off the harbor.

"Claude the sailmaker does honest work, *monsieur.* Ten deniers ought to mend your sail."

"And lodging?" Braedon inquired. "Where can we find a clean room and a good warm meal?"

Another gesture, this time toward a tall half-timbered building in a row of the same. "The Wolf's Head Inn. I'll take you there myself, if you like. You see, my cousin, he owns the place. He'll see that you and your lady are taken care of."

Braedon murmured his thanks, then shot Ariana an expectant look as he held his hand out to her. "A coin or two for this gentleman's help, my lady."

Ariana frowned at him, but did not protest the demanded expense. She was too busy worrying herself toward a swoon over what was in store for her once they docked. With nervous fingers, she dug into her small purse, withdrew a couple of farthings and handed them to Braedon.

"Come from England, have you?" asked the fisherman, his gaze flicking to Ariana before returning to Braedon and his offered coin. "The Channel is rough this time of year. You are fortunate to have arrived with merely a torn sail, *monsieur*."

"Yes, we were." Braedon replied, a note of impatience in his voice. He grabbed the cog's lines and lashed them to the dock, then retrieved a leather pack from the deck, the same one that had contained his food and wine of the past night. He disembarked, then held his hand out to Ariana to help her alight from the boat. "The inn, *s'il vous plaît*," he said to the man, not quite an order but curt enough to send the scruffy fisherman loping off ahead of them to show the way.

The Wolf's Head was one of several such establishments that catered to the busy port of Calais. Fishermen, merchants, and an uncomfortable number of grizzled, hard-eyed seamen filled the inn's main room. It was not unlike the tavern in London where Ariana and James had met with Monsieur Ferrand, an ill-fated encounter that in this moment seemed to have happened much longer ago than just a mere couple of days. Indeed, how long ago it seemed. How far she had come since then.

Mother Mary, how far she still had to go.

And to go alone, she thought with a forceful resolve as she walked beside Braedon as he approached the innkeeper.

She waited obediently as he secured them lodging for the night, her mind working on how to escape his promised—nay, threatened—talk. He would not settle for more of her evasions. He would press her about her business until she broke, she knew that about him already. He was not a man to be refused. Likely not in anything he set his mind to.

How foolish was she, to have brokered with him to bring her here? Her desperation to reach Rouen had been her chief motivation, but now she wondered if she hadn't gotten herself into a much more hazardous situation than even the one posed by Monsieur Ferrand. Braedon had delivered her to France, as she asked. Now all that remained, as he had been eager to inform her, was her promised compensation. She could not make good on what he expected, of course. No gentleman would force her to fulfill so rash a contract.

A gentleman, she thought with a miserable sense of regret. He had given her no cause to suspect he subscribed to any edicts of chivalry or genteel behavior. To think this warring man with his merciless sword arm and savage countenance would grant her pardon in her foolishness was like as not to credit that a rangy wolf might spare a trapped and bleating lamb. And to think she had been so reckless as to allow him to kiss her!

Ariana was wincing, trying unsuccessfully to blot out a sudden vision of predatory carnage, when Braedon sauntered over to her. He had paid for their accommodations with coin from his own purse, a purse she had not realized he'd carried. "I am a man of *some* means, *demoiselle*," he drawled quietly when she looked at him in mild surprise.

"This way," said the innkeeper as he came around to lead them down a hallway off the public room. He did not stop until they had reached nearly the end of the corridor, then he paused and opened the door to a darkened chamber. With a grunted "Bonjour," the portly proprietor trundled back up the hallway.

Braedon walked inside and dropped his pack on the floor. Ariana paused a moment before following him to the open door. She waited at the threshold, refusing to enter. Her stomach clenched in a tight knot of apprehension. From halfway in the chamber came the snick of a striking flint, then the warm glow of flame grew golden bright as Braedon lit a squat tallow candle. "Come in and take off your wet mantle, Ariana."

She stood firm, half in trepidation, half in haughty indignation. "What is the meaning of this?"

"It is a room, *demoiselle*. A warm, dry place with a bed and a hearth, as I didn't expect you'd like to sleep another night on the cog."

"You know what I'm asking, sirrah. Why did you secure just the one room?"

"Because it is the last available." He gave her a slightly mocking grin. "And because I like to protect my investments. Now come in, and get out of your wet clothes."

Not waiting for her either to argue or comply, he stalked to the far wall of the room where a fireplace yawned, black and cold. There was a small supply of wood on the hearth, though not nearly enough to last the night when winter was shaking the shutters and chasing a chill breeze across the rush-littered plank floor. Ariana stepped inside warily, watching as Braedon dropped down on his haunches and built a nice fire. The brittle logs crackled to life, throwing a bright, welcoming warmth into the musty little room.

Despite her wariness, Ariana surrendered to the inviting glow of the fire and walked farther within, eager to chase away some of the icy cold that permeated her clothing into her very bones. She drew off the heavy weight of her cloak and held it in her hands, uncertain what to do with the sodden garment. Braedon took it from her and dragged a wooden chair closer to the hearth. He folded her mantle over the back, fanning the large swatch of fabric out so it could better dry.

"Thank you," she murmured sullenly.

"Sit." He directed her toward the chair with a tilt of his beard-shadowed jaw. "It's time we had ourselves a little talk, my lady."

She could tell from his tone that he fully expected her to obey him, and she did, although it piqued her that he seemed to think she required such handling. It was not her nature to be difficult. Indeed, she was a quite reasonable person—perfectly sensible and forthright, she liked to think—under normal circumstances. But these were hardly normal circumstances. Nay, nothing had been normal in her life for quite some time, she reflected soberly in the moments of silence that descended while Braedon rocked back on his boot heels and stared at her, his muscular arms crossed over his chest in expectation.

As she girded herself for the worst, Ariana's gaze trailed over Braedon's light-gilded silhouette before the fireplace. She couldn't hold his piercing stare, nor could she look at the broad expanse of his shoulders and torso without knowing a sense of dread that he could keep her trapped in the tiny room for as long as he deemed necessary. Her gaze slid wearily lower to the dark stain that seeped through his tunic sleeve. His wound must have reopened while he fought the storm in the Channel. It should be cleaned again, and the bandages would need to be changed. "You're bleeding," she pointed out quietly.

He scarcely flinched. "And you are stalling, *demoiselle*. Do you wish to know my terms?"

She was very certain she didn't.

"First, you're going to tell me about your brother—about your true business here in France—and you are going to tell me now."

Ariana bristled at his highhanded command, feeling like an unruly child who'd been dragged before the castle chaplain for discipline over a transgression she had not committed. True, she had involved Braedon in her plight against his will, and true, she probably did owe him an explanation for that at least. After all, that he was standing there before her now, bleeding afresh from a wound suffered in protecting her, certainly earned him some measure of consideration.

But, saints forgive her, she couldn't give it. Not in full. As much as she appreciated Braedon's assistance thus far—reluctant as it was—her loyalty was first and foremost to Kenrick. Her commitment was centered wholly on his safety, and his safety now depended on following the set of explicit rules laid down by his captors. Rules that demanded her expedience and forbade her from confiding in anyone about the danger he truly was in at Rouen. Rules she dared not break.

Despite the logic that told her Braedon would make an apt ally in her quest to save her brother, one she could sorely use, she could not permit him to get close to the truth. Not when she was mere leagues away—a few days' travel at most—from freeing Kenrick from the villains who held him. She would have to dance around the truth as best she could, and if Braedon pressed her too far, she would simply have to lie.

"Very well," she relented with a sigh that was nearly as defeated as it sounded, "I will endeavor to answer your questions, even if they are none of your affair."

"You can start by telling me about this brother of yours."

Ariana mentally summoned a list of Kenrick's finest qualities and fed them to her brooding interrogator one by one. "My brother is the most honorable person I have ever known. He is honest and courageous, kind, considerate. He is intelligent and worldly, and as righteous as the day is long."

Braedon hardly waited for her to take a breath before he lifted one black brow and scoffed. "A veritable saint, is he?"

"As a matter of fact, 'Saint' is what his friends called him growing up," Ariana answered, meeting Braedon's dubious gaze with a smart look of her own. "Kenrick had very noble aspirations as a boy. He wanted to serve God. He tutored under our local chaplain and was prepared to take his vows of priesthood once he was of age."

He listened in watchful contemplation, as though measuring her every word. "He didn't complete his vows?"

"No." Ariana glanced down at the floor and shook her head, recalling the night Kenrick came home to Clairmont from the abbey where he'd gone as a novice but a week before. He had arrived that chilly night on foot, looking as though he'd run the whole way. She had not been privy to what was said between her father and his only son behind the closed door of the castle solar, but she had sensed the pall of shame, the rise of panic, in the air. She had sensed the close-held anguish in her brother's stoic good-bye that next day when he stood in the bailey, his face stern and blanched of color as he held the reins of his mount and prepared to leave home again. He rode through Clairmont's barbican gate without turning back, a sixteen-year-old boy heading out alone to become a soldier.

"Kenrick gave up his vows and decided to join the Knights of the Temple of Solomon instead."

"A Templar?" Braedon's sardonic mouth pursed slightly, as though the word held an unsavory taste. "Those warrior monks are not exactly known for their piety, my lady."

Ariana lifted her shoulder in acknowledgment. Of course, she had heard stories of the Knights Templar and their severe vows of poverty and chastity. She had also heard it said that those sacred vows were forsaken more often than not. They were a tight-knit brotherhood, whose arcane rituals and whispered rumors of evildoing had worsened of late to the point of outright heresy. That Kenrick was one of them troubled her, but she trusted implicitly in his honor. Whatever he was involved in now, whatever his captors wanted with him, she was certain he was guilty of no wrongdoing.

Braedon chuckled as he turned to stoke the fire. "So the saint took up the sword. For profit or for glory?"

"Neither, I'm sure," Ariana insisted. "My father encouraged him to go. I didn't see him again for eight years."

Not until the summer past. He had come home to Clairmont a changed man, obsessed with his journals and note-keeping. He had shut everyone out—his friends, his father, and Ariana. Kenrick, who had for so long been her strongest ally, was no longer willing to be bothered by the little sister who still adored him and was so thrilled to have him home. Later that autumn he was gone again, back to France, as Ariana would learn only when the messenger came with news of Kenrick's abduction. Her father had passed away soon after Kenrick had left that last time. A blessing, for it would have broken his heart to learn that his only son had met with harm.

"And that's what brings you to Rouen in the dead of winter?"

Braedon was looking at her quizzically, awaiting her answer. "T-to Rouen?" she stammered, inwardly cringing at the stutter that crept into her voice whenever she was nervous.

"The Templar fort in Rouen, *demoiselle*. Is that not where you are headed?"

"Oh. Yes," she replied, though she'd been unaware there was such a holding in the city. Her actual destination in Rouen was less illustrious than that, but she sent a silent prayer heavenward for the serendipitous information. " 'Tis just as I told you—Kenrick invited me to come and see him in Rouen."

"Urgently," Braedon added, his tone and his expression challenging. "You had to come see him urgently, was that not what you also told me when we were back in London?"

Ariana had managed to evade the need to lie to him, but he was hemming her into a corner by letting her talk freely. She held his piercing gaze and adopted what she hoped was a look of deep concern. The latter wasn't too difficult, for she truly did fear for Kenrick's life. Holding Braedon's flinty gray gaze was another matter altogether. She could almost feel him dissecting her story with each heartbeat he stared at her. Predatory, penetrating, Braedon's eyes were nearly entrancing in their intensity. "Y-yes," she stammered at last. "It is urgent I see him. Extremely urgent. I have reason to fear for my brother's . . . health."

His brow quirked at that, so Ariana rushed on to expand on the notion. "H-he was not a hearty lad growing up, you see, and winters were often difficult for him. Our dear mother perished of fever one winter when we were children." That much was true, she reflected sadly, but pushed her emotions aside upon noting the dubious twist of Braedon's mouth. "And Kenrick often doesn't take care of himself, particularly when his mind is fixed on other things. So you can see why I would be concerned," she added hopefully.

But Braedon only grunted, no doubt scenting even this mild distortion of fact. "So concerned, Lady Mayhem, that you are willing to risk your own health to get here?" He slanted her an uncompromising look. "Willing to risk something more than that, were you not?"

That he would stoop to remind her again did not surprise Ariana in the slightest. Braedon was many things, chief among them shrewd and perceptive, and it would take more than this weak attempt at deflection to throw him off the trail. Her mind raced, considering and discarding a host of falsehoods and tales that she could tell him to help explain herself. Unwanted suitors, money troubles, feuds with neighboring landholders—she cast them all aside as ridiculous, knowing Braedon would see through her the instant she opened her mouth.

She had best tread as close to the truth as possible for as long as she was trapped with him in Calais. Pray God, it would not be long. The moon would turn in just a couple weeks' time, and she had every intention of being in

Rouen that night, alone, with Kenrick's ransom, as demanded by his captors. For now, she needed to be the picture of cooperation and candor. She needed to work at putting Braedon's curiosity at ease until he transported her to Honfleur as planned. From there, she would gladly part company with her dark deliverer and continue on to Rouen on her own.

A soft rap on the door jolted her from her flimsy plans and wrung a knowing smirk from Braedon's harshly carved mouth. "I expect that will be the innkeeper. I asked him to send us up a meal. While you're chewing on your thoughts, you might as well fill your belly, too."

He strode to the door and permitted the rotund little man entry to the room. He shuffled in with a nod to both of them as he carried in the tray of steaming food. Fragrant ale sloshed over the sides of two tankards when the innkeeper set the tray down on a chest near the bed. "Will that be all, *monsieur*?"

"A warm bath and a supply of dry towels, too, if you have them."

"*Oui, monsieur.*"

As wonderful as the thought of soap and warm water sounded, Ariana tried not to think about what Braedon's intention might be where the bath was concerned. Bad enough that she be forced to dine privately with a man she hardly knew—perhaps even share the same room with him for the duration of what was sure to be the longest night of her life—but if he thought to dip so much as one naked toe into a tub of water while she was present, he was well and truly mad.

Her mind conjured the image all too readily, providing her with a mental picture of Braedon stripping off his leather gambeson and tunic to stand before her bare-chested and immodest. It wasn't hard to imagine his broad shoulders and massive arms gilded by the firelight. Nor was it difficult to conceive what the rest of his muscular body would look like, divested of its clothing. She easily recalled the sight of him at Rob and Peg's, when she had assisted with his bandages.

In a flash of fancy, scandalous enough to enflame her cheeks with heat, Ariana envisioned the wide planes of Braedon's bare chest, the tapered tautness of his abdomen cutting a firm line to his trim hips and indecently lower. . . .

The metallic clack of the latch on the door snapped her out of the wicked imaginings as the innkeeper left the room and closed them into solitude once more. Still warm from her wayward thoughts, she watched as Braedon grabbed the edge of the wooden chest and slid it nearer to the fire.

"Not exactly a seven-course supper on the dais at Clairmont, but I trust it will suffice."

The aroma of spiced meat pie, fresh brown bread, and herbed boiled potatoes steamed off the tray of viands to wreathe around Ariana's nose. Her stomach growled, piqued for the first time since its fit of revolt on Braedon's cog. With a sigh of eager surrender, she scooted off her chair and onto the floor beside the food. She broke the round loaf of bread and took a piece into her mouth, munching on the dark sourdough while Braedon placed another log on the fire.

"This is wonderful," she said when he came back and seated himself across from her at the makeshift table. Braedon took a large bite of the meat pie, then sopped up some of the gravy with a chunk of bread. He seemed to forget his irritation with her and focused instead on enjoying his meal. He sat back and sighed with pleasure, a momentary show of pure emotion that shocked Ariana.

"It's a very good meat pie," she said, letting her own guard down a notch.

"Aye, the best," he agreed. "England can never match France when it comes to good food. We had a cook in Amiens whose roasted pheasant would make you weep."

"Is that where you're from—Amiens?"

He cocked his head at her, a look of hesitancy coming over his sharp-hewn features. His dark brows knit for a moment, but then he relented with a shrug. "Yes, I was born there."

"Is it very far from Rouen?"

"Not that far. Why?"

Ariana gave a little shrug. "Perhaps you will pay a visit to your kin after we part company in Rouen." She did not expect him to laugh at the idea. "What? Why is that amusing?"

"There is nothing for me in Amiens, *demoiselle*. It was the place of my birth, nothing more."

"Have you no family there? Not your parents or siblings?"

"No." He considered for a moment, then shook his head. "In truth, I don't know. I left Amiens to squire for a minor lord in Paris when I was ten years old. Later, I took my skills to England to carve out my own life. I never went back."

Ariana reached for her cup of ale, frowning. "Didn't you miss home?"

"No."

She looked at him in question as she brought the cup to her lips, curious at the note of regret she thought she heard beneath his cool detachment. "You've never gone back in all this time?"

Light from the fire danced on the sharp plane of his

cheek as he gave her a dismissive tilt of his chin. "My father and I did not get on well together."

"Why not?"

"I suppose because I tried to kill him."

Ariana stilled suddenly, unsure what to make of his glib remark. "You're jesting."

But there was no humor in his eyes, no air of levity in his matter-of-fact tone, not even that phantom trace of regret she swore she had detected there a moment before. He looked at her with utter frankness, and Ariana felt a measure of fear worm up her spine. Had he really thought to harm his own sire? It was inconceivable to her, the sort of black-hearted passion that would have to inspire such an act.

Perhaps, warned her conscience, the less she knew about Braedon and whatever demons might haunt him, the better. She did not need to delve into the sort of hatred—or madness—that drove him. Still, she found herself drawn to the bleakness of his gaze, wondering if anyone had ever tried to reach out to him before. Wondering if, in some vulnerable corner of his heart, he might need someone to try.

She set her cup down very carefully, unable to look away from his unflinching, steel-cold gaze. "What happened between your father and you, Braedon?"

He took a bite of his meat pie, chewing slowly, thoughtfully, then he washed it down with a drink of ale. "We had an argument." He shrugged, as if refusing to revisit old memories. "It was a long time ago. It doesn't matter."

Ariana regarded him gently, accepting that he would not share his shame with her, but admitting to herself that she was never one to leave questions unanswered. As

rules were meant to be followed, puzzles were meant to
be solved. And the man sitting across from her was a mystery too intriguing to let lie. "Is that what happened to
you?" she asked gingerly. "Is that how you got your scar?"

Her question seemed to surprise him, as if while lost in
his thoughts, he had forgotten about the mark that savaged one side of his face. His hand came up, long fingers
skating over the jagged, silvery welt. "This," he said, re-
suming his air of nonchalance. "Nay, lady, this was not
my father's doing. I came by this badge elsewise."

"How did you get it?"

"Through a gross error in judgment." He looked at her
as he said it, then dropped his hand to reach for his cup
of ale. "As I recall, *demoiselle,* I was the one asking questions of you."

Ariana lifted her shoulder. "And I answered them."

"Ah. Right," he drawled, skepticism lacing his voice.
"You fed me a sketchy tale of a sainted brother, whom
you scarcely knew for all his absence from your life. A
brother who supposedly summoned you to him a half a
world away, and you set out to oblige him because you
feared he might be suffering from a head cold or tempo-
rary malnourishment." Braedon leaned back, bracing
himself on one elbow. "Your Clairmont guardsman must
have been the very embodiment of understanding to have
been willing to lay down his life to protect you in so foolish a quest."

Ariana stared helplessly at him from within the snare
of her self-spun trap, her heart clenching in guilt at the
mention of James. She fought back a prickle of sorrow,
still blaming herself for the knight's death. She should
never have allowed him to escort her to London, although it would have taken a midnight escape for her to

have ridden out of Clairmont's gates without the old guard at her side. But still she regretted having involved him, just as she wished she hadn't been forced to involve Braedon even insofar as she had already.

Although she hadn't stretched the truth too far, Braedon had not believed a word of what she'd told him—a fact that hardly surprised her. He had been questioning her veracity from the moment fate thrust them together on the docks at Queenhithe. She did not expect he would stop questioning her until she had bared every secret she held to its naked core. And that she simply could not afford to do.

Ariana dipped her spoon into the thick gravy of her meat pie, idly stirring the juicy chunks of venison and beef as she considered the strange course upon which she had set sail.

"Finish your sup, *demoiselle*," Braedon instructed her knowingly. "Perhaps you'll find a more palatable tale at the bottom of your trencher."

They ate in guarded silence, Ariana nibbling nervously, too discomfited now to enjoy the hearty meal, while Braedon wolfed down his pie and root vegetables like a growing youth without a care in the world. The bath arrived just as they were finishing up, an interruption no less welcome than the food had been about an hour before.

Two young lads carried in the big, padded wooden tub, one with a supply of folded linen towels tucked under his gangly arm. The boys were followed by four maids, each carrying a bucket of steaming water in hand. Expedient and polite, the servants filled the tub and left, the last maid offering to carry down the ravaged food tray as she departed.

"Give them a few coins for their trouble," Braedon said, tossing his purse to Ariana from across the room. She dug into the small bag and withdrew a couple of silver pennies. The girl's face lit up at the payment and she bobbed an awkward little curtsy with her murmured thanks. Ariana closed the door and turned around to face Braedon. She opened her mouth to comment on something, but just what she'd meant to say flew out of her head like a dove spooked from its roost in the eaves.

Without a care for modesty—his own or hers—Braedon stood near the steaming tub of water and shed his tunic. His leather gambeson was already beside him on the floor, removed evidently while Ariana was distracted by the departing maids. He paid her discomfiture no mind as he drew his dagger from its sheath on his hip and slipped the slim blade beneath one of the knots in his bandage. He cut each one in turn, then unwrapped the soiled linen from the wound on his arm and tossed the rags into the fire.

Ariana knew that propriety demanded she avert her gaze from his unclothed chest and torso, but she could not help looking at him. Twice in nearly as many days she had seen him in some state of undress. She should be scandalized beyond toleration, not peering surreptitiously at the hard muscle that knotted like thick ropes in his arms and shoulders. His skin looked smooth in the firelight, gilded a deep, golden bronze. She watched in unwilling fascination as he moved, his lean, strong fingers grabbing the ends of his ruined tunic and tearing it in two. He rent the cleanest section in half once more, then used his dagger to slice the swatch into several long, thin strips. He plunged one of the strips into the bathwater, then squeezed it out over his wound to cleanse it. Bloodied water dripped from his arm into the rushes on the floor. Ariana saw him grimace as the hot water washed over the deep, angry cut.

"I'm sorry you were injured," she told him from across the room. "You saved my life with Monsieur Ferrand and his men, and I never did properly thank you."

He shrugged off her gratitude and continued to work on his arm. He had sponged away most of the old blood and was now trying to wrap one of the bandages around it, pressing his elbow to his chest to hold the errant tail of the binding while he worked to wrap the length of it around his arm. The anchored end kept slipping out of its hold. After his second muttered curse, Ariana pushed aside her wariness and mistrust of him and crossed the room to take the bandage from his hands.

He merely glanced at her when she tipped her face up at him in silent command. "You'll be at this all night unless you have some help."

She set the bandages aside, then rewet the cloth and cleansed the wound again, taking care to blot tenderly as she inspected the laceration. Braedon's gaze was fixed on her the whole time; she felt the heat of it as surely as if he'd been physically touching her. The notion unsettled her, made her fingers tremble slightly as she retrieved a strip of bandage from his outstretched hand. The silence was like a weight between them, filled with awareness of the incongruous intimacy present in the tiny chamber. Ariana felt compelled to fill the quiet, hoping it would dispel some of her awkwardness.

"When I was a child," she began, speaking softly as she wrapped the clean strip of bandage around Braedon's arm, "one of our cats had a litter of kittens in the buttery off the kitchens. We kept a few around to discourage vermin, but my father refused to allow them in the keep. He had his hunting dogs—large, mean beasts that terrified

me nigh to death. I so wanted a kitten. I tried to plead
with him, as children are liable to do, but he wouldn't
hear of it."

Braedon grunted, his gaze fixed on her fingers as she
worked the bandages, but distant, as though his thoughts
tugged him toward his own memories, toward another
place and time. "Let me guess. You decided to keep one
anyway?"

"No," she denied quickly. "I couldn't. I didn't dare disobey my father. But when the mother cat died a few
weeks later and left her kittens helpless, I took it upon
myself to take care of them. Twice a day—more than
that, when I could manage it—I sneaked down to the buttery with a cup of cream and whatever scraps of meat I
could smuggle from the table to feed them. On one of
those excursions, Cook happened by the storeroom and
noticed the door was ajar. Before I could cry out that I
was there, he slammed it shut and bolted it from outside.
I beat on that door until my hands ached, but it was no
use. I was trapped."

"For how long?"

Ariana's brows knit, remembering the pitch darkness
of the storeroom, feeling the coldness of the hours she
spent behind that heavy door, alone and crying, unable to
see even her own hand in front of her face for the complete lack of light. And there were the rats. She shuddered, still able to feel the light trace of animal footsteps
pattering beneath the hem of her skirt, over the tops of
her light leather slippers. She hadn't known if they were
rats or kittens crawling on her, so she dared not kick anything away. Instead she stood in fright the whole time,
beating on the door and desperate to be let out into the
light.

"I was locked in there for two days." Two days, but

the awful terror of the incident revisited her even now, some ten years later. She could hardly enter an unlit chamber without feeling a wash of dread sweep over her. Sometimes, in the dark, her remembered fear was so strong, it robbed her of her breath.

"Good God," Braedon murmured. "Did no one wonder where you were all that time?"

"No. No one noticed." She schooled her face to stillness, trying not to wince under the sting of her humiliating admission. "My mother had already passed away, and my father . . . well, my father was a busy man. He was occupied with his own matters. I expect I could have been missing a week before he would have noticed anything amiss."

Braedon said nothing, merely watched her with an intensity that made her want to bite off her tongue. Why had she shared this humiliation with him? she wondered helplessly in the moments of silence that followed. She had never told a soul about it before, not even her small circle of friends at Clairmont. They'd all felt sorry for her that she had no mother, but she couldn't bear to admit that she'd had no father, either. She was as good as invisible at Clairmont, no matter how hard she tried to be useful and relied upon. To be needed.

It was a bitter pain she carried, yet for reasons she could not comprehend, here she was, baring her soul to this hard man, a veritable stranger. Would he laugh in dismissal, as her father had, when he learned of her foolery? She would perish on the spot if Braedon mocked her.

Eager to avoid it, she gave a little wave of her hand and picked up the last of the bandages. "No harm was done, and I learned my lesson. Kenrick was the one who found me. He was so angry he was shaking, and he scolded me quite thoroughly for making him search the castle high and low for most of the day. I think he wanted to throttle me when he pulled open the storeroom door and saw me standing there."

She laughed, but it was something of a forced sound, and Braedon did not so much as smile. "You truly would do anything for him, wouldn't you?"

Ariana nodded resolutely. "Yes, I would."

His gaze on hers, gray eyes as soft as they were thoughtful, he slowly lifted his other hand and traced the line of her cheek with a gentle caress. "Now that, *demoiselle,* I do believe."

His touch lingered. His hand was warm against her skin, the cradle of his palm cupping her jawline, his thumb idly smoothing along the slope of her cheek. He paused there for an indeterminate time, sending Ariana's heart into an anxious flutter as she recalled their kiss on the boat. She should back away now. She should turn from his unbidden caress at once. She meant to, but before she could summon the will to do so, Braedon's hand slowly fell away.

With no apology or excuse for his boldness, he stepped back a pace and retrieved his dagger from where he'd set it on the edge of the tub. Sheathing the slender blade, he bent for his satchel of belongings. He dug through the pack and withdrew another tunic, this one dyed a deep earthy brown. He donned it somewhat hastily while Ariana picked up the remaining supplies. "The bath is yours, if you want it, my lady. You should have ample time to partake of it while I'm gone."

"Gone?" Ariana glanced up sharply. "Where are you going?"

"I must see the sailmaker about repairs."

"Oh," she replied, knowing she should be relieved that

he was leaving her to her peace, even if it would be only for a short while. "How long do you think it will take before we can leave Calais and go on to Honfleur?"

"The repairs to the sail won't take too long, I expect. But it's the weather that will cause the delays. If the storm keeps up, no vessels will be safe to leave port for a week or more."

A week? A sudden swell of panic climbed into Ariana's throat. "But that's too long! I can't possibly wait that long."

Braedon's dark, considering look silenced her, but not before her worry had betrayed her to him once more. He strode toward her, that keen gaze rooted on hers, cornering her as surely as a wolf would run down a hare. "Don't think I'm unaware that you haven't told me everything, Ariana. Keep your childish loyalty to your kin. Keep your secrets, and you can take all of it with you, by yourself, to Rouen. You have until I return to decide how we proceed."

❦ 7 ❧

BRAEDON HAD BEEN prepared for more hedging and evasion on Ariana's part. He expected more vehement insistence that she was hiding nothing from him. To her credit, she had done none of those things, merely watched him in considering silence as he slung his mantle over his shoulders and left her alone at the inn. He felt the daggers of her ire jabbing at his skull for some time after he quit the place and walked the Calais streets toward the sailmaker's shop.

As much as Ariana needed him, she resented him. That much was clear.

And why shouldn't she? He hadn't made it easy for her. The way he saw it, he had no reason to. He was a man accustomed to being on his own, without the responsibilities of kin or clan. His life was simple and orderly now—the way he preferred it. The very last thing he wanted was to become any further entangled with a headstrong woman like Ariana of Clairmont on her dubious quest to tend her sainted brother.

If he were smart, he'd repair his grounded boat and leave port as soon as possible. He'd forget that the past two days had happened, forget she was waiting for him at the inn, and simply go. Divest himself of the obligation entirely.

Aye, that was what he should do. Instead, he was

standing in the musty heat of the sailmaker's shop, thinking about everything Ariana had told him, and wondering at all she hadn't said. And he nursed an irksome, continuing measure of desire for the woman that plagued him all the while he listened with half interest as the ancient craftsman inspected the torn sail and described in meticulous detail the work to be done.

"How long will it take to complete the repairs?" he asked, loath to cut the proud old man off, but in no mind to tarry much longer in the stuffy shop. By his estimation, he had been gone nearly an hour already. If his curiosity over Ariana was not enough to lure him back to the inn, a sudden nagging sense of foreboding certainly was.

"In a hurry to leave Calais already, are you?" The white-haired sailmaker chuckled as he set down his ruler and chalk. His rheumy gaze traveled Braedon's face, flicking with only the mildest interest at the cruel line of his scar. "Where do you go that you are so impatient to travel in this terrible, soupy weather?"

Although the old man gave him no reason to mistrust him, Braedon offered him a lie. "Cherbourg," he said, naming a fishing port miles away from his intended destination of Honfleur. "I have work waiting for me there."

"Ah, I see. And your wife?" At Braedon's flat stare, the old man smiled and brought a gnarled finger to his temple. "My eyes are old, but not so old that I no longer keep a watch on my harbor. I could not help but notice you and your lady as you arrived. She is lovely, sir. You are a fortunate man, indeed."

Braedon grunted, acknowledging neither Ariana's comeliness or his relationship to her. "The sail," he prompted again. "Can you have it for me on the morrow?"

"*Oui, monsieur.* I will start on it at—" A sudden light-footed scurrying noise from high in the rafters of his shop drew the old man's attention. "Damned rats," he grumbled, squinting into the shadows above their heads. "I keep a cat, but do you think that lazy old thing would trouble herself to catch them? Not one, the worthless beast, in all the five years I've had her."

Braedon glanced up toward the skittering sound that had traveled from the end of one long support beam to the other. He could have sworn he saw the reddish glow of two small eyes catch in the glint of the fireplace, but then he blinked and the beady little stare was gone. "I'll be back, then," he said to the sailmaker. "At first light, if that will give you enough time to do the work."

"Fine, *oui.* It will be ready for you, *monsieur.*" The old man nodded, but Braedon could see that he had all but lost him to the sudden pursuit of his vermin infiltrators. Picking up an oar that rested against the wall, the sailmaker stalked toward the corner of the shop, wearing a look of dogged determination. Braedon left him to his hunt, stepping out into the snowy street and closing the door behind him just as the oar crashed down with a deafening *bang!*

From the virulence of the curse that followed, Braedon guessed it was safe to assume that the old man's quarry had eluded him.

Outside, in the narrow street off the sailmaker's shop, snow fell from the darkening gray sky like a silent white rain, feather light and steady. It frosted the narrow alleyways and clung to the faces of the half-timbered buildings that lined the harbor. Nary a soul was out, despite that it was still some hours before dusk and the worst of the squall was passing.

Braedon's boots crunched in the freezing slush that

choked the street outside the inn, his steady gait the only sound, save the intermittent clank and bump of ships moored at the dock to wait out the weather. The niggling sense of unease that had followed him from the inn remained with him now, even as he left the sailmaker's shop and headed back to speak with Ariana.

And something else niggled at him now, too.

He had the sudden and distinct sense that he was being watched.

No one lingered in the street or in the alleyways he passed as he made his way back toward the inn, but that did not quell the hairs that rose on the back of his neck in warning. His instincts quivered with swift awareness. He scented the presence of someone. He was being trailed, he was certain of it. Someone hid somewhere nearby, just out of sight. Watching. Waiting.

For what?

Calais, being the closest port between England and France, was a busy place, a known haven for criminals, outcasts, and various other of humanity's more unsavory element. No doubt the hunting was poor this far into winter, but Braedon had a feeling he was being studied by someone other than a basic cutpurse, and for more than just a simple bit of petty thievery. There was deadly intent in the chill silence that surrounded him, a predatory charge in the air.

He drew up short in the middle of the street and paused there, listening. He pivoted his head, daring the shadows to materialize and confront him.

No one came.

No one was there.

Slowly, as if creeping back inch by inch, the prickling of his instincts began to subside. He turned his head back and took a step forward—then felt the stunning blow of

a heavy knife hilt smash into the side of his skull. He
went down on one knee in the slushy muck, instantly
dazed. With effort, he shook off the shattering spray of
pain and light that exploded in his brain, his bleary vision
rooting on a scuffed and wet pair of large brown boots
that stood beside him in the street.

"Where is it?" growled a rough voice from above him.
One of those sodden boots planted before him lifted to
kick him in the ribs, but Braedon saw it coming. He
grabbed the muddied heel and twisted hard as he came
up off his knees, sending his oxlike attacker to the
ground in a breathless heap. The knife flew out of his
hand and landed in a dingy clump of snow and ice. With
a roar, Braedon leaped on the man and yanked him up by
his tunic and mantle. He did not know him, he decided at
once, letting go only long enough to deliver his fist into
the miscreant's face.

"Who the hell are you?" When he did not answer,
Braedon hit him again. "Who are you, damn it? What do
you want?"

The man didn't answer, merely chuckled through his
bloodied teeth. "He's going to finish you this time, le
Chasseur."

Braedon mentally recoiled to hear his old name voiced
after so long. Le Chasseur. *The Hunter.* A name that had
once brought him glory and honor now reached his ears
like a curse. He was caught off guard momentarily, but
fury soon blazed in place of his surprise. How did this
man—this crude stranger—know him by the name he
buried nearly eighteen months ago?

"Draw your sword," he growled at the man, shoving
him back as he freed his weapon from its scabbard.

The beefy mercenary rocked back on his heels, chuckling, but he made no move to meet Braedon's challenge.

He took another step back, hardly a pace, just enough to put himself beyond arm's length.

Then, with a look of arch amusement, he bolted.

Moving with a speed and agility surprising in a man of his size and bulk, the huge assailant sprinted down the side street like a stag dashing through a thicket. Braedon started to give chase, then realized the futility in it. A few moments later, the swirling snow and foggy gray day had swallowed up all traces of the man.

Save the dagger he had dropped.

Braedon went back and picked up the intricately tooled, gem-encrusted blade. He scowled, noting the strange design of the hilt and handle—a writhing serpent wrought in silver and coiled around the weapon's grip. Nay, not a serpent.

A dragon.

With one last look down the empty alleyway, Braedon tucked the strange blade under his baldric and headed back to the inn. Whatever was going on, whatever trouble was eager to revisit him, he was certain he'd find Ariana of Clairmont squarely in the middle of it. Since he'd known her, he had been sliced at, fired at, battered about, and nearly drowned in the English Channel. Now this most recent assault in Calais. His anger had finally snapped its leash, and he would be damned if he'd let her go another minute without an explanation of just what she had gotten him into.

Braedon stalked through the inn's small public room and down the corridor to the chamber he shared with her. He drew up in front of the door and scarcely paused before he kicked it open in his fury. The feeble lock on the other side of the panel exploded from its fixtures and the door swung wide, banging against the hind wall.

Ariana's yelp of shock was echoed by another distressed scream, the second coming from behind Braedon in the hallway.

"*Monsieur!*" shouted the innkeeper, rushing up behind him upon hearing the commotion. "Oh, *monsieur*—the damage! Have a care, I beg you!"

Braedon rounded on the little man with a vicious snarl. "Leave us."

The innkeeper blinked at him for a dazed moment, then ducked and fled without a further word.

"What the devil are you doing!" Ariana gasped. She had been in her bath but a moment ago, and now stood beside the wooden tub, the ends of her honey-gold hair dripping water and naught but a sheet of white toweling gathered around her lithe, long-limbed body. She gripped the edges of the cloth tight together in a white-knuckled fist that balled over her heart. "H-how . . . how dare you barge in here in such a manner! Have you lost your mind?"

"In truth, I am beginning to wonder," he said, stalking into the small room.

Braedon had imagined she was lovely beneath her many layers of clothing and blankets, but he had not been prepared for the lissome creature that stood before him now, trembling and wide-eyed, rivulets of water tracing delicate lines of moisture down her creamy arms and slender legs. The blow he'd taken on his head had been solid, but evidently not punishing enough to keep him from indulging in a moment of thunderstruck admiration as he took in the pleasing shape of Ariana's body, so delectably draped in the small swatch of toweling.

"Get out!" she cried. "Get out at once! Have you no sense of decency?"

Braedon mentally kicked himself out of his stupor and shot her a withering glance. He was not about to leave.

"Oh, do forgive me, my lady. No doubt I lost what little consideration I had when someone attacked me and tried to crush my skull in the street a short while ago."

A twitch of confusion ruffled her outraged expression. "W-what are you talking about? Who attacked you?"

"Alas, I did not pause to get his name," Braedon growled wryly. "But the bastard knew mine. And he wanted to know where *it* was. What do you suppose he meant, Ariana?"

"I'm sure I don't know!" she shrieked as he strode forward.

"God's blood, but you are easily the most infuriating female I have ever known. Just what the devil are you about, lady?"

She frowned, taking a step away from the tub as he came farther into the room. "I-I haven't the slightest notion what you're talking about."

"Nay?" His gaze scanned the small room, fixing on the neat arrangement of her clothing near the fireplace. Her satchel lay beside her clothes, partially concealed by the fold of her drying cloak. That fat leather pouch and its damnable secrets. Secrets that might yet get her, or him, killed.

Braedon headed for the satchel, crossing the room in three angry strides.

"No—wait!" Ariana rushed after him, her bare feet padding hastily on the plank floor. "Please, you mustn't—"

Braedon seized the bag and threw open the thong and toggle that held it closed. He felt Ariana's hand frantically clutch at his tunic sleeve. He saw the wet skin of her bare arm glisten in the firelight, heard her little mewl of distress when he did not relent.

"I beg you, Braedon, do not—"

But he was undaunted by her pleas. She owed him this much, and he was tired of her evasions. Grabbing the bulky girth of the bag, he flipped it over and dumped its contents onto the floor. Behind him, Ariana sucked in her breath as the items it contained—parchments and papers and two plump leather journals—tumbled down around his feet.

"Braedon, you don't understand. I would have explained—I wanted to tell you, but they said no one was to know . . ."

He looked at her in questioning silence, then bent to retrieve one of the volumes that had broken open on the toe of his boot. The pages were inscribed with a careful hand, but the words made little sense. They were encoded somehow, penned in Latin, yet not the meticulous form Braedon had been schooled in during his youth.

He flipped the page and found something folded and tucked inside. A drawing—rather, a map. Though it was rendered with less skill than a cartographer's, Braedon still recognized England's island coastline. Several points were marked on the map: Cornwall, Glastonbury, and an area tucked into the woods of Cheshire. A line connected all three places, and beside it on the page was a complex series of figures and calculations. He fanned through more pages, finding more of the same. More cryptic text, more scribblings, more strange drawings.

Then he saw it.

A sheaf of parchment, nearly obscured by the jumble piled atop it. Braedon saw the outline sketched onto the paper, and his blood froze. He bent down and slowly drew the parchment out from under the rest of the satchel's contents.

There it was, as plain as day.

An ornate chalice, depicted in black ink and rendered in detail far too accurate to be pure conjecture. He saw the dragon image coiled around the stem of the goblet. The cup had been drawn to seem afire, with rays of light shooting from the chalice's four priceless stones embedded in its wide bowl. Stones which were purported to have powers beyond imagining.

Powers of life eternal, unstoppable might, and wealth without limit.

Braedon had to struggle to keep the fury from his voice. "Do you know what this is, Ariana?"

"I-I'm not sure. It belongs to Kenrick."

A disbelieving oath on his tongue, Braedon sharply pivoted his head to look at her. Ariana was still trembling, her eyes still glinting with reproach for his immodest intrusion, but he saw no deception in her gaze.

"I swear to you, Braedon, I do not know what any of it means. Kenrick kept it all very secret."

"These are your brother's papers?"

"Yes." She nodded solemnly. "I only know that unless I deliver that satchel to Rouen, my brother will be killed."

"By whom?"

"I don't know."

He snorted a vicious bark of laughter.

"I swear, I don't. He was here in France when someone took him hostage. That satchel is his ransom." When he stood up and let the parchment fall back to the floor, Ariana put her hand on his arm, her touch imploring him to hear her out. "They sent a message to Clairmont with word of Kenrick's capture. No one was to know about the papers—they warned me, Braedon. They said I was to deliver them to Rouen, alone, before the next full moon, or else . . . or else, I would never see my brother alive again."

Braedon did not answer her. Indeed, in that moment, he had no reply to offer her at all.

"It is the truth," Ariana insisted when he strode away from her to pick up her clothing from near the hearth. "You know everything I do now."

"Christ on the Cross." The irony of it was so rich, he could have laughed aloud. "What a damned bloody jest this is."

"You've been hounding me for answers since I met you, and now that you have them, you don't believe me?"

"Aye, *demoiselle*. I believe you."

He handed her the gown and chemise. He glanced back down at the scattering of papers and notes, at the unlikely bag of scribblings that just might be the key to a considerable fortune.

The Dragon Chalice.

There could be no mistaking it.

The cup was the stuff of legend, a folktale that got its start some hundred years before Braedon's birth. It was little more than myth and magic, oft dreamed of but never proven to exist beyond the hopes of a determined, powerful few.

Braedon ought to know.

He had once been one of them.

❧ 8 ❧

Get dressed, Ariana. Now."

Braedon's tone was clipped, on the verge of an outright
command. She bristled at the order, still rankled with
him for intruding on her bath and now committing this
greater breach of her privacy. He shoved her kirtle and
chemise at her, then paced to the room's sole window and
peered through the shutters at the courtyard below.

"If you think I'm going to dress in front of you while
you stand here, sirrah, you are mad."

"You can either get dressed and come with me, or you
can stay and deal with this trouble on your own."

"What do you mean?"

He glanced back at her and jerked his thumb toward
the window. "Two knights just rode into the courtyard—
heavily armed knights, my lady, both outfitted for war.
Any guess as to what business they are about?"

"You think they're after me?"

"You, and the information in that bag." He stared
down at the spilled contents of Kenrick's satchel, his features sharper than she had ever seen them. "They're
probably after both of us now, but I'm not staying here to
find out."

"Do you mean to say these are the same people who
hold Kenrick?"

He didn't answer, but she could tell from the grim look in his eyes that he suspected as much.

"Get dressed," he told her. "I'll pack up our things."

Any thoughts of maidenly modesty were cast to a distant second behind Ariana's primary need for survival. She hastened to the far corner of the room and quickly donned her chemise and kirtle while Braedon gathered Kenrick's papers and replaced them in the satchel. She drew her woolen hose on in a rush, then fastened them to her garters and threw down her skirts.

"Where will we go?" she asked, tugging on her still-damp boots. "You said yourself the weather will delay us from sailing on to Honfleur."

"We'll have to risk it. I don't see any other choice."

Ariana grabbed her cloak and threw it over her shoulders, then raced forward to meet Braedon where he waited at the door. It did not escape her notice that while she dressed, he had neatly appropriated her satchel.

"It will be safer for you if I carry this," he told her when she paused to question him with a meaningful glance at the pack, now slung over his arm. She might have been inclined to argue that, but he took her by the hand and led her into the hallway. "Let's go, Ariana. There must be a back entrance to the inn. We have to find it, and we don't have much time."

Together, they ran down the corridor and ducked into the kitchens of the small inn. Spice-scented steam wreathed their heads from the large cooking pots simmering over the fire. Skinned rabbits and headless chickens hung from iron racks along the far wall. One of the cooks had just returned from an adjacent storeroom with a bowl of vegetables under his arm as Braedon and Ariana crossed the kitchen. Sweating and corpulent, he barked at them to leave at once.

"Out, out! You are not permitted in the kitchens. The public room is down the hall."

"Is there a back way out of here?" Braedon inquired, giving the man a quick, conspiratorial tilt of his head. "I fear my lady's husband would be most displeased to find her here with me."

"Agh," groused the cook with a glance at Ariana and a shrug of his beefy shoulder. "That way. Through the storeroom. It will put you in the alley behind the inn."

With a nod, Braedon brought Ariana into the kitchen storeroom. It was dark and musty, lined with casks of wine and ale, and crates of winter vegetables. At the back of the small room, just as the cook had said, was the light-rimmed frame of a door. Braedon put his hand against the rough panel and carefully opened it to peer outside.

The alley was empty, save for a skinny, skulking dog that was tiptoeing through the slush and muck, his head hung low, eyes alert as he prowled the perimeter of the building for scraps. The soft creak of the door startled him, and the sudden arrival of people in the alleyway sent him off with a disgruntled whimper.

"Quickly," Braedon instructed Ariana. "Stay close."

She followed him on swift feet as he traversed one side street and then another, leading her away from the inn and down around toward the harbor, where his boat was docked. Forgetting the inclement weather, they could not go anywhere without the cog's sail. Although he had been gone only a short while, with any luck at all, Claude, the old sailmaker, would have his repairs nearly completed, or at the very least have a different sail that Braedon could take off his hands.

Along the harborfront street they ran, with Braedon often glancing over his shoulder to make certain they were not spotted. They reached the sailmaker's shop and were greeted by Claude himself, the old man having just opened his door to let out the cat. He shooed the fat tabby away none too gently with the toe of his shoe, then glanced up and gave Braedon a smile of recognition.

"Ah, *monsieur*. Back so soon, are you? And *madame*." His eyes lit on Ariana and his smile grew wider, leeringly so, Braedon would have thought, had the sailmaker been any younger. "Come in, *s'il vous plaît*. Come in, both of you."

He offered Ariana his hand in warm welcome, but Braedon held her back. Something pricked his keen senses as he peered over Claude's shoulder to the darkened shop beyond. "I don't suppose you've been able to start on my sail? We're in something of a hurry."

The old man hesitated, his gaze darting between them. "Why, yes, I have, *monsieur*. It is nearly finished. Come, I will show you."

With a surreptitious glance behind them to the street that yet remained empty of any threat, Braedon gave a nod to Ariana and they entered the shop. He kept her close, his hand on her arm. He kept his attention on the old sailmaker, watching, listening, the warning sense of danger growing stronger now that they were inside.

Claude ambled in ahead of them, taking his time as he led them into the main room of the shop. "I had hoped you might bring your lady by, *monsieur*. It is not often I get to visit with pretty ladies like this one." Again he gave her too wide a grin. "Come here, child. Let me take your cloak. Put down your burdens, the both of you. Tell me what has you in such a hurry to leave our fair city when you've only just arrived here."

Ariana returned his smile with a polite nod, but her gaze warily slid to Braedon.

"We won't be staying," he answered for her, drawing up beside her and placing his arm around her. "You said you had my sail."

"I do," replied the old man. "It is here, in the other room."

They followed him to an antechamber near the back of the cramped space, Braedon taking care to keep Ariana within arm's reach. He scanned the room but saw no sign of his sail. Another sail, a moldy sheet of leather-reinforced linen, lay across a worktable, half-finished.

"This is not mine," Braedon told him, impatience flaring in his voice.

"Are you certain, *monsieur*? Come closer and have a better look."

"That sail does not belong to me and you know it." He let his gaze roam the room, not liking the stillness of the place. It emanated silence like a tomb. "What kind of game are you playing, old man?"

"Game? I play no game."

Braedon did not believe him. The needling sense of distrust he felt at the door was amplified tenfold now that he was standing there with strange, fidgety old Claude. He noted that a candle had been tipped over on the worktable. Fatty wax lay in a splattered pool, hardened where it had landed, spread across the table and onto the edge of the sail. Some of it coated the old man's tools, which lay in jumbled disarray near his work. Odd, Braedon thought, that the proud sailmaker would allow his things to be sullied in such a fashion.

He glanced over and found the old man standing nearer to him now, looking at him.

Studying him.

His eyes slid to where Braedon had just been looking and he clucked his tongue. "Ah," the old man exclaimed. He smiled and gave a shake of his balding gray head. "That damned cat. The beast is forever getting up on things and making a mess. I don't know why I keep him."

Something peculiar struck Braedon as he held old Claude's wavering gaze. Something that made his every nerve go taut with alert. Something was not quite right about the man. Not right at all.

It was his eyes, Braedon decided suddenly.

Those smiling brown eyes, set in a wrinkled, age-spotted face, had the unmistakable glint of youth. Inexplicably, as impossible as it was to imagine, the rheumy haze that had clouded the grizzled sailmaker's eyes when Braedon first met him—little more than an hour before—was gone.

A chill swept the cramped room, settling with an unholy silence as Braedon tried to grasp what his senses were telling him. He did not trust what his eyes were seeing, but neither could he deny it.

With as much stealth as he could muster, Braedon slowly, subtly, guided Ariana behind him and turned to face the old man head-on. He gave the sailmaker a look he hoped was genial, his gaze never leaving those odd brown eyes. "A little mess can be cleaned up and forgiven," he said pleasantly, "especially when you've a hardworking animal like yours."

"Eh?" The confident, deceitful smile faltered. "Hardworking animal, *monsieur*?"

"Aye," Braedon said, testing him. "Were you not just telling me this afternoon how deft a hunter your cat was? No doubt the beast was merely chasing rats when it knocked over the candle."

"Oh! *Oui, monsieur, oui*. You are so right."

Braedon shared the impostor's false chuckle for barely a heartbeat. Then he thrust out his hand and seized the man by the throat, shoving him backward as he walked him into the nearest wall.

"Braedon!" Ariana screamed from behind him. "What are you doing?"

"*Oui, monsieur*," choked the man in a voice that was swiftly losing its rusty edge. "What is the meaning of this? Why do you wish to harm a defenseless old man?"

"What have you done with him? The sailmaker," Braedon demanded, but his instincts told him that based on the upset condition of the shop, the old man was likely already dead. "Do you mean to kill us, too?"

He struggled in Braedon's grasp, writhing and coughing, clutching at the fingers that tightened on his throat. "You are . . . choking me. . . . I beg you . . . let . . . go."

"Braedon," Ariana whispered urgently. She came up behind him and placed her hands on his shoulders. "Braedon, are you mad? Can't you see, he's just an old man!"

He shook her off with a curse. "Get back, Ariana. By all that is holy, this is no old man. This is no man at all. Are you?" he growled, squeezing his fist around the thin, withered throat. "Answer me, damn you!"

The impostor chuckled, his voice deepening in its mirth, turning guttural and queerly inhuman as it echoed in the small shop room. Braedon reached down with his free hand and drew the dragon-hilt dagger from its sheath. "Lose something today?" he asked, brandishing the weapon. "It'll be my pleasure to give it back to you."

Those strange brown eyes, beady eyes, glittered with malice and not a little enjoyment. "If you kill me, le Chasseur, there will be more to take my place."

"Let them come, then. But you die today."

He brought the blade up against the man's chest, but as he moved to drive it home, the air around him suddenly seemed to shift and shimmer. Like a river's current, the strange force flowed up Braedon's arm to encompass him. The face that looked up at him in gleeful satisfaction began to mute and twist, fading as though in a fog. The brown eyes glittered like beads of glass, lifeless and cold.

"Braedon?" Ariana gasped behind him. "Braedon! What's happening?"

He could not answer her, even if he had words to explain. It was all he could do to fight the jolting strength of whatever gripped him, all he could do to hold on to the man who was suddenly fading from his grasp like a handful of smoke. With a roar, Braedon thrust his blade homeward.

Too late.

Like something borne by the darkest brand of magic, one moment Braedon was poised to kill a man; the next he was staring at naught but empty air.

A scurrying noise drew his attention to the wide planks of the floor in the beat of astonishment and fury that followed. He looked down and his gaze rooted on a fleeing rat, ducking for a darkened corner of the shop.

"Not this time, you bastard."

Braedon released the dagger and sent it flying. It hit its mark with swift and deadly precision, skewering the rodent with a shrill squeal. It jerked and convulsed on the floor, and then it was no longer a rat, nor the startlingly real illusion of Claude the sailmaker.

Braedon walked over to where the big body of a man lay facedown with the silver dragon dagger embedded in his back. With his boot, he kicked the lifeless form over and looked down at the slackened face of the mercenary who attacked him in the street that morning.

"Mother Mary," Ariana breathed, drawing up beside him, her hand to her mouth. Her eyes were wide and disbelieving as Braedon retrieved the dagger and sheathed it on his belt. "How could he—what did he . . . what *was* he, Braedon?"

"I'm not sure," he answered honestly. "But I think we'd better get out of here before any of his friends arrive."

"What will we do about the sail?"

"Forget it. We'd be foolish to go to the boat now, anyway. They'll be expecting that, no doubt." He brushed an errant lock of hair from her creased brow. "I have another plan. Come on."

They left the sailmaker's shop and ran back to the inn, picking their way cautiously along the back of the building. Braedon crept to the corner of the place and braved a glance at the courtyard. The two horses were still there, unguarded and restlessly waiting, their riders most likely still inside searching the inn.

"I trust you ride, my lady?" he asked, throwing a glance over his shoulder to where Ariana waited for his direction.

"Yes, of course."

"Then let's go."

9

THE CRACKLE OF a small fire echoed softly in the yawning maw of a forest cavern, filling the damp, cold space with much-needed warmth. Braedon guessed they were about thirty miles inland from Calais, a taxing ride for the horses, but perhaps more so for Ariana. She hadn't said two words to him since they had left the sailmaker's shop. Now she sat a few paces away from him by the fire, a shapeless form huddled beneath a blanket.

While their wet cloaks, boots, and hose lay out to dry near the fire, he watched her quietly pick at a collection of burrs that clung to her damp gloves, absorbed in her own thoughts. She had spent the last hour or more performing the same task on her sodden skirts, which she had refused to shed, even for the welcoming heat of the fire. No doubt she feared he would ravish her on the spot, particularly after the way he had behaved that first night at sea. Not that the idea didn't hold a certain degree of appeal, but he had never laid an unwanted hand on a woman before, and he didn't intend to start now.

In truth, his mood was too grim to consider their present intimate quarters with anything more than a regretful appreciation. His gaze kept straying to the satchel that contained her brother's papers. That damnable pouch with its stock of information pertaining to the Dragon Chalice. The bag had gotten damp amid their escape from Calais; now its cryptic contents were spread about on the floor of the cave to air out.

Journals, scribblings, and sundry scribed reports beckoned his attention. What precisely had Kenrick of Clairmont been documenting? What information had he uncovered about the legendary Dragon Chalice? Braedon recalled the myth that surrounded the Chalice and its purported origins—how the bejeweled golden cup, forged in a mystical kingdom, had been stolen by a mortal man. Legend claimed the Chalice bore four sacred gemstones in its enchanted bowl, each imbued with wondrous powers. Once removed from its true home, the Dragon Chalice split apart, broken in four pieces, smaller cups that each contained one of the sacred stones. It was said that if those four pieces were reunited, the Dragon Chalice would become whole again, and whoever held it would have the powers of the ages in his hands.

Braedon might have scoffed at such fancy—indeed, he had—before he had the misfortune of experiencing some of it firsthand. It was only eighteen months ago that his life had taken an irrevocable turn. A few weeks before that he'd first heard of the Dragon Chalice when he, the celebrated Hunter, was hired to retrieve a pilfered artifact for a wealthy nobleman in Rouen. Double the reward, if Braedon also brought in the thief, which, of course, he had. The Hunter never failed.

From the time he was a boy, he'd honed his skill, his strange ability to sense things and retrieve that which was lost. Little did he know, this time he was being made a dupe. It had been a costly lesson, one that had taken many lives in the end and left his in ruin.

He never saw the betrayal coming. He hadn't thought to look. Nor did he fully believe in the power of the Chalice legend until he glimpsed into the black soul of the man who would stop at nothing to claim it.

After what happened in the sailmaker's shop in Calais, and after his unexplainable encounter with Ferrand de Paris in London, Braedon was certain of what awaited Ariana and her brother in Rouen.

Death.

It had nearly claimed him that night eighteen months ago, and now it was on his trail again. He might have blamed Ariana for embroiling him in this trouble, but the fact was that no matter where he ran or how deeply he had isolated himself from the rest of the feeling world, the Dragon Chalice was never far from his thoughts. Like a curse he could not shake, it never gave him peace.

And now, here it was again, a specter from the past, taunting him from within the most innocent, beautiful blue eyes he had ever seen.

"Aren't you going to eat?" he asked her, gesturing to the small chunks of bread and cheese that lay beside her, ignored. They had been fortunate to find food and a flask of wine in the saddle packs of the horses they took from the inn, but the stale loaf of dark bread and the ripe wedge of cheese would not go far. Braedon pulled the stopper from the hard leather wine decanter and passed the flask to Ariana. "Drink, at least. You will need the warmth of the wine."

Her weary gaze slid to him as she reached out to take the flask. He watched her tip the decanter up to her lips, watched her slender throat work as she swallowed a mouthful of the fragrant wine. She coughed a bit, pressing the back of her hand to her mouth as she passed the flask back to him. He took some, then offered her another sip. She shook her head, frowning. " 'Tis overly strong."

"That's because you have grown up on English wine, no doubt. Watered down and full of grit." He held the decanter out to her once more and gave her a stern look. "Drink, Ariana. And eat what you can. You need both to keep your strength."

She obeyed him, her delicate fingers brushing aside the little pile of plucked burrs that had gathered in her lap, before reaching out to take the wine flask from him. While she drank and then nibbled on a chunk of brown bread, Braedon strode away from the fire to tend the horses where they stood on the other side of the wide-mouthed cavern. They had been brushed and fed earlier, and watered as well, using snow he had melted in one of the soldiers' helmets, which had been strapped onto the palfreys' packs. Braedon checked their hooves, then patted the two beasts each in turn, his thoughts drifting far away from the mundane task and growing darker by the moment.

"Braedon." Ariana's quiet voice drifted across the space that separated them. A shaky little sigh chased after it. "Braedon . . . I'm scared. I don't understand what's happening. That man back there in Calais—by the saints, *was* he a man at all?"

"I don't know," he answered without looking at her. "If you want the truth, I don't know precisely what we witnessed today."

"Witchery, to be sure." Ariana's voice took on a panicky edge. "He changed form before our eyes, Braedon. That man was some manner of demon." She shivered under her blanket, and a long beat of silence grew as she gazed back into the fire. When she turned to look at him again, her face was pale with dread. "Braedon . . . what if there are more of them?"

"We're safe enough here. Calais is a day's ride behind us. You needn't worry."

But even as he said it, he knew it for a lie. The longer he and Ariana delayed in one place, the more danger they invited. Where they stopped for rest, their pursuers would not. He knew that for certain. He could almost feel them closing in with each fleeting moment. The chase would be relentless so long as they had the satchel. Their capture would be brutal, certainly. His mind raced through a host of grim scenarios, each ending with them both dead—or worse, left to live as he had been. Alive, more or less, and wishing he was dead.

They could not stay the whole of the night in the cavern. They would have to take their respite, decide on a plan, and move on before morning dawned.

"Sleep if you can," he said, turning to face her across the twisting flames of the fire. "I'll stand watch while you rest."

She gave him a sheepish look, then raised her chin. Her damp, windblown tresses slid over her blanketed shoulders in long honey-soft waves as she slowly shook her head. "You don't have to take care of me, Braedon. Please don't feel that you do. I've asked too much of you already."

"Indeed, you have," he acknowledged coolly. "But what's done is done."

Again the look of remorse. "If you want me to go, I will. I never meant to involve you in this, I swear to you. I'll understand if you want to leave me here and move on before anything worse happens."

He laughed then, wryly amused by her naïveté. His

mocking bark of laughter made her flinch. "I don't think you understand, *demoiselle*. You and I are in this together—whether we wish to be or nay. It doesn't matter if we separate or stay together. We may as well be shackled together in irons. They will be hunting both of us now." He walked toward the fire where she sat, watching her expression falter as she absorbed this news. "As for Rouen," he added, "you're not going there at all, with or without me. Naught but death awaits you there."

Now she frowned. "You have no say in what I do. You cannot keep me from going to my brother."

"I can, Ariana, and I will. I won't permit you to hand over that satchel to his captors."

"You won't *permit* me?"

"That's right. From now on, I decide our course of action. 'Tis the only way."

She got to her feet, her arms held rigidly at her sides. "What about Kenrick?"

"What about him?"

"His life depends on me delivering his ransom."

"And both of our lives are worthless if you do."

"I will deliver this satchel to his captors, Braedon. I must. You cannot force me in this."

Her rising anger did not pique him. He merely gave her a sober look and tried to reason with her, though sensing it would be futile. "You would rather willingly go to your death in Rouen?"

"I won't abandon Kenrick. He's all I have left." Her chin quivered, but the ferocity of her resolve blazed strongly in her eyes. "If you think I will let my brother die, you are more than wrong, sirrah."

"Ariana, these men have no regard for human life. If your brother yet lives, his fate was likely sealed the moment he was captured by them." She looked at him as if she did not, or could not, understand. He knew she did. She understood, but Braedon felt he had to say it anyway, to make her realize the stark coldness of what awaited her in Rouen. "They will certainly kill him, Ariana. They will have to."

"Just to get their hands on that satchel?"

"No. To get their hands on the Dragon Chalice."

"Is that what he's been studying, then—this Dragon Chalice? I've never heard of it."

"You are better off if you hadn't. It's likely too late for your brother."

"No." Her eyes took on a wild sheen. Vigorously, she shook her head. "Don't say that. Don't—"

"I'm not trying to hurt you or frighten you. I'm trying to spare you. The moment you turn over that satchel—assuming your brother is still alive at all—these people will have what they need, and they will kill him. Then they will kill you. Neither of you will be allowed to live once they have the information in that bag. You are walking into a trap, Ariana. A deadly one."

"I was assured that Kenrick would not be harmed," she replied with tenacious conviction. "I was told that neither of us was in any danger, so long as I delivered what they wanted."

"Do you really believe that? After seeing what you did in Calais, can you truly afford to believe it now?"

With a cry of distress, she turned away from him. Shrouded in the dark brown blanket, she hugged herself and took a handful of steps toward the opposite side of the cavern.

Braedon growled an oath. If he cared a whit for his own neck, he would take his stolen mount and leave her to face her business in Rouen on her own. The fact that she was learning the futility of her quest should not bother him in the slightest. He should not feel the need to comfort her. But before he could tell himself it was a mistake to reach out to her, Braedon stalked up to her trembling back and turned her to face him. Mute with her tears, she said nothing as he reached out and encircled her in his arms. Her hair was damp silk against his chin, cool and fragrant beneath his nose. He brought her closer to him, embracing her as her emotions rocked her.

"Please," she whispered against his chest, her breath warming his skin. "Take me to Rouen. Send me there alone, I don't care. Whatever happens to me, I willingly accept. I know you have no reason to help me. I know I made a bargain with you in London. . . . I know what I already owe you."

"Do you, *demoiselle*?"

"Yes."

She drew back and lifted her gaze to look at him. Braedon glanced down into that innocent face and felt a pulsing surge of hunger flood him. Mad as it was to desire her when he could all but hear the thundering approach of their pursuers, drawing closer by the moment, Braedon did desire her. He wanted Ariana with a hunger he could scarcely credit. A base part of him moved to assure him that what she said was true. She did owe him something. Something he dearly wanted to claim.

With a gentleness he would have thought beyond himself, he reached out to smooth an errant lock from her brow. Her lips parted at the contact, not quite a gasp, nor a sigh. Braedon took her face in his hands, framing the delicate bones of her cheeks as he swept her tears away with the pads of his thumbs. Her long hair, unbound and draped about her shoulders like a veil, felt soft against the backs of his hands. He let his fingers wander deeper into the glorious mass, casually fisting his hand around a thick skein of the feathery strands. Holding her thus, his grip mildly possessive, his hard gaze unable to conceal his desire, he let his free hand trace a gentle pattern along her delicate jaw and neck. She trembled under his touch. She quivered, breathing shallowly as he explored her tender skin, but she did not try to pull away. Braedon flicked a glance up to her eyes as he slid his hand along the exquisite line of her shoulder.

His hand yet bound in the silken rope of her hair, he drew her closer, pressing her curves against his rigid body. A knowing flash of anticipation darkened her eyes to a delectable shade of midnight blue as she gazed up at him. She sucked in a little breath of air as he coaxed her head back and bent to press his mouth to hers. She drew back at the first brush of their lips, a momentary hesitation, but her tension fled as quickly as it came. Braedon settled his mouth more firmly over hers, savoring the innocence, the wonder, in her untutored response to his tender assault.

It was that guilelessness that threatened to undo him. Her fearlessness, even now, when she had to know he wanted more. It was all he could do to resist the need that grew within him. With a moan, he broke away, lifting his head before he savaged her with the full measure of his hunger.

"There. It is done now," he told her, his voice husky and raw from the quickening of his body. She gazed up at him in wordless confusion, her sensual mouth still pliant and welcoming as he drew back to gaze down at her in the firelight. "Your price is paid, Ariana. Don't make any more bargains with me."

She took the warning with a flush of color filling her cheeks.

"Your debt is cleared, so you have no reason to fear my

intentions," he said, nearly growling the words. "Now, take off your wet clothes and put them near the fire."

She stared up at him, doubt flickering in her eyes.

"I'll give you a moment of privacy to change. You'll find a tunic in my pack. You can don that until your things are dry."

Without another word, Braedon turned and stalked away from her before he could give in to the desire that was still pounding through his veins. He left her in the cave alone, walking out into the night for fresh air and a clearer head. Outside in the dark, he heard her move to the fireside and drop the woolen blanket that had shrouded her like armor. Her kirtle went next. She was well out of his line of vision, but that didn't matter. Braedon's hearing was acute, accursedly so. And his hunter's mind was all too willing to play along.

With the same keenness he used to track any prey, his senses fixed on Ariana. He listened and caught the rough slide of wool skating down a lithe form, pooling softly on the ground. He heard the wispy crush of her linen chemise smoothing over the sweet flare of her hips, the curve of her waist, and the generous swell of her breasts as she drew it over her head and shed it. He breathed and scented the warm, womanly smell of her, the spicy soap she'd used in her bath at Calais still lingering on her clean skin. He could almost taste the sweetness of her on his tongue.

God knew he wanted to. And would, if he had to spend another night with her.

By the time the chemise floated to the earth at her bare feet, he had endured the sensory torture long enough. With a snarl of heated frustration, he slipped farther into the bracing night, before the tenuous leash on his desire snapped altogether.

* * *

The sailmaker's shop held the stench of death. It permeated the small, unlit abode, announcing itself the moment the door creaked open. Outside the threshold, a large black boot paused, the savage-looking spur at its heel gleaming pale silver against dark in the gathering twilight. A rolling gust of wind blew in off the wharf to snatch at the hem of a long mantle woven of rich, blood-red wool. It rippled in dark, undulating folds, the snap of heavy fabric the only sound in a street gone still and stagnant with the coming of night.

The shop's vile stench grew worse on the invading chill breeze, but the knight whose muscular frame now crowded the open doorway scarcely reacted. Only the slightest curl of his lip betrayed his revulsion. His anger was kept on tighter rein.

He stepped inside the cramped shop and took in the signs of struggle with a keen, unfeeling eye. A toppled stool, abandoned work spread out on the table, splattered candle wax coagulated and hard where it spilled across its surface. In a dim corner of an adjacent room lay an old man. He was dead and ripe going on a day, by the stink of him. His head was twisted at an odd angle, neck clearly snapped, his frail body brutalized and broken like a twig crushed beneath the heel of a bear.

The bear was, in fact, a mercenary soldier, one of three who'd been dispatched to Calais to keep a watch on the harbor's comings and goings. They had all failed in the task. Now this one was dead, lying prone on the floor of the workroom, his lifeblood spent from a dagger wound in his back. A coward's death for a barbaric man who had seemed to know no fear while he was breathing.

His commander, the tall, red-and-black-clad knight who stood over the soldier's unmoving bulk, spared his murder nary a thought. He stepped around the bloody pool and strode to the sole window in the tiny room. With a hand gloved in black leather, he wiped away a smattering of frost crystals from the diamond-cut panes of glass and let his gaze sweep the quiet harbor beyond.

"Did anyone see the girl?" he asked, addressing another knight who stood behind him.

He did not have to turn around to know that the dolt was nearly pissing himself in terror. As well he should. The idiot and his companion had left their horses unattended while they searched one of the city's inns, an error that had cost them both mounts to thievery. This one had waited for further orders, but his partner had decided it more prudent to be absent for this accounting, having evidently left to give chase on foot.

As much as he despised failure, the knight understood that it was not his place to mete out punishment. For that, he answered to a higher power. And besides, why waste precious time whipping one's hounds when the hare might yet be quivering in the bracken nearby?

"The girl," he repeated, when it seemed fear had robbed the soldier of his dubious wit altogether. "Did either of you happen to see her, or the man she is traveling with?"

"N-no, sir. The pair was gone from their room when the innkeeper admitted us."

No doubt speeding away on a couple of geldings that were all but handed to them for making their escape, the knight thought with a grim lift of his brow. They could be leagues away from Calais were that the case. If they set foot in any of the coastal towns between here and Brittany, he would hear of it soon enough, for he had taken care to post guards days ago at all the ports along the Channel.

Not that his coastal defenses were much good to him now. His quarry had fled, and had no doubt been chased inland. If she thought to head directly for Rouen—and if she knew her way around France—she could be there in a matter of days. That did not leave him much time.

"We did get descriptions of both from the innkeeper," the soldier said from behind him, rushing on to fill the silence of his commander's contemplation. "The girl is fair and petite—a golden-haired beauty, so says the innkeeper."

The leader gave a caustic grunt. "That will certainly narrow things down." He felt a bump against his calf and looked down to see a fat tabby cat twining between his feet. "And the man?" he said, hardly bothering to gauge the worthless information he was getting from the soldier. "I don't suppose we have aught to go on where he is concerned."

"Aye, well, the man should be easier to spot, sir. He bears a scar on his face, as I understand it. An old knife wound that runs the length of his cheek."

The dark head came up at that news, and although the knight registered an inward note of surprise, he gave no indication of his reaction as he turned at last to face his man. "Which side?"

"Sir?"

"His face," he growled, knowing the answer but needing to hear it voiced nevertheless. "Which side of his face was cut?"

The dullard frowned for a moment, considering. "Why, the left, sir." He nodded his big head. "Aye, the innkeeper said 'twas the left side of his face what bore the hideous mark."

Le Chasseur.

The name chased through his head like a ghost. Could

it be? he wondered. Was it merely coincidence, this scarred stranger's interference, or had the famed Hunter not learned his lesson the first time—what was it, a year ago? Mayhap closer to two years now?

The knight in the bloodred mantle began to chuckle, low under his breath. He felt certain it was Braedon le Chasseur who accompanied the girl.

It had to be.

Who else but his old friend would have the ballocks to cross him after what happened that night in Normandy?

In the cramped space of the little shop room, the soldier began to fidget under his commander's cold stare. "Do you reckon we should take word to Rouen of the girl's arrival . . . and, er, her escape, sir?"

"No," answered the knight. "Breathe naught of this to anyone." He stepped away from the window and strode past the man with deadly purpose. "I will handle it personally."

❧ 10 ☙

FOR SOME LONG hours into the night, Ariana did not sleep. She dozed once or twice but only for a duration that felt like mere moments. Most of the time, she lay awake on her improvised pallet of blankets, her mind spinning to make sense of the strange course of events that had carried her from the dull cocoon of safety she had known within Clairmont's fortress walls to this cold, dangerous place across the sea. She had gone into the task of rescuing Kenrick with a clear enough head; after all, it had seemed so simple a thing to manage. Locate the papers he had been working on, deliver them to the appointed meeting place in Rouen, then collect her brother. So straightforward . . . yet none of it had played out the way she imagined. Least of all her unwilling dependence on the scarred warrior who shared the cramped space of the dimly lit cavern.

Now it all felt to her as part of a dark dream—her ill-fated dealings with Monsieur Ferrand and James's terrible demise at the London docks, the treacherous journey from England through Calais to this wilderness, the mysterious findings contained in Kenrick's journals, the strange and deadly enemies suddenly in pursuit of her. . . .

And Braedon.

Blessed Mary, she knew not what to make of him at all,

perhaps less so now than when she had first encountered him in London. He was dangerous and forbidding; she knew that just to look at him. He had no mercy where his enemies were concerned; his wrath was swift and thorough and unforgiving. But there was a tenderness about him, too, a fact Ariana suspected he preferred to keep hidden behind the mask of detachment he wore so well.

And but a short while ago, he had kissed her for the second time.

He hadn't meant it, of course. Not really. He had done it to prove a point, to distract her from what he probably feared would be an oncoming fit of emotional hysteria, or perhaps to mock her even as he dismissed one of her many worries. But as fleeting as it had been, whether falsely offered or nay, Ariana's lips still burned with the memory of his mouth pressed on hers. To her utter bewilderment, more than any measure of fear or distress, that kiss was the true source of her present state of restlessness.

Ariana lay curled on her side, her back to the fire, staring at the dance of shadows cast on the cavern wall and high, arched ceiling. Seemingly of their own volition, her fingers released the ratted edge of the woolen blanket and slowly crept up to her mouth. She pressed her fingertips against her lips, touching the place where Braedon's kiss still lingered.

Without thinking, she flipped over on her pallet and let out a lengthy sigh. As the soft exhalation sifted into the quiet of the cave, her gaze lit on him. He had returned to the cave and sat guard while she slept, a position he maintained even now, sitting half in darkness, a brooding figure amid the shadows just outside the reach of the fire. His back was braced against the granite wall, one leg stretched out before him, the other bent at the knee to support the elbow that rested on it. Even in the dim light, she could see that his dark gray gaze was locked on her face, as if he had been watching her for some time.

"You're still awake," she whispered, rising off the pallet of old blankets to sit up. It was freezing in the cavern, she realized once her coverlet slipped off and the rush of night air seeped through the weave of her borrowed tunic. She bundled herself into the blanket's warmth and shivered off the last of the chill. "Aren't you cold? You gave me all the blankets."

Braedon didn't answer her. His dark gaze dragged from her to the crackling little fire in front of them. Ariana got up and crept closer to the flames' warmth. On the ground nearby was Kenrick's satchel and its scattered contents. She eyed the collection with more than a small bit of disdain. If not for the information it held, her brother might be safe and happy at Clairmont. James, her guardsman, would be alive, and she would not be at the mercy of the dark, unreadable man who seemed presently intent on ignoring her.

Always distant and perplexing, he had only become more so after what happened in Calais. Ariana thought she would never purge from her memory the sight of what occurred in the sailmaker's shop. Nothing she had seen, read, or heard about in all her eighteen years could explain the shifting form of the man Braedon killed before her eyes. She was not one given to superstition, nor had she ever credited such things as magic or the dark arts, but she could hardly dismiss the bizarre incident as anything less than unexplainable.

Braedon, however, seemed to take it fairly in stride. Nor had he seemed the least confused by what he had found in Kenrick's satchel. Astonished, perhaps, but she had not missed the look of stark recognition on his face after he'd torn open the bag to see what it contained. For all her fruitless searching through them at Clairmont, she had never been able to make much sense of her brother's recordings. All she saw were countless strange chronicles of miraculous healings and reports of queer occurrences mapped at various places in England and in France.

She'd wondered if there had been something hidden in his mad scribblings and calculations, or in the repeated drawings he made of a peculiar carved cup, which was depicted to be glowing with light that emanated from four stones embedded in its bowl. Ariana had thought the collection of journals and papers odd, certainly, but she could not imagine what it could mean to the men who held Kenrick. She had no idea why it could be of such worth to someone.

But Braedon knew what the information pertained to—he knew it the instant he saw it. In the cave earlier that evening, he had even given it a name . . .

The Dragon Chalice.

With a pensive frown, she reached for some of the papers and brought them onto her lap beside the fire. The ink on a few of them had smeared a bit from where the snow and rain had permeated the satchel, but all of it was still legible. Not finding what she searched for, she set aside the papers and retrieved one of the leather-bound journals.

Braedon regarded her with a measured, if speculative, gaze. "What are you doing?"

"Looking for answers."

She flipped the book open, scanning the pages for enlightenment, clues to she knew not precisely what. Kenrick's journal entries were organized by occurrence, then logged and dated, the first item beginning shortly after he entered the Templar brotherhood. There were chronicles of blind persons given back their sight; the infirm regaining their health; the lame suddenly able to walk again. The lists went on and on, concentrated in a handful of locations, some underscored or circled for emphasis, others crossed out.

Ariana recognized a few of the places with the most recurring incidents: Saint Michael's Mount in Cornwall and Glastonbury Abbey having the oldest entries. There were other sites in the notes as well, places she hadn't heard of before. One stood out among the rest, not for the frequency of its mention, but for the special attention Kenrick seemed to have given it. Nearly all of his notes in the three months leading up to his abduction centered on one entry. A queer name that sparked no familiarity with Ariana.

"Have you ever heard of Avosaar?"

For a moment, Braedon only stared at her. "Avosaar?" he echoed, his tone bland even as something flickered, considering, in his steely gaze. He blinked it away and gave her a disinterested shrug. "Nay. It means nothing to me. Why? What is it?"

"I don't know. A place, I think. Kenrick seemed very interested in it during the time preceding his abduction in Rouen. He made all these entries about miracles and unexplained occurrences, with quite a number of them referencing this word—'Avosaar.'" She held out the journal to him, but he hardly spared it a glance. "Do you think it might be the location of this cup you mentioned—the Dragon Chalice?"

"No," he said, staring back into the fire.

"Why not? How can you be sure?" She pressed on, ignoring his dismissive tone. "I think it must be important. Kenrick must have discovered something significant, perhaps something dangerous, at these places. Look, here he mentions several places in Cornwall. Another in France, at the abbey of Mont St. Michel. And this one—Avosaar."

"Let it go, Ariana. You could drive yourself mad searching for answers that likely aren't there."

"The answers are here, or why would his captors want this satchel so badly? You said it yourself. The information in this satchel is important enough to get us killed."

"All the more reason for you to leave it alone."

"I can't. Especially if what you say is true." When he shrugged off her interest, she only became more determined to prove her point. "What about these?"

She reached over to grab a handful of papers that contained Kenrick's calculations, some of which repeated the name Avosaar. She held the sheaves of parchment out to Braedon, all but forcing him to take them. He did, only to set them down without looking at them.

"In fact," she said, undaunted, "there's a map of some sort in here as well. I saw it when I first looked through the satchel at Clairmont. . . ." She grabbed one of the leather-bound journals and began to fan through the pages, searching. When she didn't find what she sought in the first volume, she reached for another. "I'll show you, Braedon. I'm certain that the points indicated on these parchments will relate back to some of the places listed in Kenrick's—"

"Christ, Ariana." Before she could open the second journal, Braedon seized her wrist in an iron-hard grasp. With his free hand, he snatched the journal back from her and threw it down beside him, out of her reach. "Enough! I said, let it go."

She flinched at his sharp tone, and at his forcible grip on her arm. He released her but offered no apology. Ariana stared at him, confused, apprehensive. "Now who's the one keeping secrets? You haven't told me everything, either, Braedon. Not about yourself, or these men who are after us—certainly not about this so-called Dragon Chalice."

"Funny," he drawled, throwing her an insolent look. "I didn't realize I was required to tell you anything, *demoiselle*."

That stung, his harsh tone and flatly arrogant glare. How easily he could shut her out. They might be on the run together now, but he was making it abundantly clear that he did not see her as an ally. Not an ally, and certainly nothing better than a dangerous inconvenience, despite that he would steal kisses from her and make her yearn for more. Peg's words came back to her now, the warning about Braedon's darkness and the advice to maintain her distance. Ariana knew she should heed the sage caution, but it seemed she had little choice. And a tenacious part of her refused to be pushed away.

"You said yourself we are as good as shackled to each other now. Don't you think I have a right to know what's going on? All of it? You've been acting strangely since we left Calais."

"Have I?" he asked mildly, although it was said with a sardonic twist of his lips.

"Yes, you have. Ever since you opened this satchel, there has been a change in you—"

He exhaled a laugh that held not a trace of humor. "If I've been acting out of sorts, dear lady, perhaps it's because I nearly had my head smashed in over the cursed thing. Because I'm getting dragged back into something I want nothing to do with."

"Dragged back?" She stared at him, latching on to his slip. "What do you mean, dragged *back* into it—into what?"

He cursed, low and roundly. "Forget it. Let's pack up our things and move on. Neither of us is going to get any sleep tonight, and we'd do better to make use of the time. We can put another ten or fifteen miles behind us before daybreak."

"Braedon," she said, gently now, refusing to acquiesce to his attempt at dismissal. "You said you are getting dragged back into something you want nothing to do with. What did you mean by that? Tell me. I need to know."

With a growl, he shoved himself to his feet and paced away from her. She expected him to bark an order at her, or to dodge her question with broody, stubborn silence. Instead he raked a hand through his dark hair and dropped his head back on his shoulders. Facing the granite wall of the cavern, he let out his breath in a heavy, burdensome sigh. "A year and a half ago I heard of the Dragon Chalice for the first time. I was approached by a man about locating a certain priceless object that had been stolen from him. He was offering a great deal of money for its return. I rose easily to the bait."

"You were hired to recover the Dragon Chalice?"

"Part of it. The Chalice treasure is, supposedly, comprised of four separate pieces. Four golden cups, bearing four priceless stones. If you believe the legend, the Dragon Chalice was rent apart by magic after being stolen from a mystical kingdom. I know, it sounds preposterous. I thought so, too, when I first heard the tale. Whether or not the legend is true, there are men who will stop at nothing to have the treasure for themselves."

"This man who hired you—he is one of them?"

"Silas de Mortaine," Braedon said, his gaze grim. "He is a very dangerous man, with a great deal of power and a great deal of wealth. And he is very determined. He wanted his trinket found, but he promised to double my reward if I also brought him the person who stole it from him."

"Did you succeed?"

"On both counts."

"And you collected your reward?"

"Oh, aye." He let out a wry grunt of humor. "I gave him his cup and his thief, and he gave me this." With the tip of his finger, he traced the silvery scar on his face. "Rob was with me that day, and so were six of my other men. De Mortaine ordered five of them killed on the spot, and I as well. His guards nearly succeeded. Only Rob and I managed to escape."

"What about the other, the sixth man?"

"Le Nantres? Alive and well. No doubt serving as de Mortaine's right arm, God rot the bastard. You see, it was he who introduced me to de Mortaine. He knew all along it was a trap. For all I know, he helped de Mortaine bait and set it."

"Why, if he was one of your own men?"

Braedon shrugged. "Who knows. Greed, mayhap. Lust for the Chalice's power. Men have fallen to lesser wants than that. I should have seen the betrayal coming, but I was too caught up in the chase. It blinded me." He turned a sober look on her. "The same way you are blinded now, Ariana."

"You think I'm a fool to want to help my brother?"

"No. I think you are courageous and bold. But you are naïve if you think this is a simple thing, to involve yourself with Silas de Mortaine and whatever sorcery surrounds the Dragon Chalice. You saw what happened to your guard from Clairmont. You saw what happened in Calais."

"Yes, I did. And I've never seen anything so frightening." She looked at him then, noting his contemplative expression, the thoughtful way he stared into the fire. "I may have never witnessed such a thing before . . . but you have. Haven't you?"

She could see that he wasn't going to answer her. He stared at her for a long moment, silent as he searched her gaze, his own shuttered and unreadable. He was keeping something from her, though whether he did so to shelter her or himself, she could not be sure. His aloofness infuriated her as much as it wounded her.

"What are you hiding from, Braedon?" The question slipped off her tongue the same instant it flitted through her mind. "Why do you strive so hard to keep everyone at arm's length?"

His chuckle held a tinge of mockery. "Why do you try to save everyone, *demoiselle*?" He held her gaze for an unsettling length of time, his gray eyes glowing in the flickering dance of the fire. "This thing is beyond you, Ariana. Beyond both of us. But you may still have a chance to get away. I advise you to take it."

"I cannot," she said, shaking her head. "If everything you've said is true, and this monster de Mortaine is the man who holds Kenrick, then I don't see how I can possibly give up now."

He exhaled sharply and gave her a skeptical look.

"Could you?" she challenged. "You could not turn your back if it were your kin being ransomed. No feeling person could be so cold."

He stared at her, unspeaking. Mother Mary, but the grimness of his features—his unblinking gaze, the harsh, unforgiving line of his jaw, the emotionless curve of his mouth—seemed to suggest that he could, in fact, walk away. Evident or nay, she didn't credit his cold silence as a true denial. And even if it were, she'd hardly let it sway her from her own course.

"I'm not giving up on Kenrick. No matter the risks. As for you, come along or let me go on alone. It makes no difference to me what you decide to do."

With his piercing gray gaze trained on her, Ariana gathered up a handful of papers from Kenrick's satchel and committed herself to reading every last word. If the bag contained anything that might help her save him, she would not rest until she found it.

Braedon watched her tirelessly pore over her brother's notes and journals for more than an hour. He knew they should ride while the weather had eased and night would conceal them on the road, before their pursuers were able to gain any more distance on them. But he felt she needed this time, too. She needed to search for answers, even if he knew it would prove fruitless in the end. As it was, she had astonished him with her deductions about the journal entries and their correlation to the treasure's whereabouts.

But none so much as her query about the reference to Avosaar.

The name given to the cup he'd been hired to retrieve for Silas de Mortaine. Avosaar. That was what the fey thief had called it, when she pleaded with Braedon to help her keep the cup from falling back into de Mortaine's hands.

Avosaar, so named for the green cabochon gem in its center, the Stone of Prosperity. One of four such stones once contained in the fabled Dragon Chalice.

He hadn't believed the girl, not until it was too late.

Soon, unless he took steps to protect her, it would be too late for Ariana, as well.

"My lady," he said, growing anxious as dawn crept closer and still she refused to give up her study of the satchel's contents. "There is yet a long road ahead. We should be away now, before it's light."

She glanced up, a faint glow of hope brightening her sleep-weary eyes. "Will you take me to Rouen, then?"

He gave her a vague nod, unable to offer more when he knew it for a lie. The coast—and a safe transport to England—was only a few days' ride at most. "Get dressed, and gather up the blankets," he told her. "I'll get the rest."

Without argument, no doubt because she was utterly spent, she donned her kirtle on top of his borrowed tunic, then collected their scant supplies and packed them onto the horses. With a twinge of remorse, Braedon looked down at her brother's satchel. He retrieved all its contents from where they lay on the cavern floor and tucked them back into the pack. Then he slung the leather bulk of it over his shoulder.

"Have we got everything?" Ariana asked from near the cavern's moonlit entrance.

He gave her a mild nod and stepped toward the guttering fire. With the toe of his boot, he kicked a mist of sandy earth over the embers, snuffing out the last of the light and heat . . . and burying the cinders of a parchment map beneath the smoke and dust and darkness.

The very map he had taken from Kenrick's satchel and burned several hours ago while, nearby, Ariana slept so fitfully.

"Yes," he said, meeting her as he strode through the lightless expanse of the cave. "That's everything, my lady."

❧ 11 ❧

THEY RODE FOR two days with only the briefest pauses for food, water, and rest. Braedon kept them under forest cover as much as possible, knowing that the danger of discovery was greater on the open, snow-covered roads and fields. It meant a slower, more arduous trip, but Ariana had accepted his advice with stalwart understanding. It wasn't until near dusk on the third day of travel that she finally began to show signs of exhaustion. She lolled in her saddle with each rut on the forest track, her slender shoulders slumped, gloved hands barely holding on to her mount's braided leather reins. With the coming of sunset, the wind rose up, buffeting them as it whistled through the trees. Ariana gave a shiver as Braedon looked over his shoulder to gauge her progress behind him. She pulled her face deep within her hooded mantle to shield herself from the harsh, wintry air.

The day was ending bitter cold and blustery, ice crystals from the previous night's storm glittering on the naked branches of spindly trees as they passed beneath. The ground under their horses' hooves was a perilous blanket of iced-over snow and unexpected drops and gullies hidden by drifts of pristine, treacherous white. Braedon rode a few paces ahead of Ariana, following the curve of a high ridge of land that rose shoulder-high above the left side of the path, carved out of the earth and edged with frozen gorse and bracken. Carefully he guided his mount through the frozen terrain while watching behind him to make sure Ariana's tired palfrey did not misstep.

"We'll stop soon," he assured her, hoping to ride another hour or so and seek their shelter at nightfall. He did not like the feel of this particular stretch of woods, and it had more to do with the prickling of his battle senses than the fact that they now trod through familiar terrain.

This very stretch of land, the thick copse that surrounded them and the Amiens meadowlands that spread out some hundred acres in each direction, held a great deal of history for him. Not far from where he now rode was the holding of his once venerable, but since deceased, sire.

As a lad, Braedon had played in these forests, dashing about the woodlands like a wildling, acting out boyhood melees and skirmishes with his friends from neighboring demesnes. It was here that he had hunted with his father from time to time, and it was here, one brisk autumn day when Braedon was not quite ten summers, that he had drawn his weapon on the man who sired him, coming within a hairbreadth of doing cold-blooded murder.

Nay, not cold-blooded, he reflected with a measure of ironic amusement, but blazing, half-crazed fury. His father might have deserved just such a bloody end, if not for his cruelty that day in the forest, then certainly for what he'd done to Braedon. And to his mother.

You're mad, boy! As mad as the hellborn witch who bore you—may she rot!

A bitter twist curled Braedon's mouth as he thrust away the remembered shouts and curses he heard nearly every day of his life while he lived in France. The whispers of queer afflictions and accusations of inherited madness that haunted him even to this day. He cast all of that aside now and focused on his surroundings, and on the slight raising of his hackles that warned of hidden, watchful eyes as he and Ariana traversed farther into the woods. He had felt this niggling awareness for some time, but he had not wished to worry Ariana with his suspicions. Unfortunately, he was certain now.

They were being followed.

Braedon's nostrils flared as he looked around and drew in a deep, chilling breath of air. He tasted danger in the draught. Death loomed in the forest hollows, behind the tangles of frozen bramble; he was certain of it. He felt it stalking closer, moving in. He could not see it, could only feel the malevolence creeping in with stealthy, predatory skill. Instinctively, his hand flexed around the hilt of his sheathed sword.

A twig snapped somewhere off to his left. Hardly a sound at all, but he cocked his ear toward it and waited, listening, watching, as his mount forged ahead through the ice and snow. He slowed the beast with a flexing of his thighs, a subtle, silent command that allowed Ariana to come up closer behind. Hanging back, he moved aside and let her palfrey draw up alongside his on the narrow path.

"Is something wrong?" she asked. "Why have we slowed?"

"Stay close to me. We may have trouble on the approach."

He heard her soft but sharp intake of breath. The cowl of her mantle framing her face, Ariana's eyes were wide, darting nervously from him to the vast stretch of forest that surrounded them on all sides. She would see no trace of the danger, this he knew. Braedon himself did not see who followed. But he felt it as surely as his skin now prickled with an animal's keen sense of warning.

Ariana's voice was a tremulous whisper from within the fur-lined folds of her hood. "Braedon, what is it? Is someone there?"

"I don't know. Whoever—*whatever*—it is, 'tis moving in quickly now."

He visually gauged the space ahead of them, then behind, calculating their options of escape, for he was certain it would come to that. He cursed under his breath. It was too narrow a path through the trees, too treacherous to send the horses into a gallop if they had to attempt flight. The forest hemmed them in on all sides. His mount became aware of the pending threat as well. The beast stamped an agitated dance in the snow, as if uncertain in which direction it might want to bolt. Skittish now, eyes rolling fearfully, the palfrey grunted and sidled on the path.

"Stay near me, Ariana," he cautioned her in a low voice, "and do whatever I tell you. Understand?"

She gave a quick nod.

Braedon drew his sword from its scabbard, the slow, lethal hiss of grating metal all but lost amid the snorting and snuffling of the worried horses. He brought his mount around front of Ariana's, shielding her as his eyes took in the darkened thicket where their attacker waited. He caught a movement up ahead, heard a rustle of crunching snow and swishing branches. A low growl sounded from within the shadows.

"Braedon, there!"

Ariana's gasp of warning was little more than a whisper beside his ear, but Braedon was already staring at the cause of her fright. Their pursuer here was not man, but beast.

Up ahead some fifty paces, watching them from atop a snow-covered rock, stood an impossibly large, seething black wolf. Its jaws were open in a snarl, teeth gleaming bone-white and deadly sharp. The animal emitted a guttural howl, its pale eyes fixed on them, daring them to move. It was looking for sport more than sustenance, standing belligerent on the rock, its muscular limbs taut and ready to spring.

"Oh, mercy . . . Braedon," Ariana breathed, and her mount began a nervous shuffle beneath her. Saddle leather creaked, metal tack jingled, as the palfrey tossed its head and started backing away from the danger. Ariana struggled to hold it, but the beast was panting already, struggling to lose its bit.

"Steady," Braedon soothed them both, barely moving his lips, his eyes never leaving the calculating gaze of the beast. "Wolves do not attack humans unless they are provoked. They would sooner run than fight."

"He doesn't look like he's going to run away from us."

"No," Braedon replied, certain that the creature he faced now had no intention of backing down. As if to confirm that suspicion, the wolf leaped down and began toward them in a slow, menacing prowl along the ridge that flanked the road like a castle's battlements. "Very slowly, Ariana, ease your mount around on the path."

"Turn around? But—what are we going to do?"

The wolf crept closer, its heavy paws and thick black nails dislodging pebbles of loose earth from the sharp promontory ledge. Braedon held his own nervous mount in an iron grip, his thighs locked tight against its sides, his free hand fisted in the reins. "I want you to ride out of here as calmly as you can, back the way we came in. I'll hold him off while you ride away. Go now, my lady."

"You want me to *leave* you?" she whispered. "No, Braedon . . ."

"Do it. Now, Ariana."

She gave a small noise of distress, and for a moment he wondered if she would defy him even in this. But then she was obeying his direction, taking a gentle hand on her palfrey and turning the agitated horse around on the road. Very slowly, with a calm that he couldn't help but admire, she set her mount to walking in the opposite direction.

The hellish beast that watched from the forest ridge bared its teeth in a grimace that seemed almost a malicious grin across the short distance that separated it from Braedon. Nostrils flaring, it let out a huff of steaming breath and emitted a low growl.

"Seems it's you and me now," Braedon taunted it, drawing the wolf's attention back to him.

It was all the warning he was to receive.

With a roar of unearthly fury, the wolf launched itself off its perch and flew at Braedon in a blur of bristling black fur and slashing claws.

Ariana had gone only a few yards when the beastly howl of rage sounded from behind her on the road. Heart freezing in her breast, she whirled around in her saddle just in time to see the huge black wolf leap down upon Braedon. She cried out, horrified as he and the wolf fell to the ground, locked in brutal combat. For a moment she knew not what to do. Braedon had ordered her to go. Every fearful instinct that quaked in terror urged her to give her skittish mount her heels and speed away. But she could not make her limbs obey the command.

She could not leave him.

"Braedon!" she shouted, wheeling the palfrey back toward the fray.

Her mount whinnied in protest, eyes rolling, as it realized what she meant to do. It took a halting couple of steps, then drew up short, shifting and sidling when she needed it to charge. The horse was too nervous, too frightened to cooperate. Up ahead on the snowy track, the wolf had clamped its jaws down on Braedon's sword arm, losing him his weapon. Growling his fury, Braedon threw his other fist at the beast's great head, knocking it to the side. He pounded it once, twice . . . but the wolf was undaunted. Slavering, teeth bared, it gnashed viciously as it made to attack again.

"Sweet Mary . . . Braedon!"

He was a strong man, with a warrior's training, but those facts did little to soothe her worry for him. This wolf had murder in its eyes, and it fought with the frenzied strength of a demon. With a cry that sounded desperate even to her own ears, Ariana threw herself down from her saddle. Braedon's own mount, now riderless and gripped in a mad panic, stomped the ground as it tried to free itself from the scuffle. Snagged by its reins, which were caught around Braedon's leg, the frightened palfrey was an added hazard to Braedon. It plunged back on its haunches, heavy hooves striking hard wherever they fell, its eyes wild and mindless.

Without another thought for Braedon's orders or her own preservation, Ariana hitched her skirts above her booted ankles and ran back up the frozen road to help him however she might. She had to disentangle the horse before she could do anything else. Screaming now, rear-ing up and pawing at the air, it nearly struck her as she approached.

Braedon must have seen her intent, even as he reached for his lost sword and took another nasty bite in his shoulder. He shouted over the horrific snarling of the wolf as it came at him in relentless attack. "Ariana, get away! God's blood, get out of here, woman!"

She didn't bother to answer him, let alone obey. Soothing the palfrey as best she could, palms held out in front of her to show it she meant no harm, she eased toward it. In the next instant, she had the tangled reins in her hand. Working quickly, she retrieved a knife from Braedon's saddle pack and sliced the narrow leather lead, severing the horse from its tether. It pitched its head to test its freedom, then fled, running off for the cover of the woods.

Behind her on the bloodstained, torn-up ground, the hellish black wolf had Braedon pinned. Its huge back bristled, spiky fur raised from its thick neck and enormous head to the muscular flanks of its limbs. Everything was happening so quickly. Braedon's hand flung out to reach his sword, but it was too far out of his reach. The wolf eyed his naked throat with a gleam of pleasure in its pale gray gaze.

"Oh, God, no!" Ariana screamed. She felt the cold hilt of the dagger in her palm and gripped it tighter, knowing at once what she must do.

"Ariana, get away. You have no idea—"

But she was already moving forward, advancing on the heaving form of the wolf. Ariana raised her hand, then brought it down in a swift arc, stabbing the beast in its side. It gave a shocked howl of pain and to her relief, it eased off Braedon.

"Go, Ariana!"

She stood firm, ready to make another strike. As the wolf spun its great, frothing head around to glare at her, its animal snarl began to take on a distinctly odd tone. The emotionless gray eyes started to change, muting from lupine shock to what could only be a human brand of rage.

Nay, she realized suddenly.

Not quite human or animal, this beast who turned its deadly gaze on her now.

"Ariana," Braedon shouted to her, holding the wolf on him when it seemed it wanted to lunge at her instead. "For Christ's sake, run!"

Dazed, she took a step back. Just one, for suddenly her limbs were not her own to command. The wolf was no base creature, she realized, shaken with the dawning knowledge of what she and Braedon were facing. As she stared, transfixed and astonished, the bristling black wolf gave a tremble of its thick fur, like a hound shaking off water.

It broke out of Braedon's strong hold as though made of air, and then it was rising up, taller and taller, changing shape before her very eyes, shimmering into another form.

The illusion passed and a hulking knight stood in its place, ugly and bleeding, his crude features twisted into a look of pure malice. His clothing was torn from his struggle with Braedon, his breath huffing from between his bruised and battered lips. He had a blade sheathed at his hip. The carved dragon hilt gleamed bright silver as he reached to draw the weapon on Ariana.

He did not get the chance.

Before he could take the first step, Braedon was on his feet and grabbing for his sword. He took it up and rounded on the man, engaging him in a vicious clash of steel on steel. Ariana watched in fear as Braedon and the shape-shifter battled a few paces before her. She wanted to help, but there was nothing she could do. Crash upon crash rang in the deserted road. Strike upon strike bloodied the trodden, muddied snow at their feet.

Braedon took another hard hit but then he was coming at his attacker like a tempest, his sword a punishing bolt, his fury rolling like thunder as he delivered a battery of maiming blows. The man went down on one knee at the last of Braedon's thrusts, a lethal slip. For in that next instant, his bellowing cry was cut short, his lifeblood spilling at his feet.

And still, Braedon kept fighting him.

Ariana crept forward once the man had gone still, her hand at her mouth, unable to utter a single word for the terror that yet held her in its clutches. Whatever it was—man or beast or hell-spawned mating of the two—it was no longer living. Braedon had slain it, yet he seemed unable to stop his blade from coming down on the carcass. He was in a blind rage, killing the beast over and over and over again as if he thought it might spring back to life if he ceased for so much as a moment.

Braedon's wrath was terrifying, but Ariana sensed the helplessness of his state and she slowly went toward him. She called his name as she approached. He did not react at all. His sword arm went up again, raising high over his head. His hand and arm were heavily soiled with blood, though whether it belonged to the dead changeling or flowed from the many lacerations and claw marks on Braedon's skin, she could not be sure. Ariana came up behind him as his blade began another relentless descent.

"Braedon," she said gently, placing her hand on his shoulder before he could land another blow. "Braedon, don't." She shook her head. " 'Tis enough."

He stilled at last, and at the sound of her voice, his head slowly pivoted away from the carnage at his feet. He looked at her for a long moment, saying nothing. Then he threw down his gruesome weapon and turned to her, pulling her into his arms in a fierce embrace. Ariana held him, too, wrapping her arms around his trim waist and pressing her cheek into his chest. He was shaking from his exertions, his breath coming fast and hard as he lowered his head and kissed her soundly on the mouth. Ariana wanted to climb into his warmth, needing the security of his arms around her. Needing to know that they both were safe and alive.

Braedon seemed to want the same assurances from her. He brought his hand up between them and tilted her chin so their eyes met. "God's wounds, woman. Why did you not run as I told you?" His voice was a harsh whisper, angry, certainly, but edged with something deeper. His gaze pierced hers even as his fingers reverently caressed her face. "Do you realize how stupid it was of you not to go when you had the chance? You might have been killed."

Ariana bit her lip at his soft scold. "I-I couldn't leave you," she confessed breathlessly. "I just . . . I couldn't bear the thought of you getting hurt."

For a long moment, he merely stared at her unspeaking. His warm gaze roamed over her face, drinking her in. Ariana thought he might kiss her again, for there was a note of something deeper than mere relief in his eyes as he looked at her, a trace of longing in his touch as his fingers skated tenderly through her hair. God's truth, she needed to feel his arms holding her tightly, needed to feel so safe and secure in his embrace. She wanted to know that she mattered something to him, too. That whatever they might face in this journey, they would face it together.

"Are you all right?" he rasped softly, taking her by her upper arms and setting her away from him, all business now, save the glowing embers in his gaze. "Were you injured at all?"

Ariana shook her head. "No. But you—"

"I'm fine." He cast a black glower at the dead man nearby and cursed low under his breath. "Let's find you someplace to clean up and get warm for the night."

Ariana followed him back to the path to retrieve her straying mount. His own horse was nowhere in sight, the terrified beast having fled without a care for its stranded rider. Braedon helped Ariana to mount up behind him, then with a nudge of his boot heels, they left the carnage and headed into town.

❧ 12 ❧

BRAEDON TESTED THE latch on the room door for the second time in what could only have been a half an hour. The old iron bolt was secure, if rusty. It would hold well enough, he decided, giving the door one final shake.

The town's sole inn was situated on the common road, and the foul weather had stranded a good number of travelers at the establishment. The public room out front bustled with activity. Raucous laughter and voices made loud from overmuch ale and cheer boomed down the corridor that separated the tavern hall from the inn's private rooms. Each time a shout went up, each time a cup crashed to the floor outside, Braedon's instincts jerked to full alert. He was edgy and on guard, and he could not ignore the niggling feeling that the shifter who attacked them on the road was not their only pursuer. There was a greater threat on the move, still advancing. Still moving closer.

He closed his eyes and rested his forehead against the cool wood of the door, training his mind to focus, to sharpen. To mentally seek out even that which sought to elude him. It was a skill he had been born with, an ability that separated him from other men. It was also his curse, and he had forsworn the peculiar gift a long time ago, when he had been a vainglorious fool, arrogant enough to whore his skills out to the highest bidder without a thought toward the possible consequences.

Le Chasseur.
The Hunter.

His reputation had brought him a certain dark notoriety, but it had also brought him pain. It had left his hands bloodied, his soul as hideously scarred as his face. But while he may have striven to forsake his strange skills, they had never forsaken him. They stirred within him, even now, on the ready, responding to his slightest beckon.

They took him back out into the cold night, onto the moonlit road, moving swiftly, scenting steel and malice in the shadows, searching for the threat that still pursued them. . . .

"Braedon."

Ariana's voice pulled him back into the room like a warm caress. He lifted his head and turned to face her. She had taken off her cloak and now stood before the hearth, her petite frame silhouetted by the orange glow of the fire that blazed behind her on the grate. She was still shivering from the cold, the golden tendrils of her hair still damp from the falling snow and drooping into her face.

"Braedon, are you certain 'tis safe for us to be here? I thought we had agreed to avoid public places until we reached Rouen. Perhaps we should continue on instead, or look for somewhere more remote to rest for the night."

She was right, of course, and logic warned him of the dangers in seeking shelter in town. He could have weathered another night outdoors, but he refused to put her through it again. Although he had not wanted to be responsible for her—for anyone, ever again—he knew he would protect her with his life. As she had tried to do for him today on the forest road.

"You're exhausted and cold, my lady. You have been

through much, and the very last thing you needed was another night in the elements." He had meant to soothe her worries, but there he was, scolding her again. After what he'd seen a short while ago in the woods, when he'd glanced up and found her wielding his dagger against the huge black beast that attacked him, all Braedon really wanted to do was gather her into his arms and hold her. In truth, he wanted to do much more than that. "Jesu, Ariana. Do you realize how close to death you came this afternoon?"

She had the good sense to lower her gaze in contrition. "We both did."

He moved away from the closed door and strode up to her. "Don't ever disobey me again, do you understand? If I tell you to do something, know that I have my reasons. I must be able to trust that you will do as I say, not question me or defy me."

A small, impatient sigh slipped past her parted lips. "I realize the danger we are in, Braedon."

"Do you?"

"Yes. I don't fully understand what is happening to us, but I'm not a foolish girl who cannot think for herself. I have been making my own decisions from the time I was young. I've had to." She glanced up then and met his gaze. Braedon smiled, for the contrition he thought he'd spied in her was something else instead, he realized now. A quiet but firm dignity lit her eyes. "I've had to take care of myself for a long time, and I don't need someone to take care of me now. If I put myself at risk today, then you must know that I did so for my own reasons—not to question you or defy you."

He could not resist the urge to sweep aside an errant wisp of hair that clung to her brow. His hand lingered against her skin, savoring the silky feel of her cheek beneath his rough fingertips. She drew in a tiny breath and held it, her gaze locked with his. "You are a mystery to me, Ariana of Clairmont. I've never known such courage—in any man or woman." He lost himself in her wide blue gaze for an indulgent moment, then reluctantly let his hand fall away from her face. "That doesn't change the fact that what you did today was reckless and foolheaded. I won't have it again, Ariana. Tell me you agree."

"Very well," she said, her tone slightly wry, matching the subtle quirk of her lips. "The next time you are attacked by a hellborn beast who means to shred you to bits, I give you my word, I shall let you have it all to yourself." She gazed up at him and gave a little shake of her head. "Impossible man. Do people always obey your every command?"

"When they don't, *demoiselle,* people get killed."

She seemed to take her time absorbing his reply, and he wondered if he had shocked her with the cold truth. She should be shocked. Indeed, she should never have been in his company in the first place. Braedon cursed the twist of fate that tossed them together that day in London. He cursed it for many reasons, but none more than the simple fact that against his will, he was becoming attached to her. Despite everything he'd done to deny it, he enjoyed being with her, and that alone scared him more than the notion that he would soon be facing his old demons again. Demons that he knew still wanted him dead.

"How long have you been alone, Braedon?"

The question surprised him. He drew back, brows knitting into a scowl. "Alone?"

"You left France as a youth, but you were alone even before that. Weren't you?" When he looked at her, his jaw clamped tight, unwilling to invite her probing, she gave him a gentle, understanding smile. "I know what it is like to be alone, too. I know it well enough to see it in another person, and I see it in you."

He exhaled sharply, not quite a laugh but a dismissing, mocking sound that felt too forced, even to his own ears. " 'Tis late, Ariana. I don't intend to waste these next few hours nattering over my poor childhood when I could be sleeping. You should do the same."

He started to turn away from her, but paused when he felt her fingers catch his arm. "You've reopened your wound. Let me take care of you for a while."

Ariana's touch remained on his arm, her slender fingers so light against him, yet holding him there, immobile. He should have drawn away. God knew he meant to, but instead he found himself reaching up to her, brushing the pads of his fingers over the velvet softness of her hand. He curved his fingers around hers and gently squeezed them, touched by her compassion.

"When I saw that shifter round on you after you stabbed him," he quietly told her as he threaded his fingers between hers, "I swear, I wanted to tear him to pieces. When I think what he might have done—" He swore a curse and shook his head.

"When did you realize it wasn't a mere wolf?"

"Almost at once. The way it looked at us. The way it was looking to attack. Wolves do not behave so boldly around humans. They know to fear us." Lost in reflection, he exhaled a deep breath. "Do you want to know the irony of this? When I was a boy, the rift that finally drove me away from my father, away from France, started over a wolf."

Ariana stroked his arm in a tender, coaxing caress. "Tell me what happened."

Braedon stared at their entwined fingers, remembering

with sudden clarity the day he nearly killed his sire. "I used to spend a great deal of time outdoors as a lad. My father and I never got on well, but it became worse after my mother left."

"She left you. . . . Why? And where did she go?"

"We never did know. My father always said she was deranged, ill in the head. I didn't care why she left, or where she'd gone." He shrugged, recalling the bitter sense of loss he'd felt when he woke up one morning and heard that she had vanished without an explanation or a word of farewell. He shoved it aside now, surprised to realize that he was still angry over her abandonment. "My father made no secret of his resentment for me, so I made every effort to maintain my distance from him. My favorite place to be was deep in the woods below our keep. One summer—my tenth year—I was running through the forest like a wildling and I stumbled on a low vine. When I came up off the ground, I found myself staring eye-to-eye with a she-wolf."

Ariana drew in a little gasp and caught her lip between her teeth. "You must have been terrified."

"I was," he admitted, "but I soon understood the wolf meant me no harm. It was an exquisite creature, with a silver-white coat and beautiful gray-green eyes. I'd never seen anything so extraordinary. It wouldn't let me near enough to touch, but it followed me to the edge of the woods that day, and when I went back the following morning, I met the wolf again. It kept itself out of my reach, but whenever I looked for it, there it was, watching over me. Protecting me, as it turned out."

"What an amazing animal," Ariana mused softly. She pushed up his sleeve and began unwrapping the bandages that covered his wounded arm. "I've never heard of a wolf befriending a person. In fact, in the villages near

Clairmont, wolves are feared to the point of hysteria for their violence toward people and livestock. They are hunted relentlessly."

"Aye. It is the same in France, too. One of the serfs out tending the fields saw me with the wolf about a month after it first appeared in the woods. Fearing for my safety, the man ran to the castle to alert my father. A hunting party was roused and mounted. Within moments, they had cornered the wolf at the crest of a steep ravine."

"Did you tell them the wolf was your friend—that it meant you no harm?"

"Oh, yes. I tried to explain. I pleaded to my father, but he wouldn't hear it. Wolves' heads fetch a healthy bounty, and he meant to have this one no matter what I said." Braedon forced out a bitter laugh. "I've often wondered if my affection for the beast only made him more determined to destroy it."

"Oh, Braedon," Ariana whispered, setting aside the bloodied strips of linen to inspect his gashed forearm. "I'm so sorry."

"It happened very fast. I tried to knock away my father's bow and he struck me to the ground. I heard the wolf growl and I cried out, for I knew it would rise to my defense. In that moment, one of the guards raised his weapon and let an arrow fly. I turned just in time to see the wolf get hit in the side. The impact knocked it back, and with a pained cry, it fell over the side of the ravine." He watched her swab at the new blood, her touch very tender and caring. "I lunged for my father," he said, relaying the memories as they came to him in vivid recollection. "I dragged him off his mount, determined to give him the same anguish he had just delivered to me. Somehow I wrenched his dagger free. I had cut him below the ear and would have sliced the blade across his neck, if his men had not been able to drag me off of him. My father was enraged, understandably. He charged that I was mad. He'd never called my mother a witch before that day, but he cursed her thus as he stood there bleeding, and he cursed me, too. He said I was her devil's spawn, and that I was no son of his. He banished me from his lands and forbade me the use of his name. I left the next day, and I never looked back."

"That's terrible. Your father couldn't have meant those hateful things, surely." When Braedon chuckled wryly, Ariana clutched his hand in hers and compelled him to meet her gaze. "What he did was wrong. What he said about you is wrong, too."

"Is it? At times, I'm not so sure. I swear, there are times I think I must be mad. To see what I have seen—"

"If you are mad, then so am I," she assured him, but he saw the tremor of fear in her eyes. Calais—and now the attack on the road—had blurred the line between what was real and what could not be explained. "You do not need to convince me that what we've been witnessing is real."

His voice growled out of him, low and deep. "Aye, very real. And I fear the stakes are getting worse with each day that passes. I can sense it. What we have seen thus far is only the beginning. Even though I cannot see it or touch it, the danger is drawing closer, even as we sit here. It is trying to elude me, but the threat is there. It is real."

"What are you telling me—that you know things others don't?"

He gave her a wry smile. "Now *that* would be insane, wouldn't it?"

For a long moment—too long—Ariana said nothing at all. She swallowed silently, her lashes sweeping down to shield her gaze. Did she mock him? What would she think if he had revealed more of his true nature? She would never understand. No one would. How could they, when he scarcely understood it himself?

"Braedon, how did you know that wolf—that creature—was hunting us today? I didn't see him until he was upon us on the path. I didn't hear a thing to betray his presence until it was too late. How did you know?"

He let her hand go and gave a dismissive shrug. "I don't know."

"Yes, you do. You knew it was there, and you knew it was no ordinary wolf—the same way you knew the man in the Calais sailmaker's shop could not be trusted. You just . . . *knew*."

Tenacious as ever, she would not let it go. "You don't see things the way I do, do you? You don't see things the way anyone else does. Tell me how this can be. I want to know."

He blew out a weary sigh. God, he was tired of running. He'd been doing it for so long, hiding since the time he was a youth. No one had ever offered him true compassion or understanding. Did he dare hope for it now?

"Braedon, you can tell me. You can trust me."

He stared into her clear blue eyes, wanting so badly to reach out to her. He realized, if it had eluded him before now, that he wanted her to know him. As he truly was, without hiding behind secrets or masks. If he could hope for anything in that moment, it was to embrace the true soul of another person and to know that he was embraced as well. He had never been compelled to try before. But then, he had never known anyone like the woman beside him now.

"Look around this room, Ariana, and tell me what you see. Listen to the space around you. Tell me what you feel."

Frowning, she slowly pivoted her head to take in the small space. "I don't know . . . I suppose I see a simple chamber, with wooden slat floors and four daubed timber walls. There's a bed over there, and a small table beside it. I don't feel anything save the warmth of the fire and the noise of conversation coming from the public room outside." She looked at him then, uncertainty creasing her brow. "Why? Do you see more than that?"

His senses took a quick account of the place, probably before Ariana even realized what he had done. He mentally sifted through them one by one now, looking for a place to start. "This room was last let a night ago. The people who were here—two of them, a man and a woman—shared a meal of roast pork and smoked cheese. They had wine. Some of it spilled on the floor over there, near the table, where the dark stain marks the seam of those two boards. Their clothes carried the scent of brine and sea air; no doubt they had traveled in from the coast. They didn't stay all night, probably only a few hours." He chuckled, leaving off there.

"What else?" she asked, watching him in rapt attention. "There is more, I can tell you are withholding something."

Braedon cocked a brow, knowing she would not give it up until he told her. "They coupled in here, more than once . . . but they didn't make use of the bed."

Her cheeks flamed a deep shade of crimson, but she did not look away. "That, sir, is a scandalous talent."

"Scandalous and inexplicable. I would give it up if I could, but it never leaves me." Silence followed, broken by his sardonic chuckle. "Ah, there, you see? Mayhap my father was right. Mayhap I am as mad as my mother."

"No. You're not mad." Her eyes locked on his, Ariana reached up and smoothed her fingers along the side of his face, along the ugly ridge of his scar. "I don't think you're mad at all, Braedon. And you're not alone anymore, either. We're in this together now."

He didn't know how long he held his breath, savoring the gentle touch of her hand on him. When he exhaled at last, it was a ragged sound, torn from him like a part of his very soul. Despite the reasoning that warned him to turn away from her at once, to reject this precious gift of compassion she offered him, Braedon tilted his face into her open palm and reveled in the smoothness of her skin against his grizzled jaw. He caught her tender hand in his and brought her fingers to his mouth, pressing a kiss to the sweet, velvety pads, then to the warm heart of her palm. She made a small noise in the back of her throat as his lips tasted her skin—a wordless whisper that seemed more longing sigh than breathless protest.

Braedon dragged his gaze to hers, all the yearning in his body pouring out to her through his eyes. He needed her. God knew how long he had needed to feel the warmth of another's touch, the sweetness of a kiss . . . the haven of a woman's yielding body.

He wanted Ariana in that moment as he had never wanted another woman before her. His desire was a savage thing that burned deep inside him, fierce and consuming.

"I don't want you to be afraid of me," he murmured, his voice thick with need. "Tell me you don't fear me now, Ariana."

"I don't," she whispered, her parted lips glistening in the firelight. "I trust you, Braedon. . . ."

Her words were lost in that next moment. Damning the conscience that urged him to keep his distance, he slipped his hand around her warm nape and pulled her into his arms. Their lips met, tentatively at first, only the merest brush of mouth on mouth, a hesitant, testing kiss that made him ache all the more for its sweetness. He brought his other hand up and framed her face, holding her gently as his tongue teased and tested the seam of her lips. She let him in with a tremulous gasp, opening her mouth as her arms went around him and caressed his back. She was clinging to him the same way he clung to her, both of them adrift and searching for safe harbor.

His pulse was roaring in his temples, his heart racing, feeding the urgency that quickened his body and left him rigid with desire. He dragged Ariana further into his embrace, letting his hands roam down the curve of her back and over the pleasing arc of her hips. She squirmed against him as he deepened his kiss, sucking at her bashful little tongue and nibbling the plump swell of her lower lip. She was melting and pliant in his arms. He was on fire, fully aroused and trembling with need of her. He broke their kiss and looked into her dusky eyes, pleading silently for release.

"Ah, God," he moaned against her, trying to hold himself in check. "This will go too far, angel. Much too far . . ."

She stared up at him and smiled a virginal smile. He had never seen anything so innocent. She was so tender and yielding. So damned soft in his arms.

"Touch me," she told him, a breathless demand. "Kiss me, Braedon . . . please."

God's truth, but he could not refuse her. He could not have denied her, even if he had found the strength to summon his voice. Helplessly, Braedon bent his head and claimed her mouth anew, kissing her with all the passion that coursed so swiftly and heatedly through his veins.

She welcomed his ardor, holding him close and opening herself to his sensual teachings. Their kiss became a dance, a heady game of conquest and surrender.

Ariana's fearless acceptance intoxicated him. It drowned out his awareness of everything else in the room, everything they had been through, everything they had yet to face outside the four walls of the inn. In her arms, nothing else existed, not even his hunter's gift and the dark foreboding it carried to his door. Braedon knew only the bliss of Ariana's hands tangling in his hair, her sweet mouth pressed so deliciously against his, her body arching into him, writhing with a virgin's hunger he longed to sate.

It was wrong to want her like he did, selfish to consider the seduction he was planning while she kissed him with such innocent abandon. But he did want her. Fiercely. He had wanted her from the moment he first saw her in the London tavern, and again when he'd carried her to bed at Rob and Peg's, thinking he could leave her there and simply forget about her. He had wanted her in Calais as well, and on his ship, when they'd watched the stars together from the stern.

"Ariana," he rasped against her throat. "My lady, this is the truest madness. I need you now. I need to feel your skin on mine."

He didn't wait for her permission. In truth, he wasn't sure he was asking for it, but she obliged him without hesitation, only trembling slightly, panting against his ear as he reached between them and cupped his hand over the soft mound of her breast. He lowered his head and nuzzled her, suckling her through the velvet of her gown. She clung to him, her head dropped back on her shoulders, her honey blond mane of hair tumbling loose in a cascade that tickled his hand where it rested against the small of her back. The lacings of her kirtle criss-crossed along the same path, ending with a series of ties at the supple curve of her derriere.

Braedon stooped before her and toyed with the little knots, freeing them with a dexterity that was surprising given his current mindless state. He loosened the lacings halfway up her back and let the fitted gown go slack. The bodice sagged in a crush of fabric, revealing the sensuous valley of her breasts. He bent and kissed her there, revel-ing in the taste of her, the feel of her flesh pressing so warm and sweet against his face.

She was looking down at him when he drew back, her eyes heavy-lidded, mouth ripe and wet from his kisses. She smiled dreamily and waded her fingers into the hair at his temple. He took her hand and kissed her palm, sensu-ally tasting her with the tip of his tongue. Then he rose up and lifted one perfect breast out of her bodice and slipped the rose-dark crest into his mouth. Every fiber in his body responded to that sweet suckling, to the pebbled hardness of her nipple as he drew it deeper into his mouth.

Ariana moaned his name, fisting her hands in the back of his tunic and arching into his embrace like a tightly drawn bow. Her legs quivered as he caressed and kissed her, her limbs seeming to weaken beneath her in her plea-sure.

"Come here," Braedon whispered as he hooked her arm around his shoulder and scooped her up into his arms. He carried her to the bed and laid her down atop the fur-covered mattress, kissing her all the while. He pressed her back with the length of his body, bearing her down beneath him, his arousal straining between the lay-ers of clothing that separated them, starving for all she would give him.

She lay beneath him in seductive dishabille, her gown

slipping off one shoulder, her hair a mussed tangle, her face flushed with arousal.

"Tell me to stop," he heard himself order her in a rough whisper. But even as he said it, his lips roamed down the graceful column of her throat, nipping at the tender flesh that pulsed so deliciously against his tongue. He dipped his head and plundered the soft swell of her bosom, gathering her breasts in his hands and pulling her free of her bodice. "Tell me to let you go, Ariana. If you do not . . . ah, God, if you do not . . ."

He had no will to wait for her denial. With a growl of pure need, he stripped her of her gown and hose, feasting his senses on the beauty spread out before him. His own clothes came off in a frenzied rush. He could scarcely hold a single thought until he was poised above her, naked as she was, his body taut and hungry. Her heavy-lidded gaze traveled the length of him, coming to rest shyly on that part of him that knew no modesty at all.

Thick and ruddy, his sex thrust out from the thatch of dark hair at his groin, straining for her touch. He took her hand and led it to his stiff member, closing her fingers around the width of him. Her hand looked very small, very pale against the flushed spear of his organ. He watched her marvel at the size of him, her uncertain caresses enflaming him to the point of breaking. "I want to be in you, Ariana. I should not ask this of you, but God help me, there is nothing I want more. Nothing I have ever wanted more."

He smoothed his hand along the lovely line of her body, delighting in the spray of gooseflesh that followed in his wake. He stroked the tender skin at her hip, letting his fingers wade into the flossy pale brown curls between her legs. She sucked in her breath when he touched her there, sliding the length of his finger between the dewy folds of her mound. Her fingers squeezed him reflexively as he penetrated her tight sheath with his fingertip. "Oh . . . Braedon . . ."

"This is where I want to be, angel."

He pressed deeper, stretching her by fractions to gradually take more of him. She gasped, biting off a soft, mewling cry as he found the pearl of her womanhood and teased it with his slickened thumb. "I want you, too," she whispered around a wondering moan of pleasure. She arched against his questing hand, guileless and needy, her body weeping in readiness. She had let go of his shaft and now clutched at him, urging him down.

"Braedon, please . . . yes . . . I want you, too." Her eyes were dazed and heavy, deepened to a sensual shade of indigo. "Please . . . I want you . . . *there*."

"Yes," he growled, shifting himself to cover her with his body. Braced on one elbow, he guided himself to the entrance of her womb. Her heat seared his swollen shaft as he slid along her silky folds, teasing before he would take her, knowing there would be pain soon to come. She watched his face with complete trust, her breath coming quick and shallow as he stroked her with the length of his sex.

He couldn't wait much longer. He leaned down and kissed her, catching her plump lower lip between his teeth. He cleaved her lips with his tongue, parting her mouth the way he parted her sex to his invading member. She opened to him like a flower, arching beneath him and crying a soft gasp against his mouth as the tip of his shaft met the barrier of her maidenhead. He couldn't have turned back if he tried. Plundering her mouth in a savage kiss, he eased himself into her sheath.

She went taut in that instant, every muscle tightening in

response to his sudden presence. He moved slowly, giving her time, kissing her all the while. "Is it all right?" he asked, looking down into her moist, glistening eyes. "I don't want to hurt you. I'll stop—"

She gave a small shake of her head. "No, don't stop. I just . . . I didn't know."

He kissed her, tenderly now, forcing his tempo to the gentlest he could manage. She was so tight around him, like a fist of wet heat. He reached between them to stroke her as he moved within her. She moaned softly, relaxing beneath him as he pleasured her with his fingers. She took more of him with each gasp and sigh, accommodating every thrust until he was plunging deep, chasing the crest of a fierce release. He felt it building, felt the rise of coming rapture, felt it tightening like a coil in his loins.

Ariana was writhing beneath him, so close to climax. He quickened his touch on her swollen nub, teasing and stroking until she screamed with her release. He followed her there in the next instant, withdrawing on a shout of harsh pleasure as his seed spurted between them in a hot, pearly stream.

For a long while, he couldn't move. He clung to her, as she clung to him, silent but for the ragged sounds of their breathing. His heart thundered in his ears. He had never felt so spent, so gloriously sated. He rose up to tell her so, but his praise died on his lips.

"You're crying. Ah, Christ. If I have hurt you—"

"No," she said, even as a fat tear rolled down her temple and into her hair. "I'm not in any pain now. Not anymore."

Had he felt glorious a moment ago? Now he felt brutish, little better than an animal. Even worse, when he drew back and saw the pink stains on her thighs and on the coverlets. Her virgin blood, smeared all over. He got up, sick with himself for what he had just done to her. Not just the blood, but everything. He had taken her innocence tonight, something he could never give back to her. He had needed, and he had taken.

Cursing roundly, he got up off the bed and yanked on his hose. He grabbed his tunic and pulled it on while Ariana sat up on the bed. She dabbed at the mess, looking sheepish and younger than he wanted to admit. He should have been the one to stop things here. He had known what he was asking, even if she hadn't. "You'll want to clean up," he said, cursing himself for noticing, even now, how delectable she looked in the middle of the bed, naked and flushed, her hair a golden tangle. He gentled his expression as he met her wounded gaze. "I'll go, and leave you a few minutes of privacy."

Her voice was very quiet. "Are you upset with me? Have I ruined this for us?"

"No. It's not you."

"Then why are you so eager to be away from me?"

"I won't be long." He didn't trust himself to touch her again, not while his body was still raging with want. He couldn't wait to get out of that tiny room, away from Ariana and the temptation she still provided, just sitting there, watching him go. "Don't open the door for anyone until I get back."

He didn't wait for her reply, merely strode out the door and closed it behind him, pausing to hear the metallic slide of the lock bar settling into place before he continued on down the corridor toward the inn's tavern room and public house.

It seemed as though Braedon had been gone for hours. Dressed in her chemise, Ariana paced the small room, marveling over the intimacy they had shared and won-

dering what she had done wrong to make him leave so
abruptly. Her mouth still burned with the memory of his
kiss, as did other, more shameful parts of her body. Her
wantonness shocked her; it was so foreign to anything
she had ever experienced before. Now that he was gone,
she felt utterly empty and confused.

She didn't know what she felt for Braedon now. All she
knew was that she missed him with a keenness that bordered on anguish, and burned with a deep desire to be
near him, even if he was scowling and brooding and striv-
ing so hard to shut her out of his heart.

She wanted to apologize for whatever she had done to
disappoint him, so when she heard his careful footsteps
in the corridor outside their room, his staccato rap on the
thick oak panel, she flew to the door and scarcely hesitated to throw open the latch and let him in.

"Braedon," she said as the door swung wide and his
broad shoulders and torso filled the frame. "Braedon, I'm
sorry. . . ."

Her gaze settled on a massive chest garbed in chain
mail and black wool. A chest emblazoned with a fierce
dragon rampant, snarling in the center of it. A low
chuckle rumbled out above that dragon's flame-breathing
mouth, the thunderous roll of laughter sounding
wickedly arrogant and menacing. Bloodred wool draped
the wide bulk of the intruder's shoulders, the heavy winter mantle falling in dark waves around his large frame
and spurred black boots. Uneasily, Ariana dragged her
stunned gaze upward, to a hard, chiseled face. Green
eyes fringed in midnight black lashes swept over her disheveled appearance in an appreciative, if uncompassion-
ate, glance.

"Nay, *demoiselle*. I am not Braedon. For once I find I
wholeheartedly regret that fact." He bared a row of

straight white teeth, a devastating smile even on a devil like the one standing before her now. Another knight moved in behind him, but her gaze remained fixed and stricken on the angel of death who stood before her, his gloved hand resting on the gleaming hilt of a sheathed broadsword. "I'm sorry to disturb, Lady Ariana, but I believe you have something I want."

❧ 13 ❧

"WHAT WILL YOU HAVE, sir?"

The innkeeper passed a bowl of pottage to a waiting patron then leaned across the scarred wooden counter to look impatiently at Braedon. It took a moment for his query to register, for all of Braedon's senses were tuned elsewhere and still ringing with want of Ariana. She was his true hunger, perhaps all the more now that he'd tasted of her sweetness. He had never known a need so strong, so consuming as that which held him when he'd been kissing Ariana. Touching her.

Desire was all he knew, even now, as he stood in the center of a busy public house, willing his blood to cool and trying to deny the power she had over him. With effort, he turned his mind away from thoughts of her and met the innkeeper's waiting stare.

"We've stew aplenty," the man offered as he filled a tankard for another lodger and handed it back, "but if you want any of the roast boar, you'd best speak up."

"Anything will do," Braedon murmured over the din of conversation that filled the smoky tavern. The establishment had been bustling when he and Ariana had arrived earlier that evening, but now the place was stuffed nigh to the rafters with travelers of all sorts, the lot of them forced to commingle while the wind howled outside. Country folk timidly sat at trestle tables with boisterous knights and haughty nobles, and in a far corner near the fireplace sat a young clergyman reading from his Bible to a group of fidgeting, restless children.

It was an unlikely assemblage, and harmless enough, Braedon thought as he let his eyes stray over the dozens of bodies and faces crowding the public house . . . but something niggled at him nevertheless. Something wasn't right.

"Give me the boar," he told the innkeeper, a prickling of unease creeping up his neck and along his spine. "And a loaf of bread if you have it; some wine, too."

As he spoke, the prickling of his senses sharpened and took root, became something colder. A warning, a sudden wash of dread. His head went up sharply, eyes keen and narrowed, nostrils flaring as he drew in a breath. It was ripe with the scent of danger.

God's blood.

They were here.

Their pursuers had found them, and he had been too blinded by lust to know it. He didn't see them in the room, but malice loomed in the air like bitter ash. They were here, and they would be looking for Ariana and the satchel. It wouldn't take them long to find her, particularly when he had left her alone in the room. Pray God he wasn't already too late.

"Ariana," he murmured, vaulting away from the counter in a rush of fury and not a little panic. He shoved his way through the knot of milling patrons, ignoring the baffled exclamation of the innkeeper behind him. Like a savage beast who'd snapped its leash, Braedon bolted from the busy public house and up the stairs toward the inn's private rooms, his boots thundering on the wooden planks as he ran the length of the darkened corridor.

His heart was pounding in his ears as he neared the

door to the room where Ariana awaited him. It was closed tight, just as he'd left it. Exhaling a breath that shook more than he expected, Braedon reached out to take the black iron latch in his hand. He squeezed it and knew a stab of ice-cold dread as the unlocked lever gave way with a metallic snick, and the door swung open.

Ariana was standing on the other side of the room facing him, her slender figure held unnaturally stiff beneath the rumpled folds of her disheveled kirtle. She stood half-ensconced in shadow, her worried face and trembling hands gilded by the glow of the waning hearth fire. Eyes wide and fearful, she mouthed his name and gave him a vague little shake of her head as he stepped over the threshold—a warning he knew he did not deserve.

It was too late to heed it anyway. The moment his boot crossed into the room, a blade came up and pressed under his chin. Ariana cried out then and moved as if she meant to come to his aid. Just as someone had been waiting for him beside the door, another stood behind Ariana. A bulky arm came out of the shadows at her back and snaked around her midsection, halting her with an ungentle tug. The guard chuckled as he pushed her forward, into the light.

"Bastard," Braedon snarled. His muscles tensed, and he felt the sharp steel of a dagger bite into his throat, encouraging him to heel. He didn't have to see the knight who held him to know who it was. With a muttered curse, he spat the name into the dimly lit room. "Draec le Nantres. Would that I had killed you all those months ago."

The mercenary laughed low, a familiar, jovial roll of humor, but the blade remained poised and unflinching beneath Braedon's chin. "Le Chasseur," he acknowledged glibly. "Is that any way to greet an old friend?

Come in, why don't you? It seems we have some catching up to do."

Despite the razor-edged threat hovering at his neck, Braedon might have attempted to escape this trap, but a quick glance in Ariana's direction gave him another reason to cooperate, at least for the moment. Draec's man also held a blade on her. The obedient glint in the blackguard's eyes bespoke the readiness with which he'd be willing to inflict harm. All it would take was a command from Draec, a man Braedon once trusted like a brother.

"Close the door behind you, Braedon, and step inside." The dagger beneath his chin eased away when Draec issued the cool command. He was no fool. No doubt he knew the knife on Ariana was as good as the one he held on Braedon. He likely sensed a bond there, and Braedon knew that was dangerous information in an enemy's hands. "I think you know why I am here."

Braedon did as instructed and came forward a step, halting face-to-face with his former friend. "Dare I hope you've come to let me settle the unfinished business between us?"

"You'd like that." Draec grunted, his cold green gaze unwavering, even as it passed over Braedon's scar. "I do understand. What I did was . . . regrettable."

"What you did cost five people their lives. Men you broke bread with, men who called you friend. And that wasn't half the wrath you brought down on us that day."

"As I said, regrettable. But then you left me no choice, did you, my friend?"

"You had a choice. You made it."

Dark acknowledgment glimmered in the mercenary's eyes, the harsh line of his mouth tightening almost imperceptibly. "What I did was necessary, I assure you. And are you really so different than me? After all, we both want the same thing. We're both here for the Chalice. Aren't we?" He slanted a look at Ariana, then turned back to Braedon with a knowing smile. "It would seem all that differs is our method of obtaining it. Tell me, Lady Ariana, what's the less ignoble approach: negotiating with cold-edged steel, or calculated seduction?"

Braedon felt Ariana's eyes root on him from across the room. She made a small noise of distress, but whether it was due to her captor's rough handling of her or Draec's crude assumption, he could not be sure. He exhaled a humorless chuckle and glared at his onetime friend. "You've got it wrong, le Nantres. I have no interest in that hell-wrought cup. I want no part of it. I had more than my fill of the Dragon Chalice eighteen months ago."

"Truly?" Draec growled, one dark brow lifting in challenge. With his dagger, he gestured to the rumpled bed, atop which was scattered the rifled contents of Kenrick's satchel. "Then where's the map?"

"What map?"

On the far side of the room, the guard brought his knife a little higher against Ariana, pressing the blade meaningfully to the bare skin above her bodice. She cried out, a sharp gasp of terror. "Braedon, this man is involved with Kenrick's capture. He wants the parchment I was looking for the other night. It's not in the satchel. If you know where it is, you must tell them!"

"Listen to her, le Chasseur. I have no wish to harm the girl, but some men's sense of sport is not so discerning, I fear. I want that map, and I want it now."

He couldn't do it. Even if he had the map in his possession, he could not willingly surrender it to Draec or his employer. He could not provide Silas de Mortaine such easy access to the Chalice. He had risked his neck for lesser goals than this. But what of Ariana? his conscience prodded. Was her life worth risking here? *Too late,* he thought, grim with the knowledge of what he might have cost her.

Braedon stared at Draec in defiance, clenching his teeth so hard a muscle jumped in his jaw. "I don't know what you're talking about. There is no map."

"Braedon!" Ariana gaped at him, incredulous. "What are you saying? I know it was there. It was in the satchel. I saw it when we spent the night together in the cavern. . . ."

Her voice trailed off into humiliated silence. In its wake, Draec chuckled. The soft mocking humor rumbled in the quiet that descended, and if it was possible, Ariana's cheeks flamed a deeper shade of red. "I see you've lost none of your charm with the ladies, my friend." He glanced over at Ariana. "Don't you know who you're with, *demoiselle*? Why, you've been in the company of none other than Braedon le Chasseur—The Hunter himself. He always gets what he's after."

"He's not after anything," Ariana said, coming to his defense even though her gaze held a trace of mounting suspicion. "He brought me to France because I begged him to help me."

"Helped you, has he? Yes, I can see that."

"You can't see anything. Before you arrived here, we were on our way to Rouen to deliver this satchel."

"Oh, yes. And did you know, dear lady, that you are some twelve hours away from Rouen? Twelve hours off, and heading directly for the coast. Toward Honfleur would be my guess. An odd path to take, for a man who's never been lost a day in his life."

Braedon could not look at Ariana in that moment. Seeing le Nantres's satisfied expression was condemning enough. He had turned them away from Rouen when they left the cavern. He'd been heading for the coast, planning to put Ariana on a boat for England to ensure her safety, whether she liked it or not. He had only meant to protect her, but now he felt her eyes fix on him in stunned mistrust.

Draec slanted him a cutting glance. "The map, Braedon. Where is it? Come now, you heard the young lady. She is counting on you to help her."

Braedon met his old friend's gaze and held it firm. Mouth twisting with the distaste of what he'd had to do, he replied simply, "I burned it."

"What!" Ariana's cry of outrage only underscored the cool reserve with which Draec absorbed the news. Her exclamation was cut short by the brutish hand that seized a handful of her hair to keep her from rushing forward in her shock.

"Unhand her," Braedon growled at the oxlike soldier, the boom of his voice carrying a savage warning. It was enough to give the man pause; a casual flick of Draec's gloved hand stayed him where he stood.

"You think you've won." Draec smiled, the glint of welcome challenge gleaming in his clear green eyes. "All you've done is delay the inevitable. We've already got Avosaar. The rest of the documents in that satchel will lead me to the remaining three stones soon enough." He shot a commanding look at the other knight. "Let the woman go, and gather up those papers."

With silent efficiency, the man did as instructed, then handed the hastily composed satchel to Draec. He took it with a quirked smile, slowly sheathing his dagger at his belt, his eyes on Braedon all the while.

"This isn't over, le Nantres," Braedon told him.

The mercenary grinned with the same charm he'd always had, his gaze lighting with the humor of the devil himself. "Oh, I do hope not."

When he opened the door and started to take his leave, Ariana rushed forward. "Wait! You have the satchel now. What about my brother? You must tell me where he is! Tell me if he's alive!"

Draec hesitated, and gave a negligent shrug. "Why, your brother is in Rouen as you expected, Lady Ariana."

"Oh, thank heaven," she breathed, clasping her hands together and closing her eyes as though to savor even this slim charity of information.

"As for his health," Draec added, looking pointedly at Braedon, "his blood, when it spills, won't stain my hands."

A terrible silence befell the room as the door closed behind the man who now had Kenrick's satchel. Ariana could scarcely breathe. Her legs threatened to give way beneath her. Indeed, they must have, for the next thing she knew, Braedon was there beside her, his arm around her to hold her up, looking at her with an expression of concern.

The liar.

Betrayer.

"Don't touch me." She backed out of his embrace as though it burned her to feel his touch. In truth, it did. She felt scorched to her marrow, yet chilled all the same. Chilled to the core of her being for thinking he might have cared for her—that what they had shared that night might have meant something to him. None of it had meant a thing. How could she have been so foolish? How could she have trusted him—Braedon le Chasseur?

The Hunter.

His name chased through her head like the cruelest

jest. Like a wolf toying with a hapless hare, he'd let her believe he would help her and Kenrick. He let her believe he might actually care for her. Mother Mary, but he'd been deceiving her even while he made love to her.

"Ariana, we need to talk."

He reached for her arm but she wrenched away from him and retreated out of his reach. "I have nothing to say to you. And I don't want to hear any of your lies." She backed farther away, as far as the little room would permit, inching toward the open door. "You weren't taking me to Rouen at all. *You lied to me.*"

"I wanted to protect you. I still want to protect you—"

"Oh. I see. And what about Avosaar? The other night, when I mentioned the name to you, you said you'd never heard of it. You knew. You knew all the time that Avosaar was not a place. It's part of the Dragon Chalice—the gemstone cup you returned to Silas de Mortaine."

"What difference does it make? It would not have helped you save your brother. Nothing will, if de Mortaine wants him dead."

"You lied to me. You burned Kenrick's map, and you lied to me."

"Only because I wanted to keep you safe."

"At the cost of my brother's life?"

"If necessary, yes."

She let out a broken cry, hurting for the foolishness that made her want to forgive him, even for something as awful as the breach of trust that might yet be the death of her brother. Her mantle was draped on a peg on the wall; she reached for it hastily and held it close to her body like a shield. "I can't be with you anymore, Braedon. Stay away from me. Just . . . stay away."

He came toward her, offering her his hand, scowling

when she could only stare at him in sickened despair. She felt as though she were living a hideous nightmare, trapped in a strangling web of fury and fear. For fear him she did. Not as she had so irrationally the day she'd first lain eyes on him, but deeper now, understanding just how ruthless—how truly dangerous—he could be.

"Jesu," he muttered, reaching out to her. "Ariana, don't. Don't look at me like that."

A sob wrenched out of her throat. "Like what—like you're a monster? A soulless beast, no different than that murderous creature we saw in Calais? Like the one that attacked us on the road? If I stand here watching long enough, will you change shape before my very eyes, the same way he did?"

He shook his head, his gaze locked on hers. "I'm not the villain you think me. And I'm not going to become something other than what I am—a man. Someone who cares—"

"No," she whispered, cutting him off before he could feed her another lie. "I was wrong, Braedon. You've already become something else. You are treacherous. You've become a snake."

The hand that waited for her to take it now dropped slowly down to Braedon's side. He said nothing more, made no move to stop her as she backed toward the open door and into the hallway beyond. She gazed at him one last time, torn between heartbreak and anger and the cold, enormous void that seemed to open deep within her at the thought of never seeing him again. So foolish, even now, she chided herself, sick with how badly she wanted to believe his excuses.

"You heard what that man said, Braedon. Kenrick will be killed for what you've done. His blood is on your hands now," she charged, nursing the anger that might well be all that would carry her away from there. "How could you? I never want to see you again!"

Choking back the cry that lodged in her throat, Ariana pivoted on her heel and fled. She ran down the corridor and into the public house. She needed to get away from Braedon and his terrible betrayal, to find somewhere safe so she could think. Somewhere she could find help and try to come up with a way to get to Kenrick, even without the damned satchel as his ransom.

14

THE OLD WOODEN cart rambled to a stop at the crest
of a small rise. The jostling of the conveyance as it came
to rest on the rutted winter road woke Ariana from a
brief doze. Bones aching from the hours of travel in the
cold, she sat up a little straighter on the hard bench she
shared with four young children and their mother. As she
moved, the woolen blanket that scantily covered the lot
of them for the duration of the night's journey slid off her
to bunch in her lap. The woman's husband, a common
man who'd been charitable enough to let her accompany
them, now pivoted in his seat up front. He gave a nod toward the misty distance just over the ledge.

"Here we are, *demoiselle*. Down there, the city of
Rouen."

In the wide river valley below, shrouded in a haze of
misty early morning fog, lay a tapestry of jagged, snow-
kissed rooftops and the soaring needlelike spires of half a
dozen churches and cathedrals.

Rouen.

At last, Ariana thought with a mix of relief and trepidation. She'd made it after all.

She had made it to the place where Kenrick was being
held, but she could not help feeling a biting misery to see
the city spread before her. What good would it do to arrive here when she had already lost her brother's ransom

to Kenrick's captors? She had nothing to bargain with now. Less than nothing, once Draec le Nantres let it be known that the map had been destroyed.

Her regret must have shown in her face. When she settled back onto the bench as the cart lurched forward once more to begin its descent down the road, the matron reached over and patted her hand reassuringly. "I pray your brother's health will recover soon, now that you are here to look after him," she said, reminding Ariana of the tale she'd given when she had literally run into the couple on her emotional flight from the tavern's public house.

Preferring to keep as close to the truth as possible, she had said only that she'd received word that her brother, away from home and serving the Knights Templar, was presently in dire straits, in need of care and ailing in Rouen. As she'd spun the tale that bought her escape from Braedon at the tavern, she had hoped the pilgrims would believe her. Now, with Rouen looming ever closer, its tall city gate rising up out of the fog like the dark, yawning mouth of a beast, Ariana worried that the stretch of fact she perpetrated was likely not at all far from the terrible truth.

"God will not abide him to suffer, *ma petite*," the woman said. "Especially not when your brother is doing the good work of the Lord."

Ariana nodded. She dearly hoped she was right. Short of divine intervention, she had no idea how she would manage to rescue Kenrick empty-handed. Perhaps it was naïve to think she had a chance, but her alternatives were few and fleeting with every day that passed. She knew not where to turn, nor whom to trust—certainly not Braedon, she thought, swallowing past the harsh reminder that stabbed at her heart.

She was alone in this now, truly alone, and short of a

miracle, she had no reason to believe she might succeed. In truth, she reflected, as the cart trundled into the city and past a glorious cathedral, perhaps divine intervention was precisely what she should seek.

Braedon's mood had not improved as the night wore on. He left the tavern soon after Ariana did, taking his horse from the stables to follow her and the family who accompanied her. He rode along, keeping a fair distance, not needing to see her to know where she was or where she was headed. More than once, as his mount sauntered a leisurely trail through the midnight countryside, Braedon considered simply giving the beast his spurs and riding out after Ariana, taking her off with him, forcing her to listen to him. But what could he say? Everything Draec had accused him of was true.

Ariana's contempt of him was understandable, especially after he'd seduced her. He could still see the hurt in her eyes, the stricken look of disbelief as she stared at him while he confessed to destroying her hopes of freeing her brother.

Kenrick will be killed for what you've done. . . . I never want to see you again!

Her tearful accusation rang in his ears. She hated him, and rightly so. She was desperate—perhaps even more desperate than the day he'd first laid eyes on her in London—but a fierce defiance sparked in her glittering gaze. She would not be defeated, no matter the obstacles tossed before her. Not Ariana. But what would she do? He hated to consider it. He knew her better than to expect her to give up and go home where she would be safe. She would only be all the more determined, all the more willing to risk her own safety to rescue her brother.

Some selfish, sane part of him urged him to wheel his

mount around and head back for Calais. He could retrieve his cog and sail off as he'd planned before Ariana of Clairmont had intruded on his life and dragged him into this mayhem. What did her owe her, after all?

He slowed his palfrey and looked back over his shoulder, back toward Calais, a simpler road by far. Mayhap he should take it. He felt certain all that awaited him in the other direction, toward Rouen, was disaster. Probably death. He wasn't a coward, but he didn't fancy himself a fool, either. He had narrowly escaped death eighteen months ago; he might not be so fortunate this time.

But then there was Ariana.

If danger awaited him in Rouen, then it awaited her, too. Perhaps tenfold, particularly when she headed into it all alone. God's blood, but he couldn't let that happen. Fool or nay, he could not let her fall victim to her brother's fate.

With a growled curse, Braedon rounded the horse back onto the road and spurred it into a gallop. Whatever Ariana was walking into, he meant to be there with her when she faced it.

The church was an unassuming place amid the soaring splendor of Rouen's many cathedrals. Squat and round, crafted of simple stone, it crouched at the end of the cobbled street like a tree stump amid a forest of tall half-timbered houses, rising church towers, and intricate spires. Ariana walked toward it, doing her best to avoid the frost-edged puddles that soaked her boots and dampened the hem of her kirtle. She held the hood of her mantle down to help ward off the bite of the morning air, squinting through the flurry of snow that had begun to fall.

She was cold, miserably cold, but she knew the chill that permeated her had more to do with what lay ahead of her than it did the February weather. All her hopes centered on the rough little church at the end of the lane. She knew of nowhere else to turn now. Summoning her resolve and whispering a plea to the heavens, Ariana entered the gated perimeter of the churchyard and walked the dozen paces to the plain door of the building. She lifted the iron knocker with her gloved fingertips and rapped uncertainly.

For a long while, only silence greeted her. Were visitors permitted here? she wondered suddenly. She did not know if the warrior monks secreted within the church would scorn the presence of a female at their door. She knew little of their code, after all. They might well turn her away, if they didn't ignore her arrival altogether.

But Ariana refused to be daunted, not when her brother could be being held somewhere not far from this very place. She reached for the knocker again and rapped harder this time, the staccato notes of her demand ringing out on the other side of the door. It opened a moment later, creaking inward and throwing a wedge of light into the incense-scented darkness within.

"Yes, yes?" A high-browed, youthful pair of round eyes came around the edge of the door, peering out at her from a head capped in close-shorn hair yet fully bearded in long, untrimmed whiskers. The young Templar cleric grunted in surprise, his inquisitive gaze widening before he quickly averted his eyes to look down at the floor. "Oh. Good morrow, then. Come to collect the alms, have you, *demoiselle*? You should know that Brother Etienne has already sent them on. Yes, yes. Good day, then."

With a humble nod of dismissal, he started to close the

door on her. Ariana placed the flat of her hand against the iron-banded oak panel before it could shut in her face. "No—wait, please. I haven't come to collect anything. I am here because I need . . ." She hesitated, wondering how best to explain her strange situation. "Please. My brother is in danger. I—I don't know where to turn. I need help."

The young monk's gaze lifted, but only slightly, as if it were forbidden to look upon a woman for more than a heartbeat. Perhaps it was, Ariana guessed, having no patience at the moment for arcane regulations. When the cleric murmured his apologies and withdrew even farther into the sanctuary of the church, she slipped her booted foot over the threshold and physically blocked the door from closing. "My brother is in grave danger, and I'm not leaving until I speak with someone. Please hear me out. His name is Kenrick of Clairmont. He was once one of your own—a Templar knight."

Like a sorcerer's key, those last few words held the power to gain her entrance. In a hushed voice, the monk bade her wait inside while he fetched his master. He was gone in a swirl of his long green robes, disappearing into a closed antechamber just off the torchlit entryway. Ariana stood there amid the quiet, hearing the monk's vague murmur in the other room, catching only brief pieces of what was being said: "female awaiting . . . most insistent . . . her brother . . . Templar, she says . . . some sort of trouble."

Silence hung in the air, thoughtful, measuring. Then, from within the chamber, the soft scrape of a heavy chair on the stone floor. The torch flames stirred as the door opened and an old man in long white robes came out to greet her. Kind-faced, spine bent with age, the Templar official shuffled over to Ariana, regarding her with the calm indulgence borne of his countless years. His underling hovered at his side, dark-eyed gaze darting to Ariana with a great deal more courage now, more open curiosity. She straightened, trying to ignore the monk's appreciative stare.

"That will be all, Brother Arnaud."

The young monk jolted out of his gaping and scurried off down the corridor without a word. Ariana watched him go, nearly expecting a similar dismissal from the old man herself, but then the wizened Templar official smiled and dipped his head in belated greeting. His wispy hair was cropped close to his skull and thinning. It gleamed snowy white in the glow of the torch lamps. "My apologies, child. I fear our more recent novitiates often find it difficult to adapt to our strict code of conduct. Especially when it comes to those edicts concerning our interaction with the fair sex. I pray you took no offense."

Ariana shook her head. "No, of course not. I am sorry if my being here is an intrusion in any way, but I am in desperate need of help, and I had nowhere else to turn."

"Please," said the Templar, slowly stretching out his arm to indicate his private meeting room. "Come in, dear girl, and tell me what is wrong."

Ariana accepted his invitation, striding past him and through the open door of the antechamber. She tried not to gape at the lavishness of the place, so incongruous to the outward modesty of the Templar church. Although compact, the room held a wealth of fine appointments. Ariana's wet boots came to rest softly on a thick wool rug that nearly ran the length and width of the floor. No less than a dozen costly candles burned in polished brass holders, their sweet beeswax scent drifting like a mild perfume on the rarefied air. The warm glow of candlelight filled the chamber, illuminating the gilt-edged spines of countless books, volumes of texts lining wide stone shelves carved into the room's very walls. At one end of the chamber stood a large wooden desk. Ornately carved and meticulously maintained, it dominated the small space. On the wall behind it hung a large tapestry depicting in colorful detail the crucifixion of Christ. Tragic though it was, Ariana all but froze, staring at the beauty of the design.

"Please," prompted the Templar official as he entered the chamber a few paces at her back. "Sit, dear child, sit."

She eased down into a small chair while the church official crossed the room to pour a cup of claret from a silver decanter. Ariana declined the drink when he offered it to her. Savoring a sip of the aromatic wine, he then seated himself at the desk, occupying a cushioned throne that would not have been at all out of place in a royal solar. "Now, tell me what brings you here, and how the brethren might help you."

" 'Tis about my brother, Kenrick," Ariana said, and proceeded to explain the bizarre series of events that had transpired since she first received word of his abduction and ransom.

"Oh, dear. Dear oh dear oh dear." Brother Arnaud dashed down the circular passageway to the back of the Templar church as fast as his feet would carry him. He ran out a darkened doorway and into the yard behind the stone chapel, the smooth soles of his leather shoes slipping and sliding in his haste to cross the snowy courtyard.

Pell-mell, breathless with excitement, he raced toward the stables and commandeered himself a mount with nary an excuse to the gaping stablemaster. Out of the churchyard he rode and up the thoroughfare of the city, kicking the swift-footed horse into a hard gallop to speed toward a huge stone castle that loomed on the outskirts of Rouen.

A shout to the watchtower guards admitted him quick entry. They knew who he was; they understood the importance of his role as spy to their powerful overlord. Lathered nearly as much as his huffing mount, Arnaud leaped to the ground of the inner bailey and vaulted up the stairs as fast as his stubby legs could carry him. Once inside, he was shuttled to the solar to deliver his valuable news.

"She's here!" he gasped, all but falling upon the door of the private antechamber, stumbling in with nary a knock of warning. Mustering his composure, he pulled himself up from his sprawl on the cold slate floor. "Forgive the interruption of your, er . . . your work, my lord, but I have just seen her. She's here. The girl is here in Rouen."

A noble head crowned in thick bright gold hair lifted from where it had previously been bent down, enjoying the bounty of a young maid's particularly ample bosom. Cold blue eyes flicked up, piercing the young monk from across the room. "The Clairmont woman?"

"Yes. Dear, oh dear, yes, my lord. She is speaking with Master Delavet this very moment—come asking after her brother, so she is."

"She is here?" demanded the man who could turn Arnaud's blood to ice with the merest unholy glance. "At the church? For how long?"

The novice Templar swallowed hard. "It's been mere moments, my lord. I came as quickly as I could to tell you. I thought you would want to know."

A black curse hissed from between clenched teeth as Arnaud's true master thrust away his pouting plaything and rose from his chair. In three swift strides he crossed the space of the chamber floor, knocking Arnaud aside as he stepped out into the corridor and shouted for someone to ready his horse.

In all his seventy-two years, the old Templar master had never before heard such a wild, strange tale as the one he'd been fed by Lady Ariana of Clairmont. He shook his head, reflecting on the distress he saw in her innocent gaze, yet unable to credit her fantastic story of mystical treasures, stolen gemstones, and men who were not men at all, but beasts of some unexplainable origin. He had listened patiently, sympathetically, while she pleaded her case, understanding of her distress even as he sent her on her way a few moments ago. That she mourned the loss of her brother was clear enough, mourned him so keenly it had affected the poor child's mind.

"God bless her, the dear, wretched thing," he murmured aloud, turning his attention to a bit of correspondence that waited on his desk. He was so engrossed in his study of the letter, he didn't realize anyone was there with him until he glanced up to reach for his quill and pot of ink.

"Oh!" he exclaimed with a start, his tired old eyes meeting with the always unsettling stare of the brethren's chief benefactor in Rouen. He stood beside the huge desk, offering nothing by way of apology or excuse, save a vague smile. On anyone else, the insubordinate stance would be construed as defiance, or worse, thinly veiled disdain. But on this man, it was merely indicative of his unflappable confidence. It was merely his way. The Templar master smiled, hopeful that this visit might signify another generous donation for the brotherhood's coffers. "Lord de Mortaine, welcome. You tread so lightly, I scarcely heard you come in."

"I understand you've had a visitor. A woman."

The old monk chuckled. "Goodness, but there is little that escapes you in this town. We did have a visitor. A most peculiar one at that."

"This woman. What did she want?"

"Ah, me. Her brother's gone missing, it seems. He was of the Order, so she came here hoping for help in finding him, although I suspect she wanted something more than that, the poor creature."

"Something . . . more?" Cool and compelling, the hard blue eyes narrowed on the old master. "Explain."

"She's not right in the head, my lord. Talking of legends and sorcery as if they truly exist. These are dangerous times to be speaking such wild notions. Someone less sympathetic than I might take her for a heretic."

"Yes," the nobleman answered, considering. "She should be careful."

"A piteous thing, to see someone so young and vibrant suffer such an unfortunate affliction. Do you know, she would have me believe that her brother is being held for ransom somewhere here in the city because he uncovered the location of a mythical treasure—some nonsense about a demon chalice."

De Mortaine gave a deep, strangely amused chuckle. "Dragon Chalice, you old fool."

The aged monk grunted up at him, dumbstruck by the malice he heard in the man's usually silky voice. "You know of this thing, Lord de Mortaine?"

His question went wholly ignored. "The chit is carrying a satchel of papers and journals. Did you see them?"

"Satchel? What papers?"

To the old man's utter shock, de Mortaine launched at him over the desk like a madman, grasping the front of his robes in his fists and wrenching him out of his seat. "God damn it, Delavet! The satchel—did she show it to you?"

"N-no! She showed me nothing—merely told me her tale and asked me to help her locate her brother. What is the meaning of this?"

"What did you tell her? Where did the foolish little bitch go?"

Master Delavet trembled to see the deadly fury blazing in the nobleman's eyes. He had never seen such evil, such black intent. Loath as he was to turn that ugliness onto another person—particularly a disturbed and unsuspecting young woman—the elderly monk realized that he was more terrified that de Mortaine meant to kill him.

God forgive him, but he was worse than terrified. He was weak, and willing to do anything to prevent his death at any moment.

Hating himself for the cowardice that cropped up in his heart, he murmured a handful of damning words. "I told the girl . . . I would send word of her brother if I . . . could. I sent her . . . to the Cross and Scallop Inn."

He spat the words out in a rush, gasping to drag in a gulp of much-needed breath. He felt de Mortaine's hands tighten around his throat. Saw the gleam of satisfaction light in the younger man's queer blue eyes an instant before he heard the violent crack of his own neck, snapping in the ruthless grasp.

❧ 15 ❧

ARIANA PICKED AT her meal of rabbit stew and hard, stale bread, having had little appetite even before she tasted the meager fare at the pilgrims' inn. The Cross and Scallop was a hive of activity. Travelers came and went all the while she sat there—a constant change of patrons, an increasingly agonizing wait as Ariana occupied a quiet corner of the tavern room, eager for word from the Templars. She was beginning to think it would not be coming anytime soon. If at all.

The aged man she had met with had been accommodating enough, but there had been an element of disbelief in his kindly old gaze as she'd explained her situation. She'd seen pity in his eyes, and now she wondered if he merely sent her off with false hope that he would inquire after Kenrick with his contacts around the city. Perhaps he expected she would simply take her outlandish tale and go away. In truth, she rather wondered if the old monk considered her completely mad. She certainly might, had she been asked to entertain so wild an account as the one she'd presented to Master Delavet that morning.

With a heavy sigh, she watched as another group of pilgrims gathered their things and bustled out of the wayside inn, making room for a new round of lodgers who filed in immediately after them. Ariana studied her con-

gealing bowl of stew as she burrowed out the center of a
stale chunk of bread. She nibbled at it, then decided she
couldn't eat after all and set the lot of her meal aside.
Sweeping away the crumbs she'd made, she glanced up to
find the innkeeper navigating his way through the thick
crowd of newcomers, his gaze searching the tavern. He lit
on her and headed her way, holding a piece of folded
parchment in his hands.

"*Demoiselle de Clairmont, oui?*" he asked as he approached.

At Ariana's nod, he handed her the missive, pausing
only long enough to sniff indignantly over her discarded
meal. She quickly unfolded the parchment and scanned
it, noting the old Templar official's signature at the bottom. A sharp glance up and across the room gave her a
fleeting glimpse of Brother Arnaud's dark green robes,
and his darting eyes staring back at her from within the
deep folds of his cowled hood. She stood up and tried to
hail him, but he ducked out of sight as if he hadn't seen
her, disappearing into the crowd before slipping out the
tavern door.

Heart pounding with hope, Ariana read the message:

> Your brother has been located. Return this evening at
> the vespers bell, and we can discuss how to best bring
> about his safe release from the men who hold him.
> Bring the satchel.

All the joy she knew as she absorbed the first few lines
of Master Delavet's missive fled the moment her eyes settled on the end of his instructions. *Bring the satchel.* The
Templar official had seemed only passing interested
when she tried to tell him about the cryptic ransom
placed on her brother's head, and he did not give her the

opportunity to explain how she had lost the selfsame ransom before sending her off with a blessing of godspeed and a vague promise that he would make some inquiries on her behalf.

Had he been in contact with Kenrick's captors, then? It seemed unlikely, or he would have to be aware that the demanded ransom was no longer in her possession. A dark thought flitted through her head, a suspicion that the old Templar might be using her somehow, testing her with this request for the satchel. It seemed unlikely, however. He had given her no reason to doubt him, and as it stood, he was her only chance of ever seeing her brother again.

It was a chance she simply had to take, she decided, when, some hours later, the bells of the many Rouen churches began to toll out vespers. Donning her mantle as though girding herself for battle, Ariana made the short trek from her corner table to the door of the inn. She passed through the crowds as neatly as she could, glad to feel the rush of crisp, fresh air as she stepped out into the street.

Night was soon to fall. The snow that blanketed the ground and spattered the facades of the tall, timbered buildings glowed an iridescent pale blue in the waning light of day. Although a fair number of people yet roamed about the streets, most of them were men, and far too many seemed to take notice of the fact that she was a woman alone as darkness began its descent.

Low murmured conversations drifted on the thin afternoon breeze, the masculine rumble of amusement and traded gibes echoing in the street behind her. Ariana quickened her pace. The Templar church wasn't far. If she hurried, she could be there while it was still light. Walking briskly now, she shot a glance over her shoulder as she turned onto the street that would take her to the Templar church. Ahead of her, just past the corner of the building she rounded, she heard a soft shift of movement.

Too late, she realized her mistake. Someone was there. A wall of darkness rose up before her, blocking her path.

She let out a startled gasp, but not before a thick wool blanket came down over her head, blotting out the scant light of the fading day. She tried to scream but when she opened her mouth, a large hand clamped down over her face from the other side, snuffing her cry of terror. Kicking, thrashing, twisting, Ariana fought to escape the iron bonds that held her prisoner beneath the large swatch of wool. All to no avail.

With one hand over her mouth, the other snaking around her waist to pull her flush against the unyielding mass of his body, her captor dragged her off the street. Ariana kept trying to scream. She kept struggling, kept uselessly trying to free herself from the person who held her in an unrelenting, merciless grasp. She heard the whicker of a horse somewhere nearby, then felt her captor's hold on her shift slightly as a stirrup jangled and he mounted the beast. Less than an instant later, she was seated up there with him, hoisted off the ground by her arm and flopped prone onto the horse's back before she knew what was happening.

A nudge of her captor's thighs sent the beast into a brisk canter. Each fall of its hooves jarred Ariana's stomach where she lay sprawled across the wide expanse of the horse's back, her assailant's strong hand the only thing keeping her from jostling off. Although she yearned to be free, Ariana clung as best she could, terrified of a fall onto the swiftly passing cobbles of the street beneath her. She felt the rider turn his mount around a corner, then felt the beat of the horse's gait grow smoother as it cleared the town gates and fell into a gallop.

She did not know how long they rode or where she was being taken. Ariana knew only that they were some distance outside of Rouen when the man who held her finally slowed his huffing mount and drew it to a halt. He leaped down, then pulled her off the back of the horse.

"Let me go!" she shouted now that she was able. "Let me—go!"

She renewed her fight the instant her feet touched ground, but when she would have struggled and thrashed to rid herself of the thick blanket that shrouded her, her captor suddenly reached out and whisked it off her head. Her gaze flew to the face of the man who kidnapped her from the city, and she let out a particularly choice curse.

"Braedon!" she gasped in outrage and confusion.

She threw a glance at her surroundings, taking in the broken, ghostlike ruins of an old abbey, half-demolished walls standing charcoal gray against the white of the snow. Nothing but desolation this far out, and, in the distance behind them, the jagged outline of Rouen. Her meeting with Master Delavet, the negotiations for her brother's release—all of it lay back there, well out of her grasp.

She looked at Braedon, panic tight in her breast. "Get away from me. How dare you do this?"

"It seemed necessary."

"You have no idea what you've done. You—you have ruined everything!" She broke away from him and grabbed for his mount's reins. "I'm taking your horse. I have to go back before it's too late—"

"Back to your meeting with the Templars, you mean?"

"What do you know of it?" The accuracy of his assumption took her aback, but a moment later anger burned through her sense of surprise. "Oh, that's right. Lest I forget, you are the vaunted Hunter. What did you do—use your strange skills to track me down?"

His answering look held a grim sort of humor. "I had no need of my skills. I could find you easily, my lady. I knew you would go to Rouen, with or without Kenrick's ransom, stubborn little fool. Your intentions were obvious when you left last night."

"As are yours, now that I know the truth about you." She turned away from him and put her booted foot in the stirrup, prepared to mount the palfrey and hie herself back to the city. She barely had her toe in the ring before Braedon reached out and snatched the reins from between her fingers.

"You know my intentions, do you, *demoiselle*? You are so certain you know what I am about?"

"I know all I need to know. You lied to me—about everything, so far as I can see. You took the map from Kenrick's satchel and you burned it."

"I couldn't let it fall into their hands."

Ariana scoffed. "You've been after the Chalice all along, just as that man—your friend, was he?—said back there at that inn. You've been using me!"

"'Twas you who came to me for help, remember? I wanted no part of this. I left it all behind me a year and a half ago. That's where I wanted it to stay."

"And yet how easily you got involved. Why didn't you just take the satchel from me? You certainly had the chance—more than once. Why let me believe that you—" She broke off, unwilling to humiliate herself with a heated challenge to his feelings. "Why let me think that you would help me?"

"I never meant to hurt you, Ariana."

She rejected his assertion with a curt shake of her head.

"You would let my brother die to make sure no one reaches that damned treasure before you do."

"Not if it can be helped. Believe me——"

"Believe you? I can never believe another thing you say. How can I ever trust you? Give me your horse. I am going back to Rouen."

"It's a trap."

She hesitated, though still intent to mount the palfrey. "It is my only chance. Let go of the reins, I command you."

"I'm not letting you go, Ariana. I'm not going to let you walk headlong into your own death at the hands of Silas de Mortaine."

"Nay, deceiver. My meeting is with——"

"Master Jacques Delavet, the old Templar official at the church in town."

Ariana whirled on him, astonished.

"You met with him this morning. I saw you leave the church; he watched you depart from the yard. Delavet didn't send you the note at the Cross and Scallop. In fact, I suspect the old graybeard is in grave danger now himself. Silas will not want to leave any loose ends."

"How could you know this?"

"The same way you suspected I found you. I watched, and I listened. That Templar cleric who brought you the missive today at the inn——"

"Brother Arnaud." She shook her head, brow pinched in sudden understanding. "Then you were there at the inn as well? It was so crowded. I didn't see you."

Braedon gave a vague shrug. "I did not want to be seen. The cleric who delivered your message left the Cross and Scallop and reported back to Silas de Mortaine."

"Why should I trust anything you say? How can I be

sure you aren't using me again somehow—using me still?"

"I only want to help you. I only want to know that you are safe."

She scoffed, resting her back against the solid girth of the horse. "I might have believed you before last night. Now I know better. Would that I had found you out before your actions put Kenrick in greater jeopardy."

"I should have told you about the map," Braedon said, his eyes lowered with a nearly convincing look of regret. "When I saw what it could mean to de Mortaine if Kenrick's ideas were correct—how easy it would make Silas's quest for the other pieces of the Dragon Chalice—I should have explained to you that it had to be destroyed."

"You had no right to touch anything in that satchel," she told him, trying to maintain her anger even though the fact that he was there, the fact that he knew where she had been and whom she had spoken with, gave her pause.

"I can help you in this, Ariana, but you must trust me. I never meant to use you. God knows, I never meant to hurt you in any way."

"Well, you have."

"I know. And I am sorry for all of it. But you must believe me now, Ariana. If you go to that meeting place today, you go to your certain death."

How foolish was she to consider his counsel after what he might have cost her? As stubbornly as she wanted to cling to her mistrust of him, she could not dismiss his warning altogether. "You are sure of this? You're saying the message I received at the inn came from this—from Silas de Mortaine—and not Master Delavet?"

Braedon nodded once, a sober admission.

Ariana frowned, considering. "I don't understand. If

that's true, why would Silas want to meet with me?" She withdrew the note from the fitted sleeve of her gown, unfolded the parchment, and handed it to him. "Why would he ask me to bring Kenrick's satchel when he already has it? Surely Draec must have delivered it to . . ."

Her voice trailed off as realization began to dawn. Braedon glanced up from reading the brief missive, a glint of cunning in his eyes. "He doesn't have it. Draec is playing some manner of game. He did not return to Rouen with the satchel last night."

"Would he try to cheat Silas, knowing how dangerous he is?"

"Draec le Nantres would cheat his own sire if it suited his purpose. Thank God," he added with a low chuckle. "He just bought us a chance to rescue your brother. Perhaps our only chance."

"What can we do?"

"Not *we*, Ariana—you. De Mortaine cannot know that I am with you. We must make sure he believes you are in Rouen alone and that you have exactly what he wants. But first we need to make sure your brother is still alive." When Ariana winced slightly and glanced down, Braedon lifted her chin on his fingertips and met her gaze. "We have a good chance, my lady. Let us make use of it."

She nodded, feeling a surge of gratitude for Braedon's presence even while she fought the warming of her heart. Despite all logic, she felt safe when she was with him. In the presence of this scarred, dangerous man, she felt protected. And though she would not permit herself to tell him, in that moment, she was so very glad he was there.

"Tell me, Ariana," he said, "is there some secret between Kenrick and you? Something only he would know—a date of some significance, or a shared jest that he might recall?"

She thought for a moment, then lit upon her answer. "A name," she said, eager to put Braedon's plan under way. "There is a name he will remember if asked about it."

"Good. That will serve as our proof. We'll take word to de Mortaine that unless we get the answer we are looking for, the satchel stays with us."

"Will it work?" Ariana asked, weathering a sudden twinge of worry. "What if he refuses to submit to our demands?"

"He won't refuse. So long as he thinks we have the satchel, de Mortaine will do whatever we ask." Braedon cupped her cheek in his palm. "Come. There's got to be a country cleric somewhere around here. We'll have him pen our demands, then we'll have the missive delivered yet this evening."

"Then what?"

"We wait."

Less than an hour after it was sent, their message to Silas de Mortaine came back with an answer. Through a hastily constructed network of messengers—one paid to wait on the missive at the Templar church, another to intercept and carry it to the city gates, and a third to bring it to Braedon where he waited under the cover of forest nearly a mile outside of Rouen—the simple proof of Kenrick's survival arrived. Braedon glanced at the single word scrawled in a bold, if somewhat shaky hand, and he smiled. With a measuring scan of his surroundings to make certain he was not being watched or followed, he gave his horse a nick of his heels and headed back for the ruined abbey to give Ariana the news.

She was waiting deep within the shell of the tumble-down cloisters, seated on a lump of blankets and furs he'd given her before he left, and warming her hands before the orange glow of a small fire as he rode within the ruin and dismounted. She got to her feet the instant she saw him and took a hesitant step toward him. Worry tightened her throat. "So soon?"

Braedon held up the folded missive. "I told you de Mortaine would oblige."

"Have you read it?" She took another step, then halted suddenly, as if she did not dare to hope. "Did . . . did Kenrick answer?"

Braedon nodded. "He is alive."

"Thank God!" Ariana ran to him, taking the piece of parchment from his outstretched hand. She unfolded it with trembling fingers, her gaze lighting on the word that came back in answer from her brother's captors. "Jonah," she said, laughing as she looked up at Braedon. "Only Kenrick would know the name of the kitten I was holding the day he found me locked in the storeroom at Clairmont. He dubbed it Jonah, for the way we were swallowed up in darkness—as though the litter of kittens and I had been trapped in the belly of a whale. Oh, Braedon," she said, circling her arms around him in a fierce embrace, "Kenrick is alive!"

He brought his hands down upon her shoulders and smiled, his gaze telling her he shared her relief. Perhaps he knew her joy, and took some measure of pride for his part in it. Ariana gazed up at him in gratitude, indeed, in something far deeper than that simple regard. She wanted no more anger between them, no matter what lay ahead of them still. She wanted no more mistrust or fear to separate them. Needing to feel the strength of his embrace, she held him tighter, resting her cheek against the solid warmth of his chest. "I want it to be over," she whispered. "I just . . . I want this all to be over now."

Braedon gently encircled her in his arms and held her close, petting her hair as he whispered soft words of comfort beside her ear. "Soon, I promise. Everything will be all right. Your brother is alive. I won't let anything happen to him now." He tilted her face on the edge of his hand and guided her misting gaze up at him. "I'll lay down my life to spare you any more pain, Ariana. You must know that."

He bent his head toward hers, and sealed his promise with a kiss. At once tender and consoling, there was also a possessiveness in the brush of contact as their mouths met. Ariana opened to him with a small gasp, parting her lips and reaching up to him with clutching, needy hands. There was a wealth of longing in her embrace, but she made no attempt to conceal it, for that same need she felt in him burned within her, too. With a groan, he dragged her farther into his arms, pressing into the soft yield of her body. He framed her face in his palms, his fingers trembling against her skin as he kissed her toward the brink of a heavenly madness.

"Ariana," he murmured against her mouth. "Would that I could take it all back. I would start over, if I could. I swear it."

She touched his cheek with her fingertips, a tender tracing of the scar that savaged his face. He was handsome, even with his flaws. Maybe more so, because of all he had been through and survived. He was a hard man, an arrogant man, but he had captured her heart like no other before him. As no other would, she admitted, if only to herself. "Thank you, Braedon," she whispered, caressing his proud jaw. "Thank you for coming after me. For being here now."

He caught her hand and held it to his mouth, placing a kiss in the tender cradle of her palm. Ariana moistened her lips, watching as he traced his lips along the inner side of her wrist. He kissed her then, once more, and she was lost. Sweeping his tongue along the pliant seam of her mouth, he suckled her, a passionate claiming that called to places deep inside her.

She should not want him so, but there was no denying the heat that beckoned her to him. There was no shred of resistance there to summon, not when she still thrummed with the stunning awakening he had brought to her body the night before. Nay, her heart yearned for him all the more, now that she was touching him, kissing him, again. With a soft cry of longing, she dropped her head back and plunged her fingers into the hair at his nape, holding him to her and reveling in the sensual press of his hips against her body.

"Braedon," she whispered. "Braedon, please . . . I need you tonight. I need you to hold me."

"Ah, my lady. Have I have corrupted you so?" he asked, pausing to wickedly stroke the delicate bones at the base of her neck.

A braided cord held her mantle securely about her shoulders. Braedon deftly loosened the little knot and let the heavy cloak fall down around their feet. The ties of her kirtle's bodice were his next course of attack. He spread the neckline of her gown, baring her skin to his gaze, and to his touch. Ariana's breathing picked up speed as he lavished a slow worship of her, tracing a lazy trail down the slope of her bosom. Her shallow gasps puffed from her parted lips, steaming in the cool night air. Braedon kissed the rise of her breast, flicking his tongue against the flushing pink of her skin.

She clutched at him with guileless, searching hands, her body trembling and quaking with his simplest touch. The stubble of his beard dragged against her skin as he

moved to sample more of her. He kissed his way to her
other breast, letting his tongue dip into the cleft of her
bosom, nipping at her and wringing a mewl of pleasure
from the very core of her being.

" 'Tis not enough to sate me," he told her, teasing her
further with his sensual kisses and a purely carnal look of
hunger. "Not nearly enough."

He slipped his fingers inside the bodice of her kirtle and
found the pebbly bud of her nipple. He filled his hand
with the warm buoyancy of her breast, caressing her,
fondling that tight pearl, which peaked and hardened under his touch. He freed her from the bodice and with an
almost savage growl, he sucked her nipple deep into his
mouth. Ariana gasped at the pleasure of it, her body
nearly melting where she stood. She caressed the back of
his skull, her fingers twining in his hair, hands fisting, as
she curved into him with a whimper.

"I need you, Ariana. I need you now."

"Yes," she gasped. "Oh, Braedon . . . yes."

He said nothing more as he bent to scoop her into his
arms and carry her to the nest of coverlets near the fire.
His gaze held hers, those mutable gray eyes hooded,
deepened to obsidian pools as he placed her before him
on her knees, then sank down with her onto the furs and
blankets. Ariana reached out to stroke his jaw with welcoming understanding, her breath rolling from between
her lips as she whispered his name once more. "Come to
me, my lord. I need you, too."

She touched him again, a feather-light grazing of her
fingers on his scar, then bolder as her hand skated down
his neck and along the front of his tunic. She caressed his
warm skin beneath the wool, allowing her hand to quest
lower, over the muscled firmness of his belly. "God help

me," he rasped, the words seeming to catch in his throat. "Do not stop there, my lady."

She knew at once what he wanted and slid her palm lower still, past the snug waist of his hose, to the swelling thrust of his arousal. She gripped him in her palm, squeezing his generous girth through the loose fabric that shrouded him, her gaze rooted on his. "More?" she asked, willfully teasing him with the friction of her hand on his member.

His reply was little more than an oath, strangled and rough with fever. Ariana stroked him more purposefully, brazen with this new feeling of power. She squeezed the rigid column of flesh, exalting in the hiss of pleasure that sifted between his teeth as he surged harder, larger, in her palm. "You will unman me, vixen."

"I think I should like to try."

"Bent on conquest, are you, lady?" He gave a deep, breathless laugh. "God's truth, but you already have me on my knees before you."

"Good," she purred, moving closer to him. "I cannot think of any better place for you, sirrah."

His slow, spreading smile held a wealth of masculine amusement. "I imagine I can think of a few better places for me. And for you." He lifted a dark brow. "Have a care, wench, or I might press you down and give you an example."

He sat back on his heels as he said it, widening his legs to give her greater access to him, clearly thrilling in his own capitulation as he thrust deeply into her commanding grasp. The wool of his clothing rasped against Ariana's palm, and against his stiffened member, which grew harder, more demanding. He groaned and closed his eyes, allowing her to drive him mindless with sensa-

tion. He watched her through half-lidded eyes as she slid
her fingers to the waistband of his drawers. His strong
hands threaded through her hair as she bent over him,
untying the laces that would free him of the restraining
clothes.

Ariana made quick work of the points and ties. With
the last undone, the front of his hose sagged low on his
hips and his sex sprang free, thick and smooth, glistening
with the evidence of his arousal. The same need throbbed
in her. The hand that had been moving in her hair now
stilled. His palm cupped the back of her skull, firm with
meaning. His eyes fixed on hers, he slowly guided her toward him. "I am desperate for you, angel. Please . . ."

She knew what he was asking of her, although a few
nights ago it would have been unimaginable to her to
think it, much less to want so badly to do it. More than
anything, she wanted to pleasure him. She needed him in
ways she could hardly fathom. Like this, she thought, admiring the magnificence of his body. She stroked his
naked member, thrilling in the tortured groan he gave
when she traced her fingers over the smooth head and
down along the rigid shaft. Licking her lips, Ariana bent
her head over him to take him into her mouth.

"Ah . . . God." Braedon shuddered as her lips closed
over his manhood. He sucked in a breath through
clamped teeth, fisting his hand in her hair. Ariana drew
on him gently at first, uncertain quite how to proceed,
but even that teasing kiss of contact seemed to enflame
him. She slid more of his length into her mouth, letting
her tongue dance along the underside of him as she grew
more bold. Gathering her hair in his hand, he lifted the
mass away from her face so he could watch her taste him.
The thought of him seeing her lips slide along his shaft
only heightened Ariana's pleasure in the act. It made her

take him deeper, each rough breath that soughed past his lips an encouragement to be more brazen. Each thrust of his hips, pumping in time with her rhythm, an invitation to be more ruthless in her assault on his senses.

Gasping, trembling, he suddenly took her by the shoulders and set her away from him. "I am your slave, lady," he said, an accusation and a plea, his voice rough with unspent passion. "Let me please you, Ariana."

He hauled her up onto her knees, framing her face in his hands as he bent down to capture her mouth with his. The musk of his body was salty-sweet in her nostrils and on her tongue. She reveled in the earthiness of their kiss, her limbs going boneless as Braedon pushed her down onto her back on the nest of coverlets. With a feral growl, he flung up her skirts, baring her to his roving gaze. He smoothed his hands up her legs, past the tops of her woolen hose, until his fingers trailed along the sensitive skin of her naked thighs. He caressed them both, then spread them wide. The backs of his knuckles skated over the thatch of springy curls between her legs, then down along the moist cleft of her womanhood. "So sweet," he praised her, "so ready for me."

With his gaze locked on hers, he slid his palms beneath her buttocks and lifted her hips off the ground, bending over her like a supplicant at the altar. He nuzzled her mound, parting her swollen folds with the tip of his tongue, cleaving her petals to find the pearl secreted within them. He suckled her as she had done him, enveloping the bud of her sex in his mouth, tonguing the tight nub until she was writhing and gasping in his arms, quivering with the impending onslaught of rapture. He sucked her deeper, ruthlessly feeding on her, holding her thighs apart and driving her toward her bliss. A shudder racked her, ecstasy so near it was dizzying. She cried his name, her back arching high, her body taut, hands clutching at him in mindless frenzy as her climax seized her.

And only then did he release her. Only when she was melting against his mouth, sated and breathless, did he relent and let her go, easing her back down onto the blankets.

With a fevered snarl, he covered Ariana and sheathed himself in one swift thrust. She cried out with heightened pleasure as he filled her, the glove of her womb gripping him in the final throes of her climax. He settled there for a moment, both of them relishing the sweet undulations of her flesh against his rigid sex. "God's love," he whispered roughly, "I cannot last now, not when you have me this close to madness."

Withdrawing in a slow, measured stroke, he brought her legs around him and filled her again, marveling aloud at the way she accommodated him, so small and tight, yet yielding, pliant. He thrust again, and Ariana felt the quickening begin to swell inside him. Faster, harder, he gave her all of him, as much as she could take. She watched, riveted, as he took her, seemingly mindless with passion, animal in his claiming of her. Panting, straining, he slid his hands beneath her and lifted her up off the ground to take him more fully. The sensation was exquisite, so raw and primal. When she began to gasp with the coming of another release, he seemed all but lost. He plunged in frenzy then, holding her gaze as the tremors of her orgasm racked her.

And then he was spending, too. He cursed, low and savage under his breath as the hot rush of his climax flooded her womb. Ariana cried out with the glory of it, her soft shout of bliss carrying into the darkened night. She held him to her, kissing his slackened mouth as they both quaked and trembled in the ebbing of shared pleasure.

Their bodies still intimately joined, Braedon rolled onto his shoulder, bringing her with him so that she now rested atop him. Ariana smiled down at him, feeling sly and disheveled, every bit the wanton. She shifted only slightly, her mound grinding against him, and the movement stirred him. He gave a deliberate thrust of his hips, grinning wickedly as his sex leaped, evidently eager for more. Pulling one of the furs over them, he settled Ariana beside him and traced the gentle slope of her cheek.

"What have you done to me, Ariana of Clairmont?" He gazed at her in quiet contemplation, his turning mind unreadable to her, even after all they had shared. "Sweet lady," he whispered. "How I wish I could promise you . . . God, promise you anything beyond this, what we share right now. I have nothing to offer . . . no future—not one you deserve."

She hushed him softly, laying her fingers over his lips. "I won't ask you for anything you cannot give. We're here now, and that is enough for me."

"No," he replied, "it is not enough. You deserve so much more than . . . this. You deserve much more than I can ever hope to give you, Ariana."

It pained her to hear him talk of all he was not, or could not allow himself to be. She loved him as he was, no matter what he could promise her, and love was all she needed of him as well. But as much as the words ached to be freed, she could not bear to speak them. Not when he might still reject her.

"This, what we have now, is enough for me," she told him, mustering a brave front as she held him a little tighter. She nestled against his warmth as he wrapped his arms around her and brought her deeper into his embrace. But he offered nothing more. Only the steady beat of his heart against her cheek, his hands tracing a soothing pattern on her shoulder as she drifted toward a sated doze.

It is enough, Ariana told herself, willing her heart to accept it.

If he could give her nothing more, then this fleeting pleasure would have to be enough.

❧ 16 ❧

SOMETIME CLOSE TO dawn, when Braedon finally allowed his eyes to close, he dreamed of the white wolf. He was sitting guard outside the narrow mouth of a rocky cleft, in a nameless forest west of a nameless town, when she came to him. Silver-furred and elegant, the she-wolf approached on silent feet, emerging like a wraith from out of the snowy thicket. No blood marred her glorious pelt, not a trace of the horrific, protruding arrows let loose on his father's command all those years past. She was as he liked to remember her: bold, inquisitive, and enigmatic. She loped right up to him like a favored hound and sat on her haunches, tilting her head at him as he slept. Her leathery black nose was cold and wet on his hand, her long tapered snout insistent as she burrowed it under his arm and nudged him awake.

Come, the compelling gray-green eyes seemed to say. *You have been asleep too long. Come with me. . . .*

And then he was following her, on his feet and jogging to keep pace as she led him soundlessly through one web of frosted branches and another, traversing the frozen forest as though on winged feet. The wolf cleared a fallen bough and paused to look back at him. It was the briefest hesitation, a glance to make certain he still followed, before she was suddenly gone, vanished in a sparkling fall of crystalline snow that filtered down from the treetops.

Braedon ran to the place where the wolf had been standing and abruptly drew back, unsteady on his feet. The toe of his boot perched at the very precipice of a deep ravine. Loose pebbles shifted underfoot and fell, noiselessly, over the steep ledge. He looked down and down . . . to the rocky, ice-slicked basin of the wide, jagged cleft. He searched for some trace of the wolf below, balancing himself at the edge of the chasm to look into it, his eyes anxiously scanning the crags for a glimpse of silver fur.

The wolf wasn't there. But he felt her keen gaze watching him from across the bottomless expanse of the ravine, where she sat, waiting for him in the roiling mist that gathered around her on the other side.

Leap, said the unblinking stare, beckoning to him, soliciting his trust. *You have the means. Accept and leap. It is safer for you over here.*

Braedon considered the advice with a reflexive stirring of doubt. He felt safe where he was, with his feet on solid, if immediately finite, ground. Below him loomed the open maw of death itself: black and cold, with hundreds of serrated teeth, eager to tear into him should he venture off the ledge. His fate was certain down there. But across the way, where the white wolf waited, there were only questions. Only mist where he would have to leap and hope to find firm footing.

Deep down, he trusted the wolf—she had always been his friend, a quiet protector to the boy he once was—but he knew that if he went to her now, there would be no turning back. He didn't know if he was ready. He didn't know if he was strong enough to accept . . .

"Braedon."

Tender, entreating, he heard the voice call to him. He paused at the chasm's edge, balanced but a heartbeat away from leaping. Then he heard it again: Ariana's voice, whisper-soft beside his ear.

"Braedon . . . are you all right?"

He came awake with a start, eyes focusing on the slightly downturned bow of Ariana's mouth. She was frowning, leaned over him in concern, her hand resting gently on his chest.

"I didn't mean to wake you, but you were breathing so strangely—as if you were running and couldn't catch your breath. Were you having a nightmare?"

"No," he said, mentally shaking off the vestiges of the queer dream. "It was nothing. I shouldn't have been sleeping so long."

"You hardly sleep at all, from what I know of you."

Ariana was cocooned with him in the tangle of blankets and furs that padded their improvised bed near the fire. The muted pink shades of dawn played over her skin as she reached out to caress his jaw. As pleasing as it was to feel her touch, Braedon turned out of her embrace and sat up, marshaling his thoughts around what lay ahead of them. "We shouldn't tarry. There is much to do this morning. Instructions for Kenrick's release must be delivered to de Mortaine, and we must make preparations for the meeting."

"Of course," Ariana agreed. "Should we go to them, do you think?"

Braedon gave a slight shake of his head, considering. "Nay. Here would be to our better advantage. After dark. We will need the cover of night to aid us in making the exchange."

"You have a plan for rescuing Kenrick?"

"A risky one," he admitted, "but I've thought it out, and I don't see any other way." He brushed his fingers over her brow, a warm caress that was both tender and fleeting. "Come. Let us get started. We'll send another message to de Mortaine, telling him how he is expected to proceed tonight. In the meantime, I will need you to help me gather as much kindling as we can find."

Bright light exploded in the darkness—blinding white, piercing—flooding in as the heavy cell door groaned open on its hinges. Kenrick of Clairmont instinctively looked away from the brilliant blast of illumination and shut his eyes. His arm went up to shield his face but was jerked back down with an abrupt metallic jangle. Ah, yes. His restraints, he realized with a dull sense of irony.

When he'd first been shackled with the iron cuffs and chains that hung from each of his limbs, they were a constant abrasion. A continuing source of fury. He had rebelled against them like an unbroken stallion fighting his first bit. Now, some untold time later—easily months, he had to believe—he often forgot they were there. Until he made the mistake of attempting to move within his cell and felt the steely bite of his bonds. His wrist burned with the new cut he'd just taken. Blood trickled along the muscle of his forearm, another laceration where he already bore many festering chafe marks.

He had been dreaming bizarre, nonsensical things in the moments before the door burst open. Not dreaming the usual assailing nightmares he had endured during his captivity, but instead of giant gape-mouthed sea creatures feasting on scrawny, mewling cats—strange musings from a mind that was likely going a little bit mad because of his confinement. He shook off the daze of his fitful sleep and squinted into the halo of torchlight that filled the cramped stone cell.

A tall, bulky shape lurked behind the flame. Kenrick recognized the air of menace radiating from the man. After consigning him to a seemingly endless solitary existence, interrupted only by frequent bouts of torture and an occasional bowl of runny gruel, Kenrick's captor appeared to have taken a sudden interest in him again. It could have only been an hour or two since the last time he'd been there, tossing him a loaf of bread with some murmurings that he would need to muster his strength. Kenrick had feigned disinterest but only until the door had closed on his captor's heels. Then he'd leaped on the bread like a ravenous beggar, wolfing the mealy loaf down so fast his starving stomach could not hold it. He'd vomited all of it up a moment later, miserable to have lost the meager meal but refusing to degrade himself with the thought of trying it again, no matter how starved he was. God only knew what this latest visit would bring. There was a measured clip of boot heels on the flagstones, the swish of silk robes as his captor came farther into the dank space.

"Back already, de Mortaine?" he drawled from the corner of his cell. "You should at least give me the proper chance to miss you. Have a care, or people will think we're in love."

Something crashed into the side of his head in reply—a fist, a boot? He couldn't be sure. Sparks danced behind his eyelids as his head snapped to the side and his neck absorbed the blow. He gave a low laugh, knowing it was his lack of fear—his carefully schooled show of apathy—that had kept him alive this long.

That, and the fact that his captors would be loath to kill him before he surrendered his secrets of the Dragon Chalice. Something he never intended to do, even if it did kill him one day.

"I see the food was not to your liking," mused the man who had hunted Kenrick down all those months ago and taken him captive. "No taste for maggots, eh, Clairmont?"

His eyes adjusting now to the light, Kenrick threw a glance at the rejected remains of the bread. His stomach heaved anew when he saw in the flickering torchlight that de Mortaine's taunt was in earnest. He steeled himself to the revolting notion, baring his teeth in a parody of a smile. "Perhaps I merely tired of them, after eating so much of the stuff in your gruel."

"So cocksure, aren't you? So damned unbreakable."

Kenrick grinned into the harsh glare of the torch, no mean feat when his jaw still ached from a recent beating. "Sorry to disappoint."

"You'll prove amusing enough, I wager, when you watch me slit your sister's throat tonight." Kenrick's gaze jerked to attention, and de Mortaine chuckled. "Oh, did I neglect to mention it before? She's here in Rouen. Your dear devoted sister, Ariana."

Now Kenrick laughed, suspecting a feint, some new ploy to get him to talk. "My sister is naught but a child. She's never ventured outside of Cornwall, much less into France. Clairmont is guarded by no fewer than one hundred knights, so unless you mean to have me think you rallied an army behind you to go and get her—"

"There was no need for such heavy-handed tactics. I merely invited her to come to me . . . and she did."

Suspicion melted into dread, an ice-cold prickle on the back of Kenrick's neck. "*Invited* her?"

"In a manner of speaking," de Mortaine purred. "Did you really think I would wait patiently for you to come around and tell me what I need to know about the Chalice? Surely you didn't expect your tiresome defiance to amuse me indefinitely. Steps had to be taken. Plans had to be made—certain precautions, if you will."

"What have you done to her?" Kenrick snarled. "If you've harmed her in any way—"

"My interest lies not in the chit herself, but in what she carries. You see, dear Ariana has brought me what you have refused to surrender all this time: your knowledge pertaining to the Dragon Chalice."

Kenrick swore an oath, glaring up at de Mortaine. "She doesn't know anything about it. I sheltered my family from knowing what I had found."

"Ah, but all those records you kept—all those journals you filled while you served the Order. They had to be kept somewhere, if you did not have them on your person. Your sister proved quite resourceful on that score."

God's blood. Ariana had found his satchel of papers. He had hidden it away when he departed for France, knowing it would be dangerous to carry the information with him. Once he realized what he'd discovered, he took measures to make sure his findings remained secure, but the bulk of his notes had been secreted at Clairmont in a satchel kept behind a false shelf in his chambers. He should have known he could hide nothing from Ariana if his determined little sister had a mind to uncover it. Clearly, de Mortaine had given her fair reason to do so. "And so you ransomed me to my family."

"Of course. Your life in exchange for your findings regarding the Chalice treasure. I told you I would have it one way or another. It is inevitable; the Dragon Chalice belongs to me. It is my destiny to possess it."

Ariana, Kenrick thought blackly. She had no idea what she had done in bringing that information to Silas de Mortaine. She was in grave danger simply for being in contact with the man, but more than that, if Kenrick's ideas about the treasure proved true—if the legend of the Dragon Chalice was at all based in fact—then in aiding de Mortaine's quest, Ariana was poised to unleash an evil like none the world had ever seen.

"I presumed this news would be of interest to you, Clairmont. I'm glad to see something has the power to deflate your overblown confidence." His eyes gleamed with malicious enjoyment. "Think on it while you wait here for me to summon you."

"Summon me to what?"

"Why, your death, of course. Your sister thinks she has the upper hand, but she'll learn otherwise. Evidently she has come to understand the value of what she possesses, and so she's begun making demands. Like her requirement for proof that you were yet alive. I did not appreciate being roused from my bed last eve to make you answer her cryptic query. You didn't appreciate it either, once we finished with you. Perhaps you don't recall; you were beaten quite senseless."

Oh, Jesu, Kenrick thought as realization dawned. His inexplicable dreams of whales and cats . . .

Jonah.

Now he remembered. It was the silly name he'd given one of Ariana's kittens some time ago at Clairmont. He remembered being forced to write it on a sheaf of parchment the night before, scratching out the name by candlelight, scarcely able to hang on to the quill. De Mortaine had knocked him into the stone wall an instant later, then more blows, until his head was ringing, until he could no longer think, and the cell went black once more.

De Mortaine was speaking again. "She's set a meeting for tonight, somewhere outside the city, where I am to deliver you in exchange for your journals and papers. I think I shall find it quite amusing to watch a heartfelt reunion of siblings . . . though not nearly as much as I will enjoy seeing your face as darling Ariana chokes on her last breath."

Kenrick knew he was being baited, and he ordered himself to stay calm. He believed de Mortaine was serious, but he would gain nothing by using the scant reserves of his strength to lash out in futile rage. The chains would bar him from reaching the whoreson, but once he was out of the cell he would have a fighting chance. He had to bide his time for now, and wait.

So long as he was breathing, de Mortaine would never get those papers.

"Well. We have much to look forward to. I won't keep you any longer, Clairmont."

De Mortaine lowered his torch and turned to depart the cell. Then, as if in afterthought, he whirled on Kenrick and landed his boot in his gut. Kenrick slumped over, clutching his stomach and tasting blood in his mouth. He spat it on the flagstones of the floor, letting his anger breed as the light in the cell was doused and the door closed tight with a bang.

Night was full upon the land, moonless, black, and still. The sky above Ariana's head was a deep, endless blanket of ebony, perforated by the pinprick whiteness of a thousand far-off stars. She shivered beneath the dwarfing vastness of it, pulling her mantle a bit tighter around her shoulders. Before her, in the roofless hollow of the ruined abbey's courtyard, a huge bonfire raged. Every twig and branch that could be scrounged from the area had since gone in to feed the giant conflagration, forming a wall of flame to serve as barrier between Ariana and the small company of riders who now approached the abbey. Over the steady rumble of the horses' hooves on the frozen earth could be heard the metallic jingle and bounce of saddle gear and weapons. Ariana's shiver became a sudden, bone-deep tremor.

The appointed hour had arrived.

Despite the sudden need for reassurance, she did not dare so much as glance over her left shoulder, toward the shadowed pillars of the abbey cloisters where Braedon waited under cover. She had to face Kenrick's captors alone, as was their original demand and present expectation, or all could be lost in a heartbeat. Ariana steeled herself as the sounds of coming riders drew nearer and figures began to take shape in the dark. Up the gently sloping rise they came, five men on horseback. Cloaked in dark habits and mantled in shadow, they rode forth with obvious purpose. Dare she hope that one of these stalwart men was Kenrick?

Peering into the lightless distance, Ariana saw now that there was a sixth man. No less substantial than his companions, this one rode in the center rear of the group, slumped forward in his saddle, broad shoulders hanging weary as though burdened with an unbearable weight. He jostled haphazardly with every stride of his mount, and it was plain that it commanded all his strength merely to stay upright in the saddle. Ariana knew in her heart this haggard prisoner was her brother, and she swallowed past a cold lump of sorrow. His subjugation would end tonight. Tightly fisting her hands to keep them from shaking, Ariana squared her shoulders and prepared herself for the confrontation that was soon to occur.

With no gate to bar them from the ruin, the troop of guards cantered their horses past the half-fallen walls of the abbey and into the wide expanse of the courtyard. The man at the head of the group halted the others without a word, merely raising his hand to stop them while he allowed his mount to advance another few paces forward.

"Well . . . Ariana of Clairmont," he said by way of greeting, addressing her from within the deep cowl of his dark mantle. His breath must have been as cold as his heart, for despite the chill in the night air, his words did not steam past his thin, cruel lips. "You've been quite a tax on my patience, girl. I hope you don't intend to let this little game play out any longer."

"Let me see my brother."

"As you wish," came the cool reply. "Bring the prisoner here."

One of the guards at the rear gave a nudge of his sword to the flanks of the horse next to him. The beast moved forward, carrying the bent figure of a man. Covered in a tattered blanket, the rags of his filthy, torn clothing visible through the moth holes and fraying, was Kenrick. Little wonder he could hardly sit upright to ride. His hands were bound before him, with no gloves to protect them, and only the thinnest scraps of leather covered his feet, the soiled bits of hide laced round and round with string to keep the soles from falling away.

Ariana let her gaze stray upward, toward the bent head and the stringy, overlong hair that drooped past his shoulders. That this abused creature was her golden, heroic brother tore at her heart like nothing she had ever known. He looked up as his mount drew to a halt beside Silas de Mortaine, slowly lifting his head. His cracked lips parted in a pained half smile. "Greetings, Ana."

"Kenrick." His name was little better than a weak croak when she saw how badly beaten his face was, how emaciated and pale her robust older brother had become since he'd been in de Mortaine's care. Ugly bruises and

slow-healing, oozing lacerations marred his cheeks and
brow. His right eyelid drooped half-closed, puffy from
recent abuse, and his lower lip was split open where a
scab had hardly formed from the last beating.

He was in a terrible state, but even with his head
slumped in submission, he held her gaze with the same
fortitude he'd always possessed. Despite the torture he
had obviously endured in his captivity, there was a spark
of fury—a glint of ready determination—in the steady
gaze that reached out to her across the distance that separated them. Kenrick might have been nearly broken
physically, but by the grace of God, his spirit remained
intact.

A swell of hot tears rushed up behind Ariana's eyes as
she took silent inventory of her brother's damage, but she
held her sympathy at bay, knowing there would be time
for emotion once Kenrick was free. For the moment, she
needed to maintain her focus, and her anger, which she
now centered wholly on Silas de Mortaine.

"As you can see, he is alive," de Mortaine said.

"Yes, barely," Ariana charged.

"Let's not quibble over details, shall we?" He took a
step forward and thrust out a gloved hand. "Bring me the
satchel, girl."

"Ariana, don't." Kenrick's order rasped between his
swollen lips. "Don't give it to h—"

De Mortaine shot a glare in the direction of the guard
nearest Kenrick, who delivered a heavy-handed blow to
his already battered face. Kenrick swayed in his saddle
but kept his gaze fixed on Ariana. Wincing in obvious
pain, he stared at her from beneath the hank of dulled
golden hair that had fallen over his scraped and bruised
brow. He gave a meaningful shake of his head, a further

silent communication that no matter what he suffered, he did not wish her to surrender the bag to his captors.

Ariana drew a steadying breath. "Release my brother and you can have the satchel. Not before."

De Mortaine's sharp bark of laughter made her flinch where she stood. "What's this—more demands? Really, now. You are only making things worse. For your brother, certainly, but also for yourself. Give me the satchel, stupid girl . . . and perhaps I will allow the both of you to live long enough to walk away from here."

"Don't believe him, Ana! He means to kill us both regardless—"

"Silence him!" boomed de Mortaine, his soulless eyes flashing hellfire. While one of the guards drew a sword and held it at Kenrick's throat, de Mortaine looked back at Ariana with a deadly smile. "The satchel, little fool. Where is it?"

She shook her head, refusing to give in to the wave of fear that rose to engulf her. "Release him now, or you will never have it."

A tendon twitched in de Mortaine's jaw as he measured her threat. Gaze piercing, thin nostrils flaring as if he scented her trepidation, he gave a cool order to his guard. "Open his gullet and let him bleed a while before he dies."

"No!"

Ariana's exclamation of horror was punctuated by a sudden disturbance of the air beside her. From out of the cloister shadows, before any of de Mortaine's men could move a muscle in obedience of his command, Braedon walked his mount into the center of the courtyard. "I wouldn't advise it, de Mortaine."

Everyone stilled as he rode out and paused near the

bonfire. He raised his left hand, which was fisted around the long strap of a brown leather satchel. In the undulating glow of the fire, the fat pouch dangled before him like the most tempting bit of bait swinging on the end of a tether. In truth, the bag contained nothing more than some of Braedon's soiled clothing and some small rocks, which they had found earlier that day while gathering kindling for the blaze that now illuminated the abbey courtyard and the disbelieving look on Silas de Mortaine's face.

With a slantwise sneer, he encouraged the guard on Kenrick to heel. "Well, well . . . le Chasseur. This is an interesting wrinkle, although not entirely unexpected. Ferrand informed me some time ago that you were still breathing. A miracle, no doubt, after the shape I left you in last time we met. And an oversight. It will be my pleasure to make sure the devil takes you this time."

"Braedon," Ariana whispered, gesturing with her eyes to where one of de Mortaine's men slyly unlashed a crossbow from his saddle and brought the weapon onto his lap.

"He won't fire," Braedon replied, his gaze locked on de Mortaine. "One false move, and this satchel goes up in flames."

"You're bluffing, le Chasseur."

Ariana felt her throat constrict at that calm assertion. She swallowed hard, trying to tamp down her worry as she fought to maintain her courage. If their ruse was discovered already, none of them would escape the night with their lives. De Mortaine's amused chuckle only heightened her fear.

"You must think me a fool to believe you'd destroy the satchel. You know as well as I the value of the Dragon

Chalice. You want to find the treasure as much as I do;
you wouldn't be here otherwise."

The breath Ariana had been holding now leaked out of
her in a quiet sigh of relief. Thank the Lord. They weren't
found out . . . yet.

"Send Clairmont forward, de Mortaine. I'd rather see
this satchel in a pile of cinders than let it fall into your
hands." As he spoke, Braedon allowed his mount to sidle
ever closer to the bonfire. "Release him. Let's have done
with this meeting."

"You say release him, and I say not until I have the
satchel. It appears we are at an impasse."

Braedon gave a grunt and shrugged his shoulder. "Nay,
I don't think so."

The long strap of the leather bag slipped through his
fingers a few inches, falling quickly. It bobbed to an end
only when the flames of the bonfire nearly licked at the
bottom of the satchel. De Mortaine's eyes followed the
downward path of his prize, his emotionless gaze flickering now with a spark of uncertainty, and, Ariana
thought, not a little worry. She bit her lip, sharing some
of that worry, praying for the moment of chance Braedon
now provoked.

"Release Kenrick of Clairmont. I won't say it again."

"Untie him," de Mortaine growled to the nearest
guard, his eyes never leaving Braedon and the satchel that
yet dangled dangerously close to the fire. To Kenrick, he
said, "You see, Clairmont? I told you I'd have it. And
know this, too: My promise to you this afternoon still
stands."

Ariana felt the danger in that promise, and she threw
an anxious look at Braedon, whose gaze remained fixed
steadfastly and unwavering on de Mortaine. Nervously,

she watched as Kenrick's bonds were cut loose from his hands. She saw her brother flex his long fingers, then caught only the briefest flash of fury in his blue eyes before he lunged for the guard's dagger and plunged it home in the man's chest.

"Ariana, run!" he shouted as he shoved de Mortaine's dead man to the ground. "Run, Ana! Get out of here now!"

"The satchel!" de Mortaine bellowed over the madness that had suddenly erupted. "Seize it from him!"

Ariana jerked in startlement as the courtyard rang with the ensuing chaos, but she didn't run. She and Braedon had wanted this sort of confusion. They had planned for it, knowing it was their only hope of getting close enough to Kenrick to assure his escape—but they had not expected him to instigate the action. Braedon sprung upon the serendipitous opportunity, ordering her to stay back, out of the fray. Then, with de Mortaine watching in wide-eyed horror, his three remaining guards rushing headlong on his command, Braedon tossed the leather satchel high into the air and let it fall deep into the center of the pyre.

"No!" De Mortaine's howl echoed with unearthly fury as the bonfire spat a plume of smoke and sparking ash high into the night sky. "Get it, you idiots! I must have that satchel!"

Everything was happening in a blur of activity. Ariana saw Braedon dispatch one of the guards, cleaving him in twain with a mighty swipe of his broadsword. Another had leaped off his mount to combat the fire with his mantle, beating the conflagration in a vain attempt to smother the roaring flames that now consumed his overlord's false prize. She saw Kenrick wheeling his mount about to grab at the reins of the dead guard's palfrey.

And there was de Mortaine, launching himself off his shying, wild-eyed steed and stalking toward the bonfire as if to conquer it by sheer force of will alone. Cursing, shaking with a rage that seemed beyond the grasp of anything human, he shed his fine mantle and threw it aside. He walked closer to the flames—right up to the very edge, unhesitating. Unafraid.

Nay, what she saw was impossible!

Frozen in astonishment, Ariana blinked away the smoke that blurred her vision, certain that the spiraling ash and churning heat was playing tricks on her eyes. It had to be a trick. Either that, or . . .

Silas de Mortaine had walked straight into the heart of the roaring bonfire.

"Ariana!" Kenrick's voice from across the courtyard rattled her stunned gaze away from the undulating flames that had just devoured de Mortaine. "Ariana—here! Hurry!"

He rode toward her with a second mount and tossed her the reins. She ran up to the horse and seated herself astride, breathless as she watched Braedon slay the last guard and wheel his palfrey around to join them.

"Are you fit to ride?" he asked Kenrick as he sheathed his bloody sword.

"I've been better, but I'll manage."

"My lady?"

Braedon's eyes were wild as they settled on Ariana. She nodded urgently, bolstered by the strength of his hand as he reached out to squeeze her trembling fingers. "Let's away," she gasped. "Let's get as far away from here as we can."

With that, the trio kicked their mounts into a hard gallop and fled the hellish inferno that roared and spat like a dragon, unleashed and rampant in the center of the ghostly abbey.

✥ 17 ✥

THEY DIDN'T DARE slow their gait until the outskirts
of Rouen lay some untold miles behind them. The horses
were lathered in a cold sweat, huffing and straining to
obey the unyielding urgency of their riders. The night itself was nearly spent as well, giving quarter to the pinkish gold fingers of dawn, which curved gently over the
horizon, turning the new day.

Although he was not convinced it was prudent to stop,
Braedon could not force them any farther. If it didn't
mean the certain death of their mounts, pushing on even
another mile stood a good chance of killing Ariana's
brother. Battered and bloodied, slumped in his saddle,
Kenrick was running on pure will alone. But like his stubborn sister, Braedon doubted very much the man would
cry mercy until he was knee-deep in the grave. While he
appreciated the stalwartness of the Clairmont line, he
hadn't gone to the trouble of finding the errant Templar
scholar only to kill him in the escape.

Braedon reined in with a low call to his wheezing
mount. Ariana and Kenrick did likewise, drawing to a
halt at the frosted edge of a wide tract of marshy land.
"There's a farm up ahead," he said, gesturing toward a
squat little domicile and an adjacent barn. "We can stop
here and rest awhile."

He procured them lodgings in the outbuilding. It was

cold and ripe with the smell of livestock, but there was a pile of winter straw that would make a soft enough bed, particularly after so many hours in the saddle. While Ariana fashioned an empty stall into sleeping quarters for her brother, Braedon tended the horses. He heard the rich murmur of her voice as she spoke to Kenrick, her many concerned questions answered by little more than grunts and nearly incoherent mumblings.

"How does he fare?" Braedon asked her when she came out of the stall a short time later.

"He was asleep nearly before his head hit the pallet. I've never seen him so exhausted and weak. He won't tell me what he endured all these months he's been imprisoned, although his mistreatment is obvious. On top of his numerous cuts and bruises, two of his fingers are broken, and the way his chest pains him to breathe, I suspect he also suffers damage to his ribs."

"He's alive."

"Yes," she said, smiling tremulously. "Thank God, he's alive. And thanks to you most especially, Braedon. I owe you so much for all you've done, for everything you've risked to help me. You have put your life in jeopardy for us, and I . . . I don't see how I can ever repay you."

He blew out a sardonic laugh as he rubbed down the last mount, thinking on all he had done where Ariana was concerned—not the least of which being his ruthless seduction of her into his bed. She had been in danger with him at every turn since the moment they met, and if he helped win her brother's freedom in the end, he reckoned she had already more than paid the price.

He walked past her to get a bucket of water for the horses. "You don't owe me anything. And you shouldn't be standing here talking about it when you ought to be trying to get some sleep, too. You're shivering."

She made no effort to move, and when Braedon looked at her askance, ready to order her beneath a blanket before she dropped like a lump of ice, he realized that it wasn't cold making her tremble. It was fear. She was quaking with it, as if she had held it at bay for as long as she could but now it threatened to devour her. She was staring at him in quiet torment, her soft blue eyes muted to a haunted shade of indigo.

"What is it? What's wrong?"

"Braedon, I saw something at the abbey tonight . . . something . . . terrible. De Mortaine. He—"

She broke off and looked at him helplessly, adrift with such emotion, he set the bucket of water down and went to her. She didn't wait for him to open his arms but wrapped herself around him, clinging to his waist as though he was her anchor. He petted her hair, smoothing it off her face as she looked up at him, jaw quivering. "I won't let him hurt you, Ariana. Don't be afraid."

"De Mortaine is dead," she blurted, shaking her head. "He walked into the center of the bonfire while you were fighting his guards. The fire swallowed him up."

"What do you mean, he walked into the fire?"

"He killed himself—I saw him! He took off his mantle and strolled into the heart of the flames after you threw the satchel in. He's dead, Braedon . . . and it terrifies me how glad I am for it."

He hugged her more tightly as he absorbed the news of de Mortaine's apparent demise, but inwardly he wondered. Hearing this now, it would be impossible not to think on another day in the past, another confrontation with the man called Silas de Mortaine. That day, it had not been flames but Braedon's sword that ended his villainous existence.

Or should have.

Braedon could still feel the queer give of his blade as it cleaved down across de Mortaine's torso . . .

And passed clean through without delivering so much as a scrape.

Unfathomable, and yet undeniable. And now this, he thought grimly, absently pressing a kiss to the top of Ariana's head, allaying her fears with the warmth of his embrace while his heart grew chilled with foreboding.

Damnation, but nothing made sense to him anymore. Not the past, and not this surreal present that kept him running, forever in hiding. Nothing made sense to him at all, save the soft, warm feel of Ariana as she clung to him in the musty chill of the barn. She was the only thing he could trust, his light in a world of dark, unexplainable treachery. He cursed himself for having brought her into that nightmarish world. Now it was too late to turn back. They were in it together.

"Think no more on Silas de Mortaine," he whispered into the silkiness of her hair. "Think no more on any of this, my lady. You're safe now. I pledge it with my life."

With a gentle touch, he lifted her chin and bent to kiss her. It was brief, for he dared take no more than the smallest taste of her lips when he longed to hold her, naked and willing, beneath him. She responded as sweetly as ever, twining her fingers in his hair and pressing her soft curves against the rigidness of his body. There was a note of disappointment in her eyes as he drew away from her.

She reached for him again, and he caught her hands to kiss each one in turn. Reading the desire in her gaze—indeed, sharing it and trying his damnedest to resist it—he gave her a slow shake of his head. "It's late, and you've been through quite an ordeal. Tomorrow we head for the coast, and, with any luck, swift passage back to England. It will be a hard ride; you should sleep while you have the chance."

"I don't want to sleep. I don't feel safe unless you're holding me." She stroked his grizzled jaw. "Will you, please . . . I need you to hold me, Braedon."

Unable to deny her, he took her back in his arms and held her for a long time. Simply held her, until she began to sway sleepily in his embrace, her head dropping onto his chest as exhaustion rose up to claim her. When her limbs went loose, he scooped her up and brought her to the mound of straw that was to be his bed that night. He laid her down on his mantle and reclined beside her, covering them both with the blankets from his saddle packs. She curled into his body as she fell into a deep slumber, holding him tight in her sleep.

His light, he thought, his lips curving into a contented, if bittersweet, smile as he enveloped her in his arms. What a fool he had been to let Ariana throw open the door to his heart. Now that she had illuminated his life in so many ways, the darkness that awaited him once she was gone promised to be all the colder for her absence.

Ash and charred rubble crunched underfoot as Draec le Nantres was admitted into the keep of de Mortaine's castle in Rouen. The pitch torches, spitting in their iron cressets on the wall, scarcely banished the darkened gloom of the place, which seemed overrife with the acrid tang of brimstone and smoke. He looked down, puzzling over the trail of cinders on the floor, which the meek, mousy little man who let him in was presently attempting to sweep away.

"Dear oh dear oh dear. What a mess, I tell you. A terrible, terrible mess."

Bent over his broom and bucket, pate tonsured like that of a monk, the man muttered further complaints under his breath as Draec walked past, heading for the great hall where he had been summoned upon his arrival at the castle. Across the wide expanse of the place, seated at the dais, was Silas de Mortaine. Golden-haired, fresh from a bath and draped in the finest silk-and-velvet robes, he stared at Draec over steepled fingers. Two large knights flanked him on either side like twin hounds of hell, arms crossed over their massive chests, dullish eyes fixed on Draec.

"Your impeccable timing seems to be failing you, le Nantres. I could have used you hours ago."

"All due respect," Draec drawled as he advanced farther into the hall, casually stripping off his gauntlets as he came to stand before his employer. "But the last I knew, my orders were to intercept a certain package en route from England."

"That package, mayhap?" Watching him closely, de Mortaine jerked his chin at a blackened lump of burnt leather sitting at the edge of the table before him. Draec glanced toward the charred pouch, then back at de Mortaine, frowning in uncertainty. "Go on, have a look inside."

Cautiously, knowing precisely what the satchel could not contain, he threw open the flap closure and briefly scanned the contents. "There's nothing in here but some old clothing and a handful of rocks. A pack of rubbish."

"A decoy, meant to distract me long enough to manage an escape," de Mortaine hissed, the venom in his voice acid enough to tell the rest of the tale.

"Kenrick of Clairmont has escaped?"

"His sister orchestrated a ruse, using that false satchel," he fumed, pointing a long finger at the charred bag as though he wished to command it to dust with his eyes.

"Clever girl," Draec remarked, thinking on the courage he had seen in the pretty blonde the night he stole the true satchel from her at the inn. The one he had been dissecting in private on his own, cryptic note by cryptic note, ever since.

"The chit is a fool if she thinks she has succeeded," de Mortaine said. "More the fool, if she and her brother intend to use what he knows to aid them in going after the Chalice stone."

"Do you credit that to be their intention?"

"I'm not willing to take that chance, particularly when I know that they are in league with le Chasseur." Slowly de Mortaine took a sip from a golden cup. "You do not seem surprised."

Draec shrugged, too late to pretend otherwise. He held himself still where he stood, careful to reveal nothing more of his thoughts to the probing gaze that watched him over the rim of the gilded goblet. "Braedon holds a grudge well, and who can resist the lure of the riches promised by the Dragon Chalice?"

"Indeed," de Mortaine mused, his cold eyes slitting to razors of warning.

"It was only a matter of time before le Chasseur came after it himself," Draec added. "If anything surprises me, it is that he survives to do so at all. We left him in a bad way that night."

"I don't detect a note of sympathy for an old friend, do I, le Nantres?"

"Not at all," Draec replied truthfully.

"Good. Because I want him dead this time—I want all three of them dead."

Although he had no taste for murder, Draec nodded in grim acceptance of his orders. He was no stranger to dealing death with his sword on the battlefield, but he had yet to stoop to delivering it in cold blood. Least of all to a woman. Or to the man who had ridden beside him into those many battles, who guarded his back on more than one occasion when death likely had the right to claim him.

He had no wish to slay Braedon le Chasseur . . . but he would, if his old friend was fool enough to stand in his way of finding the Chalice treasure. If the Dragon Chalice truly held what its legend promised—life immortal, the power of the ages—Draec le Nantres meant to win it for himself. He might even be tempted to sell his everlasting soul, did he not fear it already had been forfeited to the black-hearted creature who leaned back in his ornate chair and summoned a trembling page to bring him more wine.

"Do you think they've gone to look for one of the Chalice stones?"

"Wouldn't you?" de Mortaine queried, measuring him with a slow glance.

Draec shrugged. "I might, if I thought I had a good notion of where to find it."

"Kenrick of Clairmont seems to think he does."

"And you believe him?"

"I can ill afford not to," came the slow reply. "His work for the Templars had merit, certainly. The pattern he uncovered was one I'd never seen before, although he spared me but the briefest explanation of his discovery. I would have paid him handsomely for his findings, but he refused. Not even torture was enough to loosen his tongue." A vicious curse snarled from between de Mortaine's gritted teeth and he slammed his fist down on the table. "By nails and blood, I need that second Chalice stone. I *will* have it!"

The page who had come to replenish his wine jolted at the outburst, spilling the fine claret over the edge of the cup. De Mortaine's chastising fist cuffed the youth on the side of the head. "Clumsy idiot. Begone—and fetch Arnaud on your way out," he added in a growl as the youth hastened away with his pitcher. De Mortaine looked once more to Draec, smiling thinly. "I like you, le Nantres. You have proven your worth in the past, but I need to know I can still trust you. I need to know I have your allegiance."

"Have I given reason to doubt?" he asked, but no answer seemed forthcoming.

In the meanwhile, the double doors of the great chamber creaked open and in scurried the monkish mouse from the entry hall. Still covered in soot and grime from his task outside, Arnaud nervously wiped his hands on his long robes, then offered an awkward bow as he approached the center of the room. "Yes, yes, my lord? How may I assist you?"

De Mortaine spared the obeisant man not even the barest glance of acknowledgment. "You see, le Nantres, unlike Arnaud here, you still have a purpose. You understand the value of efficiency."

"M-my lord?" stammered the little man. "Dear, oh dear! Do I displease, my lord?"

"I can appreciate eager obedience," de Mortaine went on idly, all his focus trained on Draec. "But I cannot abide a bungler. Arnaud's sluggishness in informing me of the Clairmont woman's arrival in Rouen cost me valuable time. You will make sure it doesn't cost me anything more."

A gasp of panic sounded beside Draec as Arnaud rushed forward to plead his case before the dispassionate countenance of his master. "But—but, my lord! I vow to you—I brought you the news as quickly as I could! I tried—"

"You failed," de Mortaine stated blithely.

He looked to each of the two guards flanking his chair and gave a slight nod of command. The knights moved in unison, vaulting over the table to pounce upon the quaking Arnaud.

Except they were no longer men at all.

There, in the blink of an eye, Draec found himself staring at the horrific sight of two large wolves, slashing and tearing in a blur of black fur and gnashing, lethal jaws. Arnaud's anguished screams rang high in the rafters of the hall, scraping Draec to his very marrow.

"God's blood!" he exclaimed, leaping out of the way of the hellish beasts and turning his disbelieving eyes on Silas de Mortaine, who watched the carnage with a mild smile curving his lips. "What the devil—?"

"Merely a demonstration, le Nantres. Perhaps an overdue one."

Draec's hand flew to his weapon. An instinctive urge to assist the helpless man, some ancient code of honor that he would have thought long dead, rose in him with a fury as he looked upon the annihilation playing out before him. He drew his sword, then realized Arnaud was already dead. But still the desecration continued. "By all that is holy," he ground out, scarcely able to mask his revulsion. "Call them off, whatever they are. For pity's sake—"

"Pity?" De Mortaine chuckled. "I have none. And you'd do well to remember that while you are hunting for your old friend and his companions. I want them found at once." A snap of his fingers brought the inhuman guards to heel. Restored to the semblance they bore at the dais, the two men, blood-soaked and panting, left the broken body of the little monk. They came to stand beside Draec, awaiting de Mortaine's command. "Assemble a riding party from the garrison. These good fellows here will also accompany you on your mission. I shall look forward to your successful—expedient—return."

Shaken more than he cared to admit by what he had just witnessed, Draec sheathed his weapon and accepted his orders with a curt nod of his head. But as he quit the great hall with de Mortaine's minions hard at heels, his heart was racing as though to explode. His hands were shaking as he shoved them into his gauntlets and shouted a brusque order for a squire to ready his mount.

For the first time in all his years of knighthood and combat, Draec le Nantres had finally gotten a healthy taste of real, breath-robbing fear.

❧ 18 ❧

BRAEDON FELT A cold edge of steel come to rest at his throat as he slept. He lifted his eyelids in the gloom of the barn, determining the source of the threat even before his gaze clashed with that of Ariana's brother. He did not have to reach for the dagger he had left nearby to know that it was already lost and quite neatly turned on him. Wheezing somewhat from his injuries, if undaunted, Kenrick of Clairmont leaned over the makeshift pallet, his offended stare sliding from Braedon's face to the slumbering young woman in his arms.

"If you're going to wake me to the taste of steel, you'd better be damned sure you have the strength to use it," Braedon advised in a low murmur.

The dagger pressed closer in answer. "Get up, knave."

Extricating himself from Ariana's sleep-heavy, languid embrace, Braedon moved out from under the warm blankets. In his wake, she shifted, catlike and sensual as she slept on, her hands idly searching him out when he pivoted to the edge of the pile of straw. He retrieved his boots and pulled them on, thankful for the practicality of having decided to sleep in his clothes. Had he not, he felt certain Clairmont would not have afforded him the luxury of waking up to face his brotherly ire. He stood up and gave an obliging tilt of his chin.

"Outside," Kenrick ordered, brandishing the dagger as he followed Braedon out of the barn.

Dawn was barely a glimmer on the eastern horizon. Braedon strode a few paces away from the outbuilding and cursed the frigid cold that seeped through his tunic and into his bones.

"I know who you are," Kenrick of Clairmont said without preamble at his back the moment they paused in the yard. "Don't assume my mind is so dulled from my stay in de Mortaine's dungeon that I did not hear him call you *le Chasseur*. Your reputation precedes you, Hunter."

"Does it?" Braedon turned around to face him, his breath steaming through his curved lips as he exhaled a sardonic chuckle. "Then I expect we have no reason to stand here freezing our ballocks off over lengthy introductions."

When he moved to brush past the younger knight, the dagger came up a bit closer, cutting off his leave. "I can guess how a mercenary blackguard such as yourself would be associated with scum like de Mortaine, but what business have you with my sister?"

Braedon eyed the blade with scorn, insulted more by its insistent, needless threat than he was by Clairmont's slurs against his honor. Had he a beautiful young sister who'd become enmeshed with a scoundrel like himself, he would be equally upset and eager to do harm. But he was too tired, and too damned cold, to suffer the intended intimidation any longer. "You can either use that blade or sheath it. If we talk now, I won't do so staring down the length of my own weapon."

Reluctantly, with a glare that said this coolheaded man was as much soldier as he was scholar or saint, Kenrick of Clairmont lowered the knife. Lowered it, but held it tight in his grasp all the same. "I would have your answer, sirrah. How is it you find yourself in Ariana's company? More to the point, how do you answer to the way I found you with her on that pallet in there?"

Braedon decided to address the first part first. "You find me in her company for the simple fact that she asked me to be. She needed escort and transportation to Rouen to deliver your ransom. As I had a vessel docked in London, she hired me to bring her here . . . more or less," he amended, thinking back on the tangle of circumstances that bound them together that day he first saw her in the Queenhithe tavern.

Kenrick swore a particularly vivid oath. "Are you saying she ventured here to come to my aid without escort? By herself? Nay, Ariana is too sheltered—and she is wiser than that."

"She was coerced because of your capture. The ransom demand specified she come alone to deliver your journals and papers to an appointed meeting place in Rouen. It would have been suicide, certainly. To her credit, she brought a guard with her from Clairmont, someone she trusted, but he was killed by some of de Mortaine's spies before she left London. She would have suffered similarly if I had not stumbled upon the altercation and intervened."

"God's blood," Kenrick muttered. "I cannot believe she would be so reckless as to attempt such a thing. And surely my father would never have allowed her—"

"Your father is dead," Braedon interjected soberly. "No doubt Ariana would have wished to bring you the news in her own time, but since you would drag me from my bed to have words, I reckon you need to know the facts."

The news seemed to take him aback, diffusing some of his virulence. "Our father is . . . dead?"

"Some months ago, as I understand. While you have been chasing clues and making mortal enemies over the Dragon Chalice, your sister had to remain at Clairmont, living in the shadow of your ghost. She has much to prove—to herself, at least, as your father perished without troubling to acknowledge his pride in her. She is devoted to her family, which has come down to you alone, and nothing would have kept her from seeing you safely home. Not even the peril of facing her own death."

Kenrick was frowning now, staring at him in astonishment. "She told you all of this?"

"I've come to understand quite a bit about your sister in the time we have been together."

"Together," Kenrick repeated, his previous bewilderment replaced by a sudden, visible bristling. Doubtless he could read the meaning that Braedon did not connive to conceal. "Is that all the explanation you will give me as to the intimacy you two share?"

Now it was Braedon's turn to rankle. "In truth, I don't see how you are due a further explanation."

"I am her brother, sir. And with my father dead and gone, as you inform me, it would seem I am now the man responsible for securing Ariana's future."

"And I am the man who loves her," Braedon answered before he could bite back the confession.

"You *love* her?" Kenrick challenged disbelievingly. "She is but a child—"

Braedon shook his head, chuckling. "As I said. You have been away from Clairmont a long time, Kenrick. Ariana is no child. She is a woman full grown. The most courageous, enchanting—and, if I am being completely honest—the most perplexing woman I have ever known."

"And I suppose you are going to tell me that she loves you as well?"

"I am loath to flatter myself into thinking that she could."

Kenrick sighed at length and surrendered the dagger he gripped loosely in his hand. "You have my gratitude for offering her your sword arm and protection, but I trust you will forgive me if I say that when it comes to her future, Ariana deserves better than you."

"Yes," Braedon said, taking no offense, for he had recognized that fact himself within moments of meeting her. "I know she deserves better. And I am well aware of all that I cannot offer her. As you pointed out, my reputation precedes me."

"You will not deny that you once worked for de Mortaine?"

"I do not deny it. He hired me to retrieve something for him—"

"Avosaar," Kenrick interjected. "The Stone of Prosperity. It is one of four sacred pieces of the Dragon Chalice."

"Aye, I have heard the tales."

Clairmont's blue eyes flashed with the same intensity as his sister's so often did. "The treasure is no myth, le Chasseur. I have been studying it for years. It is real—as real as the dark magic that surrounds it. De Mortaine understands this magic, perhaps even controls it somehow. But not entirely. He is limited in his power, so long as the Dragon Chalice remains out of his grasp."

"And he will stop at nothing to have it," Braedon said.

Kenrick nodded. "When I realized what I had discovered in my work for the Templar Order, I took steps to protect my findings. I knew it wasn't safe to keep it all in one place, so I divided up my work and hid part of it away from Clairmont. The satchel Ariana delivered contained only a portion of my records. A portion, but still too much knowledge should it fall into de Mortaine's hands." He reached out and clapped his palm on Braedon's shoulder. "Thank God you tossed it into that bonfire. Better the lot of my work be destroyed than surrender any bit of it to him."

"Indeed. Would that were the case." Braedon cleared his throat and slanted a rueful look at the younger knight. "It was a false bag that went into the fire."

"What?"

"The satchel I burned tonight was nothing but a sack of rubbish meant to trick de Mortaine into giving you up. It was a ruse."

"God's blood." Kenrick's mouth quirked into the beginnings of a grin. "Then you still have it? Tell me you still have my work."

Braedon slowly shook his head. "One of de Mortaine's men stole it from us a few nights ago outside Rouen. Draec le Nantres has your satchel. I expect 'tis only a matter of time before he gives it up to de Mortaine."

Kenrick's low-voiced oath hissed between his teeth. "They will be looking for the rest of the Chalice."

"No doubt they already are," Braedon replied. "They'll be looking for us, too. We won't have much time before they rout us out."

"No," Kenrick agreed, nodding soberly. "However, there is still the matter of my sister and you. What do you want with Ariana?"

"The truth? I am no longer certain, save that I want her out of harm's way. I want her protected from all of this madness."

"Even if that means protecting her from yourself?"

Braedon met the intense blue gaze of Ariana's brother and held it.

"There is a price on your head now, le Chasseur. You crossed de Mortaine tonight. I'm sure I needn't tell you what hell that can bring."

"Nay," Braedon said, requiring no reminders. "I have seen it firsthand."

"Then you also know he must not be permitted to succeed in this. He already has one of the stones. If he recovers the three others, he will have the power of the Dragon Chalice and it will be too late. He has to be stopped now."

"Not by me. And not by you, if your sister is involved in any way. Ariana's safety is what matters most to me. If you care for her, you need to get her out of here." Braedon stared hard at her brother. "Dawn is on the rise. I want to be on the road and heading for the coast in less than an hour."

"Le Chasseur . . . Braedon," Kenrick said from behind him. "Silas de Mortaine is not a man like you or me. There is true evil in him—something . . . unnatural. I cannot walk away knowing he is out there, doing his dark work. Can you?"

Halfway to the barn, Braedon paused. "One hour," he repeated, ignoring the implication that it was somehow his concern to thwart de Mortaine's crazed intentions. But even as he thrust aside the notion, inwardly his conscience flared hot with contradiction. He squeezed his hands into tight fists and, with a muttered curse, strode into the barn to prepare to depart.

They were better than half a dozen leagues on the road that day when something pricked Braedon's instincts to alert. He said nothing to indicate his apprehension, cantering his mount alongside Ariana's on the narrow track of road that followed the Seine River, more or less, toward the coast. He quieted his senses and focused on the imperceptible stir of the air around them. His nostrils flared, scenting danger on the approach.

Death, to be sure. Riding hard, hell-bent to find them. He had but a moment to register the threat before the sound of distant, thundering hoofbeats reached his keen ears. His muttered black curse drew a worried glance from Ariana and a ready look of expectation from her brother.

"What is it?"

"Riders. Several, by the sound of it, and coming up fast." He cut a look toward a ridge of dense forest several yards off the road. "Let's go—quickly. This way!"

They turned off the empty trail and headed up the rise, where brushy-needled conifers stood evergreen and tall among their bare-branched neighbors. Weaving between them and into the cool forest cover beyond, Braedon paused to glance once more to the road. Their horses had left a climbing trail along the snowy embankment behind them. Easy evidence of the direction of their flight, but with luck and speed, they might be able to outrun their pursuers, who were still out of eyeshot but gaining fast.

Braedon led them deep into the woods, urging them to move quickly while they still had the advantage of distance. But it wasn't long at all before the sounds of riders in gear and armor rang out behind them somewhere on the road, then the shout of an outrider and a whistle alerting the retinue of the path leading into the forest. Brittle winter gorse and low-hanging branches snapped under the gait of oncoming horses . . . and now Braedon realized that it wasn't only horses and riders tramping into the woods, but something else as well.

"There they are!" one of the soldiers called.

"Braedon—!" Ariana cried, looking at him in panic. Her grip was anxious on the reins of her mount, her sudden stiffness confusing the palfrey and making it draw up on the path.

Braedon came up behind her and nudged the beast forward with his knee. "Keep going, my lady. Don't look back."

But it was too late. She had pivoted in her saddle and thrown a nervous look over her shoulder before he could stop her. "Mother Mary!" she gasped, terror vaulting in her voice. "They've loosed hounds on us!"

"Nay, not hounds," Braedon growled, reaching behind him to unlash his crossbow and slam a bolt into the chamber. "Those are wolves. Take her with you and go as deep as you can into the forest," he ordered Kenrick.

"No!" Ariana flung her hand out to grasp at his tunic sleeve. "No. I won't leave you!"

"I'll be right behind you. Now, damn it, get out of here!"

With a curse, he dropped the flat of his gauntleted hand on the rump of Ariana's mount, sending it away in a startled jolt of motion. Pausing only long enough to see that Kenrick had his sister well in hand and was swiftly guiding her into the safety of deeper cover, Braedon then lifted his weapon and aimed for the fleeting shapes of the oncoming search party. The men on horseback were several yards behind the two hellish, bounding slashes of darkness that were running, snarling, teeth bared, toward the spot where he stood.

He would have to wait a moment longer—to let the soot-black beasts race close enough that he could see the saliva frothing from their fangs—should he stand the slimmest prayer of hitting his mark with the short-shooting weapon. If only he'd had a longbow, he thought grimly, although he reckoned his skill with either contraption had long gone as rusty as his once-vaunted reputation.

The wolves crashed through the underbrush, eyes gleaming in anticipation of the kill.

Braedon stared down the length of the crossbow, finding his mark on the beast in front, aiming for the huge black chest. He waited for his chance, his jaw clamped tight, thighs holding firm to his mount as the skittish palfrey became aware of the oncoming attack.

"Easy," he muttered to the fidgeting horse, fighting hard to maintain a steady stance while his snarling target bounded closer.

Closer . . .

He squeezed the weapon's release and the bolt shot forth, a zinging flash of wood and steel-tipped menace. The metallic nick of the discharge gave his mount a start. It twitched beneath him, and sent his aim a hairbreadth to the right—grazing flesh and fur where it might have struck true in the beast's black heart. The wolf yelped in pain and went down for a moment, but as it struggled to regain its footing, its companion charged on undaunted.

"Damnation!"

It was too late to nock another bolt. Braedon slung the crossbow over his shoulder and gave the palfrey his heels. The second wolf was right upon him as he urged his mount farther into the woods, heading in the direction he had sent Kenrick and Ariana. It leaped up alongside of him, jaws snapping to gain purchase. Braedon smacked the reins against the horse's withers, pushing it harder as he reached down and freed his sword from its scabbard.

The wolf had but a moment to focus on the arc of the slashing blade before Braedon leaned over and delivered a cleaving, deadly blow.

He threw a glance behind him to where the shapes of the fanning riders were growing more distinct, their armor gleaming in the fingers of sunlight that splintered down from the forest canopy, faces taking shape across the narrowing distance. He recognized none, save the leader of the guard. He knew the face, and he knew the steely look of determination that rode on the hard line of his old friend's mouth.

Pitched forward over the neck of a thundering black charger, eyes glittering with unwavering intent, Draec le Nantres had become a harbinger of death.

Pride and fury tempted Braedon to rein in and stand his ground, to end the bitter rift with the spilling of one or the other's blood, but his foremost thought was of Ariana. Unless he knew she was safe, there would be no time for the settling of old scores.

With a narrowed glare and a snap of his reins, he sent his mount at a harder gallop, navigating the underbrush and obstacles of the forest as he pushed deeper into the woodland. Up ahead of him, visible only as intermittent flashes of streaming gold hair amid the dull brown and shadow of the trees, was Ariana. Kenrick, leading her at a swift pace through the bracken, turned and spotted Braedon behind them. They slowed long enough for him to catch up.

"De Mortaine's men," Kenrick guessed, a spark of concern darkening his glance.

"Half a dozen of them, maybe more. They're closing in on all sides. We have to get out of these woods if we stand a chance of outrunning them."

"What about—" Ariana's question seemed to snag in her throat. "Braedon, what about the wolves?"

"There's only one left, and it's wounded. But I don't expect that to slow it down too long."

"Should we split up?" Kenrick asked.

Braedon dismissed the notion with a curt shake of his head. The shouts of the guards were drawing closer. "Too risky. We're better to stick together." He nudged his horse into the lead, already searching the outlying forest for routes of possible escape. "Come on. We have to keep moving."

As hastily as they could, they resumed their flight. Tack jangling, breath misting in the cold, they ducked beneath low-hanging branches and leaped over tangled roots, plunging ever deeper into the shadowy realm of the woods. They crested a small ridge, only to be drawn up short by Braedon's raised hand. He pointed toward an oncoming guard, then just as quickly led them in another direction.

But a shout of alarm went up from the man they had eluded, and suddenly the forest erupted with the sounds of bloodthirsty knights on horseback. And then they were racing into the thicket, riding blindly as the hunting party at their back closed in. Braedon saw an opening in the tangled bracken.

"There!" he said to Kenrick, gesturing toward the darkened outlet and praying it was a way out of the woods. Braedon rode behind Ariana and her brother, watching their backs and momentarily relieved to see that they were outdistancing the knights on their bulky destriers. He followed under the natural arch of twisted vines and dormant ivy, his gaze scanning the other side for signs of danger. He sensed eyes on them but could find no immediate source of the feeling. It wasn't until Kenrick went still beside him that he knew his instinct was not in error.

"Behind you," Ariana's brother whispered. "Don't move."

With a stealth belying his scholarly demeanor, and in defiance of the injuries that battered his body, Kenrick reached for Braedon's crossbow and brought the weapon to a ready stance. He drew a bolt from the quiver and easily placed it in the channel that would soon set it flying.

Perhaps it was the confused, canine-sounding whimper that drew Braedon's head around to the place where Kenrick marked his aim. Perhaps it was the sudden sense that someone beckoned to him from within the murky shade of the forest alcove. Whatever it was, Braedon obeyed the queer sensation and turned his head to look over his shoulder, staring in astonishment at the sight that met his eyes.

As his gaze focused on the inquisitive, tilted head of the white wolf, he heard the soft click of the crossbow's trigger.

"Hold!" he ordered, bringing up his hand to knock the weapon off-target. The deadly bolt sailed off into the bushes along with Kenrick's disbelieving oath. "Hold your fire. She means us no harm."

"Braedon," Ariana whispered beside him. "Is that . . ."

With an ear twitching toward the sound of the advancing guards, the wolf rose off her haunches and trotted onto a darkened path between the trees. She paused as if to encourage Braedon to follow her, and all at once he remembered the dream he'd had two nights past. "Let's go," he said, taking the crossbow back and gesturing for Kenrick and Ariana to ride ahead of him.

"Are the both of you mad?" Clairmont asked as his sister fell in behind the wolf on Braedon's command. "We have no idea what lies ahead of us there."

Resituating the crossbow's strap over his shoulder, Braedon brought his horse around parallel to Kenrick's. "And I'd wager you have no idea what's closing in on us from behind. Nor would you want to. Let's go. It's our best option."

With a look that said he was more accustomed to giving orders than receiving them, Ariana's brother guided his mount ahead of Braedon on the path. As in the dream, the white wolf escorted them silently into the heart of the forest. As in the dream, she came to the edge of a ravine and paused to see that they followed. Braedon gave a quiet order for Kenrick and Ariana to let him pass, and he walked his horse closer.

As in the dream, a shower of ice crystals fluttered down around the wolf where she waited, the fine, filtering mist dislodged by a gentle breeze that ruffled the canopy overhead. The she-wolf vanished into the sparkling veil, but this time, unlike the dream, there was no coaxing gaze waiting for him on the other side of the ravine.

The wolf was gone, and all that awaited was the steep cleft below.

Behind them, a distance too close for Braedon's peace of mind, came the deep boom of Draec le Nantres's voice, shouting orders to his men. They had found the alcove; it would only be a matter of moments before they were full upon them. Braedon swore an oath and circled his mount around, gauging the outlying obstacles of the forest and their steadily narrowing opportunity for escape.

Too late to turn back, too risky to try to outrun le Nantres and the guards, he could see only one option.

"We have to jump the ravine."

❧ 19 ❧

W HAT!" ARIANA THREW a wild glance at him. She shook her head, certain she had not heard him aright. "Braedon, we cannot—"

He clasped the trembling hand that reached out to him, imploring. "We have to jump it, my lady. There is no other way."

Ariana's heart slammed against her ribs as he held her hand in his, her gaze commanded by fierce steel gray eyes. Breath racing, limbs trembling, all she could hear was the crashing approach of de Mortaine's men behind them, closing in, coming through the trees like a wave of malice and forcing their choices down to this impossible one.

"Do you trust me?" Braedon asked, holding her hand against the solid warmth of his chest.

"Yes." She nodded once, then again, more resolutely. "I trust you."

"I'll go first," Kenrick said, his saddle leather creaking as he drew himself up straighter in his seat. Though it would take weeks for him to resemble the robust knight Ariana had known him to be before his captivity, his courage remained unbroken. With a quirk of one tawny brow, he wheeled his mount to a spot several paces from the ledge and gave the beast his heels. The horse vaulted forward and leaped the chasm, scrambling only slightly as its hind hooves clipped the ragged edge of the ravine.

A mist was rolling in thicker now. Although she had seen Kenrick complete the jump, he was all but engulfed in the swell of haze that blanketed the other side of the chasm. She could not see the ground over there; in a few minutes even the deep ravine would be clouded in opaque whiteness.

"Now you, angel. Go—now." Braedon leaned over and kissed her soundly on the mouth, letting his forehead rest against hers for the merest beat of his heart before he released her hand and urged her to follow her brother's example. "I am right behind you. I won't let you fall."

A small, nervous cry died in her throat as she brought her mount the few paces it would need to build speed for the jump. Braedon nodded to her in reassurance, positioned at her back, ready to send his mount across the ravine after her.

"Go, my love. Now."

His voice, and his unexpected endearment, gave her strength. She shouted a cry to her mount and put her heels to its sides, sending the palfrey into a lurching vault. The horse's hooves tore up the frozen turf, and, with a sudden jarring leap, it was airborne. Ariana sucked in her breath and squeezed her eyes closed as she and the beast sailed over the cleft of the ravine. With a hard jolt, they were back on solid ground, landed safely on the other side.

Braedon's mount followed but an instant later.

"Let's get moving," he ordered, his voice quiet and nearly detached in the swirling mist that shrouded the banks of the ravine. "The fog will hide us, but not for long."

They fled at once, silent but for the heavy beats of their mounts' hooves as they escaped deeper into the woods.

Somewhere near, there was the sound of running water, a trickle of a small stream, strangely unhindered by ice or cold. Braedon led them along its shallow, steaming banks, riding against the flow to the point where the rivulet curved toward its source, a hidden spring that bubbled up from beneath a craggy wall of granite. The dark shadows on the rough-hewn rock all but concealed the narrow mouth of a cave. Ariana might not have seen the portal at all had it not been for the sudden slash of white that appeared in its space.

It was a woman, slender and ethereal. She wore a pale dove gray gown that skimmed her figure like a cloud. A mass of white hair spilled over her shoulders and down around her, framing a beautiful face and haunting silver-green eyes.

"Braedon." Ariana gestured to point her out, but he had already spied the woman.

For a moment, he did not move. Indeed, it seemed to Ariana, watching him in perplexity, that he could scarcely breathe. Stock still, staring, he said nothing as she and Kenrick drew up beside him. Then he exhaled a soft oath.

"Braedon, who is—?"

"Leave the horses," he said, her concern disregarded as he swung down off his mount. He came around to assist Ariana down from her saddle. "It's all right."

"Can you be sure?" Ariana held on to Braedon's arms for a moment after her feet touched the ground. In the mouth of the slim cavern entrance, the lady was holding out her hand in invitation, backing into the gloom of the fissure as if to show them the way. Puzzled, Ariana turned her gaze back to Braedon. "Do you . . . do you know this woman?"

"Aye," he answered, frowning with incredulity, his voice oddly wooden. "Her name is Naala. She is my mother."

A thousand questions spun in Braedon's mind as he and Ariana and Kenrick entered the mouth of the cavern cleft. That his mother was before him now, inexplicably, after so many years since she had abandoned him to his father's scorn, was like something out of a strange, forgotten dream. And thinking on strange dreams come to fruition made him think on the white she-wolf as well.

To imagine it coincidence that the wolf and his mother would appear in the same place at the same time was impossible. To imagine it anything else—to think, even for a moment, that the two were somehow connected, or, by some brand of sorcery, might exist as one—was surely nothing short of madness. In truth, after all he had witnessed since embarking on this strange journey, he had to wonder if it were no less insane to follow this white wraith as she led them farther into the unknown.

Behind him, her feet shuffling on the path, Ariana drew a shaky breath. "It's so dark," she whispered.

"Take my hand." He reached back in reassurance, clasping her fingers tight in his own as the group of them forged on.

Lightless save for the movement of his mother's pale form a few paces ahead of them, the narrow passage seemed to breathe warm air and the clean mineral scent of fresh-running water. A natural spring, Braedon realized a moment later, hearing the trickle on the other side of the moist, slanting rock wall he followed with his free hand. Descending almost imperceptibly, they turned a sharp corner and at last saw a glimmer of light at the end of the long passage. Candle glow, its reflection wobbling on a subtle curve of stone, spilled softly from somewhere at the heart of the labyrinth.

The blood in Braedon's temples yet raced from their flight into the forest. It picked up a tighter pitch of warning as they rounded the bend in the sleek granite passageway, which opened onto a dimly lit chamber. A rustle of movement within alerted him to the presence of others; his nostrils flared as he took in air, the faintest tang of unsheathed steel catching in the back of his throat. With one hand inching Ariana behind him, Braedon drew his sword before they reached the threshold. His mother was still walking, unaware that he had freed the blade from its scabbard until the barest hiss of sound rasped like a whisper in the dark passage.

"No," she gasped. Her long, silver-white hair sifted about her slight frame as she turned to shake her head at him. "Please, do not be afraid. There is no need for violence here."

"I'd rather be the judge of that," he replied, for in that same instant, as they cleared the threshold of the cavernous chamber, they were met with like preparedness, like mistrust.

Six guards—four large men and two agile-looking women—all bearing deadly, unsheathed swords blocked them off, barring entry to the room. Carved out of the granite without a single corner, the space was shaped round like a wheel, with perimeter passageways fanning out as spokes bored into the rock, their torchlit depths leading ostensibly farther into the subterranean compound. When the four men in the group advanced to challenge the outsiders, a wisp of pale, flowing silk held them off.

"It is him," Braedon's mother said, her hand raised in gentle command. The guards obeyed with total deference, withdrawing their weapons in uniform time. "This is Braedon. This is my son."

Ariana stood directly behind him, her hand clutching his arm. "What are they doing, Braedon? What is going on here?"

"I don't know." Questioningly, he looked to his mother's placid smile and welcoming expression. "Explain this. Why have you brought us here?"

"Is it not yet clear to you? I have been waiting for you to come for a long time, Braedon. We all have."

"Waiting for me?"

"You're finally home," she said, sweeping her arm out in a generous arc to the others standing before him. "These are your clan. Your kin, Braedon."

The words sank in with heavy meaning. A cautious part of him rose to deny what she said as he looked at the six pairs of pale eyes now trained on him in unblinking curiosity and waiting expectation. His clan, indeed, he thought, scoffing at the notion. He was not of this breed. He could not be. The group of guards with their dragon-hilt swords bore the trace scent of shifters: changeable, quicksilver, as mutable as the colors of their keenly watchful eyes. That same stamp of dark magic shimmered about the strange and lovely woman he'd once known as his mother.

He turned a glare on her. "This is madness."

"Is it?" she asked, almost sadly. "Can my son be so like his father that he refuses to accept that which exists right before his eyes?"

In that very moment, that fleeting space between one heartbeat and the next, Braedon's mother faded away—she shifted into the silvery form of the white wolf, then just as quickly back again. It seemed an illusion of his own confused mind, until he heard Ariana's gasp of fear behind him. "It's all right," he told her. "They mean us no harm."

Kenrick swore an oath as he came to stand at Braedon's side. "For Christ's sake, le Chasseur. They're shifters. They are under de Mortaine's command."

Braedon considered the warning, but he knew with every instinct he possessed that de Mortaine held no power over these few. There was a beastly magic here, but there was no malice in this place. As he looked into his mother's eyes, silver-green and unblinking, he felt a sense of knowing lap at him like the slow, incoming tide. Strange as she was, this creature he hardly remembered and had for so long strove to renounce, he could not deny their bond. Nor could he shake the sudden feeling that although he had never been to this place—not even in his dreams—he was somehow tied to it. And to the strangers who stared at him, now, as if he were some prodigal son returned to them after a lifetime of wandering in the world outside.

"Why did you summon me here?" he asked her. "For that is what you did, is it not? 'Twas you in my dream the other night . . . you, the white she-wolf. And it was you again out there in the forest, leading us to this place."

"Your friends need rest, and so do you," she said, moving to guide them toward the network of caverns beyond. "There will be plenty of time for talk, my son. I will explain everything to you in time."

With a look of silent command, she sent the other shifters away. The six of them dispersed, but when his mother began to lead the way toward one of the cavern portals, Braedon reached out and seized her by the wrist. "Nay, madame, this won't wait."

"Braedon," Ariana said from beside him, her soothing voice coaxing him to calm when his fingers tightened on the delicate bones of his mother's arm. The lady seemed not the least concerned, giving him a placid smile.

"Will you at least permit us to look after your friend there, before he collapses from his exhaustion? His body needs healing, and we have those skilled in such arts."

Braedon agreed to Kenrick's care with a curt nod of his head, then watched as the battered knight was assisted toward one of the torchlit passageways by two of the shifter men. The other clansfolk followed, leaving Braedon and Ariana alone with the mysterious creature who'd borne him.

"I want answers now, madame. Why have you brought me here? Why now, after all these years of leaving me to wonder if you even lived? Why do you come to me now—like this?"

"Because I could not bear your pain any longer." She withdrew her hand from his slackened grasp to reach up and trace the scar on his left cheek. "Your wounds are my wounds, Braedon, save that I wear them in my heart."

"You left me. I hated you for that."

"I know you did, but it seemed the only way. I thought that without me there, you might adjust to their ways. I . . . hoped." She slowly shook her head, as though recalling the years long past. Emotion clouded her gaze, then faded with a sweep of her lashes. "This is the only place you'll be safe . . . from them, and from those of our clan who would hunt us as they seek out the Dragon Chalice."

"What do you know of the Chalice?"

"It is the most valued treasure our people have ever known. It is the very heart of Anavrin, our kingdom." At Braedon's skeptical look, his mother explained further. "The cup was forged long, long ago, by the high mage of Anavrin and given to the ruling king as a gift of peace and a promise of protection. It was a symbol of balance and trust among the two classes of the realm—the Magics and the Immortals. Unless it is returned, Anavrin and all its people will perish."

"But if the legends are true, the Dragon Chalice is in four pieces," Ariana pointed out. "And one of those pieces now belongs to Silas de Mortaine."

"Avosaar," Braedon's mother said, nodding slowly. "The cup that holds the Stone of Prosperity. The three others, Calasaar, Vorimasaar, and Serasaar—the Stones of Light, Faith, and Peace—remain somewhere Outside. They are protected by an enchantment, but even Anavrin's magic is fragile in this world."

"De Mortaine will stop at nothing to have the treasure for himself," Braedon said. "He has killed for it already. He has a number of your own kind at his command and he has made it his mission to recover the Chalice for himself."

"Yes. And now that one of the stones has been found, the others cannot remain hidden for long."

"Do you know of any way to stop him?" Ariana asked. "Any way at all to keep him from claiming the Chalice?"

"I fear there is little that can be done to stop the cycle now that it has begun. Leastwise, not by any of us. One of our clan thought to intercede by attempting to steal Avosaar back, but she paid a terrible price. Lara knew the risks, but she did not heed them."

"Lara?" Braedon frowned. "Do you mean to say that the girl—the queer, fey young thief who raided de Mortaine's keep and took the Avosaar cup—was one of your own? A shifter?"

"Yes, she was. But not the same as those on the Outside. She was like the rest of us here, in hiding, no longer Seekers, but living away from the others as Shadows."

"Seekers and Shadows?" Braedon asked impatiently. "You speak in riddles, madame. Explain your meaning."

She gave him a placid look, her lupine gray eyes unblinking. "Twenty of us were summoned from Anavrin to walk among the Outsiders. It was our quest to seek out the Dragon Chalice and see it restored to its rightful place. However, the prophecy surrounding the Chalice decreed that as it had been taken away in an Outsider's hands, so, too, it must be returned."

"Then why don't you help us thwart de Mortaine?" Ariana suggested, her eyes brightening with hope. "If we find the three other stones, help us win back the one in de Mortaine's possession and you will have the Dragon Chalice for your people."

"It is not so simple as that, my dear. We can influence the will and actions of man, using our ability to shift forms among them—our glamour—but we cannot touch the treasure in order to bring it back to Anavrin. We were sent out as Seekers but to lay our hands on any part of the Dragon Chalice would spell our doom."

"What would happen to you?"

"She would perish instantly, engulfed in a plume of fire," Braedon answered, recalling the horror of what happened on the cliff in Brittany so many months ago. He let out a low curse, shaking his head. "The girl seemed peculiar to me, the way she'd stolen the cup from de Mortaine's keep, yet carried it in a leather pouch, refusing to touch it outright. As bold as she'd been, she was terrified as well. She had gloved her hands in two layers of thick hide just to hold the strings of the pouch that contained the pilfered cup. I didn't know why until de Mortaine ordered her death before my eyes."

"Oh, Braedon." He felt a comforting hand on his arm and looked down to find Ariana glancing up at him, her gaze filled with sympathy even though he deserved contempt for his role in the girl's demise.

"When I brought her to him to collect my reward, de Mortaine forced her at swordpoint to hold the prize she had stolen. The instant her shaking fingers touched it, there was a blinding flash of light. It poured out from the stone in the center of the cup, incinerating her as though hell itself had opened up to swallow her whole. At the time, I thought the fire to be the work of de Mortaine's wicked magic."

"No," his mother replied. "It is simply the power of the Dragon Chalice. None of us can interfere in this—not even those who are the Seekers. You have seen it for yourself, Braedon. There is a terrible price to be paid by anyone born of Anavrin who attempts to win the Dragon Chalice." Her gaze seemed to pale a bit as she looked at him. "That includes you, my son. You are no shifter, but my blood—the blood of Anavrin kings and sorcerers— runs in your veins." He grunted, still struggling to accept all that he was learning about the damned Dragon Chalice and himself. "You know it's true," she said. "It is what separates you from other men on the Outside. It is the reason you have struggled out there, among them. You don't belong there."

"And where do I belong then—here, with you? Powerless, cowering belowground in fear?"

Anger flared in his voice. His mother took a step back from him as though not quite trusting him, blood of her blood or nay. Braedon did nothing to coax her back. He'd had enough talk of magic and things he could not control. He felt adrift on a strange tide, where nothing made sense anymore. "I have heard enough," he said, his tone dismissive and brooking no argument. "Just leave me for a while—both of you. Let me think."

"As you wish," his mother replied softly.

She departed with scarcely a sound, but Ariana remained, her gaze filled with concern. "Braedon, if what she says is true, perhaps you should heed your mother's advice. After all, we have seen what Silas de Mortaine is capable of."

"You would have me hide, too?"

"*We* could, yes."

He glanced down to where she stood beside him, her hand tenderly caressing his arm. "What are you saying, Ariana? That this is the life you would choose for yourself? Nay, I don't think so."

"If this is the safest place for you—for us—then what other choice do we have? We could stay here in the caverns, or we could go somewhere else, far away from here, and forget we ever heard about the Dragon Chalice."

"Run, you mean. Live in hiding, forsaking everyone we know, as I have done for nearly two years? You would never see your brother again, or your home at Clairmont. Is that truly what you want?"

Nay, it wasn't. She would not admit it, nor did he think for a moment that she would balk if he took her up on her desperate plan that very moment. She would run with him if he asked her to. But he would never make her face that choice. He loved her too much for that.

"Tell me you'll think about it," she demanded of him, reaching up to cup his face in her palm. "Promise me?"

Braedon caught her hand in his and pressed a kiss to her fingertips. "Go see to your brother, my lady."

"What will you do?"

"Like I said, I need time to consider all of this. Alone." He touched her velvety cheek, giving her a smile meant to reassure her. "Go on. 'Tis all right."

Reluctantly, as if she feared she might never see him

again, she backed out of his arms. She paused near the mouth of one of the cavern passageways, the one down which Kenrick had been taken a short while ago. "We are in this together, do you agree? That was our pact."

He gave her a vague nod, his thoughts already spinning, contemplating his far too few options. All he knew was he would not spend another day in hiding—not from anyone or anything. Nor would he allow Ariana to be a part of the danger. This was his battle. He understood that, now that he was here in this place, confronted with so much that had for so long plagued him about who he was—about *what* he was. The fight now was his alone, and he meant to finish it. The sooner, the better.

❧ 20 ❧

THE CAVERNS WERE a serpentine maze of torchlit chambers and passageways. Countless living spaces, meeting rooms, and thick supporting pillars had been hollowed out of the rock, the whole of it warmed to a humid, nearly summerlike climate by a hot water spring that ran beneath the strange, subterranean haven. Kenrick had been tended by a healer some hours before and was currently installed in one of the private chambers deep within the place, as was Ariana, although at the moment, facing an abrupt dead end in the corridor she followed, she could not recall precisely where her quarters lay.

She had gone to fetch a pitcher of water for her own refreshment and toilette, which had seemed an easy enough task, following the healer's directions to and from the cavern well, but apparently, somewhere on the return she had strayed off course. With a whispered word of frustration, she pivoted to turn and retrace her steps.

"I trust you and your brother have been taken care of."

Startled by Braedon's presence in the passageway, Ariana drew up short. Water sloshed over the sides of the pitcher she carried, wetting the front of her gown. "Oh!" she exclaimed, brushing at the thin stain that traveled down her bodice. "Yes, Kenrick has been looked after quite well, and I . . ." She glanced down at her gown in dismay. "I was just bringing some water so I could wash. . . ."

Braedon grunted in acknowledgment as he leaned his shoulder against the corridor wall. Ariana could scarcely look at him without feeling awkwardly self-conscious, weathering a burning heat that suffused her face as he stared at her from no more than ten paces away. He unnerved her as always; even worse now, for he knew her more intimately than anyone. He knew her body, and her heart. She had willingly given him both, but in his current dark mood, she wasn't sure he wanted either.

"I must have taken a wrong turn," she said, eager to fill the silence and explain why she was standing there, fidgeting under his unsettling gray gaze. "I'm sure I can find my way back—"

When she tried to walk past him, Braedon took a step forward, directly into her path. She thought he might reach out to her, but his arms remained crossed over his chest. Like her, he had also shed his mantle in the warmth of the caverns. He stood there in his brown tunic and leather gambeson, his charcoal-colored hose still damp from their travel that day, the soles of his large black boots encrusted with mud and forest loam. He appeared tired, but now that she was looking closer, Ariana saw that there was something heavier in his features than mere fatigue.

"It has been an exceedingly strange day. Are you all right?" she asked, noting the tension in the hard line of his mouth. As uncomfortable as he made her now, she could not help wondering how he fared amid this unexpected reunion with the woman who abandoned him as a boy. "Have you thought about what she said—about what we should do?"

"I don't want to talk about her, or this . . . place," he

said in his gruff, dismissive way. He moved closer, his hands dropping down to his sides as he walked toward her. "That's not why I came looking for you."

A jolt of surprise went through her. "You . . . you were looking for me?"

He did not answer, but Ariana cursed the little thrill that raced into her veins at the mere thought of his having deliberately sought her out. She did not want to imagine—or hope—he meant anything by it, but by now she knew his moods well, and she knew enough to recognize the heat that burned in his eyes, tempered yet smoldering, as he closed in on her in the corridor. In the beginning, when her life first became entangled with his, she had shrunk away from that heat; then, soon enough, it drew her like a powerful, beckoning flame. How long ago it all seemed to her now. Now she was trapped somewhere between the two impulses: drawn yet fearful; wanting yet uncertain.

"I-I was just getting some water," she stammered, wincing inwardly to hear how she repeated herself in this present state of discomfiture. "They gave me a chamber somewhere . . . back there, I think. . . ." She gestured in the vague direction of the passageway behind him.

"I know where your chamber is, Ariana."

Of course he did. Braedon was never lost, not to his surroundings or to his emotions. He was always, aggravatingly, in control in every situation.

With a glance that caressed even when his hands would not, he said, "Come with me."

Together they walked back up the passageway. Flames from the intermittently placed torches wobbled in the disturbance of the air, sending thin snakes of smoke slithering up toward the arced stone of the corridor ceiling above their heads. For some long while, too long by half, the only sounds were the sloshing of the water in

Ariana's pitcher and the soft scuff of their boots on the dirt floor of the passageway as they walked. They passed the mouth of one corridor, then another—the one Ariana felt certain she had trod down herself on her way back from the well—before they reached an intersection of three others. Braedon turned down the farthermost left passageway without a word.

"Are you taking me back to my quarters?" she asked hesitantly as she followed after him. "Because I believe we already passed . . ."

He kept walking, obviously knowing his own path. Her advice trailed off, useless, as he led her deeper into the heart of the caverns, to where the humidity grew heavier, almost steamy, the air becoming increasingly warm and rich with the scent of moist clean earth and fresh rain. The sound of trickling water echoed off the rounded walls and along the serpentine corridor, emanating from a source she knew not where. It became clear to her but a moment later, when Braedon strode around a bend in the passageway and paused, waiting for her to follow. She drew up beside him at the entrance to a large chamber and gasped in wonder at what she saw.

Like a cavern within the cavern, the ceiling of the domed chamber arced high into the rock, but here the room seemed less an awe-inspiring creation of man than it did a phenomenon of nature. Spires of slick white stone hung down like icicles of graduating sizes, some thick as a man's arm, others no bigger in circumference than a distaff rod or walking cane. They glistened, moist from the humidity and gilded by the light from six torches housed in black iron cressets that were bolted into the rock wall several feet below.

Ariana peered down into the strange chamber, down to the base of a descending staircase carved into the stone in a spiraling curve to lessen its steepness. There at the bottom of the steps was a small pool of clear, steaming water. The surface of the pool bubbled as though boiling, the soft rumble of churning water echoing in a soothing, steady hum.

"It's magnificent," she whispered, then turned her awestruck gaze on Braedon. "What is it?"

"There is a warm water spring that runs through these caverns and on, all the way up to the woods outside."

"Yes, I know," Ariana said softly. "The healer who tended Kenrick told me about it. And I saw the heat rising off the little brook when we first rode up to the caverns' entrance."

Braedon swept his hand toward the pool below. "This is where it starts. The spring is hot, but I'm told it is most comfortable for bathing. I expect you'll enjoy it very much."

Ariana pivoted her head to stare at him, incredulous. "Bathing—in there? You can't be serious." She stepped away, backing toward safer ground near the corridor outside. "As dearly as I would love a true bath, I prefer to take mine in a tub. A nice, shallow tub made of wood, not a hole bored into the earth heaven only knows how far and filled with scalding water, bubbling up from heaven only knows where."

Braedon grunted dismissively. He unbuckled his baldric, then set the belt and sheathed sword against the wall near the chamber entryway. "The water is not scalding, nor is it that deep. And if you look, you'll see there's a natural ledge formed in the wall of the pool, just over there." The corner of his mouth quirked into a wry grin. "A perfect seat for a . . . well, a perfect seat. Go on, try it."

Ariana gave him a dubious look, fighting the smile that

his roguish flattery provoked. "Perhaps you should sample the bath first, my lord, and if you do not boil up like a stewed capon, I might consider partaking of it myself."

He made a sound of dismay in the back of his throat. "Where is your sense of adventure, Lady Mayhem?" The challenge was issued with a mocking scowl as he reached out to take the pitcher of water from her. Their fingers brushed, a bare whisper of contact, yet Ariana felt his touch sear her skin like a flame. All humor vanished from Braedon's gaze as he looked at her, his hands neither retreating nor advancing where they rested atop hers.

A question lingered in his serious gray eyes. Something he seemed reluctant to say, holding something back. He struggled with it, she thought, noting the white line of tension that rimmed his mouth. "What is it, Braedon? Is anything wrong?"

"No," he said, his voice lightly casual as he denied it, yet not entirely convincing to the woman who had come to know him as she knew her own heart. He removed the pitcher from her grasp and bent to set it down on the floor of the chamber, then took her hand in his. His fingers were warm and firm as he curled them around hers and gently coaxed her forward. "Come. Let us enjoy a few moments of privacy while we have it."

She had no will to refuse him, despite the prickling of her instincts that told her he was concealing something from her, and her uncertainty about the hot spring bath that waited at the bottom of the stone staircase. Braedon led her down the curving flight of stairs, carefully guiding her along the sloped decline, which followed the natural circumference of the domed chamber. Down and around they descended, into the gauzy cloud of steam that wafted over the clear reservoir of water and spilled onto the smooth expanse of stone that rimmed the pool's edge.

"What if someone comes in?" Ariana asked when they alighted from the last stair. "How do you know we'll have privacy?"

"I left my sword near the door as a sign to any who would approach. No one will enter, I assure you. The pool is all yours for as long as you like."

Mother Mary, but it did look inviting. Crystal clear water glistened beneath feathery steam, bubbling up softly from somewhere deep within the pale rock bowl. She could not tell how deep the pool would go, but at the bottom was a silted floor of sparkling white sand. And there, at the perimeter, as Braedon had pointed out, was a ledge hewn into the side of the rock, forming a flat slab on which to sit partially submerged in the water. Ariana went to the edge of the pool and dipped her hand beneath the surface. It was warm—quite nearly hot—but soothingly so. She turned back to Braedon with a small smile.

"Very well, you win," she told him in jest. "I'm going in."

She shucked her boots and hose, discarding them in a small pile at her feet. Ariana had lost much of her shyness around Braedon, aware there was little he did not already know about her body. But as she loosened the ties on her gown's bodice, she suddenly realized how still he had gone beside her. He watched her work to speedily undress, his gaze hooded but smoldering. She was still in her gown and chemise, but she felt naked already, stripped nude by the heat of his eyes alone. Her pulse picked up a faster beat as he stared at her, standing still as granite, stonily silent.

He desired her, she realized with a jolt of excitement. He desired her, but he was holding himself back, deliberately maintaining his distance. Ariana knew not what to make of him. Part of her knew that he had feelings for her—how badly she wanted to believe he did—yet he seemed intent to keep her at bay. It seemed the more intimate they became, the more distant he held himself emotionally. Ariana ached to feel his arms around her. She saw him retreating into his personal darkness, and she wanted more than anything to help him out of it. She loved him, even if he was determined to bar her from his heart.

Feeling sad for the hauntedness that seemed to forever follow him, she offered, "Join me in the pool, Braedon."

He shook his head. "I don't think that would be wise."

"Not wise?" she asked, trying to cajole a smile from him now that he seemed so sober. "Ah, dear. Where, prithee, is *your* sense of adventure, my daring lord? At least help me out of this gown, now that you have enticed me with the notion of a hot bath."

Facing him, she raised her arms and waited for his assistance. He obliged with a grumble issued low under his breath, gathering up the long skirts and lifting the garment over her head. He handed it to her in a large, rumpled ball, his gaze straying to the swell of her bosom at the neckline of her thin white chemise. Ariana could have walked away. Indeed, his expression seemed all but to command that she keep a wary distance, but she cared too much to turn her back on the look of loneliness that shadowed his eyes.

"Join me," she entreated him again, catching his hand and bringing the hardened knuckles to her lips. She kissed him tenderly, her gaze on his, inviting him to be with her. "Braedon . . ."

He tightened his fingers around her hand and pulled her to him. With an exhaled curse, he bent his head and claimed her mouth in a passionate kiss. Ariana let her gown drop to the ground and wrapped her arms around him, welcoming his embrace, needing to feel his lips on hers. She had never dreamed she would play the seductress, but Braedon brought out all that was woman in her. That part of her that knew the man in him, knew also that he was falling away from her somehow.

"Ariana," he whispered against her mouth. "I . . . God's blood, but I didn't come here to seduce you. I didn't want—"

He broke off with an oath, pressing his brow to hers. His hand was on her breast, toying with the tight bud of her nipple through the chemise, kneading the soft mound of flesh that ached so desperately for his touch. With more brazenness than she'd thought she possessed, Ariana stepped back and drew off her undergarment, casting it aside to stand naked before him. His exhaled breath seemed to catch in the back of his throat.

Ariana held out her hand to him. "Join me, Braedon."

Her body still thrumming and trembling from even his brief attentions, she stepped gingerly down onto the flat, submerged ledge of the pool. Warm water engulfed her to just above her calves, its silky heat like a balm to her tired limbs. Letting go of Braedon's hand, she ventured farther within and situated herself on the naturally formed seat. She had not been prepared for the sheer pleasure she felt as she sank to her breasts in the pool. Like a living blanket of heat, charged with thousands of tiny churning bubbles, the water surrounded her, cocooned her in a liquid embrace that was nothing short of heaven. Ariana reclined deeper into the warmth, letting her legs dangle over the edge of the stone precipice and into the pulsing heart of the pool. She tipped her head back and closed her eyes, unable to suppress the moan of blissful satisfaction that slipped from between her lips.

Braedon shed his clothing and stepped in beside her.

He did not seat himself on the ledge next to her, but instead hoisted himself fully into the water. It was not that deep, after all. Standing, the pool reached only to the center of Braedon's chest. He submerged himself, then came up again, sluicing water from his face and slicking back his dark hair. "You are a wicked wench, Ariana of Clairmont," he growled as he drifted back to her at the pool's edge. With a grin, he wedged himself between her knees. "You are a wicked, wanton wench, my lady, and I am a fool to think I can resist you."

"Then don't."

Ariana's amused laugh changed to a startled squeak as he seized her by the ankles and pulled her off the ledge, into his arms. She clung to him, feeling weightless as he carried her farther into the steamy pool. They kissed sweetly, mouths meshing, melding. She felt the firm ridge of his arousal pressing between them where it nestled so provocatively at the apex of her thighs. The mat of crisp hair at his chest tickled her breasts. Braedon kissed his way down her throat and Ariana leaned back in his arms, granting him further access, crying out wordlessly as he suckled her nipples each in turn.

Before she knew it, he was bringing her back to the ledge seat, lifting her onto it. He kissed his way down her abdomen and lower, pressing the flats of his palms beneath her back to arch her up out of the water. He held her thus as his head dipped ever lower. She grasped for him as he bent to suck at her woman's core. He teased her mercilessly, then plundered her with a dizzying expertise that left her quaking, gasping, her back arched tautly against the edge of the pool.

His fingers clutched her hips, lifting her out of the water and holding her fast as he ravished her with his tongue, kissing and suckling, driving her to the very brink of rapturous madness. He moaned against her tingling flesh as he laved her, his mouth searching out and finding the pearl of her womanhood. He sucked it hard, pressing the tip of his tongue against the swollen nub as he drew it into his mouth in a deep, carnal kiss. She cried out, helpless in her pleasure, her hands grasping at his shoulders, twining in the wet silk of his hair. His tempo rose to match the hungered thrust of her hips. He buried his face between her thighs, demanding her release with the questing heat of his mouth. Ariana shattered with a strangled gasp of ecstasy.

She was still climaxing, still boneless with cresting pleasure, as he drew himself up out of the water beside her to lavish her body with kisses and soft words of praise. Ariana reached for him, bringing his face up to hers. Panting and breathless, she caressed his strong jaw and the cheek that bore his silvered scar. She kissed him with all the passion that still flowed through her veins, needing more of him. Needing as much as he would give her. Glancing down the length of his warrior's body, she took in the magnificent sight of him, following the planes and striations of his muscular perfection with her hands. His sex was thick and straining at his groin, proudly risen past his navel, a thing of power and wondrous beauty. Reverently she stroked the steely velvet shaft and glistening head, palming the blunt tip of him and savoring his pleasured groan as she drew her fingers tightly around his width.

He gave her no warning, save the darkening of his changeable gray eyes, before he seized her by the wrist and turned her around on the ledge. Facing away from him on her knees, Ariana bent to the gentle command of his body as he moved in close against her back and pressed her down. His hand reached out above her head to snag the rumpled form of her gown. He slid it beneath her breasts like a cushion and eased her down over the edge of the pool.

His mouth was warm and hungry at her neck, nuzzling away the mass of her unbound hair as his lips traced a line of heat along the column of her neck to the sensitive skin at her nape. She felt the pinch of his teeth on her shoulder and she gasped, her arousal stoked brighter with the sudden shock of pleasure-pain. He covered her body with his, holding her against him with one arm snaked around her waist, the other braced beside her head on the edge of the pool as he nudged her legs wide with his knee and mounted her. The stiffness of his erection slid wetly between them, heavy and hot, pressing, insistent. Then, with a curse and a slow, seemingly endless thrust, he sheathed himself in the fist of her womb.

"Ohh, yes . . ." Ariana gasped, marveling at this new assault of carnal sensation. Eyes wide but bleary with pleasure, she could only clutch the stone ledge of the pool and hang on as Braedon moved within her, filling and withdrawing, thrusting and retreating, loving her in a manner that was primal and animal, and unspeakably arousing. His deep, urgent strokes penetrated her to her very core, a claiming so possessive, so needy, she wanted to weep with the exquisite joy of it.

Steam hazed her vision, wreathing them in a humid, dreamlike mist. The torchlight that bathed the chamber in a golden glow now cast illicit shadows on the far wall, hazy images of a couple sensually joined together, lost to passion, drowning in ecstasy. The water of the pool lapped at Ariana's stomach and thighs, churned to a frenzy by the rhythmic tempo of their lovemaking. The air around them echoed with an earthy song of muffled sighs and grunts and wordless gasps, and the steady friction of their bodies twined together and moving in the throes of climbing bliss.

Braedon growled her name like a curse and lifted her hips higher, drawing her to him so that she was farther up on her knees. He pressed her head down with a guiding kiss at her nape and drove in deeper, this new angle having tilted her to better accommodate his fervent thrusts and freeing his hands to roam her body in tactile worship. Ariana took him in, every hard pulsing inch of him. She felt her womb expand and contract with the rise of another release, felt his sex react, growing harder, thrusting deeper. She braced herself beneath him, weathering the storm of his passion, thrilling in the savage unleashing of his rigid control as he ground his hips against her bottom, then drew back, only to fill her again and again.

She splintered apart that instant, the swell of rapture breaking over her in wave after wave of mindless, bone-numbing bliss. And all the while he rode her, urging her toward a greater pleasure, branding himself on her very soul with the fierce animal joining of their bodies. Ariana sobbed her joy, going slack beneath him in quivering wonder as he chased his own release.

"Yes," she whispered. "Oh, Braedon, yes . . . don't stop. . . ."

Her breathless coaxing seemed to speed him toward completion. He pumped with wild abandon, clutching her to him like he would cling to life itself. She felt him surge harder, stronger, tighter inside her, before he shouted a savage oath and filled her with the sudden, hot rush of his seed.

"Ah—God," Braedon snarled, shuddering against the delicate arc of her spine as his body spasmed around and within her, suspended on a plane between the very heights of heaven and an earthbound hell. His fevered pulse thrummed in his temples and in points lower, as Ariana's silken sheath molded around him, seducing him of all his strength and self-control. "Ariana . . . sweet Christ, woman."

She had milked him of every dram of resolve, with her sweet entreaty to join him in the bath, her devastating siren's song. He was spent and shaking, and still he wanted her. His sex was greedy for her still, more hard than waning, more hungered now that it had feasted on her once again.

God's blood, but if anyone was doomed, Braedon thought, surely it was him. Doomed to always feel her, to always search for her in his mind, as he had in the moments before he found her wandering the cavern passageways alone on her way to find her chamber. He had hardly been aware that he was hunting her until he came upon her in the corridor. And then it had been too late for him to turn back.

His hunter's senses, so long denied, seemed to heighten with every moment since his arrival at the cavern sanctuary. In truth, they had been heightening from the moment he first set eyes on Ariana of Clairmont. With her there was no denying his true nature. She had seen through him at every turn, refusing to let him hide from her or scare her off with his bluster and growling. She brought out a fierce possessiveness in him, an animal need to keep her near, to claim her as his own and keep her by his side forever.

Impossible desires. He had known that from the beginning, when he had lusted for the intrepid girl who had thrown his world into chaos with her fool's quest to save her brother. He knew it all the more now, when he ached with joy to be there holding her in his arms, loving the enchanting woman who had somehow managed to scale the lightless fortress he'd constructed around his heart and knocked it down, brick by damnable brick.

Aye, he was doomed for certain. Ariana was in his blood, in his soul. With all the reverence he felt for her, Braedon carefully turned her around in his arms. The edge of the pool was hard at her back; he cushioned her with his arm, bringing her farther down onto the submerged seat of the pool, letting the warm water and the muscles of his forearm hold her aloft.

She smiled with lazy pleasure as she reached up and smoothed a lock of hair from his brow. Her blue eyes still smoldered, indigo dark and glossy in the flickering light of the torches. Her skin, so flawless and pure, glowed a heavenly shade of ivory, save the dusky peaks of her breasts, which bobbed prettily above the steamy surface of the pool.

"Tell me it can always be like this for us," she whispered. "So long as I am with you, it doesn't matter where we are. I never want to lose you, Braedon. I love you so much. Promise me we'll always be together."

"Ariana," he said, choked by the selflessness with which she gave herself to him. She held nothing back from him, trusting him with her emotions as she trusted him with her body. She was an angel in the flesh, and Braedon had never felt more the devil-spawned blackguard than he did in that moment, when he whispered his promise against her mouth, knowing he could not keep it.

Never had he felt more despicably unworthy than when he pressed her down beneath him and buried himself in her warmth. For he'd spoken true when he said he had not sought her out to seduce her. It had not been part of his plan at all. Indeed, he had come to find her for a far less pleasing reason.

He had come to tell her good-bye.

He was leaving on the morrow to seek Calasaar, the Stone of Light from the Dragon Chalice. He had to do what he could to put a stop to the madness the treasure had unleashed. If he could do nothing else of worth in this lifetime, he would do this.

And as he made love to her slowly in the ancient sanctuary of the pool, attending her every gasp and sigh, claiming her with a reverence that bordered on the sublime, he pledged himself to give Ariana every ecstasy, to fill what remained of the night with only pleasure. He loved her as though it were the first time . . . the last time, for indeed, it was that. Morning—and a day of reckoning that had been stalking him all his cursed life—would come soon enough.

❧ 21 ❧

HE WAS GONE.

Ariana knew it even before she woke up, alone in her chamber some hours later, after Braedon had carried her there and made love to her until she was delirious with satiation. The ache in her heart was keen as she sat up in the bed they had shared, a bed that was tangled and disheveled from the tirelessness of their passion.

Braedon had loved her thoroughly, and now he was gone. She dressed quickly, then quit her chamber, deluding herself with the idea that she might find him somewhere in the caverns and that the coil of dread she was feeling was all for naught.

It wasn't, of course. All her hopes and prayers as she dashed along the maze of passageways, peering into empty quarters, calling his name, were wasted. No amount of wishing would conjure him up. The same way that no amount of her love—no matter how deeply she felt it, or how freely she gave it to him—could have held Braedon at her side when something stronger called him.

His honor.

She had wanted nothing more than for him to see his own worth, to know the core of strength and dignity that ran so deeply within him. Ironically, it was that same gift that tore him from her now. What a fool she had been, making plans to be with him—plans to run away together or hide there in the caverns, secluded from the rest of the world. Plans that would force him to exist in the shadows, no different from the life he knew before she met him. And all the while he had let her spin her flimsy dreams, knowing he could not settle for that. Nor would he permit her to make that sacrifice herself, no matter how willing she was.

The cruelest jest was that she had meant every word. She would have turned her back on Clairmont and all the people she knew. She would have left all of it behind, including Kenrick, if she could only have been with Braedon. As his mistress, his bride, his whore . . . it wouldn't have mattered what she was to him so long as they were together. But he had not given her the choice. He had not given them the chance.

The tears that had been threatening since she woke finally overtook her as she searched out his empty chamber in the caverns and realized, without a doubt, that she had lost him. She entered on weakening legs, her soft sob hitching in the silence of the place. His bed was unturned, his sword and satchel of meager belongings gone. Not a single trace of him remained behind.

"Damn you, Braedon," she whispered, but it was she who deserved the blame. She was the fool who had been wishing he would be there, trusting that he might love her enough to keep her at his side no matter what they might face. She should have known she would wake this morning to heartache. He had left her, as she had been warned he would by Peg that first day she met him in London.

Angered as much as she was hurt, Ariana turned on her heel and fled the empty chamber.

Kenrick's quarters lay not far down the same corridor. She rushed for his chamber and found him already out of bed as well. Fully dressed and washed, he crouched on the earthen floor of the cavern room, a small chunk of charcoal in his hand. Around him on the floor was a scribbled series of words, markings, and diagrams. He looked up as Ariana entered, his coloring much improved from when she saw him last.

"Kenrick, we must—"

"You'll not believe this, Ana," he interrupted, his eyes gleaming with the spark of discovery. "It has been here before me all along. How could I have been so blind?"

"Kenrick, Braedon is—"

"Come here," he said, getting to his feet to take her in hand and guide her farther into the room. He pointed to a series of figures and lines he had drawn on the floor. Their cryptic meaning was incomprehensible to her but evidently quite illuminating to Kenrick. "Have you any idea where de Mortaine found the first piece of the Dragon Chalice?"

"No."

"Here," he said, indicating a point that sat at the top of the charcoal diagram he'd drawn. "Saint Michael's Mount in Cornwall. It was there that I first heard the name Silas de Mortaine, when I was sent to chronicle purported miracles on the Mount. In my work for the Templars, I had been sent to many such sites in England and in France, but at the time, the Order was particularly interested in my findings from this very place. They had a large benefactor, you see, and he was offering a good deal of silver for these reports."

"De Mortaine."

Kenrick nodded soberly. "I turned over my information before I realized the true weight of what I was doing. All it took was one meeting with the man to know he could not be trusted, so I refused to continue the association with de Mortaine. The Templars were upset, of course, but none more than de Mortaine himself. I secretly resumed my work without the Order's knowledge, and within a few months, I found myself staring at the dank walls of de Mortaine's dungeon."

"Your findings are what led him to the Chalice stone?"

"Yes. I may as well have handed him Avosaar with my own two hands. But I'll be damned if I will help him claim anything more." He turned his attention back to the charcoal scribblings on the cavern floor. "In fact, that is precisely what Braedon and I have been discussing here."

"Braedon and you?" she asked, confused. "The both of you have been working on this together?"

"Aye. Since he woke me some hours ago and asked me to help him assemble what we know of the Dragon Chalice thus far. Actually, without Braedon's help, I might not have seen the connection. Certainly not as clearly as it seems to me now. As soon as he mentioned Avranches, the place where de Mortaine caught up with him and Lara, the thief who had stolen Avosaar from him, I realized what it meant."

"I don't understand."

"The location of another of the Chalice stones, Ana. Combining what we both have gathered of de Mortaine and the treasure, we think we know where one of the remaining three is located. Did Braedon not tell you when he fetched you to come down here?"

"No," Ariana said sharply, realizing now what Braedon's leaving was about. "Kenrick, he did not tell me anything at all, nor did he send me here. I have not seen him since last night."

"What do you mean?"

"That is what I came here to tell you—he is gone. I checked his chambers down the hall before I came here.

He's left, no doubt to retrieve the Chalice stone on his own, now that you say he has an idea where it might be."

Scowling, Kenrick raked a hand through his overlong hair. "Christ on the Cross. 'Tis suicide to do this alone."

"Especially for him," Ariana added, worry tightening in her breast at the very thought of it. "If what his mother said is true, Braedon cannot touch any piece of the Dragon Chalice. Part of him is like the people in this cavern—half shifter, Kenrick. What happened to Lara could happen to him, too."

Her brother released a heavy sigh, shaking his head. "This is madness. What have I dragged you into, Ariana? You cannot know how sorry I am that you are involved in all of this."

"No," she said. "Do not apologize. You are my brother and I love you. I would do anything for you."

"And Braedon le Chasseur?"

"He is my life. Oh, Kenrick. He is my everything."

Kenrick's mouth curved with understanding. "He was right. My little sister has grown up in my absence. I should have been there more for you. I didn't know how things were for you at Clairmont."

Ariana shrugged, no longer haunted by the disappointments of the past when her future was still within her grasp. A future with Braedon at her side, God willing, should he want her. "None of that matters anymore. All that matters to me now is Braedon."

"Then I reckon we'd best cease talking about it and go after him, eh? He cannot be too far ahead of us yet." Kenrick moved forward to embrace her in a brotherly hug. "Don't worry. Gather up our things while I fetch our mounts."

He strode out of the chamber, leaving Ariana to collect her mantle from her own quarters and the rest of their meager belongings. She had just stepped into the corridor when she was met by a vision of quicksilver eyes and pale white silk. "You are leaving," said Braedon's mother, beautiful in the flickering torchlight of the passageway.

"Yes."

"I have lost him twice now," she said, a frank statement when her eyes were shimmering with regret. "The first time I lost my son, he was just a frightened boy. He could not understand why he was different than other children. He wasn't prepared for the legacy he had inherited from me. The legacy he had inherited from the place of my birth."

"Anavrin."

Braedon's mother smiled a bittersweet smile. "Yes. Anavrin. I could not conceal the truth from my son. He had to understand his ability—his hunter's skills—if he was to learn to use them effectively once he became a man and the corruption of the Outside sought him out. It was important that Braedon accept what he was . . . but would that I had known to conceal those skills, and their true source, from his father."

"What happened?"

"I toyed with something I could not fully comprehend—human emotion. I fear Braedon paid the price. He was young, making a game of his gift. Often he commanded his friends to hide various objects from him so he could divine their location. At first his father paid no mind to Braedon's antics, but then people outside the keep began to notice. Folk came to Braedon with pleas for him to find all manner of misplaced things: coffer keys, books, lost hounds, even straying children and spouses. Braedon's gift was unexplainable, and his father grew fearful and suspicious of him. He punished Braedon severely and too frequently. Finally I could bear it no more. I had to make him understand how special his son was."

"You told him about Anavrin?"

"I tried. He believed none of what I said. I knew the only way he would was if he saw with his own eyes that what I told him was true." The lady took a steadying breath. "There, in the bedchamber I shared with my husband, I shifted my glamour to another form. I had no idea the grave mistake I was making. My husband drove me out that very night, shouting such ugly words. He threatened to kill me, and Braedon, if I ever returned."

"Braedon thought you left because of something he had done," Ariana told her. "His father told him you were mad, and that it was your madness in him that gave Braedon his hunter's skills. He thought himself some brand of devil's spawn, for that is what he was told until the day he finally left his father's keep."

"Yes, I know. As I said, my mistake that day was grave. I tried to make it right, but I could not risk it. I did come back to see my son, but not even my glamour was enough to protect me from Braedon's father. He discovered me in the woods outside the keep and loosed his arrows on me."

Astonishing as it was to her, even though she had seen it herself the day before, Ariana nodded in understanding. "The white wolf . . . Braedon told me of the she-wolf who befriended him, and how his father wanted to slay it before his eyes. How did you escape with your injuries?"

"My clan—well, the few you saw here, that is—found me in the woods. They took me in, for they knew I would not last long on my own."

"Your wounds must have been severe."

"They were, but that is not what would have killed me."

Ariana frowned. "I don't understand."

"I had broken a covenant of my clan. I had fallen in love with an Outsider. It is forbidden of our kind, one of the conditions of our magic here on the Outside. Because my heart belonged to my husband, and to my son, I was marked for the hunt by the Seekers of my clan. Indeed, the most perilous of them all. You see, we are to seek the Dragon Chalice, above all else. I had failed in that mission. In allowing myself to love, I had become a Shadow, as are the rest of the shifters that share these caverns with me."

"And Braedon?" Ariana asked, fearful of the answer she might receive. "If he were to fall in love with someone . . ."

"Oh, he loves, my dear. Make no mistake. I see it in every glance he turns on you."

Ariana warmed to the idea, but her heart was still twisting with worry. "But the others—the shifters. Does it put him in any danger to be with me?"

"The danger my son courts has nothing to do with his feelings for you," she said, reaching out to squeeze Ariana's hand. "He needs your love, but then I suspect you already know that."

"Perhaps not as much as I need his. He is gone, my lady. He promised me we would be together, but then he left me here."

"And you do not accept that."

"No, I don't. I will not accept it," Ariana declared. "I love him—more than anything else in this world."

"Yes, I can see that you do." Now the mild expression began to warm even more, the lady's glossy white head cocking slightly to the side in curiosity. "And I can see there is still much I do not know about your kind, Lady Ariana. I admire your strength, and I am glad for the depth of your passion for my son."

As the two women clutched each other's hands, Kenrick came around a bend in the passageway. "Our mounts are waiting, Ariana. Are you ready?"

"I have to go now," she told Braedon's enigmatic mother. Impulsively, she stepped forward and embraced the lady. "You are an extraordinary woman. Be careful, and thank you for all you've done."

Braedon's mother smiled a very human, heartbreaking smile. "Take care of him, child. Make sure he knows that no matter what he might think of me, I always loved him. I always will."

"Farewell," Ariana said, then withdrew from her loose grasp and turned to follow after Kenrick.

Behind her in the corridor, she heard the muffled sound of a mother's quiet sob.

"They're on the move, Captain. Scouts spied horses and riders on the other side of the forest, running hard on the road toward the coast."

"All three of them?"

"Nay. Just two. The woman and her Templar brother, near as we can tell. Le Chasseur must still be in hiding somewhere in the woods, or perchance they have split up to confuse pursuit."

"Le Chasseur won't hide, not now. More likely he is already gone and some hours closer to finding part of the Chalice."

Draec le Nantres tossed out the contents of his drinking cup, sparing the soldier only the barest glance as he eyed him over the smoking embers of the previous night's fire. His mood was foul, helped none the least by this incompetent's report and the frigid bite of the dawning morn. He loathed sleeping outdoors, particularly when the winter chill was wicked enough to freeze a man's ballocks off. His companions in the search hardly seemed to notice the cold. Devil-spawned beasts, one and all.

Especially Ferrand de Paris, the weaselly little Frenchman who had joined up with them around dawn. Hearing the news of their quarry having set out, Ferrand's nose twitched with excitement. "How delicious to know that the Clairmont chit will soon be mine. Without le Chasseur to interfere, it should be no trouble at all to chase her down and capture her. I'll tell the others to mount up and—"

"Sit down, Ferrand." Draec's low command halted the merchant midstride. "I give the orders here—I'd advise you to remember that. I want the Clairmont woman followed, but no one touches her. In fact, I want her unaware that we are watching her at all. If le Chasseur has gone to find one of the Chalice stones—which I would wager your neck he has—then Lady Ariana and her brother will lead us directly to him."

Draec stood up and calmly adjusted his leather gauntlets. With a warning look at Ferrand, he kicked a spray of pebbles and snow over the glowing coals of the fire. Then he strode away and gave the order for the company of guards to mount up.

❧ 22 ❧

A MILE OF tidal mudflats and swampy marshland separated the city of Avranches from the island that housed the Benedictine monastery of Mont St. Michel. It was said the tides ran higher and faster here than anywhere in the world. So fast that not even a horse galloping at a dead run could beat the rush of the oncoming water to the other side. If a person set out to cross the natural causeway too late into the cycle of the tide, he risked being swept under and drowned. That was, if the pockets of treacherous quicksand didn't get him first.

But fear of dying en route did not stop the faithful from making their pilgrimages to the glittering granite marvel of Mont St. Michel. They came in droves, dozens at a time, of all ages and from all walks of life, to see the place where the archangel Michael fought the devil and won. It was said that miracles occurred in that place, and legend had it that Saint Michael himself charged the first abbot of the mount with the task of constructing the holy monument, the awe-inspiring place that had since become a site of pilgrimage for good Christians everywhere.

A score of those reverent folk now stepped off the firm shoreline at Avranches and headed out onto the muddy expanse. It was but a couple of hours this side of dusk, a dangerous time for low tide, but the pilgrims gathered to make the crossing held tight to their faith and their long walking sticks as their modest boots squished into the thick muck, beginning the hour-long trek to the abbey.

Braedon dismounted and held fast to the reins of his horse. The skittish beast seemed none too sure of the merit in making the trip, and Braedon had doubts of his own. Mont St. Michel loomed like a ghost before him, shrouded in a heavy fog, an unwelcoming slab of steep rock and forbidding waters. But it was here he might find Calasaar, and so he went, bringing up the rear of the group, a conspicuous bristle of sharp-edged steel and dark intent amid the knot of hymn-singing, prayer-murmuring pilgrims.

The assembly was not quite halfway across the muddy seabed when a distant shout from behind them brought the party to a halt. A sharp blast from a pilgrim's horn went up from someone near the head of the group, a warning call that went unheeded by the two riders who had ventured onto the sand from the Avranches shore.

"Go back!" one of the pilgrims shouted. "You will not make it in time!"

"Saint Michael save them—the tide is already coming in!"

But the riders were too far back to hear the warnings, and taking the flats at too urgent a speed. They kept coming, unaware of the danger until all at once one of the horses tilted wildly to the side. Its foreleg sunk into a deep pocket of quicksand. Jarred and stumbling, the beast went down, tossing off its rider with a shrill whinny of fright. Braedon knew who fell even before he saw the tangle of blond hair spill out of the hooded mantle as the woman hit the ground.

"Ariana," he breathed, his heart jolting in his chest.

He ran to his mount and leaped onto it, kicking the

beast into a lurching gallop back toward Ariana and her brother. He managed to avoid the treacherous dangers of the sand. As he neared the place where Ariana lay, he jumped down off his huffing mount and raced to her side. Kenrick was there, too, on his knees, digging at the hole of muddy quicksand that swallowed his sister's leg to mid-calf.

Braedon joined him, dropping down to take Ariana's face in his hands and stare at her with disbelief and bone-deep fright. "Ariana—God's blood, woman! What are you thinking? Why did you come?"

"You left me!" she charged, anger blazing in her eyes. "You said we were in this together—to the end, you said—and then you left me!"

"Jesu, Ariana. I left you only to keep you out of harm's way—because I knew you would be foolish enough to do something like this."

"Was it your intention that I sit idly by and wait for word that you had gotten yourself killed? Was I supposed to be better off left to wonder what might become of you?"

"Yes, damn it," Braedon answered, his tone hot, although he found it difficult to hold his anger—or his concern for the rising tide—when he was looking into such beautiful, determined blue eyes. He bent down and kissed her fiercely on the mouth. "Little fool. I shouldn't be so glad to see you here."

She gave him a wobbly smile, then reached up to throw her arms around his neck, hugging him tightly. "I want to be with you. I love you, Braedon."

With a curse, he shot a woeful glance at Kenrick. "Couldn't you talk sense into her?"

"Don't think I didn't try. You're the one who told me just how headstrong she is once she sets her mind on something. I'll not argue that point ever again," he added as he freed her foot from the quicksand.

With Ariana loosed and out of danger, the two men turned their attention to her downed horse. The mount was skittish, but unharmed, and once it was released from the quicksand, it seemed eager to be off the mud-flats and back on solid ground. As were they all.

Remounted, the three of them set out for the conical jut of granite, still half a mile away. The tide was coming in quickly; already Mont St. Michel seemed to float above a mirrorlike haze of water in the distance. The pil-grims were small clumps of darkness in Braedon's line of vision as they reached the mount's shore and climbed up to safety. Their warnings of fierce currents ringing in his ears, he looked to Ariana and her brother as he wheeled his mount around to take the lead.

"The going will be hazardous—all the more so because we will have to ride, and ride fast. Follow my lead pre-cisely. Do not let your mount stray off the path I lay out for us. Kenrick, you ride in the rear and keep your eye on Ariana. And you," he said to the woman who held his heart so fully, "you stay with me and don't ease up on your horse for a moment. Do you understand? The tide moves swiftly. We won't have time for error."

She nodded, reaching out for his hand. Braedon squeezed her gloved fingers, hearing the roar of the en-croaching ocean over the steady pound of his own heart. He kissed Ariana's hand, then gave the order for them to set off for Mont St. Michel at all haste.

From the mainland shore, Draec le Nantres watched as the tide swept in to fill the causeway and separate the mountain crag from Avranches. At a full mile out and night fast approaching, it was difficult to tell whether the three riders made it safely to the other side or were engulfed by the treacherous incoming current.

Not that it mattered.

Not now.

The fact that Braedon was headed to Mont St. Michel was evidence enough to bring a smile of victory to Draec's lips. There was only one reason that his old friend would return to the abbey on the mount. Only one thing that would compel him to go to the place where he had nearly lost his life some eighteen months ago. And now that he thought on it, Draec wondered why he hadn't seen the truth of it before.

Braedon knew where one of the Chalice stones was hidden. God's blood, but he would wager the enigmatic bastard had known all this time.

Now, so too did Draec.

"Go back to the village and secure a boat," he ordered one of his men. "We're going to Mont St. Michel."

"But the tide's still coming in, Captain," came the edgy protest. " 'Twill be another two or three hours before the sea's right for travel."

"Do it, I said." Draec's low growl sent the guard scrambling away to carry out his command.

Gaze narrowed, mouth twisted in dark satisfaction, he stared at the pyramid of coal gray granite rising up out of the water like a rugged jewel. The full moon climbed higher from behind the island, a pale, glowing beacon amid the gathering twilight. The Chalice stone was secreted away somewhere in that abbey fortress, and Draec le Nantres meant to have it.

Tonight.

❧ 23 ❧

BY THE TIME they reached the rocky shore of Mont St. Michel, the sea had risen to the height of Braedon's knees. Dismounted the last several yards and walking, as were Kenrick and Ariana, Braedon led them with their horses up out of the churning tide and onto the granite outcrop at the base of the mount. It had been slow going on the muddy strand, an exhausting trek that might have killed them had they lagged at all in the crossing. But they had made it. They passed through the massive stone gate that stood as sentinel for the island fortress and its inhabitants, leading their horses along the shaded arch and onto the path within.

And now they faced a steep, arduous climb to the abbey. A solitary road led through the thickly settled village and up to the crest of the granite crag. The last of the group of pilgrims were just reaching the first corner of the winding incline as Braedon, Ariana, and Kenrick paused to let the horses catch their breath before they pushed the beasts to continue.

"If we don't wish to cause a stir," Kenrick said from beside Braedon, nodding toward the robed travelers, "it might behoove us to enter the abbey amongst a large group."

Braedon paused, considering his options as he watched the pilgrims round a bend in the moonlit path and step out of sight. "Following the pilgrims into the abbey will likely be too conspicuous for my purposes. I need to be able to move about with as little notice as possible."

"There is another way in," Kenrick said. "An older entrance, to the north. It was once the almonry, but it was long unused when last I was here. You'll have to scale the rough side of the mount to reach it, but if you mean to slip in unnoticed, I wager 'twill be your best chance."

"Agreed. You and Ariana go on ahead up the road with the horses. Just gain entrance as quietly as you can, and keep yourselves safe until I find you."

Kenrick gave him a nod of agreement, but Ariana's face seemed less amenable. "I don't think we should split up. Surely we can enter discreetly enough with the other pilgrims, then slip away to search for the stone."

Braedon shook his head. "The peace-minded Benedictines would doubtless find it hard to ignore my savaged countenance," he explained, surprised he still had to remind her of the scar that ended all hope of his ever entering any place discreetly. Ariana had accepted his face—his scars, both seen and unseen—but she was an exception in a world frightened by the strange or the different. He saw her fear now, her reluctance to leave him even for a moment, and it touched him to feel the depth of her love. He reached out to smooth away a wet tendril of hair that had flown across her brow, plastered to the white of her skin by the sea spray. He smiled, bringing her close and lifting her gaze to meet his. "This is the best way, I promise."

Her dubious pout only made him want to kiss her more. He would have, if not for Kenrick standing nearby, endeavoring not to notice them. Ariana huffed a little sigh, scolding him in a frustrated whisper. "I didn't come all this way to find you, only to let you leave me again."

"And I am still cross with you for risking such foolery, so don't remind me," Braedon chided, breathing in the warm scent of her in the moment before he released her from his embrace. "Let's get moving. The sooner we are in, the sooner we can be out. Go with your brother. I'll meet up with you inside as quickly as I can."

"Be careful," she told him, holding on to his hand as she stepped away from him and distance finally separated them.

Braedon tossed her an easy smile, but inwardly his gut was warning that all would not go as smoothly as he hoped. He felt malice hanging on the wind, a sense of foreboding coming from the general direction of the night-engulfed Normandy shore. A glance at Kenrick lifted the knight's head from where he stood, sloughing down the thick gray mud that clung to the horses' legs. Braedon drew him aside with a tilt of his chin.

"Were you followed to Avranches?" he asked quietly, careful not to let Ariana overhear his concern.

"Not that I saw. We took the main road, but it was empty most of the way, and we were riding hard. If anyone trailed us, they were as stealthy as ghosts."

No doubt they were, Braedon thought, his mood darkening. He unfastened his sword belt and handed it, weapon and all, to Ariana's brother. "Take this, you may need it."

Kenrick fixed the baldric around his waist. "You're anticipating trouble?"

"I fully expect it. I'm counting on you to keep her safe for me. And if I don't meet up with you by high tide, promise me you'll find a way to take her off this island and get her home. Don't wait for me beyond midnight—do I have your word?"

"Aye," Kenrick agreed. "I don't have to tell you that she won't like it."

"Don't give her a choice."

"You're a good man, le Chasseur." Kenrick held out his hand, a gesture of his apparent regard. "Godspeed you on your path tonight. Wherever it may take you."

Braedon clasped the outstretched hand with a brief nod of acknowledgment. Then, with a final glimpse of Ariana's beautiful face emblazoned in his mind, he left for the shadowy north side of the mount, and whatever destiny awaited him inside the abbey fortress.

It took nearly an hour for Ariana and Kenrick to make the laborious ascent to the abbey. The road leading up the steep incline of the mount was a narrow, winding path that seemed to go on without end. Walking the horses, for the beasts had been too taxed from the crossing to carry riders, they passed row upon row of timbered residences and a handful of closed shops. The street was dark, their trek lighted only by the milky glow of starlight and the full moon, which seemed enormous and eerie that night, looming above the island in a cloudless black sky.

It was that wash of moonlight that gave Ariana her first niggling of apprehension as she and Kenrick began up another steep climb in the road. The moon's pale rays glinted on the inlaid mother-of-pearl hilt of Braedon's sword, which was sheathed at her brother's hip. Braedon imagined there might be danger awaiting them at the abbey, or he would never have surrendered his weapon. And that left him with only a dagger, Ariana realized, a feeble implement of defense, should he encounter trouble of his own while he was searching for Calasaar.

At last they reached the crest of the mount. The wind

blew in strongly off the sea, salty and cold, buffeting the towering structure of the abbey marvel and snatching at the edges of Ariana's cloak. Gaping at the awesome sight of Mont St. Michel, she reached up to catch her flapping hood, which billowed like a sail before it was snagged off her head by a gust of briny air. Kenrick was at her side, but he seemed unmoved by the wintry gales or the sheer immensity of the holy place before them. His gaze was turned outward, overlooking the expanse of glittering black water that now filled the space between Avranches and the mount. He swore a profane oath.

"What is it?" she asked, following his line of vision.

"There. Halfway across the bay."

He need not say any more, for Ariana's gaze settled on the orange glow of a single torch, bobbing along on the water. A small boat was approaching, and above the roar of the waves and the bitter howl of the wind, she could just make out the sound of men's voices.

" 'Tis them."

"Le Nantres?"

"I'm sure of it. Braedon thought he might have followed us to Avranches."

"Oh, God," Ariana whispered. "What should we do?"

Kenrick turned away from the promontory to take her by the arm. "Let's get inside before they see us."

"We'll be safe from them inside, won't we? You don't think le Nantres and his men would dare breach the sanctuary of the abbey to come after us?"

"Come on," Kenrick said, offering her no assurances as he led her to the huge oak doors and gained them entrance to the abbey's almonry.

As Kenrick had instructed, Braedon found the old entrance on the north side of the abbey abandoned to time and the elements. The muscles in his calves and arms burned with the exertion it had taken to scale the rocky back of the mount, but the strain and trouble of the climb paid off tenfold when he tried the weather-beaten door of the old Romanesque structure. Unbarred, unguarded, it gave without protest, save for a groan of its rusted hinges.

Inside, the vaulted stone crypt was unlit and cold, a forgotten chamber that seemed ancient compared to the intricate design of the abbey's marvel. Braedon took a moment to let his eyes adjust to the gloom before he closed the door behind him, shutting out the moonlight and the howling Aquilon that blew in off the open sea beyond. In the dark, his mud-encrusted boots falling softly on the dusty slate floor, he crossed to the rear of the narrow, pillared vault.

A set of stairs led to the floor above. Braedon followed it, pausing when he detected the low murmur of voices and the soft crackle of a warm fire. Illumination glowed from within the elongated chamber, stretching thin fingers of light across the gleaming tiles of the floor. Braedon came to the top stair in silence and peered around the corner into the hall beyond. Three rows of columns ran the length of the scriptorium, dividing the chamber and its twin fireplaces built into the outer wall. Huge, high-set windows seemed to grow out of the groined ceiling. Their arched maws of glass gaped black with the deepness of the night sky above.

Below them, suspended by cording between the pillars that marched the length of the room, hung a number of tapestries. They had been affixed beneath the capitals like curtains, makeshift partitions that provided a level of solitude for the monks who worked so diligently at translations and manuscript illuminations within the tomblike quiet of the scriptorium. Two of those monks, young clerics in the black robes of the Benedictine order, made an abrupt exit from behind one of the tapestry partitions. Braedon moved back into the shadows as they crossed the open floor. The pair was too engrossed in scholarly discussion to notice the watchful, steady gaze that followed them as they quit the hall. An instant later, Braedon crept out of the darkened stairwell. Hastily he crossed the length of the scriptorium.

"Brother Raimond," a monk called, the detached voice trailing Braedon as he stole past the wall of tapestries. A chair scraped away from a table behind one of the curtains. The voice came again, shrill with censure. "Brother Raimond, you've carried in mud on your shoes again. That's the second time this week. . . ."

Braedon reached the anteroom door and slipped outside, narrowly escaping before the angry monk could finish his erroneously placed scold. Bypassing a corridor where a group of brethren stood to converse in low-toned Latin, he pivoted in the opposite direction and skirted along the shadows of yet another pillared hall, this one curving around toward what appeared to be an infirmary. Braedon navigated his way through that room, then a chapel lit by scores of candles held in large iron candelabras. Adjoining this worship hall was an ossuary, the place where the monks stored cemetery remains removed from the limited grounds of the burial plots.

He entered the dank, musty chamber, certain he was getting close to where he needed to be. He could almost feel it, the Stone of Light—Calasaar—clutched in the talons of a serpentine dragon that snaked around the stem of the mystical vessel. He could visualize the golden cup, one-fourth of the Dragon Chalice, its power guiding him.

Calasaar was near, he would stake his life on it.

Then he spied something promising: a plain, unassuming door at the far end of the ossuary. Five long strides carried him to the small portal. He tried the latch and cursed. Locked. He rattled the ancient panel of black oiled wood, testing the hinges. The door would not give. Not unless he meant to smash it in. He considered doing just that, but in the moment it took for the thought to enter his mind, a disturbance made him still where he stood.

Draec le Nantres was inside the abbey. Braedon sensed his movement. He willed his mind to focus and counted three others with him: shifters, all of them—one with the verminous stench of Ferrand de Paris. Braedon felt their malevolent presence stir the air, although their glamour seemed dimmed by the sanctity of the holy place. But they were well armed, and they were on the hunt inside the almonry.

Ariana.

Braedon trained his senses on her, searching for her with his mind. He felt her fear at once, felt her moving deeper into the abbey with Kenrick. They, too, knew le Nantres was there. Infiltrating the crowd. Searching for his quarry. They could elude him for a while, but how long?

He wouldn't have much time.

Bracing his shoulder for the impact, Braedon rammed his body into the small oak door and splintered it off its hinges.

❧ 24 ❧

NOT EVEN THE tight huddle of mingling humanity could conceal them from the cold green eyes that searched the crowded space of the almonry. Ariana stuck close by her brother's strong arm as he led her farther into the long gathering place with its central support of six tall pillars. Kenrick guided her to the back of the nearest one, some halfway down the length of the place, and inserted them into a small circle of pilgrims who stood, heads bowed, murmuring in a language she did not recognize, ostensibly absorbed in a moment of shared prayer.

A nod from Kenrick directed Ariana to pose likewise. She whispered a prayer in earnest as he carefully peered around the granite column to assess their position regarding le Nantres and the men who accompanied him. They had arrived a short while ago, Draec and a small number of armed knights who scarcely attempted to hide their purpose in coming to the abbey on the mount. Like stealthy forest predators, they moved about the crush of people who were taking alms and receiving blessings and lodging from the Benedictine abbot, their gazes searching, relentless as they split up to comb the almonry.

Ariana could not stand the fearful anticipation any longer. Lifting her head only the barest fraction, she whispered to Kenrick, "Where are they now? Have they seen us?"

"I can't be sure. But we can't stay here waiting for them." He ducked back around the pillar, the tendons in his proud jaw drawn tight. "Braedon told me to take you out of here at the first sign of trouble."

"Leave?"

She opened her mouth, ready to protest that she would go nowhere without Braedon, but Kenrick was already shaking his head, his decision made. "It doesn't matter. It's too late to try to leave the abbey. They would spy us for certain. Which means we'll have to press farther in and look for a place for you to hide until this is finished."

"Until it's finished? What do you mean—Kenrick, what will you do?"

She did not have to see his hand tighten around the hilt of Braedon's sword to know that her brother wouldn't hesitate to use it. He threw a quick glance over his shoulder toward the buzzing throng of pilgrims, then took her hand to lead her away. "This way, little sister. Quickly."

They made their way to a darkened stairwell leading to the floor above. Fleeing as swiftly and as quietly as possible, Kenrick brought her out into another chamber, then down a hallway. Behind them, footsteps followed, the fall of heavy boots echoing off the stone. Kenrick broke into a run, dragging her along behind him as he dashed through one torchlit chamber to another.

At the end of the last, they entered a tall domed crypt. Its rotund perimeter was lined with thick pillars of smoothed stone, situated close together like the trunks of massive trees. The vault seemed to be an intersection of sorts, for spaced around it were several doors and access ways. Before they could decide which one to try, their pursuer—the largest of le Nantres's men, an ugly, black-bearded brute—thundered in behind them.

He made a grab for Ariana, but Kenrick swept her out

of reach and drew his weapon with a warning hiss of un-sheathed steel. "Go, Ana! Hide yourself."

She numbly shook her head, hating the thought of saving herself when Kenrick, and very likely Braedon, would stand to defend her to their deaths. For a moment she stood frozen, watching her brother circle around the other man, Braedon's sword gleaming like molten silver in the torchlight. Kenrick was normally strong and fit, but he was still suffering from his mistreatment by his captors, and he was more accustomed to wielding an ink quill than he was a sword. She gaped at him in horror, certain he was going to get himself killed while she watched.

"Go, Ariana! Now!"

The sheer ferocity of his shouted order jolted her into action. She skirted between two of the fat pillars and fled into the darkness of the corridor as the first clash of steel rang out. Kenrick bit off an oath, hissing in pain. Dear God, had he been struck? The chilling thought shook her to her core as the violent grate of weapons continued. Ariana ran down the lightless passageway in terror, praying the night would not cost the lives of either one of the men she so dearly loved.

It wasn't there.

With one of the ossuary torches in hand to light the crypt, Braedon stood in the center of Mont St. Michel's treasure room and swore a vivid oath. He searched the domed alcove once more, but met with frustration and anger, and not a little confusion. Impossible as it seemed to him, he had been wrong.

Calasaar was not there after all.

The vault held a number of other treasures: jewel-encrusted crosses, exquisite sculptures—even an age-darkened, punctured skull that sat atop a pedestal like the holiest of relics. A small wooden casket adorned with brass fittings held a place of prominence on a carved stone altar placed beneath the sole window of the vault. Made of costly stained glass, the window fractured the moonlight that spilled in from it like multihued gemstones, varied and brilliant. The colors danced across the altar, glittering in rainbow reflections on the polished bowls of several priceless-looking cups and goblets.

But none of them was the cup containing the Stone of Light.

Braedon raked a hand through his hair, looking around him for something he might have missed. He had searched every alcove, examined every paltry treasure in the vault. To no avail. It simply wasn't there.

And yet . . .

He scowled, stunned to think he had been wrong. Could he be missing something? He pivoted, shining the torchlight in a wide arc around him. Nothing was illuminated further, save for the smooth brick of the crypt's stone walls and high, arched ceiling. His hunter's senses— that accursed gift he had finally come to embrace—had, in the end, deceived him. The irony of the situation wrenched a huff of laughter from his throat.

After all he had been through in the journey from London's docks to this very moment, he had failed. His chance to do something good—his determined grasp at redemption—had been for naught. Just when he had begun to believe it, to trust in it, his hunter's gift had proven a jest.

But where it failed to direct him to Calasaar, the fickle gift rose up like a herald's call to warn him that Ariana was in imminent danger. Somewhere in the abbey, she was in mortal fear. In the short time he had wasted

searching the crypt in vain, Draec's men were closing in.
Braedon felt them moving along the corridors. He
scented fresh blood in the air, Kenrick's blood, let by an
enemy blade. He could feel the clash of steel somewhere
in the abbey, could almost hear Ariana's panicked
breathing as she fled deeper within the labyrinth, searching for someplace to escape the danger.

"Run, my love," he quietly intoned. "Hide yourself,
and wait for me."

She found an alcove tucked into a shadowy corner of
an empty room some length down one of the passageways. Heart slamming against her ribs, Ariana scurried
inside the meager hiding place and waited, willing her
breath to calm lest the sound of her fearful panting betray her. She knew not how long she hunched there in the
dark, flattening herself against the cold granite bricks of
the wall. It seemed hours, an endless time of worry, of
wondering.

Was Kenrick all right?

And what of Braedon?

Heaven's mercy, but if she lost either one of them now,
she knew not how she would bear it. Fear for her own life
paled when she thought of the two men she loved more
dearly than anything, both out of her reach and facing
danger of the worst kind. Would that she could be with
them, that she could help them in some way. As she fought
to contain the tumult of her emotions, she realized the din
of clashing swords had quieted at the far end of the corridor outside. There was only silence now. Only darkness in
the tomblike room in which she hid. She listened, straining her ears for any hint of what lay beyond the chamber.

"Oh, Kenrick," she whispered, praying he escaped the
altercation with minimal harm.

Every instinct urged her to go to him, to see for herself if he yet lived, or . . .

"Ariana?"

The low-voiced summons sounded just outside the dark little room.

"Ariana, 'tis all right, little sister. Are you near? Come out."

With a soft cry of relief, she all but stumbled out of her concealment. Kenrick was at the door to the chamber, throwing her a lopsided grin as she ran to him and flung her arms around him. "I was so worried! Are you hurt?"

"Nay. Come with me."

He took her by the wrist, his strong fingers gripping her tighter than needed as he brought her out into the torchlight of the corridor. Now she could see that he was indeed unharmed. He was perfectly well, save for the lingering bruises of his captivity. Thank heaven, she thought, feeling some of her alarm ebb as he led her along the passageway.

"Where are we going?"

He didn't answer her, merely hushed her with a hiss of warning tossed over his shoulder. "This way," he said, and suddenly they were turning toward the vaulted crypt where he had just battled one of le Nantres's men. "Kenrick, wait. This path will only lead us to—"

The words choked off in her throat that next instant, for standing before them, gilded in the wobbling glow of torch flame was Draec le Nantres himself.

She jolted back, but Kenrick's grasp on her wrist prevented her from moving more than a pace. She wrenched against that biting hold, and threw a confused glance at him. "Kenrick . . . ?"

Emotionless eyes stared back at her—eyes that she could now, in the light, see were not the clear blue they should be, but rather a dullish black. Vacant. Cruel in their fathomless apathy. But the smile he gave her was far from unfeeling. Wicked, full of arrogance, the beast who held her bared his teeth in a leering grin of malicious satisfaction.

"Let me go!" she cried, fighting the bruising hold. At first she thought the pressure had lessened, for a spread of queer tingling began to creep up from her wrist. The sensation traveled higher, intensifying, and when Ariana looked up, it was no longer Kenrick's face staring back her, but another. A face that put a knot of revulsion in her stomach.

"Ah, you see, *ma belle petite*?" The shifted countenance of Ferrand de Paris laughed now. He hauled her spine against the front of his fleshy body, chuckling as she fought in vain to break free. "I promised you we would meet again."

"What have you done with him? You devil's spawn— what have you done to my brother?"

Wrenched around and taken into a pinning hold against Ferrand's immovable girth, Ariana started to scream. His sweaty hand came down over her mouth. Hard fingers clamped firmly over her lips. Ariana bucked. With her struggles, Ferrand's iron clasp on her face grew more punishing. His fingers, fat as sausages and sour with the tang of sweat and steel, tightened to a bruising vise over her mouth. Her teeth scored her lips beneath the pressure, the taste of her own blood making her heart beat faster, her frantic struggling growing more desperate.

Draec le Nantres smiled his devil's smile as his gaze settled on her. "You must think me the worst sort of blackguard, the way we keep meeting up under less than pleasant circumstances."

Ariana dearly wanted to tell him what she thought of

him, but the meaty brace of Ferrand's hand had not eased even a fraction. She glared at le Nantres over the stubby fingers clamped over her face, reining in her fear and anger lest the fury of her emotions command her wits.

"Let her speak," Draec ordered the greasy Frenchman. "She won't be fool enough to scream. Not when her beloved brother has a blade to his throat."

Ariana looked in horror to where Kenrick was now being brought toward them. The remaining two of le Nantres's men held him between them, hands tied before him. One of his captors pressed a dagger beneath his chin. His tunic was splattered with blood. For a terrified instant, Ariana feared it was a mortal injury, but a quick glance at the rest of his person showed he bore no serious wounds. Not yet, she amended, her gaze rooted to the deadly length of steel poised so hazardously against his skin.

Ferrand's hand dropped away from her mouth, and le Nantres came closer. "Now, why don't you tell me where le Chasseur has gone, Lady Ariana?"

She dragged her attention away from her brother. "I don't know."

Deep black lashes swept down lazily to shutter le Nantres's intense green eyes. If he was angered with her answer, his blithe expression betrayed nothing. Nor did his calm voice, uttered but a hair above a growl. "I know he's come here to retrieve one of the Chalice stones. I need you to tell me where he is. It will be easier on all of you that way, I promise."

"Your promises mean nothing. I have heard enough of what your word is worth to know it cannot be trusted." She sent a worried look toward Kenrick and caught the nearly imperceptible nod of his head. He shared her judgment, as he shared her conviction that the Dragon Chal-

ice must never fall into le Nantres's clutches—or his ne-
farious employer's. "I wouldn't tell you where Braedon
was, even if I knew. If you mean to kill us, you'll do it regardless of what I say now."

"Your fire is admirable, dear lady, but do not presume
to know my methods . . . or my motivations. The mistake you make here would be grave, I assure you."

He stared at her, chilling her with the depth of bleak
detachment in his gaze. If Draec le Nantres had a heart
at all, surely it was buried beneath a mountain of cold,
hard stone. His mouth was his warmest feature. It
curved into a smile that bordered on the sensual, a pro-
fanity of nature, when it could so easily deliver the black
threat that still lingered in the hallowed corridor of the
abbey.

"You know I mean it," he said. "And you are afraid."

She could not deny it. Her heart was racing. Her
breathing was becoming erratic and shallow the longer le
Nantres watched her, waiting for her to comply with his
orders. He could wait to eternity, she decided, trying
without success to tamp down the rush of panic that kept
threatening to overtake her. To her further alarm, the
dark-haired knight strode up to where she stood, imprisoned by Ferrand's unyielding grasp around her waist.
Like a bird of prey sizing up its quarry, le Nantres moved
in with light, predatory ease.

She considered lashing out at him, alive with the need
to strike something. If not for Ferrand trapping her arms
at her sides, she would have done just that. Jaw clamped
so tight it hurt, Ariana glared at le Nantres in mute rage.
Reflexively, her fingers curled into fists. The object of her
contempt merely grunted in response, not missing even
that small act of defiance.

"Rash behavior will only bring you trouble," he told

her. He threw a look at Ferrand. "Secure the lady's hands."

"Leave her alone," Kenrick snarled as the order was quickly carried out. He, too, bore a look of murder, pointed at Draec le Nantres. "Damn it, leave her alone." He tested his captors' hold on him and was rewarded with a knee driven into the small of his back. He arched taut with the blow, restrained from falling by the rough hands gripping his arms. The breath he dragged into his lungs soughed sharply in the quiet of the passageway.

Ariana winced to see Kenrick in renewed pain. A tear flooded her eye and spilled down her cheek. Le Nantres caught it on the tip of his finger with all the gentleness of a lover. He was standing before her now, scarcely a hand's width separating them. Ariana could hardly breathe for the subtle invasion of the air around her. Le Nantres reached out and took her chin in his hand, tipping her head back until she was staring up into his hell-born gaze.

"Perhaps you don't have to tell me where Braedon is," he said, studying her at length. He stared into her eyes, as though stripping away her flimsy veneer of bravery and seeing straight to the depths of her panicked heart. He lifted his hand to touch her. Ariana flinched away, an instinctual reaction that he seemed to find amusing. Or advantageous. The profane smile widened. "Perhaps le Chasseur—the acutely perceptive Hunter—can be persuaded to come to us instead."

"He already has."

Braedon's deep voice came from down the length of one of the darkened corridors. Ariana turned her head toward the sound, relieved to hear him, yet fearing what danger awaited him now that he was found out. He stood in a slim wedge of light near the end of the passageway. Flick-

ering torch glow poured out from the doorway behind
him, haloing his wide shoulders and warrior's stance. Unearthly, radiant with the light that broke all around him,
he had never looked more fierce. Or more avenging.

"Let them go, Draec. This is between you and me
now."

Le Nantres chuckled as he took a careful step down the
corridor. "Between you and me? Well, now. My employer
would likely argue that point. He wants the Dragon Chalice; I am merely the tool by which he'll get it."

With an ungentle shove, Ferrand set Ariana walking
down the passageway, their pace slow behind Draec's calculated swagger. She could just see Braedon's face past le
Nantres's thick shoulder. He watched the group of them
approach, his teeth now bared in an antagonistic grin.

"You're out to serve yourself, Draec. I know you too
well to think otherwise. I knew it the moment I realized
you hadn't returned the satchel to de Mortaine. If you
seek the Chalice, you do so for your own purposes."

"So you want to paint me as a villain, do you?" Le
Nantres shrugged insolently as they advanced toward
where Braedon waited. "No matter. I certainly don't intend to explain myself to you, old friend. Let's end this,
before someone gets hurt."

"Release Ariana and her brother, and we can end it
here and now."

The edge of Braedon's mantle shifted as he spoke, skating ever so slightly with the movement of his body. That
hint of movement would not have caught Ariana's notice
at all, save that the subtle shift of light from the chamber
at his back betrayed an object that Braedon hid behind
him. Shiny. Golden. Barely visible for how he tried to
conceal it behind his back, the object glinted like a beacon in the torchlight. It was a glimmering golden cup.

For one astonished instant, Ariana wondered if it was the Calasaar cup. But no, she thought, recalling the warnings of Braedon's mother. With his shifter blood, he could never touch any part of the Dragon Chalice, so this must be . . . dear God, it was a ruse.

But le Nantres and his men knew naught of Braedon's legacy. Their eyes were on the prize, greed for the Chalice treasure overshadowing caution.

"He holds something behind his back," Ferrand advised Draec in a smug whisper. "Do you see it there?"

"That's right," Braedon said, utterly calm in his deception. "If you want Calasaar, le Nantres, then come and get it."

❧ 25 ❧

As intended, Draec and his men began to close in. Braedon tilted the brass goblet he held behind him, inviting the light from the ossuary to glint once more on the hammered gold bowl. Taking the goblet from the treasure room had been an impulsive bid for leverage, seized upon the instant he realized Draec had captured Ariana. He could not hope to pass off the rather unremarkable cup for the ornate, mystical Calasaar, but then he had no intention of trying. All he needed was a diversion.

He backed into the ossuary, then farther still, leading them into the dim crypt of the treasure room. Draec followed willingly enough, his gaze never straying far from the cup Braedon secreted behind him. Le Nantres stepped over the threshold of the vault, followed by the others. Ariana looked worried, more for him than herself, despite Ferrand's bruising hold on her. The bastards had bound her hands. The leather cording was cutting into the delicate skin at her wrists, leaving red chafe marks. Ferrand seemed only too eager to worsen her discomfort. He drew her arms tight, ensuring her abrasions would hurt her all the more. Braedon wanted to cut the Frenchman down over the very idea, but he had to keep his head. He had to proceed with caution.

Positioning himself far into the chamber, he watched as Draec came to stand some half a dozen paces before him.

Ferrand held Ariana to Braedon's left, well out of reach. Kenrick and the two guards on him took their place on the right, effectively hemming him in, should he entertain the idea that he or his companions could attempt flight.

Le Nantres crossed his arms over his chest, arrogant now that he was in control. That was one of his greatest flaws, Braedon recalled. Arrogance was a warrior's most crippling weakness, and well he knew that. It could make a man careless. Even a man as cunning and controlled as Draec le Nantres.

"So Calasaar was here all along," Draec remarked.

Braedon did not answer. He was careful to keep the cup out of direct sight, lest his ruse be discovered too soon.

Le Nantres held out his hand, expectant. "Give it to me."

"I will. But not until you release the woman and her brother. I want no harm to come to them."

Draec's expression grew deadly serious. "The one in harm's way is you, old friend. Give me the cup, or you force my hand. How it ends tonight is up to you."

Braedon kept his gaze trained on the dark knight, giving him nothing. "Tell me one thing."

Le Nantres quirked a raven brow, an affectation of patience, though Braedon could tell what little he possessed was beginning to wear thin.

"The day you betrayed me and the rest of our men. How long had you been planning it? It was you who first told me about the Dragon Chalice. And it was you who convinced me to meet with de Mortaine about the first stone. You knew I would go after it, just as you knew de Mortaine would be waiting to kill me—to kill all of us—once we returned."

"You make it sound simple. It wasn't."

"I am glad to hear that," Braedon drawled sarcastically.

"There was little I could do once it had all started. Silas de Mortaine is a dangerous man. He made it clear that I was either with him, or against him."

"I've never known you to cow before anyone, Draec. Do you mean to tell me that you feared de Mortaine so much, you willingly brought about the slaughter of your brothers-in-arms?"

"It wasn't fear," Draec said at length.

"Then what?"

"Have you any idea what the Dragon Chalice will mean to the man who finally claims it? We are talking about wealth and power beyond imagining. We're talking about the prospect of life immortal. I won't be stopped in this. Not by you, nor anyone else. I must have that Chalice."

"Don't you mean de Mortaine must have it?"

Draec's mouth curved into a dragonlike smile. "It is time for you to decide, old friend. Do you give me Calasaar, or do I take it by force? How do you wish this to end?"

Ferrand, obviously gleeful at the notion of imminent bloodshed, wrenched Ariana tighter against his portly body. Lips flattened against his teeth, he chuckled when she tried to pull away from him. To add further insult, Ferrand grinned at Braedon, then crudely licked the side of Ariana's neck from base to ear. She cried out, revolted, and every muscle in Braedon's body went taut with the need to kill.

No more waiting. He would end this now. On his terms.

"Very well," he ground out from between gritted teeth. He tightened his fingers around the cool metal of the cup at his back. Slowly, he began to bring it around. "You want the damned cup, le Nantres—then have it."

As Draec came forward to seize the cup, Braedon jerked his arm upward, releasing the goblet to the air. It hurtled high above their heads, cartwheeling top over bottom into the arced space of the crypt.

"You bloody fool," le Nantres growled, turning to follow the soaring path of the cup. "Get it!" he shouted to Ferrand as the goblet sailed toward him through the air.

But the Frenchman seemed unable or unwilling to move, let alone comply. His eyes went wide with horror as the golden vessel spun toward him. In the instant his attention was stolen away, Ariana lunged out of his grasp. She needn't have bothered, for Ferrand was already shoving her aside to escape the path of the cup he feared would incinerate him on contact.

An instant later, Braedon caught her in his arms. "Are you all right?" he asked, whipping his dagger free of its sheath and slicing away her bonds.

She nodded. "Be careful."

In that moment of chaos, Draec vaulted forward to catch the goblet as it dropped. Kenrick used the diversion to his advantage as well, ramming his elbow into the chest of the guard who held him at knifepoint. While the dullard coughed from the blow, Kenrick wrenched the weapon from his slackened grasp and rounded on the second man, gutting him in one swift blow. The first guard moved quickly then, drawing his sword with a roar of rage.

Braedon saw the deadly attack coming. Although he knew it would be to his best advantage to fell Draec, or even Ferrand, he could not stand by while Ariana watched her brother take a lethal blow. His dagger cool and heavy in his hand, the sole weapon he had in that moment, Braedon took quick aim and let the blade fly. It arrowed across the ossuary and struck home, planting to the hilt in the heart of its target. The big knight went down with a curse on his lips, dead before he hit the ground.

Kenrick threw him a look of gratitude, but it turned to stricken alarm an instant later.

Behind him, Ariana cried out a warning. "Braedon! Look out!"

He turned his head, too late. Ferrand's sword came at him in a flash of steel, a sure strike to his midsection. But in the instant it would have torn into him, something stopped it—Ariana's slender form. She came in front of him, too abruptly for him to react, her arms spread wide, spine pressed against him like a fragile shield. Everything happened in a blink, yet the motions played out in sluggish horror, as though time crept forward in agonizing slowness.

Braedon saw the long blade protruding from beneath Ariana's rib cage. He heard her gasp of startlement, saw her arms drop down limply at her sides. He felt an excruciating wave of anguish—of wordless shock—as Ferrand withdrew his weapon and stumbled back on his heels. His sword came away from her, stained with blood. Ariana's blood, which was spilling out of her and onto the slate tiles of the ossuary floor. When he might have advanced, Draec held Ferrand off with a look.

"*No!*" Braedon's voice was a pained howl, booming in the sudden pall of the chamber as Ariana's legs gave beneath her. "Oh, God—no!"

Eyes wide with shock, Ariana began to sink slowly to her knees. He held her, easing her down, every part of him—his every instinct—clawing at him with the bone-deep fear and pure, overwhelming grief of losing her.

Now, after everything. Before he'd had a chance to tell her how much she truly meant to him. How very dearly he loved her, and always would.

"Braedon," she whispered, her voice thready as she gazed up at him.

"I'm here, love."

"Am I . . . bleeding?"

"Shh," he soothed, unable to form words as he knelt down beside her and carefully cradled her in his arms.

She moaned softly, wincing, struggling to draw air into her lungs. Her hands came up as if she meant to assess for herself what had happened to her. Braedon gently guided her away, closing his fingers around hers before she could feel the terrible truth of her injury.

"Oh, angel, nay . . . just lie still."

The wound was bad. Worse than bad, he acknowledged with a grim sense of understanding. Kenrick dropped down on the other side of his sister, offering quiet words of reassurance. His face was ashen, however, and his hands trembled as he drew aside her mantle and looked upon her bloodstained gown.

"Jesu," he hissed.

That softly uttered word confirmed Braedon's worst fears. He sat there, numb, then shook his head in denial.

No. Not her.

Not Ariana. Not like this.

A wave of raw fury built in him, swelling past his grief, a need for swift vengeance. With a vicious snarl, he shoved to his feet and whirled to face Ariana's assailant. God help him, he would tear Ferrand's throat out with his bare hands. He would slay them all. He lunged forward, but three blades held him at bay. Draec and Ferrand and the last remaining guard all stood before him, weapons poised for attack.

Draec gave him a grave look, saying nothing as he took in the severity of Ariana's wound. He knew, too. Braedon could see the truth of it in his old friend's eyes. "It didn't have to come to this, you know."

"No, it didn't, you bastard."

Ferrand began to chuckle, clearly enjoying the misery he had dealt.

"You could have stopped it," Draec said, sharing none of his associate's amusement. Indeed, his face held a surprising degree of remorse, his sharp green gaze darkened and grim. "You could have prevented this, Braedon. All you had to do was tell me where to find the damned cup—"

"To hell with you and the Dragon Chalice!" Braedon roared. He turned his fury on the vermin grin of Ferrand de Paris. "There is a score to be settled here now, Goddamn it."

"Yes." Draec nodded. "You are right about that."

With measured civility and an utter lack of warning, he pivoted toward Ferrand and slashed his blade across the shifter's throat. The chortling humor flushed to a slackened gurgle, then a rasping, dying sputter. He slid down to a lifeless slump on the floor, his dull black eyes wide and unseeing.

"Your score is settled now, friend. All that remains between us is the matter of the Chalice stone." Ferrand dead and already forgotten, Draec held out the false cup. "Calasaar, is it?" he asked Braedon, who was still held at the end of the last guard's blade. "You know as well as I that the true cup will have a dragon wrapped about its base, the same as the other. Like Avosaar, the true cup bears a dragon clutching one of the Chalice stones in its talons."

The plain brass chalice hit the floor with a clatter. Draec stared hard. Outside, the full moon shone like a ball of white fire through the narrow arched window of the crypt. The bright spangles of light spilled over le Nantres's face, illuminating what seemed a mask of barely contained rage. But his eyes flashed with something stronger still. Desperation, Braedon realized, looking into the haunted visage of his old friend, his old betrayer. More than greed or want of glory, what drove le Nantres now was a steely, desperate need.

Braedon thought to call it fear, but he had spoken true when he said he'd never known the brash knight to be afraid of anything. Least of all, the wrath of another man. Draec did not seek the Dragon Chalice so much for his shadowy employer as he did for himself. The question was, why?

"Where is it?" Draec demanded. The guard's sword edged closer, biting into Braedon's chest. "God damn it, do not be a fool. Where is Calasaar?"

"Obviously not here."

"You're lying." Le Nantres stormed to the reliquary on the altar and threw open the lid with a bang. He plunged his hand into the treasures housed within and stirred the lot of them, careless in his haste to have what he had come to claim. "Worthless trinkets, all of this," he hissed. He gave up on the casket of artifacts and church baubles, pivoting to face Braedon once more. His gaze slid to a priceless urn that sat on the deep embrasure beneath the window; an instant later, he sent the vessel crashing into the opposite wall. The ancient earthenware shattered in a thousand pieces, punctuating Draec's vivid oath. "I need that cup, you understand? I won't leave here without it."

"Braedon." From behind him, on the floor with Ariana, Kenrick called to him in a quiet, strangled voice. "We don't have much time," he said when Braedon turned his head to look at them. "She's fading."

Like a hundred-stone weight, those words pressed down on his heart. Bleak and hopeless, too impossible to believe. By the Cross, but if he had the Calasaar cup—if he'd had the accursed Dragon Chalice in whole—he would give it to Draec now. He would give him anything, if only Ariana weren't slipping away from him in a pool of blood at his feet. She was his light, his heart—God's love, she was the very meaning of his life—and he was losing her.

Ignoring le Nantres's demanding presence, in total defiance of the sword that was a mere hairbreadth from ending his suffering, Braedon turned around and knelt beside his beloved. So much blood. Her breath was naught but quick, shallow pants. Her beautiful blue eyes kept dimming beneath the heavy droop of her lids. Somehow she managed a small smile for him.

"Braedon," she said, though it was a soundless word on her lips, little better than a sigh.

"I'm here," he told her. "I'm here. I'll never leave you, Ariana. Never."

Her chin trembled. "It's . . . so cold."

"I know, angel." He brought her into his arms, gingerly, lest he cause her any further pain. "I'll keep you warm. Don't worry. Just be still."

Kenrick gave him a sympathetic look, sorrow drawing a thin line at the corners of his mouth.

"Le Chasseur," Draec warned from behind him, "our business is not finished."

"I say it is." Braedon refused to give another thought to le Nantres or anything else. His focus was on Ariana entirely. If Draec meant to run him through in reprimand, so be it. He didn't care. He'd rather take his death right there than live a moment without her. "If you mean to kill me, Draec, then do it. You have already taken the one thing that matters to me."

For several heartbeats, Le Nantres stood quiet, contemplating. "Nay, I'm not going to kill you, old friend. That's never been my aim. All that matters to me, you see, is the Dragon Chalice." He blew out a sighed curse. "You say you were wrong about Calasaar being somewhere on the Mont, but your instincts led you here. I'd sooner trust that than your word any day."

Braedon kept his gaze trained on Ariana, his fingers stroking her face and the cooling skin of her hands. "Go to hell, le Nantres."

"Yes, probably." Draec's humorless chuckle rumbled in the pall of the crypt. "I trust you'll save me a place at table whenever I might arrive. Let's get out of here," he said to the remaining guard. "That stone is somewhere in this abbey. I want it found. *Now.*"

Ariana wanted so badly to close her eyes. She wanted to sleep, for every bit of strength she possessed seemed to have fled her, leaving her heavy and listless in Braedon's arms. She felt his hand on her brow, a warm, soothing presence now that darkness was creeping in. She heard movement near the door: the scuff of boots and the shift of fabric, the chink of spurs on stone, as Draec le Nantres and the other soldier departed to search the Mont for Calasaar.

When she opened her eyes again, it was to see Braedon's face above her. His proud jaw was held tightly, clenched as firmly as the hand that held hers against his chest. She could feel his heartbeat thudding beneath her palm. Steady, strong, she focused on that beat of life, drawing strength from it, reassurance that nothing bad could happen to her when Braedon held her in his arms. But something was wrong. The gray gaze she knew so well seemed too bright, too sharp with emotion. There was fear in Braedon's eyes, and a sorrow that broke her heart.

"Am I dying?" she asked him, needing the truth. "I feel so . . . strange . . ."

"Ah, love. You won't die. Don't say it."

"The blade . . ." She nodded weakly, recalling the moment she was struck down. "It hurts."

"Shh, I know. I'm so sorry, angel."

Ariana tried to tell him it was all right, but the breath soughed through her teeth wordlessly, a monumental effort just to stay awake. She reached up to touch his cheek, but her arm would not cooperate. It rose only a fraction from where it rested at her side, heavy as a lance. Braedon saw her struggle. He wrapped his fingers around her hand and brought it to his lips, pressing a warm kiss into the center of her palm. He was so tender. So comforting and strong. She never wanted to let him go.

But she would have to, she knew. Darkness was encroaching. The full moon, which had seemed so unbearably bright not a few moments before, had since begun to dim. Shadows crouched in to fill the corners of her vision. A trick of her weakening body, no doubt. Soon she would see nothing but darkness. She forced her eyes to remain open, forced her blurring gaze to stay rooted on Braedon's face.

"Ariana, stay with me," he urged, squeezing her hand and smoothing his fingers through her hair. "Stay with me, my love. Kenrick, go get help. There must be something the Benedictines can do for her."

Even in her weakened state, Ariana could see the morose look her brother gave him. Although doubt filled his eyes, Kenrick nodded to Braedon, then offered her a stern, brotherly order. "You stay strong, Ana. You stay with us, understand?"

"I don't know if I . . . can. So tired, Kenrick. I want to sleep."

"No." Braedon jostled her slightly, startling her back to wakefulness. "No sleeping yet, my love. You must stay awake."

She sighed, feeling darkness flood into her vision. "Tired, Braedon . . . I want to go home."

"Shh," he whispered. "I know. I'll get you there. I promise."

"Don't let me die here, Braedon. Please . . . take me out of here."

He looked at her for a long moment, stroking the back of her hand, his gaze willing her to keep fighting the sleep that beckoned so strongly. "All right, angel," he managed to croak, seeming to force the words past his parched lips. Kenrick had since gotten to his feet and now stood beside Braedon, resting his hand on his shoulder in a show of support. Braedon glanced up at him. "Let's take her home, as she wishes. It's nearly midnight; the tide will be at its peak."

"I'll see if I can find us a means off this crag," Kenrick said. "There were some boats docked down at the base of the Mont . . ."

Braedon nodded. "Hurry."

❧ 26 ❧

SHE COULDN'T DIE.

God help me, Braedon silently intoned, *do not let her die!*

Was this the terrible price his mother warned him he would pay for his pursuit of the Dragon Chalice? Would that he had known it would be so steep. Cursing himself for not heeding the warning, he removed Ariana's mantle and laid it aside so he could inspect her wound. It was still bleeding. It wouldn't stop, and with each passing moment, he could see Ariana's strength drain. Her eyes kept drifting closed, slower all the time, her focus steadily weakening.

"Stay awake, my love. Please . . . you must stay awake."

How could his voice sound remotely calm when his heart was banging around in his chest like a drum? He mustered every ounce of composure he possessed, holding back his fear to show Ariana a confidence he did not truly feel. What he felt was terror. Marrow-deep, consuming terror. She was slipping away, and it was all he could do not to roar his grief that he was losing her. It was getting queerly dark in the small chamber, dimming gradually but as surely as the life was ebbing from Ariana's frail body.

Her thready voice reached out to him in the gathering darkness. "I love you, Braedon . . . so much. Love you . . ."

"Ah, sweet." He gazed down at her, regret lacing every breath he dragged into his lungs. "I love you, Ariana. I adored you from the moment I first saw you. You must know I loved you from the start."

She shook her head, weakly, a wistful smile tugging at the corner of her mouth. "Noble liar . . . you didn't love me . . . thought I was naught but . . . trouble." A small laugh puffed past her lips. "More bother than I was worth. That's what you said."

He cursed, then gave her a rueful smile. "Did I say that? I vow, I don't recall it."

"Certainly . . . did." She closed her eyes as he ran his fingers over her brow, smoothing back a dampened lock of her hair. "Stubborn-willed, idealistic . . . you said . . . you said I was the most infuriating female . . . you'd ever met."

"Bluster, all of it," he admitted now. "You should have known I didn't mean a word. You're an angel. My angel." He touched his fingers to his chest. "You're my heart, Ariana."

"Now you . . . tell me?" She gave a choked little laugh. "I might have known you'd . . . choose a moment like this to try to endear yourself to me. Now, when I am—"

"No," he said, cutting her off before she could say it. "I should not have let a moment go by without telling you what you mean to me. I'll tell you every day, if it makes you happy."

"Mmm," she moaned softly. "It would . . . very happy."

"Then stay with me now, Ariana. I'll take you home, and I swear to you I'll tell you every day how much I love you. How much I adore you, and cannot live without you."

"You . . . promise?"

"Yes. God, yes. Anything you want."

The chamber was growing inexplicably darker. Thick shadows crept in from all sides, blotting out the moonlight. Only the slimmest shaving of light remained, and that, too, was slowly becoming faint. Braedon kept his attention rooted on Ariana. He caressed her delicate cheek and that pretty, stubborn chin, needing to touch her, needing to hold on to her. With her name a sorrowful whisper on his lips, Braedon stretched out beside her on the hard, cold slate of the treasure room floor. He gathered her close to him, giving her the warmth of his body.

"Shall I tell you how life will be for us once we're away from here?" he asked, needing to fill the quiet with lighter thoughts. With some glimmer of hope, even if that hope seemed only a fragile illusion. He pressed a kiss to her dampened brow. "Would you like to know how I intend to woo you, dear lady, and win your heart forever?"

"You have my heart," she whispered. "You . . . always will."

Undeservedly, he thought, looking at her fragile, broken body and hearing the life slowly ebb from her with each passing moment. "I mean to earn your love, Ariana. I'll never be worthy, but if you promise to stay with me now—to fight this, and let me take you home to Clairmont—I vow I will spend every day of my life devoted to you in all ways."

"Mmm . . . like the sound of that," she sighed.

"I give you my oath, lady. I will never let a single day pass without telling you that I love you. And a kiss," he added, "every day, you shall have a minimum of one kiss. Starting now." Lifting himself to his elbow, he pressed his lips to hers, savoring the sweet, tender feel of their mouths brushing together. He could hardly summon the will to break the contact, lingering there as though to never part with her.

When at last he did draw back, it was to find her watching him, a pleasured look in the shadowed blue of her eyes. "And children?" she asked.

"Of course. As many as you like."

"I would have liked to have had your children, Braedon."

"Then so you shall," he told her. "A dozen, if it makes you happy."

She smiled. "A dozen would be acceptable . . . to start."

"As you wish. Anything you wish."

"And . . . you'll marry me?"

"I wed you here and now, my lady." He brought her hand to his lips and pressed a kiss to her pale fingers. "If you'll have me, Ariana, I would be proud to take you as my bride. I love you. God knows, all I wish is for us to be able to hold each other, to love each other, for the rest of our lives."

She gave him a sad little smile. "Nay, my lord." She shook her head, faintly denying this last request as her eyes began to drift closed once more. "Braedon le Chasseur . . . lord of my heart . . . I will love you forever."

Although he tried, Braedon could not hold back the stinging tear that streaked down his face as Ariana slipped toward unconsciousness. She was still breathing, but for how much longer, he could not be certain. She had lost a great deal of blood. The sword wound was brutal, more brutal than many he had seen in combat. No amount of promises or praying would see her through this trial. He was losing her, right there. Right now. Sorrow, raw and shattering, choked him. He fought the anguish with all he had, but it was stronger than him. He held on to Ariana, ordering her to fight, to hang on, but he could feel her slipping away.

Dark and darker his world became—the darkest hour of his life. He did not think he could endure this abyss of pending loss. As if to echo the gloom that swelled within him, the chamber light now seemed all but doused. A deep blackness pervaded the space around them, plunging the room into an eerie, almost lightless chasm. Even the full moon could not penetrate the queer, coming darkness. The glowing orb seemed all but as snuffed outside the window, visible only as a sliver of white.

The strangeness of it drew Braedon's attention to the mullioned pane of glass above the altar. He rose to his feet and walked to peer outside.

"What the devil . . . ?"

The moon was gone.

Full and round but a short while ago, now only the barest edge remained. That edge of milky white burned bright, but it was being slowly devoured by an encroaching shadow of black. It was like a cloud, only he had never seen a cloud so thick or so uniformly round as the shadow that began to slide farther over the moon. As he watched, unsure what to make of the anomaly, the blackness covered the last of the light, plunging the abbey chamber and everything outside into complete and utter darkness.

"Braedon . . . are you here?"

"Yes, love. It's all right. I am still with you."

"Dark," she said, her voice sounding faint behind him, parched and thin with fear. "It's getting very dark."

He knew how she disliked the dark, and he would not permit her to suffer a single moment of apprehension. Not now. "Don't be afraid. I'll get a light from the other room," he said, turning his attention away from the deep night sky and its suddenly missing moon.

All he took was one step. One step, and then he saw it. The smallest, faintest glimmer, emanating from the far wall of the chamber. He paused where he stood, peering suspiciously into the dark as the glimmer swelled to life. Like orange embers drawing flame, behind the bricks in the wall, slowly, steadily, the glimmer became a glow. Braedon walked toward it, drawn as though entranced. Warmth emanated from the smooth wall of stones. Light broke through in fingers of illumination, a line of flame-bright heat that seemed to form an arch in the wall.

A door, he realized in astonishment.

A door that was no door at all, but a part of the wall itself, its hidden frame outlined now by the breaking prisms of light.

"My God. Ariana, do you see this?"

Drawing his breath in wonder, he lifted his hand to touch the wall, to determine if what he was seeing were real. He pressed the flat of his palm to the warm stone, cautiously, amazed by the power he felt vibrating from the other side. It was so pure, so strong—

The bricks beneath his fingertips suddenly began to tremble.

Braedon drew back at once, wary. But the bricks kept trembling, shifting as though the mortar could not hold them. And the light behind the wall grew brighter, blinding. Braedon turned his face away from the piercing rays that seemed to hold the force of a hundred flames. He heard the stone wall begin to scrape on itself, the sound of pebbles breaking loose, crumbling onto the slate floor at his feet. He shielded his eyes with his forearm and watched in sheer amazement as the center of the ancient stone wall rattled and shook . . . then fell to dust before him.

Behind it now, in the gaping arch left by the rubble, was a door. Light still burned on the other side of that wooden portal. Mystical, beckoning. Braedon touched the latch on the small wooden panel, and the door swung wide without a sound. He stepped forward into the arched space that had only a few minutes ago been sealed by two solid feet of stone and mortar. He entered through the hidden door, and looked down a steep flight of granite stairs. The light was brighter down below, as though pulsing from the heart of the Mont itself.

With a word of reassurance to Ariana, Braedon entered cautiously. He put his hands out at his sides, feeling along the wall as he began his descent. Peculiar etchings marked the smooth wall of the stairwell. They looked to be letters and strange little shapes, carved into the granite with stunning precision. The markings were graceful and artistic, but their meaning was indecipherable to him as he continued down, awestruck and anxious as to what he might find at the base of this secret passageway.

"Calasaar."

His voice was a gasp of awe as he reached the final step and came to stand before a raised pedestal of shining glass-smooth stone. Atop the small altar was a cup. A golden cup with a dragon coiled about its stem. And in the beast's talons was a stone of pure crystal white light.

"Calasaar," he said again, astonished beyond further words.

By the saints, he had found the Stone of Light!

With leaden legs and sweating palms, he ran to the pedestal. He thrust out his hand, ready to grab the cup . . . and there he paused.

His fingers hovered just above the mythical treasure,

less than a breath away from seizing it. His blood pounded in his temples—the very blood that might now seal his doom.

Half shifter, his conscience warned.

If he touched any part of the Dragon Chalice, he could perish on the spot. He might meet the same fate as the thief who'd stolen the other stone from de Mortaine all those months ago. The memory of it rose up in swift clarity—the girl's screams as she was forced to hold the Avosaar cup, the blinding ball of flame that engulfed her on contact, like dragon's breath, reducing her to ash in mere moments. That same fiery end might wait for him now, in the shimmering glow of the Stone of Light.

And yet . . .

If the Dragon Chalice and its four enchanted stones truly did hold the power of the ages, if it could truly give life as the legends said, then it might also give him a chance to save Ariana.

Dear God, it might be his only chance.

"For her," he said, flexing his fingers as he drew closer to the cup.

The woman he loved—the woman who meant everything in the world to him—was dying in the crypt abovestairs. If he died now for daring to defy his destiny, then so be it. His life meant nothing without Ariana.

Girding himself for what may come, Braedon spread his hand over Calasaar's golden bowl. Heat radiated from the cup, meeting his palm with the strength of a thousand fires.

"For her," he said, resolved beyond any degree of apprehension. "Anything for her."

He slowly closed his fingers around the dragon base of the cup.

A charge not unlike a bolt of lightning surged up his

arm. His palm and fingers burned, searing under the force of the treasure's power. Pain lanced through him, spreading from his arm, which shook and trembled as he fought to hold the cup.

But the hellish flames did not come.

No incinerating ball of fire rose up to take him, despite the unceasing lash of heat that swelled to fill his body and, it seemed, his very soul. Excruciating and thorough, the pain nearly robbed him of his breath. But he was alive, by God, and he had the Calasaar cup.

"Hold on, Ariana," he prayed as he dashed back up the narrow passageway. "Don't let me be too late."

Awash in the black opacity of the moonless night, the room took on the glow of the Calasaar cup as he came up the stairwell. Soft shades of gold illuminated Ariana's delicate form, lying so forlornly in the center of the crypt. Braedon ran to her side and knelt next to her. "Ariana," he said, bending down to kiss her pale lips. "My love, can you hear me? Are you still with me, angel?"

She didn't answer. Her eyes were closed, her limbs lax and unmoving. She had gone utterly still.

Braedon's heart lurched in his chest. "Ariana!"

He bent over her, pressing his ear to her breast. Thank the saints, she was still breathing. Her heart was still beating, but faintly. And not for long, he was certain. He had to give her a drink from the cup and pray for a miracle. Pray for some bit of magic, for that was the only hope he had left.

He scanned the dim chamber for a water flask or wineskin. There was neither. But there was an ewer on the table in the adjacent room. He raced to it and grabbed the earthenware pitcher. It could weigh no more than a soldier's helmet, but it took all of his strength to lift the vessel and pour some of the water into the Calasaar cup.

His hands were shaking as he brought it back to Ariana. He fed her from the enchanted bowl, lifting her head into the crook of his arm and pressing the rim of the cup to her parched lips.

"Drink, love. Please, you must drink."

The water trickled over the seam of her mouth and down her chin. He tried again, coaxing her to take a swallow, even a small one. Ariana parted her lips and drank a bit. She choked, but then she took another drink.

"That's it," he whispered. "Take some more if you can."

She swallowed again, then turned her head away without opening her eyes. Her skin was fading to a paleness that terrified him. Braedon waited, watching for any sign that she might be all right. Her breaths were growing even more shallow. He held her hand, kissing her fragile fingers, and feeling his heart break further as her grasp steadily weakened.

He closed his eyes, unable to hold back his grief. It clawed at him, stronger than the searing waves that yet assailed him from the touch of Calasaar's power. The fabled cup slipped out of his hand and fell to the floor beside him. It no longer mattered to him. None of it did, if he could not share his life with Ariana. Heart heavy, eyes burning with the stinging swell of his sorrow, he laid his head down on Ariana's breast and swore a bitter oath.

He didn't know how long he held himself there, mourning all he had lost. He held Ariana against him, wishing he could trade his life for hers. He clutched her tightly, wanting to warm her coldness away, fearing the thought of letting her go.

"Braedon," came a feathery whisper beside his ear, so

soft he thought he'd imagined it. "Braedon . . . you are crushing me."

He drew back with a disbelieving gasp. "Ariana!"

Her beautiful eyes were open now, becoming clear and alert in the soft glow of Calasaar's light. "Are you crying?" she asked, life coloring her face once more. She reached out to brush away the moisture on his cheek. "Whatever is wrong?"

"God's love, Ariana." He released a shout of immense joy. "Are you all right?"

She smiled at him as if he had lost his mind. "Of course I am." When she reached for his hand, the one that had held Calasaar, she frowned. "Oh, mercy. What happened to you?"

"I found the Stone of Light, angel. There was another chamber within this one—a passageway leading down to a hidden crypt. . . ."

He pointed behind him, to the pile of rubble that had fallen to reveal the secret door. But the rubble was no longer there. The wall was restored to its previous solid form, as if the portal behind it never existed—as if the light behind the bricks had never been there. All evidence was gone . . . save the golden cup with the dragon and its glowing stone.

Braedon drew back to assure himself that Ariana was well and truly healed. He tore open the punctured bodice of her gown, impatiently moving aside the bloodied fabric that was covering her wound. Hardly a trace of the savage laceration remained. It was healed as though a year had passed and it had only been a scratch. All that was left to mark it was a silvery wedge of scarring.

"It's gone," he breathed, filled with relief. "Your wound—Ariana, my love, it's *gone*."

She glanced down, touching the new skin that glowed a

healthy pink beneath her fingertips. Staring at him in obvious wonder, she let out a gasp of shock. "Oh, Braedon!"

He caught her in his arms and kissed her, and he immediately forgot all about secret passageways and doors that appeared behind walls of solid granite, and the searing, humming force that still echoed in his veins. All he knew—all that mattered—was this woman. Ariana was alive.

They were still embracing, still kissing madly, when the sound of urgent footfalls approached in the corridor outside.

"Braedon," Kenrick called as he entered the chamber. "We must be off at—" He drew up short and stared at them, agape. "What is this? How did you—how did she . . . ?"

Braedon could not help but beam. Keeping one arm locked tight around Ariana, he gestured to the cup that lay beside them. "Calasaar," he said. "The Stone of Light was here all along. The magic truly exists."

Kenrick strode into the crypt, shaking his head in evident disbelief. He took the cup from the floor and held it up before him. "Incredible. And you?" he said, looking to Ariana. "Your wound—"

"It's healed, thanks to the power of the Dragon Chalice. And thanks to Braedon."

With a gentle stroke of his hand at her nape, Braedon brought her to him for a slow, passionate kiss. "I love you," he murmured, staring deeply into her eyes.

"You made me some promises tonight, my lord."

"Yes, I did." He kissed her again, with all the joy and affection that swelled in his heart. "I've just satisfied one of my daily vows. I cannot wait to start on the others." Her blue gaze shimmered, full of life and welcoming sensuality. "A dozen, did you say?"

Her laughter warmed him like a balm. "Aye, my lord, a dozen . . . to start."

"Kenrick," he said, never taking his eyes off the lady who held his heart in her tender hands. "What about that boat?"

"There is one tied up on the north point, the seaward side of the mount. Unless I miss my guess, it's the very boat that le Nantres commandeered to get here from Avranches. If we hurry, we can put in while he's still chasing his tail here in the abbey, looking for this cup. The Channel Isles are only a couple hours out, so long as the weather continues to hold."

"By all means, let's hurry and get that boat to England," Braedon said, grinning as he rested his forehead against Ariana's. "I have given a lady my vow, and I mean to keep it. As soon as possible."

Together the three of them made their way out of the abbey, their escape aided by the prolonged distraction of the queer night sky. The moon, which had been full and shining earlier that night, was still absent, but in its place glowed an orb of deepest red incandescence. All the pilgrims who had gathered at the abbey and most of the resident Benedictines now stood gaping out of windows and crowded shoulder-to-shoulder in the doorways to observe the strange phenomena.

Amid their state of awe, no one noticed the humble trio who slipped out of the crowd on silent, stealthy feet. Nor could they guess at the true miracle that had just occurred within the walls of the mountain chapel. That miracle, Braedon thought, was not so much the magic of the Calasaar cup as it was the extraordinary woman who held the treasure tight beneath her mantle.

Ariana was the greatest magic he had ever known. Her

love was more powerful to him than any legend or sorcerer's spell. She was his destiny, and his future. She was his very soul.

And as they climbed into the small, abandoned boat at the base of the mount and pointed it toward the open sea, he knew that a lifetime of miracles awaited him . . . beginning with making Ariana his bride.

❧ EPILOGUE ❧

Clairmont Castle, England
May 1275

SPRING BREEZED IN on an angel's breath, warm and pleasant, lofting down from a cloudless sky of palest blue to embrace the countryside in verdant promise. Lady Ariana of Clairmont closed her eyes and savored the bliss of the morning as she and her beloved new husband reclined atop a blanket in a secluded pondside meadow in the heart of the expansive demesne. Her body was still singing from his attentions, her bare skin still heated and flushed from the shattering release that had left her weeping and sated but a moment before. She nestled deeper into the strong curve of Braedon's arm, sighing with the lazy, sensual peace of a woman well pleasured.

"Have I told you yet today that I love you, wife?"

"Mm, yes you have, husband," she murmured against his warm, strong chest.

"And I've kissed you?"

"Thoroughly." She smiled with wanton delight, recalling the many ways—the many wicked places—his lips had pleased her with their touch. "You have been most vigilant in keeping your promises."

"Good," he growled with masculine pride. "I wouldn't want to disappoint."

"Nay," she sighed. "Oh, nay, never that, my lord."

He stroked her bare shoulder in a languorous caress that stirred her even as it soothed. "There is still the matter of those dozen babes, however. It has been nearly four weeks that we've been wed. I'd hate for you to think I am any less than committed to fulfilling all of your demands, my lady."

"Oh, trust me, my lord, when I say that your commitment has been duly noted . . . and appreciated."

With a brazen slide of her hand, she reached down the length of his lean, muscled body. His sex was hard even before she touched it; with her fingers wrapped around the heavy shaft, it surged fuller, thrusting in her palm. She rose up on her elbow, watching pleasure play over his expression as she drew her hand up the stiff length of his arousal and down to the thick root of him. "I would say, my dear husband, that the length . . . and breadth . . . of your commitment is—"

"Yes?" he prompted.

She leaned down to kiss the curving corner of his sensual mouth. "Well, it is most impressive."

He groaned as she turned into him and slid her leg over his hips, coming up on her knees to straddle him. Teasing him shamelessly, she seated herself just below his pelvis, cradling his jutting shaft at the moist juncture of her thighs. "As for the depth of your commitment, sir, I'm afraid I couldn't be sure just yet."

He grinned, flexing his hips beneath her and creating a delicious friction of their bodies. "Perhaps my lady requires another demonstration?"

"Oh, yes," she purred. "I think another demonstration is definitely in order."

He pulled her down atop him and claimed her in a passionate joining of mouths and limbs and wrenching, unparalleled rapture. She was still panting and breathless when she took his hand to her lips and kissed the center of his scarred palm. The silvery marks bore the curving lines of a dragon, etched into his skin when he had taken the Calasaar cup from its hiding place at Mont St. Michel in order to give her a lifesaving drink from the treasure. He had borne unspeakable pain for her.

"It was worth it," he said, knowing her so well he was able to divine her thoughts merely by looking at her. "Our life together—all that we share—was worth everything that happened."

Ariana held him closer, knowing just how much he had lost in saving her. He had paid a terrible price—just as his mother had warned—in daring to touch that missing piece of the Dragon Chalice. For more than his burns, which were severe, his act of sacrifice in the abbey had also cost him his hunter's instincts. He swore he was glad to be rid of them, but Ariana knew he would say that only to keep her from feeling guilt for any part of his suffering.

"Any news from your brother?" he asked, no doubt attempting to guide her away from troubling thoughts.

"No. Not a word since he left for Cornwall."

Kenrick's health had improved since his rescue and return to Clairmont, but along with his healing came a dogged determination to find another of the Dragon Chalice stones. He had a strong will, much like his sister, Braedon had often reminded her, and there was little anyone could do to sway him from his course. Ariana had tried, but he only waited long enough to see her wed before he was gone once more. She missed him, and she worried, but she also understood. And now she said a silent prayer for him, hoping wherever he was, that he was safe.

"You are quiet, love." Braedon smoothed his hand along her face and paused when his fingertip trailed through a track of moisture on her cheek. "I thought we agreed, no more of these."

"I know," she said, sniffling. "Sometimes I just can't help it."

More and more lately, she thought with a sense of frustration. Her emotions were as unpredictable as her appetite the past several days.

Braedon pressed a kiss to her brow. "Shall we see if there are any fruit tarts in the kitchens today?"

"Nay, not for me." The very picture made her stomach clench queerly. "But I do wonder if Cook might warm some of that blood pudding for me, left over from last eve's sup."

"Blood pudding," he drawled, clearly revolted, which was no mean feat with a man of Braedon's fondness for a good meal. "You have yet to break your fast today and you are craving blood pudding?"

"Mm-hmm. It sounds delicious."

"Well," he said, chuckling, "who am I to refuse a lady and her stomach?"

"Indeed, my lord. You have vowed to oblige my every whim—or do you forget your promise?"

"I will never forget my promises to you, love. You need only whisper your heart's desires and I will do my utmost to fulfill them . . . no matter how peculiar. Or wicked."

Ariana smiled as he pressed down with a searing kiss. "Oh, I do like the sound of that, my lord. I like that very much."

Read on for a sneak peek at the
next enchanting romance
in the Dragon Chalice series

HEART OF THE FLAME

Coming in early 2005

Cornwall, England
May 1275

HE ENTERED THE place slowly, his footsteps hesitant now that he had breached the threshold. After so long an absence from his Father's house, he was not at all sure he would be welcome. He doubted he would be heard. But embraced or nay, his heart was heavy, and he knew of nowhere else to lay his burdens. The blame here, however, was wholly his own; he reckoned he would carry that for the rest of his days.

Fine silver spurs rode at the heels of his boots, ticking softly on the smooth stone floor as he advanced, their tinny music the only disturbance of sound in the vacant chamber. Unwarmed, unlit, save the overcast glare that washed in through a high window, the vaulted space held the cool stillness of a tomb. Fitting, he thought, his eyes yet burning from the sight that had greeted him upon his arrival.

For a moment, as he reached the end of his path, the knight could only stand there, his limbs leaden from his days of travel, his throat scorched and dry like the bitter chalk of ash.

Golden head bowed, he closed his eyes and sank to his knees on the floor.

"Pater noster, qui es in caelis . . ."

The prayer fell from his lips by rote, familiar as his own name. Kenrick of Clairmont had said this prayer a thousand times, nay, countless repetitions—a hundred times a day for seven days straight, as was required every time one of his Templar brethren had fallen. Although he was no longer of the Order, he wanted to believe that where his vow was broken, some scrap of his faith might still remain. The prayer he recited now was for a friend and that man's family, for Randwulf of Greycliff and the wife and young son who once lived here.

Each breath Kenrick drew to speak held the cloying tang of smoke and cinder. Soot blackened the floor of the chapel where he knelt, as it did the walls of the small tower keep beyond. The place was in ruin, all of it dead and cold some weeks before he had arrived.

Rand and his cherished family . . . gone.

All because of him. Because of a secret pact he had shared with his friend and brother-in-arms, a pledge sealed more than a year ago at this humble manor near Land's End. God's blood. If he had known what it would cost Rand, he never would have sought his help.

" . . . sed libera nos a malo . . ."

Too late, he thought, bitter with grief and remorse. For a moment, he allowed his gaze to settle on the wreckage of the place, at the modest gold crucifix hanging above the altar, unscathed. He bit back the wry curse that rose to his tongue, but only barely. Not even God could stop Silas de Mortaine from visiting his wrath on these noble folk. But he would dwell no longer on regrets, nor could he afford his grief. There would be time for both once his business here was concluded.

"Amen," he growled, then brought himself to his feet in the charred nave of the chapel.

As eager as he had been to arrive earlier that day, now he longed to be away. His scalp itched beneath the cropped cut of his hair, a lingering effect of his captivity, when his head and beard had crawled with lice. He had cut it all away at first chance, preferring to be clean-shaven, his dark blond hair kept shorter than was stylish, curling just above the collar of his brown tunic and gambeson. He scratched at his nape, cursing the reminder of his incarceration.

On second thought, perhaps the niggling crawl of his scalp had more to do with the sudden feeling he had that he was not alone in the abandoned keep. There seemed a mild disturbance in the stillness of the air, as though someone—or something—breathed amid the death that permeated the place.

"Who is there?"

From the corner of his eye, he caught an unmistakable flicker of movement. His head snapped up, his gaze cutting sharply over his shoulder. Damn it, he *was* being watched.

A fleeting splash of color moved near the entryway of the chapel. Kenrick caught a momentary glimpse of pale white skin and wary, wide green eyes. A mere blink was all the time she paused—just long enough for him to register the delicacy of a heart-shaped face caught in a startled expression as the woman looked back at him in that frozen instant. A drooping mane of unbound auburn hair framed her striking countenance, the rich russet-red tangles glowing like fire against the persistent gray of the morning.

As tense as he was, his blood seething over the loss of his friends and the grim purpose that brought him there, Kenrick was not immune to the beauty of this unexpected intruder. Indeed, he was tempted to stare at finding such incongruous loveliness amid the smoldering ruins. His observer seemed in no mind to afford him the chance. She lunged, as quickly as a sprite, and dashed into an antechamber of the chapel.

"Stop," he ordered, knowing he would be ignored, and already leaping to his feet in pursuit. His quarry was far lighter of foot than he, simply there one moment and gone the next. But there were few places to hide in the small chapel. "Show yourself. You have nothing to fear," he said, stepping into the vaulted antechamber. "Come out now. I wish only to talk to you."

The barest shift of sound came from a toppled cabinet to his right. The door to the piece hung askew on its hinges. Though too small to hide but a child, it afforded the sole spot of concealment in all of the chapel. From the darkened wedge of space at the top, Kenrick saw the glint of a wary stare watching him as he approached.

"Who are you?" he asked, coming to stand there. He wished not to frighten the chit, but he wanted answers. Needed them. "What do you know of this place?"

When no reply came, he reached out with his booted foot and began to move aside the broken door of the cabinet to reveal its cowering occupant. There was a whine, then a fearful, animal growl as he bent down to peer inside.

"Jesu Christe."

It was not his stealthy observer after all. A small red fox glared at him with hackles raised and teeth bared, trapped between the unyielding back of the cabinet enclosure and the man who blocked its easy escape. The instant Kenrick withdrew, the little beast dashed out and fled the chapel for the safety of the outlying moors. Kenrick turned and watched it go, letting out his anxiety in a long, heavy sigh.

Where had she gone?

Whoever the woman was, she had managed to vanish. *Into thin air,* he was tempted to think, as he scanned his surroundings and saw no trace of her whatsoever.